# Praise for DEBORAH CROMBIE's
# WATER LIKE A STONE
## and her previous Kincaid and James crime novels

"[Crombie] makes various psychological motives believable and is a master of the cliffhanger."

*Virginian Pilot*

"Crombie has an uncanny affinity for the English detective genre. She [creates] a believable mystery in a realistic setting. Her characters are three-dimensional and are drawn with compassion and sensitivity."

*Dallas Morning News*

"Comparisons with Martha Grimes and Elizabeth George are inevitable. . . . Crombie's emotionally intense, quietly yet exquisitely wrought gems have taken on new brilliance with each offering."

*Times of London*

"An American mystery novelist who writes so vividly about England, she might have been born within the sound of the Bow Bells. . . . [Crombie] has the remarkable knack of summing up a character in a very few words, making each of them count."

*Cleveland Plain Dealer*

"A masterful novelist."

*Denver Post*

"A writer who turns out singularly skillful mysteries
steeped in British locales. . . .
Crombie [always writes] an engaging, richly peopled,
satisfying mystery."

*Houston Chronicle*

"Crombie keeps this series on its toes with her smooth
procedural techniques and engagingly eccentric characters."

*New York Times Book Review*

"In the style of P.D. James, Crombie explores character
as much as circumstance."

*Calgary Sun*

"A master of the modern British mystery . . . one writer
who gets better with every book."

*Harrisburg Patriot News*

By Deborah Crombie

WATER LIKE A STONE
IN A DARK HOUSE
NOW MAY YOU WEEP
AND JUSTICE THERE IS NONE
A FINER END
KISSED A SAD GOODBYE
DREAMING OF THE BONES
MOURN NOT YOUR DEAD
LEAVE THE GRAVE GREEN
ALL SHALL BE WELL
A SHARE IN DEATH

Forthcoming in hardcover

WHERE MEMORIES LIE

# WATER LIKE A STONE

## Deborah Crombie

**AVON**

*An Imprint of HarperCollinsPublishers*

AVON BOOKS
*An Imprint of* HarperCollins*Publishers*
10 East 53rd Street
New York, New York 10022-5299

Copyright © 2007 by Deborah Crombie
Map drawn by Laura Hartman Maestro
Excerpt from *Where Memories Lie* copyright © 2008 by Deborah Crombie
ISBN: 978-0-06-052528-6
www.avonmystery.com

First Avon Books paperback printing: January 2008
First William Morrow hardcover printing: February 2007

Avon Trademark Reg. U.S. Pat. Off. and in Other Countries, Marca Registrada, Hecho en U.S.A.
HarperCollins® is a registered trademark of HarperCollins Publishers.

Printed in the U.S.A.

10  9  8  7  6  5  4  3

# *Acknowledgments*

Thanks to all the usual suspects: my husband, Rick; my daughter, Kayti; my agent, Nancy Yost, for her unfailing support, acumen, and good humor; everyone at William Morrow whose combined efforts bring a novel to life—my incomparable editor, Carrie Feron; also Lisa Gallagher; Tessa Woodward; Danielle Bartlett; Virginia Stanley; Christine Wheeler; and Victoria Mathews, whose copyediting no doubt made *Water Like a Stone* a better book.

My readers are indefatigable: Steve Copling, Dale Denton, Jim Evans, Viqui Litman, and Gigi Norwood, patient members of the Every Other Tuesday Night Writers' Group; my friends Diana Sullivan Hale, Marcia Talley, Kate Charles, Tracy Ricketts, and Theresa Badylak, all of whom read the manuscript and offered advice and encouragement.

On the other side of the Pond, thanks to Sarah Turner at Pan Macmillan, Arabella Stein at Abner Stein, and all those who provided information or hospitality; Richard Abraham, financial investigation officer, North West Surrey Fraud Team, Surrey Police; Neil and Kathy Ritchie at Tilston Lodge, Tilston, Cheshire; Georgina West at Stoke Grange Farm, Barbridge, Cheshire; and the Olde Barbridge Inn, Barbridge, Cheshire, and the Salt City Jazzmen, to whom I hope

I've done justice. (If the Olde Barbridge Inn doesn't have a mummer's play on Boxing Day, they should!)

And a special thanks to illustrator Laura Maestro, who has once again graced my book with her enchanting map.

Any mistakes I have made in procedure or geography are entirely my own.

# WATER LIKE A STONE

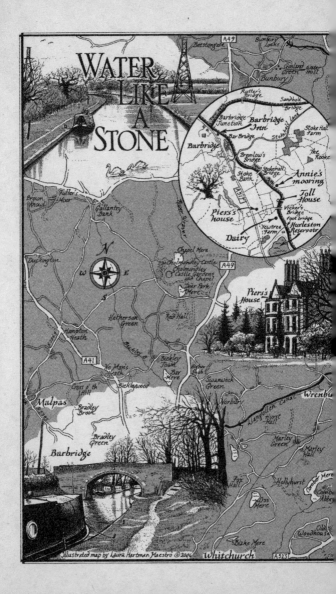

Illustrated map by Laura Hartman Maestro © 2006

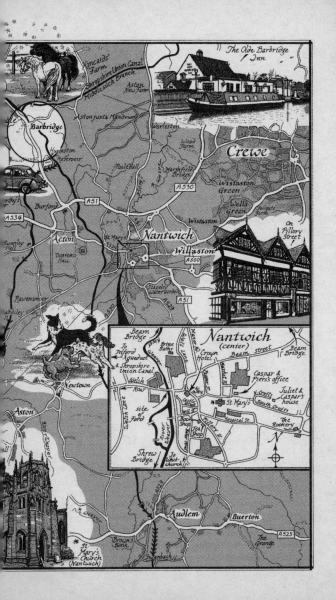

The Olde Barbridge Inn

Kincaids' Farm
Shropshire Union Canal
Aston New Farm
Middlewich Branch
Aston juxta Mondrum
Worleston

Barbridge

Crewe

Hurleston Reservoir
Poolehall
Wood Farm
Marshfield Bridge
A530
Wistaston Green
Wells Green
Tollgate Farm

A51
Burford
Acton
St Mary's Ch.
Nantwich
Wistaston
Willaston
A500
On Pillory Street

A534
Swanley Hall
Dorfold Hall

A530
Stapeley Water Gardens
A51

Ravensmoor
Baddiley

Nantwich (center)

Newtown

Beam Bridge
To Telford Aqueduct Shropshire Union Canal
Brine Baths
Crown Hotel
Beam street
Beam Bridge
Bank Lane
Caspar & Piers's office
Juliet & Caspar's house
Welsh Row
Castle
St Mary's
crafts
South Crofts
The Rookery
site of Ford
Book Shop
Hospital St.
Tea Shop
Pillory St.
Shrew Bridge
To Whitchurch
River Weaver

Aston

St Mary's Church (Nantwich)

R. Weaver
A529
Audlem
Buerton
A525
Brown's Bank
The Grange
Swanbach

# Prologue

❧

*Late November*

MIST ROSE IN SWIRLS from the still surface of the canal. It seemed to take on a life of its own, an amorphous creature bred from the dusk. The day, which had been unseasonably warm and bright for late November, had quickly chilled with the setting of the sun, and Annie Lebow shivered, pulling the old cardigan she wore a bit closer to her thin body.

She stood in the stern of her narrowboat, the *Lost Horizon,* gazing at the bare trees lining the curve of the Cut, breathing in the dank, fresh scent that was peculiar to water with the coming of evening. The smell brought, as it always did, an aching for something she couldn't articulate, and an ever-deepening melancholia. Behind her, the lamps in the boat's cabin glowed welcomingly, but for her they signaled only the attendant terrors of the coming night. The fact that her isolation was self-imposed made it no easier to bear.

Five years ago, Annie had left behind her husband of twenty years as well as her job with South Cheshire Social Services, and had bought the *Horizon* with money accumulated from her interest in her family's shipping business. She'd imagined that the simplicity of life on a boat sixty feet long by a mere seven feet wide, and the physical demands of working the boat on her own, would keep her demons at bay. For a while it had worked. She'd developed a deep love of the

Cut, as the traditional boating people called the canal, and an unexpected strength and pride in her own skills. Her explorations of the inland waterways had taken her from Cheshire to London, then back up the northern industrial route to Birmingham and Manchester and Leeds, until she sometimes imagined herself adrift in time, following the route of all those hardy people who had gone before her.

But lately that ghostly comfort had begun to fade, and she found herself returning more and more often to her old haunts, Cheshire and the stretch of the Shropshire Union Canal near Nantwich. Her memories came thronging back. Against the horrors she'd seen in child-protective services, the measure of her own life seemed woefully inadequate. She'd been too afraid of loss to make her own mark against the darkness, to stay in her marriage, to have a child, and now it was too late for either.

She turned back towards the lamp-lit cabin, drawn by the thought of the white wine chilling in the fridge. One glass, she told herself, just to ease the evening in, but she knew her discipline would fail as the long hours of the night ticked away. Just when, Annie wondered, had she become afraid of the dark?

Ahead, the Cut curved away between the overarching trees, offering the elusive promise of vistas unseen, unexplored, and a chill little wind snaked across the water. Scudding clouds blotted the rising moon, and Annie shivered again. With a sudden resolve, she leapt to the towpath. She'd take the boat up the Cut to Barbridge before the light faded completely. There, the bustle and sounds from the old canalside inn would provide a welcome distraction. Perhaps she'd even go in for a drink, leave the bottle of wine safely corked, a panacea for another night. Then first thing in the morning she'd move on, away from this place where the past seemed so much more present.

Kneeling in the soft turf with her hand on the mooring strap, she felt the vibration on the path before she heard the rapid footfalls, the quick pant of breath. Before she could move, the hurtling shape was upon her. She saw the boy's wild, white face, felt the lash of his sodden clothing as he stumbled past her. He muttered something she didn't quite catch, but knew it for a curse, not an apology.

Then he was moving away from her, and she imagined she heard the sound of his footsteps long after his slender shape was swallowed by the darkness.

# 1

*December*

**GEMMA JAMES** would never have thought that two adults, two children, and two dogs, all crammed into a small car along with a week's worth of luggage and assorted Christmas presents, could produce such a palpable silence.

It was Christmas Eve, and they'd left London as soon as she and her partner, Duncan Kincaid, could get away from their respective offices, his at New Scotland Yard, hers at the Notting Hill Division of the Metropolitan Police. They had both managed a long-overdue week's break from their jobs and were on their way to spend the holiday with Duncan's family in Cheshire, a prospect that Gemma viewed with more than a little trepidation.

In the backseat, her five-year-old son, Toby, had at last fallen asleep, his blond head tilted to one side, his small body sagging against the seat belt with the abandon managed only by the very young. Geordie, Gemma's cocker spaniel, was sprawled half in the boy's lap, snoring slightly.

Next to Toby sat Kit, Duncan's thirteen-year-old, with his little terrier, Tess, curled up beside him. Unlike Toby, Kit was awake and ominously quiet. Their anticipated holiday had begun with a row, and Kit had shown no inclination to put his sense of injury aside.

Gemma sighed involuntarily, and Kincaid glanced at her from the passenger seat.

"Ready for a break?" he asked. "I'd be glad to take over."

As a single fat raindrop splashed against the windscreen and crawled up the glass, Gemma saw that the heavy clouds to the north had sunk down to the horizon and were fast obliterating the last of the daylight. They'd crawled up the M6 past Birmingham in a stop-and-start queue of holiday traffic, and only now were they getting up to a decent speed. "I think there's one more stop before we leave the motorway. We can switch there." Reluctant as she was to stop, Gemma had no desire to navigate her way through the wilds of Cheshire in the dark.

"Nantwich is less than ten miles from the motorway," Kincaid said with a grin, answering her unspoken thought.

"It's still country in between." Gemma made a face. "Cows. Mud. Manure. Bugs."

"No bugs this time of year," he corrected.

"Besides," Gemma continued, undeterred, "your parents don't live in the town. They live on a *farm*." The word was weighted with horror.

"It's not a working farm," Kincaid said, as if that made all the difference. "Although there is a dairy next door, and sometimes the smell does tend to drift a bit."

His parents owned a bookshop in the market town of Nantwich, but lived in an old farmhouse a few miles to the north. Kincaid had grown up there, along with his younger sister, Juliet, and as long as Gemma had known him he'd talked about the place as if it were heaven on earth.

By contrast, having grown up in North London, Gemma never felt really comfortable out of range of lights and people, and she wasn't buying his glowing advertisements for country life. Nor was she thrilled about leaving their home. She had so looked forward to a Christmas unmarred by the calamities that had shadowed last year's holidays, their first in the Notting Hill house. And she felt the children needed the security of a Christmas at home, especially Kit.

Especially Kit. She glanced in the rearview mirror. He

hadn't joined in their banter, and his face was still and implacable as he gazed out the window at the rolling Cheshire hills.

That morning, as Gemma had attempted a last-minute sort through a week's worth of neglected post, she'd come across a letter addressed to Kincaid and bearing Kit's school insignia. She'd ripped it open absently, expecting a fundraising request or an announcement of some school activity. Then she'd stood in the kitchen, frozen with shock as she scanned the contents. It was from Kit's head teacher, informing Kincaid of her concern over the recent drop in Kit's academic performance and requesting that he schedule a conference after the holiday. Previous notes sent home with Kit by his teachers, the head had added, had come back with signatures the staff suspected had been forged.

Gemma had waited with tight-lipped restraint until Kincaid got home, then they'd confronted Kit together.

Things had not gone well. Kincaid, his anger fueled as much by Kit's duplicity as by concern over the boy's school performance, had shouted at his son while Toby and the dogs had cowered in the background. Kit had gone white and balled into himself as defensively as a threatened hedgehog, and Gemma found herself the peacemaker.

"It's too late to ring the head now," she'd said. "We'll have to wait until term takes up again after the holidays. Why don't we all calm down and not let this spoil our trip." Glancing at her watch, she added, "And if we don't get off soon, we'll never make it to your parents' in time for tonight's dinner."

Kincaid had turned away with a shrug of disgust to load the last of the luggage, and Kit had retreated into the stony silence he'd maintained since. It was ironic, Gemma thought, that although it was Kit who'd been called on the carpet, she felt that she and Duncan were the ones who had failed. They should have discussed how to handle things before they talked to Kit; perhaps they should even have spoken to the head teacher before tackling the boy.

Having recently come to at least a temporary resolution in the custody battle with Kit's maternal grandparents that had consumed much of their last year, they'd allowed themselves to be lulled into a false sense of security. Kit had at last agreed to have his DNA tested, and when a match proved Duncan was his biological father, the court had awarded him custody dependent on the continuing evaluation of the boy's well-being and the stability of his home life.

They should have known better than to take that achievement for granted, Gemma thought. It was too easy, and with Kit, things were never going to be easy. A simple paternity test was not going to magically erase the damage he'd suffered from his mother's death and his stepfather's abandonment.

As she glanced at Kincaid sitting beside her, she guessed his uncharacteristic display of anger stemmed from the fear that they might lose everything they had gained.

A rustle and a yawn came from the backseat. "Are we there yet?" piped up Toby. "I'm hungry."

"You're always hungry, sport," Kincaid answered. "And we're close. Just a bit longer."

"Will Grandma Rosemary have mince pies for us?" Toby, as always, had jumped from a sound sleep to a high-energy state of alertness.

Gemma found it both amusing and touching that Toby, who had never met Duncan's parents, had adopted them as comfortably as if they were his own family, while she, who had at least met Duncan's mother once, felt as if she was facing a root canal. What if they didn't like her? What if she didn't live up to their expectations for their son? Kit's mother, after all, had been an academic, a well-respected Cambridge don, while Gemma had gone straight from secondary school into the police academy, and no one in her family had ever graduated from university. Her parents were bakers, not intellectuals, and her mother's most literary endeavor was an addiction to *Coronation Street*.

"Yes, lots and lots of mince pies," answered Kincaid. "And turkey tomorrow for Christmas dinner."

"What about tonight? I'm hungry tonight." Toby leaned as far forward as his seat belt allowed, his eyes wide with interest.

"Your auntie Jules is cooking tonight's dinner, I think, so you'll just have to be patient. And polite," Kincaid added, sounding a little uneasy. He didn't often talk about his sister, and Gemma knew he hadn't seen Juliet or his niece and nephew since the Christmas before last.

Toby drummed the toes of his shoes into the back of Gemma's seat. "Why? Can't she cook?"

"Um, she was always better at making things with her hands when she was a little girl," Kincaid said diplomatically. "But, hey, if Gemma can learn to cook, anything is possible."

Without taking her eyes off the road, Gemma smacked him on the arm. "Watch it, mate, or you'll get worms in your food from now on." Toby cackled, and to Gemma's relief, she thought she heard a faint snicker from Kit.

"How is Father Christmas going to find me if I'm not at home?" asked Toby. "Will I have a stocking?"

"Don't be such a baby," said Kit. "You know there's—"

"Kit, that's enough," Kincaid said sharply, and the slight rapport of a moment ago vanished instantly.

Gemma swore under her breath and gripped the steering wheel a bit tighter, but before she could think how to mend the breach, Toby shouted, "Look, Mummy, it's snowing. It's going to be a white Christmas!"

The large flakes drifted into the windscreen one by one, light as feathers, then came more thickly, until the swirling mist of white filled Gemma's vision.

"A white Christmas," Kit repeated from the backseat, his voice flat with sarcasm. "Oh, joy."

"Bloody Caspar." Juliet Newcombe swung the pick hard into the three-foot swath of mortar in the wall of the old dairy barn. "Bloody Piers." She swung again, with equal force, enlarging the hole left by her first blow.

The light was fading fast, and the bitterly cold wind blowing off the canal held the metallic scent that presaged snow. She'd sent her crew home hours earlier, to spend Christmas Eve with their families, and it was only her stubbornness and her fury that had kept her on at the building site long past knocking-off time.

Not that she didn't have a good reason for working late. The conversion of the old dairy barn on the Shropshire Union Canal, between Nantwich and Barbridge, was the largest commission she'd landed since striking out on her own in the building business, and a spate of unseasonably bad weather earlier in the month had thrown the project weeks behind schedule. She leaned on her pick for a moment, surveying the progress they *had* made.

Set where the gentle sweep of pasture met the canal, the place would be a small gem when it was finished. The building was a single story, constructed of traditional Cheshire redbrick, and slate roofed. At some point in its history, outbuildings had been added to the original single-roomed barn so that the structure now formed a U, with the wings facing the pasture. The main building hugged the edge of the Cut, and the windows they'd set into the frontage gave a wide view of the water and of the arch of the old stone bridge that crossed it.

Of the half dozen narrowboats moored below the bridge, only one sported a welcoming light and a wisp of smoke from its chimney. Perhaps its owners lived year round on the boat and were making preparations for a cozy Christmas Eve.

"A cozy Christmas Eve," she repeated aloud, and gave a bitter laugh. Her eyes prickled as she thought of her children—Sam, with his ten-year-old's innocence still intact, and Lally, fighting to maintain her wary, adolescent cool against the excitement of the holiday. They were at her parents', waiting to meet their cousin, her brother Duncan's newfound child.

*Cousins,* she supposed she should say, recalling that the woman her brother lived with had a small son of her own. Why hadn't they married? she wondered. Had they discovered that the secret of a happy relationship was not taking each other for granted? Or were they just cautious, not wanting to make a mistake that could bind them to years of misery? She could give them a bit of advice, if they asked her.

Then, guiltily, she remembered that she had no corner on misery. They had lost a child this time last year, a baby born just a few weeks too early to be viable. Her face flushed with shame as she thought of her failure to call, or even to write. She had meant to, but somehow she could never manage to find the words to bridge the gap that stretched between her and the older brother she had once adored.

And now they would be here, tonight. They were all coming to her house for a festive Christmas Eve dinner before midnight mass at St. Mary's, and she would have to play "happy families."

Caspar would be civil, she was sure, the perfect host, and no one would guess that her husband had just that afternoon accused her of sleeping with his partner, Piers Dutton.

Rage swept through her again and she swung the pick hard into the crumbling mortar. She had to go home, she had to face them all, but first she would finish this one task, an accomplishment that was hers alone and untainted by lies. She would breathe with the rhythm of the blows and think of simple things, making a doorway from the front room of the barn into what had once been a feed store. The old barn's history stretched away from her like a ribbon; the generations of farmers who had found shelter here on frosty mornings had huddled inside on evenings like this.

One of them had mortared over what she guessed had been a manger, leaving a smooth, graying swath that broke the uniformity of the redbrick walls. It had been a good job, neat and careful, and in a way she hated to destroy it. But the barn's new owners wanted a doorway from what would be their kitchen/living area into the back of the house, and a doorway they would have.

As the hole in the mortar widened enough to give her purchase, she hooked the tip of the pick into the mortar and pulled. A piece came loose, but still hung, attached by what looked to be a bit of cloth. Odd, thought Juliet, peering at it more closely. The barn had grown dim with the approaching dusk. She extricated the tip of the pick, then switched on her work lamp and trained it on the wall. She touched the stuff with her fingers. Fabric, yes—something pink, perhaps?

She inserted the pick again and pulled, gently, until she dislodged another piece of the mortar. Now she could see more of the material, recognizing the small pattern as leaping sheep, a dirty white against stained pink. It looked like a blanket her children had had as babies. How very odd. The fabric seemed to be nestled in a cavity that had been only lightly covered with the mortar. Shifting her position so that her body wasn't blocking the light, she tugged at the material, freeing a little more. It seemed to be wrapped round something, another layer of cloth . . . pinkish cloth with a row of rusted snaps.

It's a doll, she thought, still puzzled—a black baby doll in a pink romper suit. Why would someone put a doll inside the wall of a barn?

Then, she realized that those were tufts of hair on the tiny head, that the face was not brown plastic but leathery skin, that sockets gaped where there should have been eyes, and that the tiny hands curled under the chin were curves of bone.

# 2

❧

HUGH KINCAID climbed up on the ladder once more, adjusting the strand of fairy lights he'd strung over the farmhouse porch. Above the rooftop, the sky had turned the ominous color of old pewter, and his nose had begun to run from the biting cold. He didn't dare free a hand to wipe it, however; his position was precarious enough and becoming more so by the minute as the light faded.

His wife stood below him, hugging her jacket closed against the wind. "Hugh," she called up to him, "come down from there before you break your bloody neck. They'll be here any moment. Do you want your son to find you sprawled on your backside in the garden?"

"Coming, darling." Giving the strand one last twitch, he made his way carefully down to stand beside her. She hooked her arm through his, and together they stepped back to admire the sparkle of lights against the dark red brickwork. The house was unadorned, foursquare in the style of the Cheshire Plain, but comfortable—if a little worn around the edges, as Hugh liked to think of himself.

"It looks a bit pathetic," he said, eyeing the lights critically. "One lonely strand. I should have done more."

"Don't be silly." Rosemary pinched him through the thick cloth of his coat. "You're behaving like a broody old hen, Hugh, and you're *not* getting up on the roof." Her tone was affectionate but firm, and he sighed.

"You're right, of course. It's just that . . ." For an articulate man, he found himself unaccountably at a loss for words, and unexpectedly nervous about meeting his grandson. It wasn't as if he didn't have grandchildren, Juliet's Lally and little Sam, who were even now waiting inside for the expected arrival. But there was something—and God forbid he should ever admit this to anyone, even Rosemary—there was something about his son's son that felt special to him, and he wanted everything to be perfect.

It shocked him that he, who had always thought himself such a progressive, emancipated man, should harbor such a sentiment, but there it was, and he found himself wondering if the boy would ever consider changing his name so that the Kincaid line would go on.

Hugh snorted aloud at his own vanity, and Rosemary gave him a questioning look. "I'm a silly old fool," he said, shaking his head.

"Of course you are, but it will be all right," she answered, and he knew she had sensed what he'd left unspoken, as she always did.

He took his handkerchief from his coat pocket and blew his nose. Rosemary was right, he decided. The fairy lights did look cheery, and from the sitting-room window the Christmas tree twinkled as well. "What did you do with the children?" he asked, wondering why they hadn't come out with their grandmother.

"Sent them to watch a video. They were driving me mad, and there was nothing left for them to help with in the kitchen." She pushed up her sleeve to glance at her watch. "It's odd we haven't heard from Juliet by this time," she added.

He sniffed, catching the tang of impending snow beneath the scent of wood smoke emanating from the kitchen stove. Through the bare trees he saw lights begin to blink on in the neighboring farmhouse and knew full dark was fast approaching. "Snow's coming. If they're not here soon—"

"You think your police-superintendent son can't find his way home in a snowstorm?" Rosemary interrupted, laughing. Before he could protest, she tensed and said, "Shhh."

At first, he heard only his own breathing. Then he caught it, the faint whisper of tires on tarmac. A pinprick of light came from the direction of the road, then another, as the beams of the oncoming car were sliced by the intervening trees. It made Hugh think of Morse code, a distant SOS.

The car progressed so slowly that Hugh thought they must be mistaken, that it was only an elderly neighbor creeping home from shop or pub, but then it slowed still more and turned into the farmhouse drive, bumping along the track until it rolled to a stop before them.

The front passenger door swung open and his son emerged, smiling, though his face looked more sharply etched than when Hugh had seen him last. As Duncan hugged his mother and pumped his father's hand, saying, "Sorry we're so late. Traffic was a bit of a bugger," a small blond boy erupted from the back, followed by an equally bouncy blue roan cocker spaniel.

Hugh's heart gave an instant's leap before he realized the boy couldn't be Kit, he was much too young. Then the other rear door opened and a boy climbed out, clutching a small, shaggy brown terrier to his chest like a shield.

"Dad, this is Toby," said Duncan, with a gentling hand on the small boy's shoulder, "and this is Kit. And Gemma, too, if she can get her bits and pieces together," he added, smiling, as a young woman came round the car from the driver's side. "She decided not to let me drive the last stretch, and I think our country roads have left her a bit frazzled."

Hugh greeted her warmly, taking in her attractive, friendly face and the coppery glint of hair drawn back with a clip, but he couldn't keep his eyes from the boy—his grandson.

Rosemary had warned him, of course, but still he found he was not prepared. The boy had his mother's fair coloring, but was so like his father in the stamp of his features that Hugh felt he might have been seeing Duncan again at thirteen. Such resemblances were not uncommon, he knew, but awareness of them is usually dulled by daily proximity. It seemed to Hugh he'd been offered a rare glimpse of the march of generations, and he felt a twinge of his own mortality.

"Come in, come in," Rosemary was saying, "I've got the

kettle on, and the children are dying to see you." She shepherded them all into the front hall, but before she could divest them of their coats and luggage, Sam came galloping down the stairs, followed more slowly by his sister, Lally.

Lally's face was set in a pout and Sam was holding the phone aloft, waving it like a trophy wrested from the enemy. "Granddad, it's Mummy. She wants to speak to you."

"Tell her we'll ring her back in five minutes, Sam," said Rosemary, "As soon as we've—"

"She says it's urgent, Nana." His mission accomplished, Sam handed the phone to Hugh and sidled down the last few steps, his curious gaze fixed on Kit and Toby.

"Juliet," Hugh said into the phone, "what is it? Can't it wai—"

"Dad, is Duncan there yet?" his daughter broke in, her voice sharp and breathless.

"Yes, he's just come in. That's what—"

"Dad, tell him I need him to come to the old dairy—he knows where it is. Tell him—" She seemed to hesitate, then said, on a rising note, "Just tell him I've found a body."

"Bugger," Kincaid muttered as he squeezed under the wheel of Gemma's Ford Escort and slid the seat back far enough to accommodate his longer legs. His sister hadn't stayed on the line to speak to him, but before disconnecting had told their father that her mobile battery was running low.

Was this some sort of joke, he wondered, her revenge for all his teasing when they were children? Surely she couldn't actually have found a body? His father had made light of it, with the children listening, but if it was true, he felt he must be the victim of a cosmic rather than a sibling prank.

Nor had she said whether she'd called the local police, so he'd decided to check out the situation before notifying them himself. He didn't want to add embarrassment to aggravation if it turned out she'd discovered the remains of some stray animal in the old dairy.

His father had filled him in briefly on Juliet's renovation project, and Kincaid remembered the place well. He and Jules had spent a good part of their childhood rambling up and down the canal towpath, and the dairy had been a familiar landmark. He would have much preferred, however, to take a trip down memory lane on a bright, sunny day rather than a miserably cold evening, and Christmas Eve to boot.

Nor was he happy about leaving Gemma and the boys after only the briefest of introductions. Glancing at the house once more as he backed out of the drive, he saw his dad still standing at the open door, gazing after him. Kincaid waved, then felt a bit foolish, knowing his father couldn't see him. Then, as he watched, his dad stepped inside, the door swung closed, and the last vestiges of light and warmth vanished.

The dairy, he remembered, was on the main branch of the Shropshire Union Canal, near Barbridge. In fact, they had passed right by it on the way to his parents' house. As children, he and Jules had reached that stretch of the Cut by crossing the fields and then the Middlewich branch of the canal that ran nearer the farm, but tonight he would be taking the road.

As he eased the car back out onto the main track, a few snowflakes drifted against the windscreen, and he swore. They'd outrun the snow near Crewe, but it had caught up. Heavier now, the flakes disintegrated beneath the wipers, and the tarmac gleamed wetly in the headlamps. When he reached the Chester Road, he turned back towards Nantwich, and when he had passed the turning for Barbridge he slowed, looking for the small lane he remembered.

It came up on him suddenly and he swung the wheel hard to the left. A house loomed out of the darkness, dark spikes of chimney pots briefly visible through the swirl of snow. A Victorian lodge, neglected in his childhood; the sort of place one approached only when bolstered by a playmate's bravado. It was occupied now, though—he'd glimpsed the glow of light in a ground-floor window.

The house fell away behind him as the hedgerows and trees reached round the car like skeletal arms, and he navigated the track's twists and turns as much by memory as by sight. Then the terrain leveled out as woods gave way to pasture, and ahead he saw the flicker of a lamp. Easing the car over the last few rutted yards, he pulled up beside a white builder's van. He could see the silhouette of the old dairy now, the light clearly coming from its open doors, but as he climbed out of the car, the van door swung open and his sister jumped down from the driver's seat.

"Jules." He drew her to him, feeling the slenderness of her shoulders beneath her padded jacket, and for a moment she relaxed into his arms. Then she drew away, establishing a distance between them. Her face was a pale blur against the frame of dark hair that straggled loose from a ponytail.

"Thanks for coming," she said. "I didn't know who else to call."

Kincaid bit his tongue on the obvious—he wouldn't pass judgment until he'd seen what she had to show him. "What are you doing out here?" he asked instead. "Staying warm?" He brushed at the snowflakes settling on his cheeks and eyelashes.

Juliet shook her head. "No. Yes. But it's not that. I couldn't stay in there. Not with—" She gestured towards the barn. "You'd better come and see for yourself. You can tell me I'm not crazy." Turning from him, she started towards the light, picking her way through the slushy ruts. He followed, taking in the jeans and the heavy boots that accompanied the padded jacket, marveling at the transformation in his sister since he had seen her last.

His mother had told him, of course, that Juliet had left her job as office manager of her husband's investment firm and started her own business as a builder, but he hadn't quite been able to visualize the accompanying transformation.

Juliet stopped just inside the door of the building and Kincaid stepped in, looking around. The light came from a battery-powered work lamp set on the dirt floor. He lifted it, chasing the shadows from the upper part of the room. Windows had been framed into the dark redbrick of the canal-facing wall, and he knew that under better circumstances the view would be spectacular. Some framing had been done on the inside as well, marking out obviously preliminary room divisions, and a few feet from the back wall, a pick lay abandoned in the dirt.

He saw the swath of mortar set into the dark brick, a jagged hole in its center where the pick had done its work. And there was something else—was it fabric? He moved in closer, raising the lamp so that the area was illuminated clearly. Gingerly, he reached out with a finger. Then, in spite of the cold and the wind that eddied through the room, he caught an all-too-familiar whiff of decay.

"Is it a baby?" said Juliet, her voice sounding thin in the frigid air.

"Looks like it." Kincaid stepped back and put his hands firmly back into the pockets of his overcoat. He needn't have worried about his sister's failure to call the police straightaway. "It's been here a good while, I'm afraid."

"Is it—it wasn't a newborn—" She gave him a stricken look, as if she'd realized the subject might be painful for him.

He leaned in to examine the small body again. "No, I don't think so. Less than a year old, would be my guess from the size, but then I'm certainly no expert. I don't envy the forensic pathologist trying to make a determination on this one."

"But why would—how could—" Juliet took a breath and seemed to make an effort to pull herself together. "What do we do now?"

Kincaid had already pulled out his phone. Punching in 999, he gave her a crooked smile. "We ruin someone else's Christmas Eve."

The small entrance hall was a jumble of noise and movement, filled to bursting with adults, children, and dogs. One part of Gemma's brain registered the smell of baking mingled with fresh evergreens, while another took in the pale green walls hung with framed illustrations from children's books, an umbrella stand crammed full of brollies and walking sticks, and pegs draped with coats. Holly intertwined with gold ribbons and the deep red berries of yew wound up the stair rail.

The boy who had brought the phone—Gemma guessed he must be Duncan's nephew, Sam—was shouting something, striving to be heard over the high-pitched, frenzied barking that came from the back of the house. As Geordie and Tess joined in the chorus, Gemma tried to hush the cocker spaniel while Kit soothed the terrier in his arms.

Rosemary Kincaid had urged her son to at least have a cup of tea, but he'd demurred, saying the sooner he looked into things, the sooner he'd be back. When he'd pressed Gemma's shoulder with a whispered "Sorry," she'd gripped his arm and murmured, "I'll go with you."

"No. Stay with the boys," he'd said softly, with a glance at Kit. "I can manage this, and they need you."

She'd subsided in unhappy silence, watching him go with a sense of mounting panic. Surely he hadn't walked into a murder on the first day of their holiday; that was too unfair for belief. It could be anything, she told herself—in her days on the beat she'd had more than one call from citizens convinced the remains of a stray dog were human. Now it was only because she'd worked so many homicide cases that the word "body" automatically conjured up murder.

"Gemma, boys," Rosemary was saying, "come back to the kitchen. I know it's a bit late for tea, but I suspect none of us will be getting dinner anytime soon." Kincaid's mother had greeted her warmly, as she had the only other time they'd met, at Kit's mother's funeral. Although Rosemary's chestnut hair had perhaps gone a bit grayer, she had the strong bone structure and fine skin that aged well, and she radiated a wiry energy.

As Gemma responded, she was aware of her own accent, her North London vowels sounding harsh and flat compared with Rosemary Kincaid's educated Cheshire tones.

She glanced at Kincaid's father, who had watched Duncan drive away but now came back into the hall and closed the door. Hugh Kincaid was tall, like his son, with a jutting forehead and chin and a prominent nose. His brushed-back gray-streaked hair and roll-neck fisherman's jumper seemed to exaggerate his features, making his face seem severe. Then he smiled at her, revealing an unexpected charm, and Gemma found herself suddenly enchanted. Smiling back, she felt herself begin to relax.

"You'd better do as she says," Hugh warned, with a glance at his wife, "or there will be consequences." Gemma found she hadn't expected the faint trace of Scots in his voice, although she knew he came from near Glasgow. It made her think of Hazel Cavendish, so far away in the Scottish Highlands, and she felt a pang of longing for her friend.

"Don't pay him any mind," Rosemary countered, laughing. "Lally, Sam, come and introduce yourselves properly." She put a hand on the boy's head, as if holding down a jumping jack. "This is Sam. He's ten. And this is Lally," she added, glancing at the girl, who still hovered a few treads up the staircase, "who must be just a few months older than Kit, here."

Giving the girl all her attention for the first time, Gemma noticed first the inch of midriff bared in defiance of the weather, then the shoulder-length dark hair and oval face, the lips curved in a tentative smile. Gemma's breath caught in her throat. The girl was striking, beautiful in that heart-piercing way possessed only by girls on the cusp of womanhood, innocence poised on the brink of knowledge.

"Hi," Lally said, and grinned, an ordinary teenager, and Gemma shook off her flight of fancy.

"Come and see Jack," Sam said, raising his voice over the increasingly frenzied barking from the back. "He's our sheep—"

He was cut off by a thump and a crash, and a blur of black and white came barreling down the hall towards them. "Sheepdog," Sam finished, grinning. "He doesn't like to be left out of things."

Tess launched herself into the melee from Kit's arms and the three dogs jumped, circled, and sniffed, a shifting mass of canine pandemonium.

"Well, that seems to be all right, then," Rosemary said in the sudden quiet, eyeing them critically. "I thought we should let them get acquainted gradually, but Jack seems to have taken care of the formalities. Let's go see what sort of damage he's done to my kitchen." She took their coats and added them to the already overloaded pegs, then led the way towards the back of the house.

Still chattering, Sam latched onto Toby. "There's geese,

too, and ponies. Do you want to see them after tea? What are your dogs called? I like the little one—she's cute."

Toby answered him happily—or at least tried to, between questions—but Gemma noticed that Kit, having fallen in next to Lally, didn't speak. She couldn't blame him for feeling a bit intimidated meeting so many new family members at once, but hoped that he would soon relax.

When they reached the kitchen, they saw that Jack had hurled himself against the door so hard that it had slipped its latch, banging open and causing a slight dent in the hall plaster. Rosemary grumbled something under her breath that sounded like "Daft bloody dog," then herded them all into the room, as efficient as a sheepdog herself.

Gemma looked round in delight. The room was wide rather than deep, and she suspected it stretched across most of the back of the house. To the left was the cooking area, dominated by a cream Rayburn range and an old soapstone sink. Open shelves held a selection of dark cobalt-blue china in a calico design, and a few pieces in other blue-and-white porcelain patterns Gemma didn't recognize. To the right was a long, scrubbed pine table, surrounded by mismatched pine chairs, all with tie-on cushions covered in a blue-and-cream floral print. The back wall held a nook for cut firewood and a small wood-burning stove. The smell of fresh baking was mouthwateringly intense, and Gemma realized she was ravenous.

While Hugh fed the stove, Rosemary filled two teapots from a kettle steaming on the Rayburn, then pulled a plate piled with scones from the warming oven. "I don't suppose you like scones," she said to Kit, who was standing near her, "or homemade plum jam, or clotted cream."

"But I do," answered Kit, returning her smile and adding, "Can I help you?"

Gemma breathed a small sigh of relief as Kit helped ferry plates and cups to the table, carrying on a quiet conversation with his grandmother. Within a few minutes, they were all squeezed round the table, with the dogs tussling on the floor by the fire and the lubricant of food and drink beginning to loosen human tongues.

Seated between Toby and Rosemary, Gemma watched her son's manners anxiously, hoping he wouldn't stuff his mouth too full of scone, and worse, talk through it. Kit sat on the other side of the table, between Lally and his grandfather, while Sam had wedged himself into the small space at the end.

Kit was answering his grandfather's questions about school politely—if, as Gemma now suspected, less than truthfully—but she noticed he still hadn't made direct eye contact with Lally.

She shifted her attention back to Rosemary, who was saying, ". . . we'd planned to go to midnight mass after dinner at Juliet's, if that's all right with you, Gemma. It's a bit of a tradition in our family."

"I know," said Gemma. "Duncan told me. We meant to go last Christmas, but things . . . intervened." It had been work, of course, that had interrupted their Christmas Eve, and matters had gone steadily downhill from there.

A shadow crossed Rosemary's face. "Gemma, dear, I've never had a chance to tell you in person—"

"I know. It's all right." Gemma made the response that had gradually become easier, and that realization gave her an unexpected sense of loss. Her grief had given her something to hold on to, an almost tangible connection with the child she had lost, but now even that was slipping away from her.

Casting about for a change of subject, she asked, "Do you always have your Christmas Eve dinner at Juliet's?" Her own family usually went to her sister's, although Gemma considered an evening with Cyn's overexcited, sugar-fueled children more an ordeal than a celebration.

"Yes, she's insisted, ever since the children were small." Rosemary gave a worried glance at the large clock over the Rayburn. "I can't think why she would have stayed so late at the building site on her own, and today of all days. And what could she possibly have foun—" She stopped, her eyes straying to the children, then said instead, "Do you think they'll be long?"

Gemma hesitated over the truth. If Juliet had in fact found

a body, missing Christmas Eve dinner might be the least of her worries. "I really can't say. Is there anything we could do to help, in the meantime?"

"No. It's just ham and salads, and those Juliet will have made ahead. Nor would Caspar thank me for messing about in his kitchen uninvited," she added with a grimace. "Although he's happy enough to help himself to my punch—" This time it was her granddaughter's quick glance that silenced her. "Let's give it a bit," she amended. "Surely we'll hear from them soon."

The younger boys having divided the last scone between them, Sam stacked his plate and cup and pushed away from the table. "Nana, may we be excused? Can I show Toby and Kit the ponies?"

"You won't be able to see a thing," answered Rosemary, but Sam had his argument ready. "We'll take torches, and Jack will find the ponies. May we, please?"

Toby was already bouncing in his seat with excitement, and Kit looked interested. "Mummy, you'll come, too, won't you?" asked Toby, pulling at Gemma's hand.

"Yes, if Grandma Rosemary says its all right," she answered, and found she had used Toby's form of address for Kincaid's mother quite naturally.

After another quick look at the clock, Rosemary gave in gracefully. "All right, then. But bundle up, and be sure to put the other dogs on leads. You don't want them taking off across country in a strange place."

"I should stay and help you," protested Gemma, but Rosemary shook her head.

"Go with the children. This washing up won't take but a minute, and Hugh will help with the table. Won't you, dear?" She raised an eyebrow at her husband, and the gesture reminded Gemma of Duncan.

"Now you see how I suffer for my sins," Hugh said with a grin, beginning to clear the table. Trying to imagine her dad doing the same, Gemma shook her head. In her family, even though her mother worked like a demon in the bakery all day, her father expected to be waited on at tea.

When Gemma and the boys had put on their coats and

collected the dogs, she saw that Lally, who had slipped away up the stairs, had returned dressed for the outdoors as well.

The old scullery off the kitchen was now used as a boot room, and Hugh suggested they trade their shoes for pairs of the spare wellies that stood lined up on a low shelf. Gemma, having struggled with boots that were a bit too small, was last out. She found that Lally had hung back, waiting for her, while the boys ran ahead. Jack dashed around them in circles, barking excitedly.

"Oh." Gemma drew a breath of delight as she looked about her. "How lovely." The snow must have been falling heavily since they'd arrived, and now muffled the countryside in a thick blanket of white.

"Did you know that it's only officially a white Christmas if a snowflake falls on the roof of the BBC in London on Christmas Day?" asked Lally as they started after the boys, the snow squeaking as it compressed under their boots.

"That's hardly fair, is it?" Gemma thought of the occasional London snow, quickly marred by graffiti and turned to brown slush. This was different, a clean white silence stretching as far as she could see, and she was suddenly glad she had come.

The dog stopped barking, and in unspoken accord, she and Lally halted so that not even the rhythmic squeak of their boots disturbed the peace. They stood together, their shoulders touching, and let the still-falling snowflakes settle on their faces and hair.

Then, faint and far away, Gemma heard the wail of a siren, and her heart sank.

*He discovered the joy of possession when he was six. It had been the first day of term after the Christmas holiday, the class fractious with memories of their temporary freedom, confined indoors by the miserable weather, a cold, gunmetal sleet that crept inside coats and boots. Sodden jackets and mittens had steamed on the room's radiators, filling the air with a fetid, woolly odor that seemed to permeate his sinuses and skin. Odd how smell provided such direct and concrete link to memory; the least scent of damp wool brought back that day instantaneously, and with the recollection came emotion, tantalizingly intense.*

Their teacher—stupid cow—had encouraged them to show off their favorite Christmas gift. He'd had the latest toy, but so did most of the others, so no one was suitably impressed. But a toady child called Colin Squires—fat, with oversize spectacles—had opened a leather pouch filled with agate and cat's-eye marbles.

Both boys and girls leaned closer, reaching to touch the swirling colors of the agates and the strange, three-dimensional eyes. Colin, perspiring with pleasure, hadn't been able to resist clicking the marbles enticingly inside his pocket long after show-and-tell was over, and at break he had demonstrated marbles games to a group of admirers.

He, however, had stood back at the edge of the circle, watching with feigned disinterest. Even then, he'd understood the necessity of planning.

Three days later, when Colin's fleeting charm had waned and the other children had gone back to their usual games, he brushed up against Colin on the playground and came away with the bag of marbles transferred to his own pocket.

He kept his acquisition to himself, gloating over the marbles only in the privacy of his room, where he could fondle them without fear of interruption.

He knew, of course, that he had done something taboo, and that secrecy was the safest policy. What he didn't realize until he was a few years older was that he hadn't felt, even then, the prescribed emotion, what other people called "guilt." Not a smidgen.

# 3

**THE UNOPENED BOTTLE** of ten-year-old Aberlour stood on Ronnie Babcock's kitchen table, its ready-made red bow still attached. Babcock regarded it sourly as he added the day's post to the already toppling pile beside the bottle, then tossed his coat over a chair filled to overflowing with unopened newspapers.

The scotch was a gift from his guv'nor, Superintendent Fogarty, and you could always trust the super to judge the appropriate level of gift giving to a T. Not a blended bottle of Bell's, which might make it seem he undervalued his team, but nor could he be bothered to spend a quid or two extra on the twelve-year-old Aberlour. No point in splashing out more than was absolutely necessary, he would say. A diplomat to the bone, was Fogarty—no wonder he'd gone far in the force.

Not that Fogarty was a bad copper, as much as it sometimes galled Babcock to admit it. He was just a better politician, and that was what up-to-date policing required. Fogarty played golf regularly with the right county officials; he lived in a detached bungalow in the toniest part of suburban Crewe; his unfortunately bucktoothed wife appeared often in the pages of *Cheshire Life*. The Fogartys' life had, in fact, been Peggy Babcock's ideal, and she'd told Ronnie often enough what a fool he was not to emulate it.

Babcock had sneered at that, and look where it had got

him. Alone in a sedate semidetached house on the Crewe Road outside Nantwich, a house he had hated from the day the estate agent had shown it to them. And Peggy, who had insisted they buy the place, had packed her bag and walked out, straight into the arms—and the flat—of the same estate agent.

He gave a convulsive shiver as the cold began to seep through the thin fabric of his suit jacket. The central-heating boiler had been wonky the past few days, but he hadn't mustered the time or energy to have a look at it, and tonight it seemed to have gone out altogether. Now there was no chance in hell of getting the heating man to come, which meant it was going to be a long, cold Christmas.

Slipping back into his overcoat, Babcock tore the bow off the bottle of Aberlour, but stopped short of breaking the seal. The question was, did he put himself out of his misery now and suffer the hangover on Christmas morning, when he had to pay a courtesy call on his aged aunt, or did he put it off until he'd discharged his one social obligation and could sink as deep as he liked into alcohol-induced self-pity?

There were a couple of beers in the fridge, if not much else—he could make himself a sandwich and drink them while he watched Christmas Eve rubbish on the telly. Either choice was pathetic.

He'd volunteered for the holiday-call rota rather than face the evening on his own, but the citizenry of South Cheshire seemed remarkably well-behaved this Christmas Eve, more's the pity, and he had finally given up a hope of action and left a stultifyingly quiet station.

For a moment he toyed with the idea of calling Peggy to wish her a happy Christmas, but that meant he'd probably have to carry on a civil conversation with Bert, and he doubted his Christmas spirit would stretch quite that far.

Beer and telly it was, then, and he'd better bring the duvet down from the bedroom for a little extra warmth. He'd hate for his officers to find him frozen on his sofa when he didn't turn up for work after the holiday. Serve Peggy right, though, the cow, he thought with a snort, if she had to make social capital out of his embarrassing demise. On the other hand,

"Killed in the line of duty" would provide her with conversational fodder for years, and he didn't intend to give her the satisfaction.

He had opened the fridge, groaning when he saw only a solitary can of Tennents and an open packet of ham that curled up at the edges, when the mobile phone clipped to his belt began to vibrate. Even before he glanced at the number he knew it was Area Control—no one else would be ringing him on Christmas Eve.

"Thank you, God," he said with a sigh, and raised his eyes heavenward in salute as he flipped open the phone.

They sat huddled in Juliet's van, with the motor running in hopes of coaxing a little warm air from the heating vents. The windows were already fogging from their breath, and outside, the snow still drifted down, cocooning them from the outside world.

Kincaid found himself thinking of the time when he and Jules, as children, had managed to get themselves locked in their neighbor's coal cellar for an afternoon. He'd been devouring science fiction at the time, and as they'd sat scrunched together in the dark in what had seemed utter isolation, he'd imagined they were the last two people on earth. Fortunately, the neighbor had come home and heard their shouts, so they'd got off with no more than a bollocking and a missed meal, but he'd never forgotten the exhilarating terror of those long hours.

Beside him, Juliet took off one glove and held her bare hand in front of the vent, then grimaced and pulled it on again. "It's bloody freezing," she said. "Do you think the police will be long?"

Remembering how she had always refused comfort, he didn't give her a reassuring answer. "Quite likely. They'll be short-staffed tonight, and the bad weather won't help." After notifying the local police, he'd rung Gemma and his parents to explain the situation, but when he'd offered his phone to Juliet and asked if she needed to call Caspar, she'd said no.

Kincaid had never been particularly fond of his brother-in-law—he found the man's supercilious attitude exasperating—but he was distressed to hear the evident unhappiness in his sister's voice. He knew better than to pry, however—unless he did it very tactfully.

"How's your new business going?" he asked.

From the look on Juliet's face, it had been the wrong question. "This was my first big commission. We were already behind schedule because of the weather, and now with this—" She gave a despairing little shrug. "What makes it worse is that the client is a friend of Piers—" A few more strands fluttered loose from her ponytail as she fell silent, shaking her head. "Oh, God, listen to me. I'm a selfish cow to even think about my problems, when that poor child— What do you think happened to it, Duncan? And the pink suit—was it a little girl?"

"We can't know that yet," he answered gently. "But try not to think about it. Whatever happened was a long time ago—"

"Not that long," she broke in, surprising him. "That blanket—the children had one in the same fabric when they were small. It must have been Lally's, I think, because it was pink, but we used it for Sam as well."

"Do you remember where it came from?" he asked, unable to damp down the quickening of his pulse as his investigative instincts kicked in. This was not his case, he reminded himself—it had nothing to do with him.

"The supermarket, maybe. Or one of the chain baby shops. It was nothing special."

He pictured the child only a few yards distant, its flesh wasting away from its small bones, and wondered at the care with which it had been wrapped in the cheap blanket. But he had seen parents batter their children to death, then cover them tenderly, so he knew it meant nothing. Nor did he want to think about those things, not here, not now.

"How do you do it?" Jules said softly, as if she'd read his mind. "How do you deal with things like this every day, and still put your children to bed at night without panicking? They're so fragile, so vulnerable. You think it's the most frightening when they're babies, but then they get old enough to be out of your sight, out of your care, and you know that anything can happen . . ."

He thought immediately of Kit, and of his own failure to anticipate trouble in that quarter. And his niece, he remembered, was almost the same age. "Jules, are you having trouble with Lally?" he asked.

"No. No, of course not." Juliet pulled off her glove again, but this time, after testing the vent, she stripped off the other glove, too, and rubbed her hands together in the airstream. After a moment, she said, "It's just that . . . a month ago, a boy from Lally's school was found in the canal, drowned. He was fourteen. They said there was alcohol involved." She looked up at him, her hands still. "He was a good kid, Duncan. A good kid, a good student, never in any kind of trouble. If it can happen to a child like that . . ."

"I know. It means none of them is safe." It occurred to him then that he didn't know his niece at all, that he couldn't begin to guess whether or not she was at risk. "Is Lally all right? I'm sure it was very upsetting for her."

"I don't know. The school provided counseling for those who wanted it, but I'm not sure if she went. She doesn't talk to me anymore. But she's seemed different the last few weeks, more withdrawn." Juliet sighed. "Maybe it's just her age. I suppose I was difficult at fourteen, too."

"Worse than difficult," he said, teasing. If he had hoped for an answering smile, he was disappointed. Juliet flashed him a look he couldn't read, then yanked her gloves on again and huddled deeper into her jacket.

Why was it, Kincaid wondered, that he always managed to put his foot wrong with his sister?

Ronnie Babcock felt his adrenaline start to pump as he backed out of his drive. As glad as he was of any excuse to avoid his own company, he'd expected nothing more exciting than an alcohol-fueled domestic, or perhaps a burglar taking advantage of someone away for the holiday. Certainly when his phone rang he hadn't imagined the interred body of a child—at the least a suspicious death, at the most a homicide.

He forced himself to slow the powerful BMW. It was still snowing and the roads would be growing treacherous. Although he liked to drive fast, he was careful of his car—God help anyone who put a nick or dent in the Black Beast, as he liked to call it. He'd bought the 320 used after Peggy had walked out, and if there were whispered comments about the male menopause around the station, he didn't care. He'd been a poor kid, and to him the car represented everything he'd never thought he could achieve.

Not that he thought of himself as middle-aged, mind you. As he slowed for the A51 roundabout, he tightened the knot in his tie and glanced at himself in the driving mirror. At forty-one, his hair was still thick, springing from the widow's peak on his brow, and if there were a few gray threads mixed with the blond, they didn't show. He'd kept his footballer's physique, too, as well as the broken nose and the scar across his cheek where a football boot had caught him full in the face. His rather battered visage often came in handy in the interview room, and he liked to think there were women—his ex-wife notwithstanding—that found it attractive.

The traffic was lighter than he'd expected, and he had an easy shot of it to the location of the call, skirting the north side of Nantwich on the A51. At the Burford roundabout the A51 turned north, towards Chester, and the visibility dropped to near nil in the blowing snow. He crawled along, swearing under his breath, thinking about the logistics of getting the crime-scene unit out in this weather. From the brief report he'd been given, he wasn't sure if the actual site of the corpse was sheltered from the elements.

His swearing increased in volume as he saw the turning too late to negotiate it. He had to drive another mile into Barbridge before he could find a place to turn the car, and this time he crept back towards the farm track at a snail's pace. His moment of triumph was short-lived, however, when he discovered he couldn't even see which way the track turned. Nor was the high-powered BMW designed for driving in accumulating snow on unpaved roads. He coasted to a stop, wondering if he was going to have to get out and leg it the rest of the way with the help of a torch. His overcoat was lightweight; his shoes were new and expensive and would be soaked through in minutes.

Then, as he checked the batteries in the torch he kept in the door pocket, the curtain of white surrounding his car began to thin. After a moment, it was once more possible to pick out individual flakes, and then there were only a few solitary, erratically drifting crystals.

Babcock suspected the reprieve was temporary, but he could now see the road a few yards beyond the car's bonnet, and he meant to take advantage of it. He put the BMW into gear again and crept along the track, and soon he saw the panda cars' blue lights flashing like beacons.

When he came out into the clearing, he saw that the head-lamps of the patrol cars illuminated a Ford Escort and the sort of white van used by builders and plumbers. One of the patrol officers stood talking to two civilians, and as he drew nearer Babcock could see that the taller figure was a man in a City overcoat, and the smaller, which he had first assumed to be male, seemed to be a woman dressed in rough clothing. Behind them, torches flashed within the shadowy huddle of outbuildings.

What a godforsaken place, and how had these people come to discover a body here on Christmas Eve? He picked his way across the snowy ruts, careful of his shoes although he knew it was a hopeless prospect. At least he wouldn't be the only one with ruined footwear, he thought with some satisfaction, considering the cut of the other man's overcoat.

The woman was quite pretty, dark-haired, and there was something about her that tickled his memory. Then, as the man turned towards him, his face fully illuminated in the glare of the lights, Ronnie Babcock gave an involuntary grunt of surprise. What the hell was *he* doing here?

"Well, I'll be buggered," he said as he reached the waiting group. "If it isn't my old mate Duncan Kincaid. Trouble himself."

Her skin was pale, and felt clammy to the touch. Worse, even in the dim light of the cabin, it seemed to Gabriel Wain that his wife's lips were tinged with blue. When he smoothed her dark hair from her brow, she moved restlessly under his touch and opened her eyes.

"Gabe, you won't forget, will you?" she whispered. "They'd be so disappointed—"

"Of course I won't forget, woman. I'll do it as soon as they're asleep, I promise." From the next-door cabin, he could hear the rustlings and occasional giggles of their son and daughter, awake past their bedtime with Christmas Eve excitement. The stockings would be laid at the ends of their bunks, even if the knitted socks held only oranges, boiled sweets, and a few knickknacks from the shop at the Venetian Marina.

There were a few other surprises wrapped in colored paper and tucked away in the main cabin: crayons and paints, some clever three-dimensional cards depicting canal life that the children could tack up by their beds, a book for each of them. And for seven-year-old Marie there was a doll; for nine-year-old Joseph, his first pocketknife. To provide these things, Rowan had worked extra hours painting the traditional roses-and-castles canalware she sold to supplement their income, and the effort had exhausted her.

Not that it took much to exhaust her these days. Worry gnawed in his belly like a worm, and his helplessness in the face of her growing weakness made him so angry his hands had begun to shake continually, but he tried to hide such feelings from her. He knew why she wouldn't seek help at a hospital or clinic—he understood the consequences as well as she did. So he did what he could: he managed the boat and the locks with only the children's help, he'd taken over almost all the domestic chores as well, and he did what he could to comfort the children and attend to their lessons.

But it wasn't enough—he knew it wasn't enough, and he knew he would be lost without her.

He shifted a little on the bed's edge so that he could pull the blanket more firmly over his wife's shoulders. Even through his thick wool jumper he could feel the chill creeping into the boat. The narrowboat's only heat came from the stove in the main cabin, but he dared not add more wood this late in the evening. He stored a supply on top of the boat, both for their own use and to sell to other boaters, and with the Christmastime slowdown in odd jobs, he couldn't afford to burn their only source of cash. Nor would he be able to forage easily for more wood with snow on the ground—if the cold snap lasted more than a few days, they would be in real trouble.

Rowan's eyelids had begun to droop again. "You sleep now, do you hear?" he whispered. "I'll take care of everything." And he would, too—it was just that it was becoming harder and harder to see how he was going to manage it.

Rowan was asleep, her breathing shallow but regular, and from next door the children's voices had faded from drowsy whispers to silence. Giving his wife's shoulder a squeeze, he moved quietly through the children's cabin and into the stern.

He stood for a moment, gazing at the remains of the stew he'd made for dinner, still standing on the hob; at the lace-ware and brasses decorating the polished wood of the cabin walls; at the bright detail of the castle scene Rowan had painted on the underside of the drop table. The children had strung tinsel and a red-and-green paper chain over the windows and Marie had tacked up a drawing she'd made of Father Christmas wearing a pointed red hat.

Only embers glowed in the stove. With sudden decision, Gabe took a log from the basket and fed it into the fire. It was Christmas Eve, and he'd be damned if they'd spend it freezing. Maybe tomorrow the weather would break. Maybe he'd find a carpentry job before the New Year. He had contacts here—it was the only thing that had brought him back to the Nantwich stretch of the Cut.

Right, he thought, with the wave of bitterness that swamped him all too often these days. Maybe Father Christmas would come. Maybe the boat's makeshift loo would work properly for once. And maybe his wife would miraculously get better, instead of more frail by the moment.

Tears stung his eyes and he blinked furiously, stabbing at the fire with the poker until the heat scorched his face. She was slipping away from him and he couldn't bear it, not after everything they'd been through.

There was only one option that he could see. He could sell the boat. There were always collectors sniffing around the

Cut, looking for traditional working narrowboats built before the 1950s, the less altered, the better. Willing to pay a handsome price to do without plumbing or central heating, they would restore the boats to their original state and show them off at boat shows. Never mind that entire families had lived in seven-by-eight-foot cabins and babies had played on top of the sheeted coal or cocoa in the cargo space—that only added to the romance.

Gabe snorted in disgust. They were fools, playing at being boatmen, and he'd not give up the *Daphne* to the likes of them. He'd been born on this boat, as had his father, and now his family was one of the last still clinging to the old way of life.

And selling the boat would only be a stopgap measure at best—he knew that. Where would they go? What would they do? They knew nothing else, and there was nowhere else they would be safe.

He thought of the face from the past that had appeared so unexpectedly today. The woman had been maneuvering her boat round the angle where the Middlewich fed into the main branch of the canal at Barbridge; skillfully, he thought, for a woman alone. Then she had looked up.

It had taken him a moment to place her in the strange context, and then he'd felt the old, familiar lurch of fear. She had recognized them as well, and had spoken to Rowan and the children in a friendly way, but he didn't trust her. Why should he, even after what she had done for them?

She and her kind, no matter how well-meaning, meant nothing but trouble—had never meant anything but trouble for him or his people. *He'd* been the fool to think they could run away from it forever.

Moving slowly back into the children's cabin, he stared down at their sleeping forms. The light reflecting off the snow came through the small window more brightly than a full moon. He knelt, touching his daughter's curls with his large, calloused hand, and a fierce resolve rose in him.

He knew one thing, and it was enough. He would do whatever it took to keep what remained of his family from harm.

# 4

❧

**FROM THE MOMENT** he had looked up and found her watching him from the stairs, Kit thought that Lally Newcombe was the most beautiful thing he had ever seen. He was afraid to look at her, afraid his face would betray him, yet he hadn't been able to tear his eyes away. Around him, the commotion of dogs and greetings faded to an incomprehensible babble, and when Tess leapt from his arms, he'd felt as if he'd been stripped naked, defenseless before the dark-haired girl's remote and considering gaze.

The entrance of Jack the sheepdog and the group exodus from the hall gave him a respite, but even then he'd been aware of Lally's movements, as if he'd developed remote sensors on every inch of his skin. He trailed after the others, feeling as if his hands and feet had suddenly become enormous, awkward appendages more suited to a giant.

Once in the kitchen, he tried to ignore Lally, tried to look at anything other than her face and the slice of bare skin showing in the gap between her shirt and her jeans. When Rosemary spoke to him, he forced himself to focus, and to answer, pushing his voice past the lump in his throat and keeping it level.

Rosemary—his *grandmother,* he reminded himself. He still couldn't quite get his head round it, even though he'd met her once before, at his mum's funeral. Although he hadn't known then that she bore any relation to him, she had been kind to him, and had stood up to Eugenia. It had been the one bright spot in that horrible day.

Eugenia, his *other* grandmother, his mother's mother. Would he ever be able to hear "grandmother" without thinking of her? She was the only grandmother he had known until now, and his mother's dad, Bob, the only grandfather.

As he helped Rosemary carry the tea things to the table, he glanced up at Hugh, his new grandfather, with curiosity. Hugh Kincaid was a tall man, with a lean, beaky sort of face, and a comfortable aura of the outdoors about him. But there was a bookishness, too, a hint of the faraway about his eyes, and Kit thought he might be the sort of person who held long conversations with himself.

Just now, however, he was laughing and joking with the younger boys, and Kit's face flamed with envy. In that moment he hated Toby, hated the easy way he made friends so easily. Then he flushed again with shame, hating himself for the thought, hating himself for being so cruel to the smaller boy earlier that day.

He didn't know what had got into him lately. Sometimes it seemed as if something alien lived between his brain and his mouth, out of control, just waiting to take over whenever he spoke. And then there were the dreams. He'd had them the first few months after his mother died, and now they had come back, worse than ever. He woke from them sick and sweating, afraid to go back to sleep, and afterwards he carried a lingering queasiness with him all through the day. Maybe he would be all right here, away from home, away from school.

The thought of school brought back that morning's confrontation with Duncan and Gemma, and he cringed inwardly. Kit had known he would get caught out, had thought that before it happened he'd find an opportunity to confess, to explain. But the time had somehow never come, and when he'd been taken by surprise, all the words he'd prepared vanished like wraiths and left him stupidly, painfully silent.

The clatter of dishes jerked Kit back to the present. The meal was finished and Hugh was clearing away the tea things. When Sam suggested they go outside, he was glad of any excuse to get away from his thoughts.

It was both a relief and a disappointment when Lally hung back with Gemma. He wanted to be near the girl, wanted to speak to her, yet he didn't know what to say. But as he trooped ahead with Sam and Toby, stomping footprints in the freshly fallen powder, he began to forget his discomfort. For the first time since they'd arrived he was able to take pleasure in the moment.

The field sloped down to a distant dark smudge of trees, and halfway across it he saw two shaggy shapes that must be the ponies, one dark, one light. Jack had bounded ahead and was now circling the ponies, yipping and lunging. The dog's white markings seemed to disappear into the snow, so that the moving black patches of his coat looked strangely disembodied. Kit stopped a moment, watching, feeling the cold sear his lungs as he breathed. The snow and the sharp, smoky, night air were glorious, London and school seemed a universe away, and the holiday felt suddenly full of promise.

Kincaid grasped the hand held out to him, studying the man with dawning recognition. "Good God, it's not Ronnie Babcock, is it?"

"That's Chief Inspector Babcock to you, old son," Babcock said jovially, but his voice held the hint of self-mockery Kincaid remembered from their school days. He hadn't seen Babcock since he'd left Cheshire for London more than twenty years ago, and the last he'd heard, Babcock had been looking at a promising career in professional football.

"I'll be damned. I'd no idea you were on the force, Ronnie. What happened to the—"

"Knee," Babcock interrupted shortly. "I thought I should look for something with more long-term benefits—although at the moment I couldn't tell you what they are." He grinned and gave a shrug that took in the snow and the surroundings, and Kincaid remembered his unexpected charm.

He'd never known Babcock really well. Their friendship had been an odd one, and had come about by chance. Babcock had been a tough, working-class kid with an attitude, and his social circle had not naturally intersected with Kincaid's. But more than once, Kincaid had seen him stand up for a kid who was being bullied, and had witnessed an occasional gruff and rather awkward kindness, quickly masked by teasing.

Then, one day, Kincaid had gone into his parents' bookshop after school and seen Ronnie Babcock at the cash register, finishing a transaction with one of the shop assistants. Babcock had looked furtive, and Kincaid, his curiosity aroused, had moved close enough to glimpse the other boy's purchase as it went into the bag. The volume was not something risqué, as he'd half expected, but a battered, used edition of James Hilton's *Lost Horizon*.

Kincaid had opened his mouth to rib Babcock about his taste in reading material when something in the boy's expression stopped him. When Babcock had finished counting out his coins and stuffed the book into a jacket pocket, he moved away from the counter and said quietly to Kincaid, "Look, you won't tell my mates at school, will you?"

"But—"

"It's a poncey book, see," Babcock added with a look of pleading. "I'd never live it down."

Kincaid did see. He'd grown up tainted by the aura of his parents' profession, as well as by the folly of his own occasional displays of knowledge. He'd been labeled an anorak, a bookworm, and no matter how well he did at games or how tough he was on the playground, it had stuck.

"Yeah, all right," he'd said, grinning. "But only if you promise to tell me what you think of the book."

After that they had talked when they'd run across each other in town, and Babcock had often come into the bookshop when he knew Kincaid was working after school, but that had seemed the natural limit of the relationship. Babcock had never invited Kincaid to his home, or vice versa, and they'd had no reason to keep up after leaving school.

Babcock had aged well, Kincaid saw now. He still looked fit, and even with his pugnacious boxer's face, he'd acquired an air of polish unimaginable in the teenager.

"Chief inspector?" Kincaid said, raising an eyebrow. "Aren't you a bit elevated to be taking a call on Christmas Eve?"

"My inspector's got kiddies at home. My sergeant, too." Babcock shrugged. "And besides, it's not often something as interesting as a mummified baby turns up on my patch."

Beside him, Kincaid felt Juliet flinch, and saw Babcock eyeing her with interest. He wondered if the callous reference had been deliberate on Babcock's part.

Babcock pulled his overcoat collar a little higher on his neck and gave Kincaid a sharp glance. "Now, as much as I'd like to stand around all night in the bleeding snow waffling on about old times, why don't you tell me exactly what you're doing here. Scotland Yard isn't in the habit of calling *us* to report a body."

"You know I'm with the Yard?" Somehow Kincaid had expected Babcock to be as ignorant of his profession as he had been of Babcock's.

Babcock smiled at Kincaid's consternation. "It's still a small town, mate. And I still pop into your dad's shop now and again. You'd made superintendent, last I heard. So have you added psychic detective to your accomplishments?"

The dig was unmistakable. Kincaid realized that Babcock might not be thrilled to have Scotland Yard nosing about, especially if his dad had been painting him as the town's golden boy. "Look," he said, "I'm just here for the holiday with my family. It's my sister who found the body. She called me at my folks', and I rang 999—"

"After having a thorough poke round and contaminating my crime scene," Babcock finished sourly.

Kincaid raised an eyebrow. "You'd have done the same. For all I knew, it was a prank." When Babcock nodded a reluctant acknowledgment, Kincaid went on, "You remember my sister, Juliet?" He touched Juliet's shoulder, urging her forward.

Babcock gripped her hand in a belated shake. "I thought I recognized you. You're Mrs. Newcombe now. I know your husband." There was a reserve in his second comment that sounded less than reassuring, but he went on with evident sincerity. "So sorry you've had to deal with all this, and to-night of all nights. Can you tell me exactly what happened?"

Juliet looked white and pinched, but she answered strongly. "I'm a builder. I'm renovating the old barn for my clients, a couple from London named Bonner. I was working late, try-ing to finish up a few things before the holiday."

"On your own?" Babcock's voice held a note of skepti-cism.

Juliet stood a little straighter. "Yes. I'd sent my lads home. I was hoping to finish tearing out a section of mortar before the light went. And then I found . . . it . . . the baby."

"And you didn't ring the police right away?"

"No." For the first time she sounded less confident. "I—I wasn't sure—I wanted—I knew Duncan was expected at our parents', so I thought . . ."

Babcock considered for a moment. "You said the new owners? How long have they had the place?"

"Just a few months. They're boaters. They bought it with the idea of turning it into a second home, with a good moor-ing for their narrowboat."

"And they've no previous connection with the property?"

"Not that I know of."

Babcock looked at the figures moving in the light spilling from the old dairy, then peered up the lane into the dark-ness. "So these Londoners, who did they buy the barn from? The people in the big house at the top of the lane?"

"No." The sharpness of Juliet's answer caught Kincaid by surprise. "No. There's a farmhouse just at the bend in the lane, about halfway down. I think the owners—the Fosters—bought the farm directly from the people who had owned the farm and the dairy barn for years. Then, last year, they de-cided to subdivide the property and sell off the barn and surrounding pasture. The market's booming, with any old tumbledown outbuilding being hyped as 'suitable for renova-tion.' The dairy was a real treasure and they knew it."

"What happened to the Smiths, then?" Kincaid asked. He remembered the old traditional Cheshire farming fam-ily who had had the place, and who had tolerated his and Juliet's exploring the property.

"Sold up about five years ago," Jules answered. "Retired and moved south. Shropshire, I think."

"Smith? Bugger," Babcock muttered with feeling, then glanced at the barn again. To Kincaid, he said, "Any idea how long—"

"Not a clue. Maybe your pathologist can hazard a guess. Is he a good man?"

Babcock smiled. "In a manner of speaking. But don't tell her I said so."

Embarrassed by his unconscious sexism, Kincaid grimaced. Fortunately, it seemed to have passed Juliet by. Stomping her feet to warm them, she pulled back her jacket cuff and squinted at her watch. "Look. It is Christmas Eve, and we've got family waiting. I don't know what else I can tell you."

"I'll need a proper statement from you, but I can get that tomorrow," Babcock conceded.

"It's Yew Cottage, near the end of North Crofts."

"I know the place." Babcock turned to Kincaid. "What about you, Duncan? Ensconced in the familial bosom?"

"Yes." Kincaid gave brief directions to his parents' house, although it wouldn't have surprised him to find that Babcock knew perfectly well where they lived—then fished a card from his coat pocket. "Here's my mobile number. If you could—" He stopped as the flash of car headlamps coming down the track caught his eye.

As a white van emerged from the trees and rolled towards them, Babcock turned to look. "That'll be the SOCOs. Dr. Elsworthy won't be far behind."

A man climbing from the van called out, "Hey, boss, what have we got?"

Babcock raised his hand in acknowledgment, answering merely, "Meet you at the barn."

"Right," he added briskly to Kincaid and Juliet. "I'll be in touch. Mrs. Newcombe, I'll need the names and contact information for anyone working with you on the premises, if you could get that together for me by tomorrow." He held a hand out to Kincaid. "Good to see you, old son."

Babcock might as well have said *Run away and play,* so

obviously had his attention moved on. Kincaid felt a flare of irritation at being cast aside like a used tissue. He knew all the things running through his old friend's mind—Babcock would be deciding how to organize the crime scene, structuring the interviews of the property's present and former owners and of the neighbors, making arrangements for the examination of the remains—all the things Kincaid would be doing himself if it were his case.

The gears in Kincaid's mind clicked over, his adrenaline pumped, and the exhilaration of the chase kicked into his system like a drug. He wanted to look over the crime scene with Babcock and the SOCOs, he wanted to see what the pathologist had to say about the body of the child. It was on his lips to ask Juliet to go on without him, to tell Babcock he'd stay, when he glanced at his sister.

Hunched against the cold in her padded coat, she looked more vulnerable than he had ever seen her. She was regarding him with a puzzled expression.

"Duncan, can't we go?" she asked.

*We've got family waiting,* she had said to Babcock. He thought of Gemma and the boys, marooned at his parents' as Christmas Eve ticked away, and cursed himself for a selfish bastard.

"Of course," he said, and to Babcock he added, "Good luck with it, then."

He turned and walked Juliet to her van, but as he started to get into his own car, he couldn't resist a look back at the scene.

Babcock was still standing in the same spot, watching him, his lips curved in a knowing smile.

"Where the hell is she?" Caspar Newcombe slammed the phone back into its cradle on his desk. "It's nearly eight o'clock and not a word from her, and we're supposed to be serving dinner for her whole bloody clan before midnight mass."

"Have you tried ringing her mother?" His partner, Piers Dutton, settled himself a little more comfortably in one of the client's chairs across from Caspar's desk and arranged one ankle over the other. Fed up with pacing round the empty house and ringing his wife's unresponsive mobile phone, Caspar had walked the short distance to his firm and found Piers there, finishing up some paperwork. Seeing Caspar's expression, Piers had got up from his desk and followed Caspar into his office.

Newcombe and Dutton, Investments, occupied the ground-floor premises at the end of a Georgian terrace near the town square, just a few yards from St. Mary's Church. The building was a gem, and Caspar took great pride in their acquisition of the office suite. He'd also expected his wife to share his feelings, and to look on her position as office manager of Newcombe and Dutton as a privilege.

Instead, she had walked out on them without so much as giving notice, and had *borrowed* money to set herself up in business as a builder. A builder! If she had intended to humiliate him, she couldn't have made a better choice. Not that she hadn't always been handy around the house—in fact, he'd been pleased when she'd tackled projects that would have required calling in a professional—but this was beyond the pale. And now—now he found she'd done worse.

"I shouldn't have to be chasing after her like she was a wayward child," he said sulkily to Piers. Caspar eyed his own chair, an executive leather model that had cost the earth, but felt too irritated to sit. Instead, he crossed the room to the drinks cabinet and poured a good finger of Dalwhinnie single malt into two crystal tumblers. These were not just any tumblers, of course, but Finnish crystal in a contemporary design. Waterford was passé, in Caspar's opinion, and he made a point that everything in the firm's offices should reflect the best and most up-to-date.

That included himself, although he was forced to admit that even in the finest wool trousers and a pale yellow cashmere jumper, he still looked like the accountant he was, no matter how glorified his title. He was too tall, too thin, too dark, with fine-boned and serious features that had not been designed for the sort of nonchalant charm his partner radiated so effortlessly.

"Cheers," said Piers now, as Caspar handed him a whisky. He sipped and took a moment to savor the taste before giving his verdict. "Very nice. You shouldn't let Juliet raise your blood pressure, you know," he added, peering at Caspar over his glass. "She's probably just got hung up with family. Didn't you say her brother was arriving? He could have been delayed by the weather."

Caspar was not to be mollified. "I don't see how that excuses her turning off her phone. It's inconsiderate, under any circumstances. And that's not to mention her inviting them all for Christmas Eve dinner without consulting me."

"It's Christmas, Caspar. If I can achieve détente over dinner with my lovely ex, then you can certainly put up with the in-laws. You make it sound as if they have the plague." Piers downed another third of his drink. He was a big man, with thick fair hair that sprang from his brow in a leonine wave, and if he had begun to put on a little weight as he entered his forties, he carried it well. Tonight he wore a long denim coat over a nubby green sweater, and looked every inch the country squire.

Stinging a bit from Piers's criticism, Caspar changed the subject. "Is Leo already at Helen's, then?" he asked.

Leo was Piers's fourteen-year-old son, Helen his ex-wife. Piers and Helen shared custody of the boy, but since Piers had bought the Victorian manor house a few miles from town and begun playing at country gentleman, Leo spent most of his time with his father.

Piers supported Helen very well, however, in a mock Tudor cottage on the west side of Nantwich, just the other side of the river, so perhaps Helen found it wise not to protest. Helen, unlike his own recalcitrant wife, knew on which side her bread was buttered.

"Oh, yes. Leo's grandparents are there as well, and he's on his best behavior. Hoping to increase the size of his Christmas check, I should imagine," Piers added with an air of satisfaction. Leo Dutton had inherited his father's good looks, and was already well versed in using them to his advantage.

Piers polished off the last third of his whisky, stretched,

and stood. "I'd better be off. If I make Helen keep dinner waiting, I'll have to endure injured looks the rest of the evening. We'll see you at church later on, shall we?"

Caspar doubted that Piers felt any more religious impulse than he did, but several of their clients were churchwardens or members of the congregation, so it behooved them to put in an appearance. Nantwich was still a small enough town that the social lives of those with money to spend on investments were closely intertwined, and the firm's business depended on their keeping and strengthening ties with those in prominent positions.

"If we make it," responded Caspar, with another glance at his watch. "At this rate—"

Piers turned back from the door with a sigh of exasperation. "For heaven sake's, man, ring your mother-in-law. If you're worried—"

"I'm not worried," Caspar said mulishly. He downed half his drink in a rebellious gulp and felt the fire burn all the way down to his gut.

"Caspar." Piers eyed him speculatively. "You've had a row, haven't you? A flaming row." His heavy brows drew together as he frowned. "You didn't tell Juliet about our little talk, did you? That was to be just between us. You agreed."

Now Caspar was torn between guilt and a desire to vent. "It just came out," he admitted. "I didn't intend it. She had the gall to say she'd always tried to do her best by our marriage. Bitch." He swallowed the rest of his drink, and this time he barely felt the burn.

"Goddamn it, Caspar." Piers no longer looked amused, and Caspar suddenly felt crowded by the other man's physical presence. "I'd no intention of making things worse between you and Juliet. I was just looking out for your interests, because you're my friend as well as my partner. If you couldn't keep your mouth shut, I won't be responsible for the consequences." He turned away, and a moment later, Caspar heard the outside door open and then slam firmly shut.

He stood, his empty glass dangling from his nerveless fingers. Now he'd torn it. Piers was right, he should have kept his mouth shut. The last thing he'd wanted was to make

Piers angry with him, or to betray his trust. He couldn't remember Piers ever raising his voice towards him before.

But it was odd, he thought, swaying slightly as he made an effort to set the glass neatly on his desk. Piers had been angry, there was no mistaking that, but just as he'd turned away, Caspar could have sworn he'd seen a gleam of satisfaction in his partner's eye.

Annie Lebow had no trouble getting a mooring at Nantwich Canal Center. On Christmas Eve, most sane boaters were happily landlocked with family or friends.

The canal center occupied the old Chester Basin, once the terminus of the Chester Canal. Finished in 1779, the canal had been cut wide to accommodate the barges carrying heavy goods, including the famous Nantwich cheeses, across the Cheshire Plain from Nantwich to Chester. After years of decline, the basin had been resurrected in the nineties by an industrious couple, becoming an important center for boat-building and boat repair, as well as providing everyday services for boaters.

Annie needed some work done on the *Horizon*—the electrical system had developed a glitch—and Nantwich had seemed the obvious choice. Or so she had told herself, disregarding the fact that she was unlikely to find anyone to do the necessary repairs during Christmas week. The truth was that she found herself more and more often drawn back to the scenes of her working life, the very places she had once so desperately wanted to put behind her.

How odd that today she had seen the very family who had been primarily responsible for her leaving her job, and who had also inspired her to take up the boating life. She'd been tempted to tell Gabriel Wain that she owed him a debt of gratitude, but suspected he'd think her daft.

No matter how competent or how experienced she'd become, she'd never really belong to the world of the traditional boat people. Not that there were many like the Wains left on the canals. She'd wondered, in the years since she'd handled their case, if she'd let her fascination with their way of life affect her judgment.

The sight of the children today, so obviously happy and healthy, had relieved any nagging doubts. The mother, however, had looked wan and ill—and frightened. Annie had known better than to comment—she understood the reason for the Wains' distrust all too well. She'd told herself it was none of her business, but it seemed that once a social worker, always a social worker, like it or not, and she found it hard to let go of her concern for Rowan Wain.

With the boat safely moored in the quiet marina, she'd used her torch to pick her way along the towpath and onto the aqueduct that carried the Shropshire Union over the Chester Road. The Shroppie, as the boaters affectionately called it, was actually a connected system of canals built at different times by different canal companies. It was here at Nantwich that the old Chester Canal met the narrow Liverpool to Birmingham Junction Canal, built by the Scottish engineer Thomas Telford in the late 1820s. While the iron aqueduct was not as impressive as Telford's stone aqueduct at Pontcysyllte, in Wales, Annie had always loved its soaring lines. This aqueduct and the Birmingham Junction Canal had been Telford's last projects—he had, in fact, died before their completion—and that somehow added a bittersweet touch to their beauty.

It had been Rowan Wain who had told Annie about the Pontcysyllte Aqueduct, which carried the Llangollen Canal across the entire span of the Dee Valley. The first time Annie had taken the *Horizon* down the Llangollen and worked up the nerve to cross the aqueduct, she'd been terrified and exhilarated. The boat seemed to float in midair like a spirit, high above the valley, and it was like nothing else Annie had ever experienced. Afterwards, she felt she was a true boater.

From where she stood now, she could see the snow dusting the rooftops of Nantwich, and she thought she could just make out the dark shadow that was the tower of St. Mary's Church. Even as a child, visiting from her home near Malpas, in southern Cheshire, she'd been fascinated by Nantwich. The black-and-white-timbered shops facing the green had made her think of a picture on a chocolate box, and she'd liked the way the massive red stone bulk of St. Mary's had balanced the prettiness of the surrounding buildings.

Once, she'd asked her parents to take her to Christmas Eve mass at St. Mary's. Her mother had refused, with her usual scorn, saying there was a perfectly good church in Malpas that they were expected to attend and it would be idiotic to consider driving twenty miles through darkness and bad weather to go somewhere else.

It had been no less than Annie had expected, but to her surprise, her father had agreed, and they had gone, just the two of them. Annie had known, even then, that her father would suffer the consequences of her mother's anger for days, but her guilt had not been able to dampen her pleasure. It had been one of the few times she'd spent alone with her busy father. They hadn't talked much, but there had been a shared sense of adventure between them, spiced by the re-belliousness of defying her mother. She couldn't remember another occasion when she had felt so close to him.

Years later, living with her husband in the house she'd inherited from her parents, she'd thought of asking him to go with her to midnight mass at St. Mary's. Roger, cheerful atheist that he was, would have indulged her, but it was that very indulgence that had made her decide against it. Roger had viewed all her passions with an air of affectionate but slightly amused condescension, and that particular memory had been too precious to taint with ridicule.

Still, after five years of separation, and knowing Roger as well as she did, the temptation to confide in him was strong. She'd wanted to tell him about her encounter with the Wains, about her fears for Rowan Wain's health. She'd even gone so far as to punch his number into her mobile phone, but at the last minute had disconnected.

It was Christmas Eve. Roger would interpret a phone call as an admission of loneliness, perhaps even an admission of defeat.

Loneliness, yes, but she'd been lonely when they were to-gether, sometimes more than she was now. Defeat, no, not yet, even if she hadn't found the peace she'd sought in her roving life on the Cut.

The muted throb of a diesel engine signaled the progress of a narrowboat. Looking back towards the basin, Annie saw a light moving low on the water. As the boat entered the aqueduct and glided past her, close enough to touch, the muffled figure at the tiller nodded a silent greeting. Annie watched the boat's light until it disappeared, then turned back to the glimmering rooftops of Nantwich. She no longer felt so alone.

There was nothing stopping her, she realized, other than a brisk and solitary walk through the streets of the town. She would go to midnight mass at St. Mary's, and she would celebrate in her own way those things for which she was thankful.

# 5

**BABCOCK CHUCKLED** aloud as he watched his old friend drive away. Having caught the brief, unguarded expression on Kincaid's usually composed face, he had recognized naked lust for the chase. He felt a surprising satisfaction at having discovered a kindred spirit, rising so unexpectedly from the ashes of his past life.

Brushing at a feather touch of damp on his cheek, he realized it was snowing again. "Sod it," he said aloud, casting a glance at the sky, which seemed to loom within touching distance. He scrubbed the accumulating flakes from his hair in irritation and set off after his crime-scene techs, his amusement forgotten.

He stopped at the open doorway of the barn, nodding at the constable standing watch. What *would* be the doorway, Babcock amended, as he could see now that the opening was merely roughly framed. The interior was littered with the debris of construction—a few planks and pails lay scattered about, and a power saw had been propped against the leg of a wooden sawhorse. Near the far wall, a pick had been dropped on the dirt floor, its blade catching the light from the battery-powered lamps.

Clive Travis, his chief forensics officer, stood just inside the door, struggling to get his paper suit on over bulky warm clothing. Travis was a small, lean man who wore his thinning sandy hair pulled back in a ponytail, and whose energetic personality mirrored his whippet-like appearance. Tonight, however, he looked anything but happy, and his fellow officer seemed no more cheerful. Sandra Barnett, the scene photographer, was quick and competent, but always appeared as if she'd rather be doing something else. Tonight, her broad face looked positively funereal.

"So, what do we have here, troops?" Babcock asked. After slipping off his overcoat and handing it to a constable, with a grimace he accepted gloves and another paper suit from Travis. Protecting the evidence from contamination was a bloody waste of time, he was sure, in an old scene that had been openly accessible, but it had to be done. It would be his head on a platter if there was a balls-up, and he hadn't got where he was by indulging his rebellious streak—at least not very often.

"Have a look for yourself, boss." When Babcock was properly suited, Travis slipped a torch into Babcock's freshly gloved hand. "A babe in a manger, you might say."

Sandra Barnett glanced at Travis and thumped down her camera case with unnecessary force. Babcock supposed he couldn't blame her for being irritated by Travis's irreverence, but it was one of the reasons he liked the man, that and Travis's appreciation of the bizarre—and bizarre this case certainly was.

From where he stood, Babcock could see the pickwork in the far wall, and in the opening, a scrap of pinkish cloth and what looked like a cluster of tiny brown twigs. Maneuvering carefully around the dropped pick, he stepped closer as Travis repositioned a light so that it provided better illumination. Suddenly, his brain assembled the component parts of what he was seeing into a coherent whole.

"Jesus," he said involuntarily, not caring if it earned a glower from Barnett. The twigs were the curled brown bones of a tiny hand. What he had seen as a clump of root filament was the tuft of fine hair left above a wizened face. The empty and sunken eye sockets seemed to peer back at him.

No wonder Juliet Newcombe had seemed shaken. Babcock had seen much worse in the course of his career, in terms of blood and mutilation, but there was something

WATER LIKE A STONE

pathetically vulnerable in this little corpse. Who could have done such a thing to a child?

The lower half of the child's body was still encased in its mortar shroud, but from what Babcock could see, there was no obvious sign of physical trauma, nor any bloodstains on the blanket or clothing. Voices at the doorway alerted him to the arrival of the Home Office pathologist and he turned away, glad enough to have someone else take over the examination.

Dr. Althea Elsworthy strode into the barn, disdaining Travis's offer of a paper suit with an irritable flick of her wrist. She always carried her own supply of latex gloves, and paused just inside the doorway to stuff her heavy woolen pair in the pocket of her coat and puff air into the latex replacements before pulling them on. "Mummified, is it?" she said, directing her inquiry in Babcock's direction, although she hadn't acknowledged him. Before he could finish nodding, she continued, "No point bothering with the astronaut gear, then, and I'm not taking off my coat in this bloody cold. I'll be buggered if I'm courting pneumonia on Christmas Eve without a bloody good reason."

As she paused to take stock of the room, Babcock studied her with the amazement he always felt. Tonight, her tall, thin figure was enveloped in what looked like a man's ancient tweed overcoat, and her flyaway gray hair was covered by a navy wool watch cap. Her face, however, was as stern and uncompromising as ever. Although from her vigor he guessed her to be in her sixties, her skin was so webbed with fine lines that it resembled tanned leather.

As she passed by him, he caught a faint whiff of dog. Her dog accompanied her everywhere, in all weathers, stolidly waiting in the back of her ancient moss-green Morris Minor car. The beast appeared to be a cross between an Irish wolfhound and the Hound of the Baskervilles, and Babcock had been known to speculate as to whether it was actually stuffed and permanently bolted into place as a deterrent against car burglars.

But that the dog was alive and not taxidermically enhanced he could personally testify. He'd once made the mistake of accepting a lift from the doctor, and the dog's hot breath had prickled his neck all the way back to the station. He could have sworn a few drops of saliva dribbled down his collar. Riding in Elsworthy's car had been a mistake in other respects as well—the upholstery had been so coated with dog hair that its original color was indistinguishable, and it had taken him days to remove the thick gray mat from his suit.

Tonight, he thought he detected an odor other than eau de dog emanating from the good doctor—the sharp tang of whisky. But the doctor's eyes gleamed with their usual intelligence, and her manner was as brisk as ever. Had she been celebrating, Babcock wondered? Was there a Mr. Elsworthy waiting at home? It was not the sort of thing one would ever dare ask her, and he couldn't imagine her offering a personal confidence. Nor was he sure he really wanted to know.

He stepped farther back, giving the doctor room to work. Stooping like a bulkily clad crane, she carefully eyed the body, then probed gently here and there with a gloved finger. She offered no commentary—small talk was never the doctor's habit—and after a few minutes Babcock couldn't contain his impatience.

"Well?" he asked. "How long do you think it's been here? How old is it? Is it male or female?"

The look she shot him might have been aimed at a schoolboy talking out of turn in class. She turned back to the gaping mortar. "You might assume from the clothing that the child is female," she said at last, with only a trace of sarcasm. "Further than that, I can't say until I can do X-rays and a proper examination." She peered down into the lower part of the wall cavity. "From the length of the body, I'd guess the infant was less than a year old, but not newborn."

Babcock snorted. "Very helpful."

"You were expecting miracles, Chief Inspector?"

He thought he glimpsed a flash of humor in her eyes. "I wouldn't mind."

"As to your first question," she continued, "once your technicians have finished documenting the scene and we can remove the remains, I'll do the preliminary exam at the morgue. Then we'll see." Elsworthy straightened up and peeled off her latex gloves, stuffing them into another capacious pocket as she moved towards the door.

He had reached for his mobile phone to request reinforcements, uniforms to man the perimeter and begin the house-to-house, when the doctor turned back.

"I can tell you one thing," she said, and he paused, phone open in his hand. "This was no casual burial, no callous dumping of a corpse. If you want my opinion, I'd say it was a ritual interment."

When Gemma and the children returned from their trek to the pony pasture, they found the kitchen tidy again and Rosemary gathering the ingredients for punch. There had been no word from Kincaid or his sister.

Sam led the children off to see his hoard of presents under the tree, and Hugh had gone up to his study, for "just a few minutes," Rosemary informed Gemma with a roll of her eyes, adding, "He's just acquired a rare edition of one of Dickens's lesser-known Christmas stories. Once he gets immersed in a book, he'll forget to eat if I don't remind him. I suppose that sounds rather charming, but in reality, it's quite irritating."

Gemma had seen the same sort of single-minded focus all too often when Kincaid was working a case—in fact, it had recently almost cost him the custody of his son. She, on the other hand, found it difficult to compartmentalize the different aspects of her life. Even while concentrating on work, some part of her mind would be wondering what sort of day Kincaid was having, and whether there was something in the fridge for the children's dinner. She'd seen it as a curse, this inability to shut down her emotional radar when she wanted so badly to succeed at her job.

But lately she'd begun to think that the feminine hardwiring of her brain might have its compensations. The personal ones were more obvious—God forbid that *she* had failed to turn up at Kit's custody hearing—but there were professional blessings as well.

Her promotion had required her to learn to lead her team effectively, and she'd discovered that her awareness of their moods and shifting allegiances was an invaluable tool. She was also finding that an ability to see the big picture, to synthesize, sometimes allowed the disparate pieces of an investigation to slip into place.

Now, if she could just apply some of those same skills to navigating the complexities of Duncan's family, maybe she would actually get through this holiday. She liked Rosemary, although she didn't know her well. Their phone conversations had consisted of superficial chitchat. Gemma had no idea what lay beneath this woman's competent exterior.

"What are you making, exactly?" she asked, watching Rosemary transfer an assortment of bottles into a box for easy carrying to the car.

"It's called cardinal's hat. Very festive—and lethal if overindulged in." She touched the bottle tops in turn. "Claret. Cognac. White rum. Red vermouth. Cranberry juice. Rose water." Reaching into the fridge, she pulled out a bottle of champagne and held it aloft like a trophy. "Champagne. And"—she reached into the fridge again and removed a plastic bag—"rose petals to float on the top. Scavenged from my friend the florist on the square."

Gemma couldn't remember her parents ever drinking champagne. From the photos, she knew their wedding had been strictly chapel, a tea-and-cake affair, and any family gatherings where alcohol was served tended to run to beer and port. "Sounds very elegant just for us," she said, glancing a little uneasily at her casual slacks and sweater. The punch sounded as if it called for a velvet dress.

"It's a bit much for Juliet's taste, to be honest," Rosemary told her, placing the rose petals carefully atop the bottles. "But Caspar likes the show."

Gemma's curiosity prompted her to forget her caution. "You didn't sound earlier as if you were much bothered by what Caspar thought."

"Oh, dear." Rosemary glanced up, a guilty expression on her face. "Didn't I? In front of the children?"

Gemma nodded. "Maybe I misinterpreted—"

"No." Rosemary sighed. "Although I do try not to do that. It's very unfair to Lally and Sam. He *is* their father, and the past year or so has been difficult enough for them without my adding to it."

"Um . . ." Gemma hesitated, not sure of the line between polite concern and nosiness. On the job, she'd have had no such scruples. Temporizing, she said, "I understand Juliet changed jobs this last year?"

"That's a very tame way of putting it," agreed Rosemary, pushing the box out of the way and sitting across from Gemma at the big scrubbed table. "Juliet had served as general dogsbody for Caspar's business since he and his partner set up on their own a few years ago. 'Office manager' was her official title, but she did everything from answering the phone to making appointments to keeping the books, and Caspar paid her a minimum wage. He said she benefited by the firm's overall profitability, so it would be like robbing Peter to pay Paul to give her a decent salary. And while that may have been true, at least in part, it certainly did nothing for Juliet's self-esteem.

"She was content enough at first, because it allowed her some flexibility with the children, but then I could see it wearing away at her. Anyone could guess it was only a matter of time before she bolted."

"But setting herself up as a builder, and with no experience? Wasn't that a bit—"

"Risky? Impractical?" Rosemary's smile, so like her son's, lit up her face. "I'd even say foolhardy. But she'd managed quite complicated DIY projects on their own house for years, as well as acting as an unpaid contractor for her friends, and it was what she'd loved doing ever since she was a child."

Gemma wondered if Rosemary felt a little envy for the daughter who had turned away from the family business to make her own way. Had Rosemary dreamed of a life that held more than raising her children and helping with her husband's shop?

"Our banker, an old friend of Hugh's and mine, loaned her the start-up money. Caspar was livid, and even though she's kept her head above water so far, he hasn't forgiven her. I think his pride is more damaged than his pocketbook.

He sees it as a sort of defection." Rosemary looked a little abashed. "I'm talking out of turn. It's just that—well, I can't say these things to Juliet, and I certainly can't discuss it with friends in town. Everyone knows everyone's business here. But I'm worried about Juliet, and the children. Lally especially—it's such a difficult age. And her father spoils her, which only complicates the situation further."

"He doesn't sound the type to spoil his children," said Gemma, thinking that what he sounded was a right prat.

"Oh, well, fathers and daughters." Rosemary smiled. "To his credit, I think he does love the children. And he can display a certain earnest charm."

Gemma must have looked askance, because Rosemary let out a peal of laughter. But before she could speak, the phone trilled and she rose to answer it. After a murmured conversation, she rang off and turned back to Gemma.

"You'll get a chance to see for yourself, soon enough," she said briskly. "That was Duncan, calling from his mobile. We're to meet them at the house."

From the moment Kit stepped into his grandparents' sitting room, he felt he'd known it his whole life. The shelves of books and the faded Oriental rug reminded him of Gemma's friend Erika's house, except that here the space was dominated by two large, scuffed brown leather chesterfields rather than a grand piano. The little wall space not filled with books held framed cartoons of odd-looking people and even funnier-looking dogs. A low fire burned in the grate, and a large fir tree had been jammed into the corner nearest the window.

Sam crouched beneath the tree, sorting packages into a pile. "I've got more than anyone else," he crowed as he delved under the branches for another gift. Toby knelt beside him, and Kit could tell from his brother's expression that he was wondering if there were any packages under the tree for him.

"You do not," said Lally. Perched on an ottoman, she watched her brother with an expression of disdain. "And nobody cares, anyway. You're a wanker." She glanced at Kit from under her lashes, as if to see whether he was impressed with her vocabulary. He was. Hoping she couldn't see him blushing, he gave an involuntary glance at the door. Gemma would box his ears for saying something like that, and he didn't want her to think badly of Lally.

"Am not." Sam stopped in his pawing to glare at her, while Toby, losing interest in someone else's loot, wandered over to the hearth.

"You don't even know what it means."

"Do so. It's—"

Before Sam could enlighten them, Toby interrupted. "Kit. Kit, look. They've got our names on them." He was pointing to the stockings hanging from the mantel. There were four, each a different Christmas tapestry, and names were embroidered across their velvet tops. He reached up, tracing the lettering on the last one. "It says 'Toby.'" At five, he was very proud of his rudimentary reading skills.

Moving closer, Kit saw his name beside Toby's, and Sam and Lally's on the other two.

"Nana didn't want you to feel left out," Lally informed them, which made Kit feel more awkward than ever, rather than included. The last thing he wanted was anything calling attention to the fact that he didn't belong, or anyone feeling sorry for him.

Having lost the focus of attention, Sam had risen from his pile of gifts and was jiggling impatiently. "Come see my Game Boy," he demanded. "It's upstairs. My dad gave it to me for my birthday."

"Kit doesn't want to see your Game Boy," said Lally, with undeniable finality. "You take Toby."

Sam hesitated, his inner struggle showing clearly on his face. He wanted to show off his toy to Toby, but he hated giving in to his sister's bossiness. Pride of possession won. "Okay. But we'll be right back. Come on, Toby."

Kit felt his breath stop with terror as the door closed behind the younger boys. What would he find to say to Lally alone? He needn't have worried.

"I know where Nana keeps the sherry," Lally announced. "We can have a sip, but not enough so that she'll notice the level's gone down in the bottle."

"Sherry?" Kit made a face. He'd been given a taste once at Erika's. "But that's nasty. Tastes like cough medicine. Why would you want to drink that?"

"It does the trick, doesn't it?" She slipped off the ottoman and opened a cabinet near the fireplace. "Granddad keeps his whisky in here, too, but it's really expensive, and he says he checks it to make sure it's not evaporating."

Kit stared at her back as she reached up for a bottle. Could that possibly be a tattoo, just where her shirt rose to reveal the top of her jeans and an inch of bare skin? She turned back to him, bottle in hand, and he tore his eyes away from her midriff.

She pulled the cork and took a drink, but he noticed it was a very small one, and she had to hide a grimace. Holding the bottle out to him, she said, "Sure you don't want some?"

Kit shook his head, blushing. Would she think him a total prat?

"Don't tell me you never get into your parents' drinks cabinet at home?" Lally wiped the lip of the bottle with the hem of her shirt and recorked it.

"They don't keep much," Kit answered evasively. Duncan usually had a bottle of whisky in his study, and there was often a bottle of wine or a few beers in the fridge, but he certainly wasn't going to admit it had never occurred to him to sneak any. Besides, Duncan had let him have a taste of watered-down wine when they had friends over for dinner, and he hadn't cared much for it.

"You have to develop an appreciation for the finer things," said Lally, coming back to the ottoman, and Kit had the feeling she was repeating something she'd heard often. She sat, drawing her knees up under her chin, and scrutinized him.

Feeling like a specimen under the dissecting microscope, Kit squirmed and searched for something—anything—to say that might impress her.

Lally's rescue left him feeling even more confused. "Do your parents fight?" she asked.

"I—sometimes, I suppose." Did Lally know that Gemma wasn't his real mother, that his mum had died? If not, he wasn't going to tell her.

He thought of the tense silences that sometimes happened between Duncan and Gemma since she had lost the baby, and felt a coldness in his chest. He didn't want to talk about that, either.

"My mum and dad fight all the time," Lally went on, as if she hadn't expected an answer. "They think we don't hear them, but we do. That's why Sam's so hyper, you know. He didn't used to be like that. Or not as bad, at least. Mum's never home after school anymore either, since she started her business. Do you think my mum really found a body?" she asked, sitting up a bit straighter.

Not having really given it much thought, as his parents seemed to find bodies on a daily basis, Kit answered, "She said so, didn't she? So I suppose she did." It didn't seem the sort of thing one would make up.

"What do you think it was like?" Lally's eyes sparkled.

Kit flashed on the one thing he couldn't bear to think about, the image as vivid as the day it had happened. He felt the nausea start, and the prickle of sweat on his forehead. Desperate to change the subject, he said, "Where's your house, then?"

"Nantwich, near the square." Lally appeared to notice his blank look. "You don't know the town at all, do you? It's dead boring. But you can find things to do. Once we get dinner over with tonight, we'll go out. I'll show you round a bit."

The sitting-room door swung open with a bang, making Kit jump, and Sam looked in.

"Uncle Duncan just rang. We're going to our house, all of us, in Granddad's estate car. Nana says we have to leave the dogs."

"My dad doesn't like dogs in the house," Lally explained, jumping up. "Let's get our coats. If we hurry, we can get the best seats."

And Kit, who never willingly left his little terrier, trailed after her without a word.

*He discovered the pleasure of cruelty at eight. His mother had promised him a special treat, an afternoon on their own, the pictures, then an ice cream. But at the last minute*

*a friend had rung and invited her out, and she had gone
with nothing more than a murmured apology and a brush of
her hand against his hair.*

*He'd felt ill with fury at first. He'd screamed and kicked at
the wall in his room, but the pain quickly stopped him. It
was not himself he wanted to hurt.*

*Nor was there anyone to hear him. His mother would
have asked their neighbor Mrs. Buckham to look in on him
and give him his tea, but for the moment he had the house to
himself. He straightened up and wiped his runny nose on his
sleeve.*

*Slowly, he made his way to his mother's room. Her scent
lingered, a combination of perfume and hair spray and
something indefinably female. The casual clothes she'd
donned for her afternoon with him lay tossed across the
bed, discarded in favor of something more elegant. Her face
powder had spilled, and fanned across the glass of her vanity table like pale pink sand. He wrote "bitch" in the dust,
then smeared the word away—even then, he had known
that crudity brought less than satisfying results. And he had
seen something else. Her pearl necklace, a favorite gift
from his father, had slipped to the floor in a luminous tum-
ble. He lifted it, running the smooth spheres through his
fingers, then rubbing them against his cheek, feeling an unexpected and pleasurable physical stirring. With his pulse
quickening, he glanced round the room. His gaze settled on
just what he needed—the hammer left behind after his
mother's recent bout of tacking up pictures.*

*First he took the pearls in both hands and jerked. The
string snapped with a satisfying pop that flung the beads to
the carpet in a random cascade. Then he lifted the hammer
and carefully, thoroughly, smashed every pearl into a splash
of luminescent dust.*

*A gleam caught his eye—two had escaped and were nes-
tled against the leg of the vanity, as if hiding. He raised the
hammer, then stopped, struck by a sudden impulse, and
scooped the pearls into his pocket. They felt cool and solid
to his touch. He would keep them as souvenirs. Only later
would he learn that such things were called mementos.*

*The satisfaction that coursed through him after his act of destruction was unlike anything else he'd ever known, but that had been only the beginning. He awaited discovery, trembling with dread and excitement. His mother came home and went upstairs, but there had been no explosion of anger. Instead, she locked herself in her room, complaining of a headache. It wasn't until the next morning, when he'd faced her across the breakfast table, that he'd seen the fear in her eyes.*

# 6

**"I'M TOO BIG** for riding in laps." Toby squirmed half off Gemma's knee, but she hooked her arm round his middle and pulled him firmly back.

"You'll just have to make the best of it, won't you?" she said, taking the opportunity to nuzzle his silky hair, something it seemed she seldom managed these days. "And what about my poor knee, having to put up with such a big boy on it? Do you hear it complaining?" She bounced him and he giggled, relaxing against her.

"Knees don't talk, Mummy," Toby said with assurance.

"Mine do," Rosemary chimed in from the front passenger seat. "Especially when I've spent all day in the garden."

Hugh Kincaid's old Vauxhall estate car could theoretically have held seven comfortably, but the third seat had been filled with cartons of books. Hugh had managed to shift them so that Kit could squeeze in the back, leaving Sam, Lally, Toby, and Gemma to jam into the center seat as best they could.

It had begun to snow again, and the car was cold in spite of the number of bodies. "We'll soon get the heater going," Hugh said cheerfully as he turned up the blower. The blast of frigid air made Gemma even colder and she hugged Toby to her until he wriggled like a hooked fish.

For Gemma, already disoriented by the unfamiliar terrain and her limited vision from the rear seat, the journey into town merged into a swarm of onrushing white flakes, punctuated by the yellow glare of the occasional sodium lamp and the wet gleam of black road. Ordinarily preferring to drive, she disliked the sensation of things being out of her control, and she felt a little queasy from the motion of the car.

Then, as they passed beneath a dark arch, Sam said, "Look. There's the aqueduct. The canal goes over the road."

"You mean the boats go overhead?" asked Kit, sounding intrigued.

"Can we see?" added Toby.

"Not tonight," said Rosemary. "But maybe tomorrow, if the weather clears."

There were houses now, crowding in on either side, and Sam continued his narration. "This is Welsh Row, where the Welsh would march in to kill the English. And not far from here were the brine works, where the Romans made salt. The 'wich' in Nantwich means salt, you know."

"Who appointed you tour guide, Sam?" Lally said waspishly. "I'm sure they're perfectly happy not knowing." Lally and Kit had been talking as they left the house, and Gemma wondered if Lally was cross over having had to sit beside her brother rather than her new friend. At any rate, Gemma was glad to see Kit overcoming his shyness with his cousins.

Toby tilted his head back until he could whisper in Gemma's ear. "Who are the Welsh, Mummy? Do they still kill the English?"

Gemma stifled a laugh. "The Welsh are perfectly nice people who live in Wales, lovey. And no, they don't kill the English. You're quite safe." Wanting to encourage Sam, who had subsided into hurt silence, she peered out the window at the classical fronts of the buildings. "From what Duncan's said, I thought Nantwich was Tudor, but these buildings look Georgian."

"Most of Welsh Row is Georgian," Hugh answered, and although Sam jiggled with impatience, he didn't interrupt as his grandfather went on. "But the town center has an exceptional number of intact Tudor buildings. It was built all of a piece, after the fire of 1583, a good bit of it with monies contributed by Elizabeth the First, who wasn't known for her generosity. It's thought that she feared the Spanish would invade through Ireland, and Nantwich was the last important stop that provisioned the soldiers garrisoned at Chester."

Gemma could easily see where Sam had got his interest in local history.

"There's no access to the town square by car," Hugh added as he stopped at a traffic light, "but I'd be glad to take you for a little tour after dinner, if you'd like. We can walk easily from Juliet's, and of course we'll be going to the church."

"There may not be time before mass," put in Rosemary, sounding a little anxious. The box of punch ingredients clinked as she adjusted it on her knees.

"Well, if it's possible, I'd like that very much," Gemma told Hugh. They were passing along a very ordinary shopping precinct now, and glimpsing a Boots and a Somerfield's supermarket among the nondescript postwar shop fronts, she felt unexpectedly disappointed.

Hugh made a quick right turn, causing Rosemary to clutch her box a bit tighter, then another, and then he was pulling up in a quiet cul-de-sac. To one side, Gemma saw ordinary redbrick terraced houses, their porches sprinkled with colored fairy lights, their postage-stamp lawns and common green muffled with snow. On the other side of the street stood a high garden wall with a wrought-iron gate at one end, and it was towards this that Hugh led them like heavily padded ducklings when they had piled out of the car.

Although it was masked by evergreens, Gemma could see that the wall was built of a dark brick, as was the house that rose behind it. Near the gate, a narrow path overgrown with foliage led straight back from the cul-de-sac.

"The town center is only a five minutes' walk that way," Hugh said cheerfully, nodding at the path as he opened the gate, but Gemma could only think that she wouldn't care to walk there alone. The atmosphere of the entire place struck her as secretive: the dark tunnel of the path, the house brood-

ing like a fortress behind its high wall. Nor did the sight of
the garden improve her first impression. Small and enclosed,
it was planted entirely with shrubs sculpted in different shapes
and sizes. No patch of lawn welcomed dogs—or children,
for that matter.

But she could see that everything was immaculately maintained, and there were footprints leading to the door and
welcoming lights in the windows. Sam charged ahead and
flung open the front door, shouting, "Mum!"

It was Duncan, however, not Juliet, who came hurrying
into the hall to meet them. "Jules is changing," he explained,
"and Caspar seems to have gone walkabout."

"Did Mummy really find a body?" asked Sam, hopping
from one foot to the other with impatience.

"Yes, I'm afraid she did," Kincaid answered gravely. "I'll
let her tell you about it if she wants."

"But what did it—"

Rosemary, still holding the punch box, forestalled her
grandson. "Let's get these things in the kitchen. Gemma, I'll
do the honors for Juliet. Take off your coats—there's a cupboard just to your right."

While Sam and Lally shoved their things into the cupboard willy-nilly, followed a little more carefully by Kit and
Toby, Gemma took the opportunity to look about her. The
sitting room to her right had forest-green walls and pristine
white sofas, while the magnificent Christmas tree in one
corner was decorated with white silk roses and shimmering
crystal drops. The dining room on the left was just as elegant, but done in deep reds, and the long mahogany table
was already set with china and crystal, as if awaiting a feast
for ghosts. The rooms had none of the slightly shabby comfort of the Kincaids' house, and none of the effortless style.
It made Gemma think of a stage set, and she could see why
Juliet was happy to spend her days mucking about on a
building site.

When their coats were stowed—and Gemma realized that
here nothing would ever be tossed casually over the back of
a chair—Hugh took the box from his wife, saying, "Just tell
me where you want this."

"In the kitchen, of course," she snapped, but Gemma had the feeling that her sharpness was not really directed at her husband. She seemed ill at ease, and Gemma suspected it had to do with her son-in-law's absence.

"Come see our rooms," Sam demanded of Kit and Toby, and as the children trooped obediently after him up the wide staircase, Gemma found herself momentarily alone with Duncan. He seemed to slump a little, as if glad of a respite.

"Are you all right?" he asked, touching her cheek. "Is Kit? I'm sorry it took longer than I expected."

"What was—" she began, but he interrupted her.

"A baby. But it had been there a long time, probably years. Jules is a bit upset." He didn't quite meet her eyes, and his face wore the careful expression she had come to recognize.

God, how she wished he would stop treating her as if she were made of glass, and would shatter at the mere mention of an infant. She was about to protest when she heard a rustling on the stairs. Looking up, she saw a dark-haired woman coming down, dressed in just the sort of red velvet dress Gemma had imagined appropriate for the evening. While Gemma would have recognized her from the few family photos Duncan had shown her, she had not envisioned Juliet Newcombe's delicacy, nor the haunted look about her eyes.

"You must be Gemma," said Juliet as she reached them. She took both Gemma's hands in her own, and although her smile seemed to take an effort, her voice held genuine warmth. "I'm so glad to meet you."

At that moment, Gemma realized that she had been prepared to dislike Juliet, and felt a rising blush of shame. "I'm sorry you've had such a difficult night," she told her, giving Juliet's small, cold hands a squeeze before letting them go.

"Not the best of circumstances," Juliet agreed. "But still, I'm glad you're here, both of you." She turned to Kincaid. "The children—I thought I heard—"

"Upstairs. Sam's acting the tour guide," answered Duncan.

"And Caspar— Has he—"

Duncan shook his head. "Not here yet. You should have rung him, Jules. Maybe he's out looking for you."

"I doubt that," she answered, and this time her smile was as brittle as ice.

"Look," Duncan said into the awkward silence that followed this conversation stopper, "Mum and Dad are in the kitchen making the famous punch. Can we help with any—"

The front door opened and Juliet froze as a man stepped into the hall, her hand raised to her breast in an unconsciously defensive gesture. "Caspar."

Tall and thin, dark haired like his wife, Caspar Newcombe was fastidiously dressed and wore expensive-looking rimless glasses. His rather patrician good looks were marred, however, by the peevish set of his mouth and the cold glare he directed at his wife. He neither greeted nor acknowledged Gemma and Duncan. It was only when he took a step forward and listed dangerously to one side that Gemma realized he was drunk. He put a hand to the wall and propped himself up with deliberate nonchalance.

Juliet returned the glare and took the offensive. "Where have you been?"

"The Bowling Green." Caspar made no effort to keep his voice down. "Having a bit of Christmas cheer, which I'm not likely to get at home, am I, my dear wife? I could ask you the same, but at least I know you've not been dispensing your favors to my partner, because he was in the office with me. But maybe you've been having a bit of rough-and-tumble with one of your lads? Or is the correct term 'coworker' these days?" He smirked at his own cleverness.

"You bastard," Juliet said quietly. "Did Piers just happen to suggest that to you, too, over a confidential drink? Or did you think of it yourself?"

Out of the corner of her eye, Gemma glimpsed a movement at the top of the stairs. Looking up, she saw the treaded bottom of a trainer and a ragged denim cuff disappear round the landing. Lally. She'd noticed earlier that the bottoms of Lally's jeans were fashionably shredded. She reached out to Juliet in warning, but Juliet was speaking again, her attention so focused on her husband that the house could have come down round their ears before she noticed.

"You're a gullible fool, Caspar," said Juliet, her voice rising now. "But whatever you think I am, and whatever you think I've done, *I'm* not a liar and an embezzler."

At least he was warm, thought Ronnie Babcock as he stood in the Fosters' sitting room, although he suspected that soon his damp clothes would start to visibly steam. Tom and Donna Foster had invited him in, albeit grudgingly, but had not taken his coat, or given him a seat. Nor had they offered that most obvious of courtesies on such a miserable night—a drink. Maybe they'd simply thought he'd refuse on principle, but that was a charitable interpretation.

He guessed the couple to be in their mid- to late fifties, townies who had embraced the country life and brought their slice of heaven along with them, transforming the interior of what must once have been a charming traditional farmhouse into a replica of the most banal suburban semidetached.

The electric two-bar heater that had been pulled in front of the empty brick hearth radiated waves of a harsh, dry heat that had at least defrosted Babcock's extremities, even though half blocked by Foster's considerable bulk. The wife was thin, with a tightly drawn face and hair lacquered a very unnatural shade of red. The sparkling sequined reindeer on her jumper was by far the most cheerful—not to mention the most tasteful—thing in the room. She'd perched on the edge of the sofa, part of a hideous three-piece suite done in peach plush, and kept glancing at the large television hulking in one corner of the room, its sound muted, as if she couldn't bear to tear herself away.

Tired of standing around waiting for frostbite to set in while he watched the techies do their jobs, Babcock had decided to call on the previous owners of the barn. He'd gone on his own, intending to give his subordinates the rest of their evening off before the investigation swung into full gear tomorrow, but he'd begun to wish he had brought along a friendly face.

"I'd very much like to know what's going on, Inspector," demanded Tom Foster, as if he had summoned Babcock for an interview. "You lot have been up and down our lane all night, making a muck of things. We'll be lucky to get our car out in the morning." His accent was broad Mancunian. Babcock didn't know about the wife's, as she hadn't spoken, even though her husband had included her in his perfunctory introductions.

"It's Chief Inspector," Babcock said mildly, but he didn't apologize for the inconvenience. "Mr. Foster, I understand that, until recently, you owned the old barn down by the canal."

"That's right," agreed Foster, his bald head gleaming in the glare of the ceiling light. "Bought the property as an investment five years ago, didn't we?" If he'd hoped for confirmation from his wife, he was disappointed, as her eyes had swiveled back to the girls in skimpy Santa outfits parading across the telly screen.

"Figured we couldn't lose, with the property market going up, and we didn't, oh no." Foster allowed himself a satisfied smirk. "Made as much on the sale of the barn and surrounding pasture as we spent on the whole place, including this house. Of course, the house was in a terrible state, and the owners left it full of moldy old bits. Had to call the junkman to haul them off.

"We've done the house up proper since. All the mod cons." Foster looked round with the pride of a monarch surveying his kingdom.

Babcock realized he was beginning to grind his teeth, and that he was sweating inside his overcoat. He made a conscious effort to relax his jaw and unfastened the top button of his coat. "Mr. Foster, has the barn been in use since you bought the property?"

"What's all this about the barn, Inspector?" Foster's temporary joviality vanished. "Have those kids been getting into things? I won't have them crossing my property—I've told them often enough—and if they've been trespassing down the building site, the Bonners have a right to know."

"It's not kids, Mr. Foster. The builder, Mrs. Newcombe,

made a discovery. Someone mortared a baby into the barn wall."

In the shocked silence that followed Babcock's announcement, he heard a faint squeak, like the mew of a distressed kitten. He'd succeeded in removing Mrs. Foster's attention from the television.

"What? What did you say?" Foster shook his head as if he had water in his ears.

"A baby," whispered Mrs. Foster. "He said they found a baby. How horrible."

Babcock relented a fraction. "It's been there a good while, Mrs. Foster. Perhaps years." On second thought, he wasn't sure why the passage of time made the child's fate any less terrible, but Mrs. Foster nodded, as if he'd said something profoundly comforting. Neither husband nor wife expressed any concern for Juliet Newcombe's ordeal.

"Before our time, then." Foster seemed to find some personal satisfaction in that.

"We won't know for sure until the experts have examined the child's remains," said Babcock smoothly. He wasn't about to reveal to the Fosters that the experts' opinions might not give him a well-defined time frame, nor did he intend them to know how handicapped he was by the lack of that knowledge. "That's why I need to know if there's been any activity in the barn in the time you've owned it."

"Never go down there, myself," said Foster. "But we see if anyone goes up and down the lane. And we'd see lights if there was any funny business at night."

Babcock had surveyed the prospect from their front garden himself, and felt quite sure that the bend in the lane would block any view of lights in the barn. "So you're saying you haven't seen anything?"

The struggle between the desire for importance and the wisdom of noninvolvement was clearly visible in Foster's face. Caution won out. "No. No, I can't say as we have."

"When exactly did you sell the property to the Bonners?"

Foster screwed up his already round face in concentration, so that he looked like an overripe plum about to burst. "Must be just on a year, now. After Christmas. Old hulk of a place—

we thought sure the Bonners would raze it and build new. And why on earth would they hire an inexperienced girl as a contractor? We said as much, but they paid no heed. Taken leave of their senses, if you ask me."

Juliet Newcombe must be in her late thirties, Babcock calculated, and he doubted very much that she would think being referred to as a "girl" a compliment. "Why *did* they choose Mrs. Newcombe against your advice?" he asked.

"Referred by his high muckety-muck up the lane," said Foster, jerking his head towards the Barbridge road. "Dutton. Piers Dutton. Though if you ask me, he'd like you to call him Lord Dutton."

"We've asked him for drinks a half dozen times. He always has some sort of excuse," added Mrs. Foster. Babcock felt a twinge of sympathy for the neighbor, stalked by the social-climbing Fosters, who had undoubtedly been angling for a return invitation and a look at the Victorian manor house.

Piers Dutton . . . an unusual name, he thought. Then a gear meshed in his brain and he realized where he had heard it. Piers Dutton was Caspar Newcombe's partner. Perhaps Dutton had felt more sociable towards the Bonners, and it was only natural that he should recommend his partner's wife to his new neighbors—although considering that his relationship with the Bonners would be ongoing, he must have had confidence in Juliet's ability to do the job.

"And the people who owned the property before you? The Smiths, wasn't it? If you could give me a contact address for them—"

"But we haven't heard from them in years," said Mrs. Foster. "Have we, Tom?" Babcock pegged her as one of those women who wouldn't like to say the sun was shining without confirmation from her husband. When Foster nodded in agreement, she went on. "You see, we came along just as they'd put the place on the market. They'd expected to take their time looking for something else, but as it was, they went into rented accommodation—a flat here in Nantwich, I remember. We sent them a Christmas card that first year, but we never heard from them after."

"Have you any idea where they meant to go?" asked

Babcock. It seemed the simplest things always turned out to be the most difficult.

"I know they had a grown daughter in Shropshire, but they hadn't decided what they wanted to do. Only that they'd had their fill of farming, and they'd made enough on the sale of the property to give them a quiet retirement."

"If you have the address of the rented flat, perhaps they left forwarding instructions."

Mrs. Foster looked stricken. "But I'd not have saved it, not when we didn't hear from them the next Christmas."

"Of course not." Babcock had the disheartening vision of names of unresponsive recipients crossed off the Christmas card list, year after year. "What about the estate agent who handled the sale?"

"Craddock and Burbage, on the High Street," said Tom.

Babcock made a note in his notebook, although he doubted he'd forget. Jim Craddock, like Kincaid, was an old schoolmate—one who, unlike Kincaid, had stayed in Nantwich and taken on the family business.

He'd have to hope the Smiths had left forwarding information with the estate agent, or that they'd remained on friendlier terms with some of their other neighbors. And that was assuming, of course, that they were both still living. "They were an older couple, then, I take it?" he asked. "No children left at home?"

"I only heard of the one daughter. But they did say something about being nearer the grandchildren," answered Mrs. Foster. Then she gaped as the realization struck her. "You surely don't think the Smiths had anything to do with the child you found? But that's—that's—"

"We have to examine all the possibilities." Babcock thought it likely he could rule out the Fosters themselves. Still, he couldn't resist the opportunity to put the wind up these two, if only for the momentary satisfaction of wiping the smug expression off Tom Foster's face. "And you, Mr. and Mrs. Foster?" he said. "Do you have any children?"

The snow had stopped but for the occasional flake drifting erratically through the air, like a sheep straying from its flock.

Hugh Kincaid led Gemma through the shrouded garden, his jacket brushing miniature flurries from the shrubs as he passed. When they reached the street, he paused and gazed up at the star sparkling clearly in the eastern sky.

"I think that's it for tonight," he said. "The storm seems to have blown itself out—just in time, too. I hate to think of the roads blocked on Christmas."

Gemma took a deep breath, shaking off the atmosphere of the house, and the frigid air rushing into her nasal passages seemed to sear straight into her brain—a result, she suspected, of drinking too much of Rosemary's lethal punch. Making an effort not to wobble on her feet, she glanced back towards the house and said hesitantly, "Are you sure we should go? I feel we should be helping tidy—"

"Not to worry. I promised you a tour of the town, and it's the least I can do to make up for the first impression you must have of us," answered Hugh, sounding pained. The subject of Juliet and Caspar's behavior, and the fiasco that had been dinner, hung awkwardly in the silence that followed his comment.

Gemma hated to embarrass him further by agreeing, yet to pretend the evening had gone smoothly would be akin to ignoring an accident in the middle of the road—and a bloody accident, at that. "It must be difficult," she ventured after a moment. "For you. And for the children."

Earlier, Rosemary had put a stop to the shouting match in the hall, coming in from the kitchen with the fury of the Valkyries blazing in her face. "Whatever this is about, you will stop it this moment, and behave in a civilized manner," she commanded. "The children will hear you, and you have guests, in case you'd forgotten."

Juliet flushed as scarlet as her dress and looked round, belatedly, towards the top of the stairs. Caspar glared at his mother-in-law, as if he might rebel, but after a charged moment, he stomped off to his study and slammed the door.

"Thank you for reminding me, Mother," Juliet had said stiffly, but without apparent sarcasm, and she then led the way back into the kitchen. There she'd organized the food and passed it to Duncan to carry to the table, all without speaking an unnecessary word. With her head up and her back held ramrod straight, she'd seemed almost to vibrate with repressed tension and anger.

Gemma had found herself wanting to offer a touch or a word of comfort, but had no idea how she might approach this woman she barely knew—or whether her sympathy would be welcome.

When the meal was ready, Rosemary had called the children, while Hugh had tactfully volunteered to fetch Caspar. Caspar had not appeared until everyone else was seated, then had taken his place at the head of the table with all the grace of a petulant child. He toyed with his food and downed liberal glasses of punch, the combined actions being unlikely, in Gemma's opinion, to improve the situation.

The dinner—cold ham, a stuffed, sliced breast of turkey, and beautifully composed salads—had been delicious, but might have been sawdust for all the enthusiasm displayed by those gathered round the table. Even the children had seemed subdued, and Gemma wondered if Lally had shared what she'd overheard.

Duncan and his parents had made a valiant attempt to carry the conversation, but when every effort to include Caspar and Juliet had fallen flat, Hugh resorted to telling them in great and excruciating detail about his acquisition of the rare Dickens Christmas story.

As soon as the meal could decently be declared over, Caspar had retreated to his lair again, and Lally had asked if she and Kit could go early to church to save seats for the rest of the party. Juliet had agreed, and Sam, rather to Gemma's surprise, had seemed quite happy to stay behind with Toby. Duncan had offered to help his mother and sister with the washing up and had rolled up his sleeves with aplomb.

Now Hugh hooked his gloved hand through Gemma's arm and steered her, not towards the car, but towards the dark path that led away from the gate.

Gemma yielded reluctantly to the pressure. "Is this—um, are you sure it's safe?" she asked.

"Safe?" Hugh glanced down at her in surprise. "Well, we might get a bit of the white stuff down our necks, but doubt we'll be mugged, if that's what you're thinking." He smiled. "This *is* Nantwich, not London, and North Crofts is a very respectable avenue."

"Avenue?" Gemma repeated curiously, now that she had a chance to look about her. What she saw resembled nothing she would call an avenue. The little lane, accessible only to pedestrians, was fenced on the right, and on the left had houses set back behind long, narrow walled gardens. A light showed here and there in a window; otherwise the lane seemed as deserted as the moon. "Difficult to get the shopping in, I should think," she said, and even her voice seemed muffled by the snow and silence.

Hugh chuckled. "Spoken like a true Londoner. But there's an alleyway behind the houses that serves both North and South Crofts. The houses on South Crofts have some lovely Victorian decorations—stained glass, mosaic tiles."

Soon the lane curved to the left—the bottom of the horseshoe formed by the two streets, Hugh explained—and they passed the alleyway he had mentioned. Hugh steered her gently again, this time towards the dark mouth of a tunnel formed by overarching greenery. The snow was lighter, but footprints were still visible in the dusting of powder.

"Public footpath," he explained. "It connects the Crofts with the center of town. The children will have come this way before us."

Gemma ducked and pulled up her collar as a clump of snow fell from one of the overhanging branches. "I thought public footpaths crossed farmers' fields."

"This one probably did, at one time. Now, however," he added as they emerged from the tunnel, "it brings us to Monk's Lane. There are very fine Georgian buildings here." Gemma looked where Hugh pointed, but again her view was blocked by a wall. Walls, tunnels, secrets, and enveloping deathly quiet—Gemma wasn't sure she liked this place at all.

"Caspar's office is just there," Hugh said as they reached the end of the row, his tone indicating that Caspar didn't deserve to have an office in a hovel, much less a fine Georgian building. "And off to the left is the Bowling Green pub, where Caspar stopped off on his way home."

"Does he make a habit of it?" asked Gemma.

"I don't know. I'm not usually privy to Caspar's habits. Although we work such a short distance apart, I seldom see him except for family occasions." He paused, then said more slowly, "I hadn't realized how bad things had got. Juliet doesn't talk to us about it—or at least not to me."

Gemma recalled that she'd said nothing to her parents about the problems she and Rob were having until she'd filed for divorce—she'd been too humiliated to admit to her parents that her marriage was a failure. She considered sharing this with Hugh, but doubted he would find it comforting.

Hugh stopped, hands in his pockets, staring up at the dark mass of the church now rising like a fortress above them. Even in the dim light Gemma could see that his face looked drawn. "I should have stopped it tonight. She's my daughter, for God's sake. He practically called her a whore."

"You couldn't have known what he was going to say."

"No. But I could have waded in afterwards, not left it to Rosemary," argued Hugh. "Rosemary doesn't have to think out what to do, she just goes ahead and does it."

Gemma knew from personal experience that acting before you thought could have regrettable consequences, and, emulating Duncan, had tried to learn to rein in her more impulsive tendencies. Odd that his father disliked in himself one of the qualities she'd admired in his son.

"Duncan and I stood by, too," she said. "Sometimes domestic situations blow out of control more quickly than anyone expects."

"Of course, you're right," said Hugh, but Gemma sensed he was merely agreeing out of politeness. "Poor Gemma," he added, touching her elbow again to draw her on. "Here I said I meant to make up for our bad impression, and I've gone and aired the family's dirty laundry. Must be Rosemary's famous punch. Either that or you have a talent for eliciting confidences."

"A bit of both, I expect," Gemma said with a smile. He might have had too much punch, but his footsteps were steadier than hers, and he was very perceptive.

They passed the church, then a snow-covered expanse

emma assumed must be the green. Their street intersected another at the green's end, and there Gemma stopped, her mouth open in an "O" of surprise and delight. This was what Duncan had described, what she had imagined. The buildings ran together higgledy-piggledy, black-and-white timbering against Cheshire redbrick, gingerbread gables, and leaded windows winking like friendly eyes.

This was the High, she saw from a signpost, but she would have known instinctively that she stood in the very heart of the town. The shops were ordinary—a WH Smith, a Holland & Barrett, a newsagent's—but they had been tucked into the lower floors of the original Tudor houses, and so were transformed into something quite magical.

The movement of the buildings over the centuries had caused the black-and-white timbering to shift a little, giving the patterns a tilted, slightly rakish air. Snow iced the rooftops, Christmas lights twinkled, bundled pedestrians hurried through the streets, and from somewhere came the faint strains of "God Rest Ye Merry, Gentlemen." Gemma laughed aloud. "It's perfect. Absolutely. The best sort of Christmas-card perfect."

"It is rather lovely," agreed Hugh, the pride in his voice reflecting her delight. "That's the Crown Hotel." He pointed to a particularly fine example of half-timbering. "Built in 1585, after the Great Fire. It's famous for its continuous upper-story windows. And down this way is Pillory Street, and the bookshop." He urged her on, and a few moments later she peered into the window of a less remarkable shop front. The windows, however, were dimly lit, and Gemma caught a glimpse of aisles of books, invitingly arranged.

"You do like books?" Hugh asked suddenly.

"I do," answered Gemma, laughing. "But I didn't grow up with them, so I haven't read all that much. Not like Duncan. And with my job, and the children . . ."

"I was afraid I might have bored you, at dinner."

"Not at all. Will you keep it? The Dickens?"

"It's tempting," Hugh admitted with a sigh. "But it's valuable, and it's finds like this that pay the bills. Besides, it's the discovery as much as anything—the thrill of it."

Gemma thought of the moment of illumination when the parts of a case came together, and imagined that the instant when you realized the book you held in your hands was something special must be the same. "I can understand that."

Hugh gave her a searching glance. "Yes, I think you can. Duncan and Juliet take books for granted, you know. They've lived with them all their lives.

"But my family were shopkeepers in a small Scottish town—they had the newsagent's—and other than the papers, the most challenging things I saw in print were comics and a few pulp novels. I was good at my schoolwork, however, and won a place at a grammar school. My English teacher encouraged me, and I've never forgotten how I felt when I discovered there were more worlds at my fingertips than I had ever imagined, more worlds than I could ever explore . . ." He stopped, looking abashed. "Oh, dear. I'm pontificating. A very bad habit, when I've so willing a listener. And I'm going to make us late," he added, glancing at his watch. "It's almost eleven. We'd better go back. I'll show you the shop tomorrow, if time permits, or the next day."

They were quiet as they walked back down to the High, but now Gemma felt comfortable with the silence. She'd found unexpected common ground with Hugh Kincaid.

There were more people in the square now, gathering, she guessed, for the midnight service at St. Mary's. Hugh had started to lead her across the High when Gemma saw a flare of light from the corner of her eye. It had come from the direction of the Crown Hotel, a match or a lighter, perhaps, she thought as she looked back. Two figures—no, three— were silhouetted briefly in an archway beside the hotel's front door. Teenagers, Gemma felt sure, from their slenderness, and a certain slouchy cockiness in their postures. There had been a hint of furtiveness as well, she thought as they disappeared into the darkness of what she now realized must be the old carriage entrance. Or was that just her, bringing the job with her?

She shrugged and turned away—it was none of her business what kids got up to here—then stopped and looked back

nce more. The girl—yes, she was sure one of the three had
een a girl—had been dark haired, and the boy she'd seen
most clearly, blond. Lally and Kit? But they were in church,
he reminded herself, and the boy had been too tall, too thin.
Nor would Kit have been smoking—he hated it with a passion. She was letting her imagination run away with her.

"Gemma?" Hugh's voice came warmly beside her. "Are
you all right?"

"Yes." She took the arm he offered and smiled up at him.
"I'm fine."

The smell of old incense, woodworm, and damp stone hit
Kincaid like a sensory bomb as he followed his family into
the porch of St. Mary's. It happened when he entered any
church, the scent-triggered barrage of memories, but it was
most intense at St. Mary's.

He had grown up in this place—the cathedral of South
Cheshire, it was often called. Although in truth it was only a
town church, it was one of the finest in England, built on the
scale of a cathedral by masons who had worked on York
Minster, then later completed by men who had built the ca-
thedrals at Gloucester and Lichfield.

It was a cavernous church, but to him it seemed intimate,
comforting even. If he closed his eyes, his feet could find the
worn places in the stones unaided, his fingertips the nicks
and gouges made by bored children in the backs of the
pews. Here he had been baptized and confirmed.

His father, who had rebelled early against his Scots Pres-
byterian upbringing and declared himself an "intellectual
agnostic"—or had it been "agnostic intellectual"?—had
protested, but his mother insisted that the human animal
had a need for structure, for ritual and discipline, for the
ties with the community that the church provided, and for a
sense of something larger than itself. His mother had won,
as she usually did, but it was the sort of argument that had
often echoed through house and bookshop in his childhood.

The porch, crowded with congregants jostling to break
through the bottleneck into the nave, smelled of sweat and

wet wool. Before him, Kincaid could see his parents, then the top of Juliet's dark head. He knew that Sam, although momentarily invisible, was clinging to his mother's hand. Rather to Kincaid's surprise, Caspar had joined them on their walk to church, but he seemed to have disappeared in the shuffle through the porch doors.

Kincaid's fingertips rested on Gemma's shoulder as insurance against separation, and Toby, his view limited to waist-bands and coattails, butted against his leg like a frustrated calf.

"Where's Kit?" Toby asked, picking at Kincaid's trousers, his voice rising perilously close to a whine. "I want to see Kit."

It was long past the five-year-old's bedtime, and Kincaid suspected they'd be lucky to get through the service without a meltdown. Bending over, he hefted the boy to his hip, a harder task than it had been only a few months ago. "We'll look together," he suggested, "and if you find him first, I'll give you a pound to put in the collection box. Deal?"

"Deal," agreed Toby, looking much happier now.

At that moment, the organist launched into a Bach prelude and the sound rolled over them like a thunderclap, vibrating teeth and bones. Kincaid felt an unexpected lurch of joy, and tightened his grip on Gemma's shoulder. She looked back at him in surprise, and he saw his delight mirrored in her face.

"The organist was always good," he said, with proprietary pride, but she was gazing upwards, transfixed.

"The windows are wonderful. But look at that one"—she pointed—"it's modern, isn't it?"

Kincaid's gaze followed her finger. "Ah. That's the Bourne window. It's my favorite, although it was installed just about the time I left home for London. It's a memorial to a local farmer named Albert Bourne. It depicts God's creations." He pointed in turn. "See, at the very top of the arch, God's hand? And below that, the swirl of the cosmos, then the birds of the heavens and the creatures of the sea, then the world's wildlife." His hand had traveled two-thirds of the way down the window. "But here's the surprise. Here the designer moves from the general to the particular. Those are the rolling hills of Cheshire. And the house, there in the center, that's Cheshire brick. Then the animals of farm and field and thicket, and there, on the right, the very best bit."

Gemma searched for a moment, then gave a laugh of pleasure as she saw what he meant. "It's a man, walking his spaniel through the field."

"Bourne himself. No man could ask for a more fitting memorial—or woman, either," he corrected quickly, as she turned on him a look of reproach. "Although I suspect the dog is a springer, not a cocker like Geordie."

"There's Kit!" called Toby, who from his elevated height had been peering through the crowd shuffling in front of them. "And Lally."

The teenagers were not near the front, as Kincaid had expected, but halfway down the nave on the outer aisle. There was a gap of several feet between, and when Kincaid neared the spot, he saw that they had filled it with coats, hats, and gloves.

"It's the best we could do," Lally said to her mother as their group reached the pew. "The church filled early. And people are giving us dirty looks."

"Never mind," Juliet told her. "We're here now. We'll squeeze in as best we can."

"Where's Dad?" Lally asked, as Kit stood aside to make room for them.

"Oh. He's here somewhere," Juliet said, as casually as if she had mislaid a handbag, but Kincaid thought no one was fooled, particularly Lally.

"I want to sit with him."

"Well, you'll have to make do with me for the moment," snapped Juliet, her attempt at calm normality slipping. "You're not to wander off looking for him. The service is about to start."

Any further argument was quelled as the organ stopped and a hush fell on the congregation. As the family jammed into a space meant for half as many people, Kincaid with an arm round Gemma's shoulders and Toby half in his lap, the processional began.

Kincaid slipped easily into the familiar rhythm of lessons and carols. He was home, and nothing had changed—or at least the things that had changed were for the better. He had his own family here now, Gemma and the boys, and he felt that at last all the pieces of his life had come together.

As if to punctuate his thoughts, the choir launched into "O Holy Night," one of his favorite carols, and the congregation followed suit. Behind him, a clear alto voice rose. The voice was untrained, but powerful and true, with a bell-like quality that sent a shiver down his spine.

His curiosity overcoming his good manners, he turned round until he could see the woman singing. She was tall, with short blond hair going gray. Lines of care were etched into a strong, thin face he suspected was not much older than his own, and she seemed unconnected to the family groups around her.

As she became aware of his gaze, the woman's voice faltered, then faded altogether as she stared back at him.

Embarrassed by the alarm in her eyes, Kincaid nodded and gave her what he hoped was a reassuring smile, then turned round and joined in the carol. After a moment, she began to sing again, hesitantly at first, then more strongly, as if caught up in the music. Through the remainder of the service, he listened for her, but dared not risk another glance. He felt as if he'd stumbled across a shy animal that mustn't be spooked.

Only one thing marred his pleasure in the mass. The last of the carols was "Away in a Manger," a piece he had always disliked. He thought the lyrics saccharine, the tune impossible, and tonight it conjured up an image he'd tried to suppress. He glanced at Juliet and saw her standing tight-lipped, her face strained, her hands gripping the top of the forward pew. So she had thought of the child in the manger as well, this one no cause for celebration.

Then the recessional began and they filed slowly out after the choir, joining the queue of those waiting to pay their respects to the priest. Kincaid spotted Caspar Newcombe standing to one side, shaking hands and chatting with passersby, ignoring his wife and family as if they didn't exist. Beside him stood a large, handsome man whose well-cut clothes didn't quite disguise the fact that he was running to heaviness. His good looks and wavy fair hair made Kincaid think of a matinee idol, from the days when film stars had looked like men, not androgynous boys. He, too, was meeting and greeting, but not alone. Beside him stood a tall boy with the stamp of the older man's features beneath his bored expression, and fair hair that might wave if not cut stylishly short.

"Who's the bloke with Caspar?" he whispered to his mother, who stood nearest him in the queue.

Rosemary looked at him in surprise. "That's Piers Dutton. Caspar's partner. I didn't realize you'd never met him. And that's his son, Leo. He and Lally are in the same class."

So this was the partner with whom Caspar had taunted Juliet during their row. At first sight, Kincaid couldn't imagine a man less likely to appeal to his sister—but then he'd not have wagered on Caspar, either.

"Caspar and Piers never miss a chance to oil their connections," said his mother, the softness of her voice not disguising the bite. "The churchwardens are good clients."

"Somehow that doesn't surprise—"

Kincaid looked round as he felt a bump against his shoulder, followed by a murmured apology. A woman had nudged past him, slipping out of the queue and making her way towards the porch doors. Although she moved with her head ducked, avoiding eye contact with those she passed, he recognized the slightly untidy short hair, the slender body whose movement hinted at unexpected fitness.

It was the woman who had sung so beautifully, leaving as she had come, alone.

# 7

THE NEWCOMBES had walked back from church, the four of them together, Sam and Lally forging ahead with their father while Juliet lagged behind. They would have looked a proper family to anyone watching, thought Juliet, the children boisterous with the cold and the excitement of the occasion, the father doting, the mother tired from the day's preparations.

But when they'd reached the house, Caspar had disappeared into his study without a word, and Juliet had gone up with the children. Then, when she'd seen Sam and Lally settled and kissed them good night, she'd gone into her bedroom and carefully, deliberately, locked the door.

She leaned against it, breathing hard, her hands trembling and her heart pounding in her ears. It was over. Her marriage was over. She couldn't deny it any longer. She'd lived with the sarcasm, the veiled accusations, the ridicule, refusing to acknowledge the extent of the rot.

But tonight Caspar had gone too far. The things he'd said to her, his humiliation of her in front of her family, were unforgivable. There could be no going back.

But how could she manage if she left him? What could she do? She had virtually no income; drawing a pittance of a salary, she only barely managed to keep her fledgling business out of the red. Of course, she could do the sensible thing. She could give it up, find an ordinary, respectable office job that would bring in a regular paycheck.

But oh, she loved her building work with a passion she'd never expected, loved even the days spent in blistering sun and freezing rain, days she came home so exhausted she fell asleep over her dinner. She had a knack for seeing what things could become, and for bringing brick and stone to life under her hands.

No, she wouldn't let it go, wouldn't let Caspar take that from her, too, not if there was any way she could help it. What, then? Ask her parents for help? Bad enough that she would have to admit she had failed at her marriage, without begging for money as well.

Of course, she wouldn't be penniless. Caspar would have to give her some financial assistance. But she knew him now, knew he would use his connections to find the best solicitor, knew he would juggle funds to reduce his apparent means and that Piers would help him, regardless of the cost to the children.

And the children—dear God, how could she tell the children she meant to leave their father? Lally would never forgive her. And Sam, what would it do to Sam, so vulnerable beneath his constant chatter?

But she could see now that she'd been a fool to think the children didn't know what was happening, a fool not to realize that Caspar was poisoning them against her every day in little, insidious ways, and that he was prepared to do worse.

She had to think. She had to come up with a strategy that would protect her and the children. Steeling herself, she unlocked the door, switched off the light, and climbed into bed, her body tense as a spring. But there was no tread on the stairs, no click of the doorknob turning.

Slowly, the traumas of the day caught up with her. Her body warmed under the duvet, her muscles relaxed, and against her will, her eyelids drifted closed. Hovering in that halfway state between sleeping and waking, she knew when the dream began that it was a dream.

She held a baby in her arms . . . Sam . . . no, Lally . . . She recognized the pink blanket with its leaping white sheep. The child stirred in her arms . . . She could feel the warmth of it against her breast . . . Then, as she looked down, the tiny red face melted away, bone blossoming beneath the skin, eyes sinking into the gaping pits of the sockets.

Juliet gasped awake and sat up, panting in terror. It was a dream, only a dream of the poor child she had found. Sam and Lally were safe. "Only a dream," she whispered, easing herself down under the covers again. "Only a dream."

But as her heart slowed, her senses began to register the faint pre-dawn creakings of the house. She had slept longer than she thought, and the night was almost over. Caspar wasn't coming to bed at all.

A wave of fury washed over her, leaving her sick and shaking, slicked with sweat. He'd never meant to come up, never meant to face her after the things he'd said. Avoiding a confrontation was his way of punishing her, of keeping the upper hand.

Now she would have to get up in the morning, go down, and manage Christmas for the children as if nothing had happened, and he would be smug and vicious in his little victory.

And then a new thought struck her. Was he ahead of the game? Was he plotting already, calculating the damage he could do? And the children—there had been something sly tonight in the way he had sucked up to Sam and Lally, complimenting and cajoling them.

The children. She clutched at the bed, as if the room had rocked on its foundations. What if he meant to take the children?

Christmas morning dawned cold and clear, with a sparkling layer of frost laid over the packed snow like icing on a cake. Ronnie Babcock greeted the beautiful day with a distinct lack of appreciation, and a reminder to himself to dig out his sunglasses or he'd have a permanent squint. His central-heating boiler had not miraculously repaired itself in the night, and after sleeping under every spare blanket and duvet he could find, he'd plunged out of bed with the temerity of an arctic

explorer, bathing (thank God for immersion heaters) and
having with dangerous haste. His reward for his fortitude
was a seeping cut on his chin. Lovely, just bloody lovely.

And to top it off, he knew he couldn't forgo his duty visit
to his great-aunt Margaret, case or no case, and he had better get it over with before his appointment with Dr. Elsworthy at Leighton Hospital.

Margaret was his mother's mother's sister, and the only
link remaining to his family. Nor had she anyone else. A
childless spinster, she had been a fiercely independent career
woman, overcoming her working-class background as her
sister and his mother had never been able to do. Ronnie had
admired her, even as a child, although he couldn't say that
he had known her well. Great-aunt Margaret hadn't been a
woman with a knack for children, and it was only in the last
few years, with his mum gone, that he had begun to develop
a relationship with her.

Unfortified even by his usual coffee—it was too cold in the
kitchen to stand about while it brewed, much less drink it—he
shrugged into his overcoat and headed for the door. But with
his hand on the knob he hesitated, then, with another curse,
turned back and picked up the single-malt whisky, red bow
and all. He could always buy himself another—and better—
bottle, but he couldn't go calling on Christmas morning without a gift.

The private care home was on the outskirts of Crewe, in a
neighborhood of quiet and prosperous semidetached houses.
He knew the place wasn't bad as far as care homes went—
he'd had enough experience in his job with council-run establishments that skirted the health-code criteria—but no
amount of wood polish and fresh flowers could quite disguise the underlying odor of human incontinence and decay.

It was early for visitors, but he knew the residents were
given their breakfast at what Great-aunt Margaret always
called an uncivilized hour, and he also knew that Margaret
would be most alert early in the day.

Although the matron, a large and obnoxiously cheerful
woman, greeted him with even more than her usual bonhomie, he'd taken the precaution of slipping the whisky bottle

into a shopping bag. The residents were not supposed to have alcohol on the premises, but he sidled past Matron with a smile and not the slightest twinge of guilt.

He found Margaret alone in the residents' sitting room, her chair tucked in beside a gaudy artificial tree. In a bright red woolen suit, she looked like a present left behind by an absentminded Father Christmas. Her fine white hair had been styled into a wreath of curls, her nails varnished in the same cheery color as her suit.

"You look fetching," Ronnie told her, bending to kiss her papery cheek.

"For all the good it does me." Her voice was still strong, with the slight huskiness he suspected was due to the unfiltered cigarettes he remembered her smoking when he was a child. Her bones, however, had felt fragile as dried twigs when he'd rested his hand on her shoulder, and she looked frailer than the last time he'd seen her.

"Where are the other inmates, then?" he asked, pulling the nearest chair a bit closer to her. It was one of their standing jokes, and she smiled appreciatively.

"Off enduring their families for the day, most of them. Makes me glad I've only you to torment me." She never said she liked his visits, or asked when he was coming again, but he suddenly guessed that the bright suit, the nail varnish, the freshly styled hair were all in his honor. She had looked forward to his coming, and he felt a rush of shame.

To cover his discomfort, he rustled in the bag and revealed the bottle of whisky. "Thought you might want to keep this a secret from Matron," he whispered.

"Too bloody right," agreed Margaret. Taking the bag from him, she tucked it beside her in the wheelchair and gave him a conspiratorial smile as she covered it with the rug she kept over her knees. "There should be some use for being crippled, I always say.

"Now," she said, fixing him with a beady gaze, "tell me what you're doing here at this ungodly hour on your holiday. Has that wife of yours mended her ways?" Margaret had never had anything good to say about Peggy, but at least now Babcock wasn't obligated to defend his ex-wife.

"Afraid not, Auntie."

"Lucky for you," she sniffed. "So it will be work, then, unless your prompt appearance is just an excuse for avoiding our little Christmas feast."

Babcock colored, knowing he would have made an excuse if one hadn't presented itself. Murder scenes were one thing, but mealtimes at the care home were beyond his powers of endurance.

His struggle must have been apparent, because she sighed and said, "It's all right, boy. I can't say I blame you, especially considering the state of Reggie Pargetter's bowels these days. Why don't you tell me about your case?"

He could see no need for secrecy, as what little he knew would be public knowledge as soon as the local presses recovered from their Christmas hiatus. So he told her what they had found, and where, ending by saying, "I'm just on my way to Leighton for the postmortem."

Margaret sat silently, her head bowed, for so long he thought she had lost the drift of the conversation, or perhaps even dozed. But then she looked up, and he saw that although the lines in her face seemed etched more deeply than before, her eyes gleamed with understanding.

"It was an act of desperation," she said softly. "Do you see? Whoever buried that child suffered an unthinkable grief."

The dream began, as it always did, with Kit running through the Cambridgeshire cottage in search of his mother. He felt an increasing sense of urgency, but the rooms seemed to elongate ahead of him, as if he'd fallen into the wrong end of a telescope. He ran faster, his panic mounting as the rooms seemed to stretch into tunnels. Suddenly the kitchen door appeared before him. He stopped, his chest aching, seized by a dread that froze his fingers even as he reached for the doorknob. His mother needed him, he told himself, but his hand felt leaden, his feet rooted to the floor. His mother needed him, he knew that, but he couldn't make himself go farther.

Then, before he could back away, the door swung open of

its own accord. Kit swayed as he saw the room before him.
The floor and walls curved upwards like the sides of a bowl,
and at the bottom lay his mother. She lay on her side, her
knees drawn up, her head resting on one arm, as if she had
just lain down for a nap.

It's a cradle, he thought, the room was her cradle and it had
rocked her to sleep. He would wake her. She was depending
on him to wake her and he mustn't fail.

But when he knelt beside her and brushed back the fine
fair hair that had fallen across her face like a veil, he found
that her skin was as blue as glacier ice, and felt as cold to the
touch. The sound of his own scream echoed in his head.

Kit's eyes sprang open and he kicked and pummeled the
bedclothes as if he could free himself from the nightmare's
grip. As the cold air hit his sweat-soaked T-shirt, he shivered convulsively and came fully awake. For a moment, the
dream's disorientation continued, then he realized that not
only was he not in the Grantchester cottage where he had
grown up, but he wasn't in his room in the Notting Hill
house, either. He was in Nantwich, at his grandparents', in
Duncan's old room.

Jerking himself upright, he peered at Toby, still sleeping
soundly in the next bed. Good. That meant he hadn't
screamed aloud. He didn't want to think of the humiliation
if he'd brought the whole bloody house running. He wiped
his still-damp face with the corner of the duvet and considered the slice of light showing through the gap in the curtains. It seemed to be morning, but there was no sound of
movement in the house, and Tess still slept curled in a hairy
ball at his feet. Beside her lay a dark oblong. Squinting, Kit
edged his foot closer to the object, until he could feel its
weight and its odd-shaped lumps. His sudden spurt of fear
resided and he felt an idiot.

It was a stocking. Now he saw that there was one across
the foot of Toby's bed as well. Someone had come in while
they slept and left them. It was Christmas.

He started to reach for the stocking, but his hand trembled.
He lay back, pulling the duvet up to his chin. The dream was
still too close.

The wave of homesickness that swept over him was so intense that he bit back a groan. He wanted to be in London, in his own room, in his own bed, with familiar sounds and smells drifting up the stairs from the kitchen. Sid, their black cat, would nose open the door and stalk across the room with his tail waving, his way of telling Kit it was time to get up. Kit would go down and help with preparing the Christmas dinner, and their friends Wesley and Otto would drop by to exchange gifts while Gemma played the piano . . .

As hard as Kit tried to sustain it, the comforting fantasy evaporated. He knew too well that being home wouldn't have stopped the dream—hadn't stopped it these past few months. It had come often, in various guises, in the weeks after his mother's death. Then the dream had faded and he had begun to hope it had gone for good, that he could tuck it away along with the images he couldn't bear to remember.

But it had returned, in isolated snatches at first, then with more detail and greater regularity. Now he counted the nights he *didn't* have the dream as blessings, and he dreaded sleep. His heart was beginning to race again as the distorted scenes flashed through his mind, and he felt his throat close with the familiar choking nausea.

To distract himself, he looked round the room. Toby had pulled the covers up over his face, but a cowlick of blond hair rose from the top of the duvet like a feather, and Kit was glad of his sleeping presence.

It was a calm room, with French-blue walls and white trim. Kit wondered if it had looked this way when it had been his dad's. There were a few framed prints of famous locomotives, but most of the available wall space was taken up by bookcases. He'd had a quick look at the titles the night before. There was science fiction, fantasy, detective stories, as well as childhood classics he recognized, like Arthur Ransome's *Swallows and Amazons* and the Narnia books, but he'd also seen volumes of history and biography and a book of famous trials. Were these things Duncan had read, or did Hugh use the room these days as storage?

Tess raised her head and yawned, showing her small pink tongue, then stretched and padded up the duvet to settle next to his side. Freeing an arm from the covers to stroke her, Kit let his mind wander further. What had his dad been like when he'd slept in this room at thirteen? Had he known what he wanted to do with his life? Had he kept secrets from his parents, and got in trouble for it? Had there been a girl, like Lally?

But that idea made him flinch, and his hand fell still on the dog's flank. He shouldn't even be thinking of Lally that way. It was wrong. She was his cousin, and his face flamed at the thought of anyone in the family discovering how he felt.

Besides, last night he'd realized what a fool he'd made of himself when he'd met Leo Dutton.

Things had started to go wrong after they'd got to Lally's house. They'd been in Sam's room, admiring the younger boy's collection of Star Wars action figures with varying degrees of enthusiasm, when Lally had heard the sound of the front door.

"My dad," she'd said, slipping from the room with the quickness of anticipation. Then Kit had heard raised voices, the words indistinguishable, and a few moments later Lally had come back in, much more slowly, her face shuttered.

With the same sort of sibling radar Kit sometimes experienced with Toby, Sam stopped in the midst of demonstrating an X-wing fighter and looked questioningly at his sister.

"Mum and Dad are having a row." Lally had shrugged, as if it didn't matter, and perched nonchalantly on the edge of Sam's bed. But after that there had been an edginess to the atmosphere and Lally had begun to tease her brother so mercilessly that Kit found himself coming to the younger boy's defense.

Dinner was even worse. It was a relief when the meal was over and Lally pulled him aside, whispering, "Come on. We'll say we're going early to save seats at the church, but we'll have time to have a smoke."

"Smoke?" Kit said, before he could think to hide his surprise.

"Don't sound so shocked." Lally's conspiratorial little smile turned to a pout. "Don't tell me you don't have a fag now and then."

"No," he said honestly. "I don't like it." He couldn't tell her that the smell reminded him of his grandmother Eugenia, and made him feel physically ill.

Lally regarded him coolly. "Well, you can do what you want, as long as you're not a telltale. Are you game?"

"Yes, okay," he'd agreed, hoping that once they were away from the house she wouldn't be so prickly. To his surprise, Sam had not asked to go with them, but had given Lally a look Kit couldn't fathom.

He had little opportunity to enjoy his time alone with Lally, however, as her mum had given her a package of leftover food to deliver to an elderly neighbor, and by the time the task had been accomplished, she'd hurried him down the dark path into the town. "I promised to meet a friend at the Crown—that's the old coaching inn," she explained as they reached the square.

Then, when the tall blond boy appeared from the shadowed archway that ran alongside the old pub, Kit gave a start of surprise. He'd assumed the friend was female, and his heart sank.

"So this is the little coz," the boy said, without introduction. He pulled a packet of cigarettes from his jacket pocket, gave one to Lally, then extended the pack to Kit.

Jamming his hands farther into his pockets, Kit shook his head. "No, thanks." To Lally, he added, "What's your friend's name?"

"Leo."

"Aw, it's a sissy boy." Leo's smile showed even white teeth in his thin face. "It even has manners."

Kit knew there was no good answer.

Unexpectedly, it was Lally who rescued him. "Leave it, Leo," she said. "We don't have much time." She fished in her handbag and pulled out a disposable lighter.

"Did you bring my stuff?" Leo asked sharply, as if annoyed at her defection, and Lally looked up at him in surprise.

"We barely got out of the house. And it's Christmas Eve, for Christ's sake. We have to sit in church next to our parents in a half hour's time. That's pushing it, even for you."

She tucked her hair behind her ear, then cupped the tip of the cigarette with one hand while she flicked the lighter with the other. The brief orange flare illuminated the planes of her face but left her eyes in darkness.

The smell of the burning tobacco was pungent in the cold air, and Kit had to stop himself backing up a pace. As Leo reached for the lighter and bent over his own cigarette, Kit took the opportunity to study him. In spite of the other boy's height, he didn't think Leo was actually much older than he was. There was a stretched quality to him, as if he'd grown faster than his bones could tolerate. His blond hair was buzzed short, and he wore a navy wool peacoat that looked like those Kit had seen in expensive London shops. Kit was suddenly painfully aware of his serviceable padded anorak, bought a size too big so that it would fit over his uniform blazer. He looked like a geek—worse, a geek wearing hand-me-downs.

"Are you in the same class at school, then?" he asked, trying to mask his discomfort by taking the initiative.

Lally answered without looking at him. In spite of her bravado, she stood with her back to the arch of the old carriage entrance and kept her eyes on the square. "Yeah. We go to Marlborough School, not the comprehensive. We passed it on the way into town. But we were in primary school together, so we've known each other for yonks, since we were in nappies, practically."

"Speak for yourself," said Leo, mocking. "I'm sure I never wore the things."

Was it possible that Lally and Leo weren't a couple? Kit wondered. That if they'd known each other for years, they were just friends who hung out together? They hadn't touched, or shown any signs of wanting to sneak off for a snog. Kit felt a leap of hope that he didn't care to examine too closely.

"Oh, shit," hissed Lally, startling Kit out of his daydream. Before he could respond, she grabbed him and yanked him back into the shadow of the archway, dropping her half-smoked cigarette to the ground in the process. "There's my granddad. And your mum."

"She's not my mum," Kit responded automatically, then felt a stab of guilt for disowning Gemma so publicly. "I mean—"

"Did they see us?" Lally interrupted, her voice rising.

Leo looked casually out towards the square. "Don't think so. They've gone on, although the woman looked back. So that's your stepmum?" he said to Kit, his eyebrows raised in appreciation.

"Yeah," Kit answered shortly. Not only did he not intend to explain his complicated family situation to Leo, he felt protective of Gemma. He hadn't liked Leo's salacious leer one bit. He was about to add "Mind your own business" when he caught sight of Lally's tense face. For someone who had said she didn't care what her parents thought, she was awfully worried about getting caught.

"We'd better get to the church," she said. "There'll be hell to pay if there aren't any seats left."

"Oh, I'm sure you'll think of something to explain it, Lally, darling." Leo's grin was knowing. "You're good at making up stories."

Kit thought he saw Lally's face darken at the dig, but instead of answering, she peeked out to ensure that the coast was clear, then towed him across the square, leaving Leo to trail in their wake.

When they reached the church, the pews were already filling and Lally swore again, this time under her breath. As she craned her neck, trying to find the best spot, Leo said, "I'd better find my dad, then. He's expecting me to meet and greet and press the old birds' willing flesh."

"Leo, that's disgusting," whispered Lally, but she was distracted by her search for seats.

"Get your dad to let you come to my house tomorrow," said Leo, unperturbed. "We'll show coz here a good time." With that worrying remark he'd disappeared, and Kit had watched with a frown as the other boy slipped through the crowd.

Now, in the clear light of morning, the prospect had not improved. Kit had had enough experience with boys like Leo at school—they had made his last few months a misery. He knew he was on dangerous ground, that if he made one wrong step, Leo would crucify him in front of Lally.

A sleepy voice interrupted his troubled thoughts. "Is that bacon?" said Toby as he threw back his covers and sat up, his hair standing on end like a little blond hedgehog. Kit realized that beneath his preoccupation he'd been aware of the smell of bacon frying, too, and his stomach rumbled in response.

The household was stirring. Kit could smell coffee, now, too, and hear an occasional muted laugh from downstairs. It was time to get up, to see what the day had brought, and he found he was glad of an excuse to think of nothing more complicated than presents and food for a few hours.

"Look, Toby," he said as his brother spied the stocking, "Father Christmas found you after all."

The distinctive low-throated rhythm of a diesel engine came first, then the rocking wash that followed the passage of another boat through the canal basin.

Annie, who on the boat usually woke with the dawn, opened her eyes and blinked against the brilliance of the light spilling through the window over her bed. For a moment she felt disoriented, then memory flooded back. It was Christmas, and she had been late back from the midnight mass at St. Mary's the night before.

She lay quietly, letting her eyes become accustomed to the light, enjoying an unexpected sense of well-being. She had, she realized, slept deeply and dreamlessly for the first time in months. Had it been the singing? If so, she should do it more often. She'd wanted to sing as a child, but it hadn't been an accomplishment her parents thought important.

When her need for coffee overcame her unaccustomed laziness, she threw back the covers and pulled on several layers of fleece. First she turned up the central heating, sending up a silent prayer of thanks for generators, then she stoked the woodstove. Assured that the ambient temperature in the boat would eventually rise above arctic, she put water on to boil and ground her coffee beans.

Fresh filter coffee was one of the small luxuries she allowed herself. Even though she'd read somewhere recently that filter pressed was less healthful than coffee brewed using drip or percolation, she loved the thick, syrupy strength of it. She drank it without sugar, but when she could get cream, she kept a small carton in the boat's fridge. Marina shops weren't always that well stocked, and not all towns on the canal system offered moorings as convenient to the shops as Nantwich.

With her coffee in hand, she opened the salon door and stepped out onto the deck. Sun glinted off snow on the towpath, and from the accumulation on the decks and roofs of the unoccupied boats. Although the weather had cleared, the temperature had not risen enough to cause a significant melt. The basin seemed oddly deserted, even considering the weather. No smoke rose from any chimney other than hers, and there was no movement on the towpath.

Of course, those who kept the narrowboats as second homes would be spending Christmas in their primary residences, and even most of those who lived marginal lives on the boats had someone to go to at Christmas.

Not that she'd been without an invitation, she reminded herself as the abyss of self-pity cracked open before her. Roger had asked her to come, as he always did, and she had refused, as she always did. What would he do with her, she wondered with grim amusement, if she should change her mind?

He had stayed in her family home when they had separated. It had seemed a sensible solution to her at the time, as she wasn't ready to sell the property but didn't want to leave it unattended. He paid her a nominal rent, and she'd told him that if they divorced and decided to sell, she would give him first option to buy the place. She didn't like to think that only self-interest had kept Roger from dissolving their marriage, although she knew that, realistically, it was unlikely he could ever pay her what the house was worth.

Nor could she deceive herself into thinking he missed her terribly. Roger was an even-tempered man who disliked disruption as much as he liked his creature comforts—living with her had not been easy for him. Still, he was thoughtful when it suited him, and she remembered that he had sent her a Christmas gift.

Nipping back inside, she retrieved the package from the drawer where she had stowed it and took it out into the sunshine. It was neatly wrapped in hand-printed paper, and she felt sure Roger had done it himself. He was a competent, thorough man with an artistic flair, all qualities that made him a good journalist—and a good husband. It was she who had not been able to function in the marriage.

Carefully, she pulled loose the package's taped ends and peeled the paper off without tearing it. "Oh!" she said aloud as the gift slipped from its wrappings. That it was a book didn't surprise her—that much she'd guessed from the package's shape and weight—but this she hadn't expected. Checking the flyleaf, she saw that it was a first edition of Tom Rolt's *Narrow Boat,* printed in 1944. The book, an account of the author's exploration of the canal system on his refurbished narrowboat, the *Cressy,* was one of the seminal books on boating life, and Rolt himself had been one of the founders of the Inland Waterways Association.

Annie owned a modern copy, of course, and had reread it many times for its lyrical prose and haunting evocation of bygone days on the canals, but she had never seen an original edition. How like Roger to have found it for her—she would have to ring and thank him. Perhaps she'd even suggest they meet for a holiday meal.

Slowly, she leafed through the volume, examining the woodcuts that prefaced each chapter. The artist, Denys Watkins-Pitchford, had captured the essence of life on the canals with a lovely economy of shape and line. She remembered reading in her modern edition that the drawings had been based on photographs taken by Angela Rolt, Tom's wife.

There was a traditional Buckby water can, the top lock at Foxton, a heron poised in marshy grass, the long-vanished warehouse that had spanned the Shropshire Union Canal at Barbridge . . . As Annie gazed at the images, they brought back all the enchantment she had felt at her first introduction o boating life, and that she had owed entirely to her contact with Gabriel Wain and his family.

Of course, she had seen the canals and boats all her life, had occasionally walked a towpath or stopped to watch a boat going through a lock at Audlem. But she had never set foot on a narrowboat until the day she had been sent to interview the Wains.

How odd that she should have seen them again just yesterday, after all these years. The worry that had nagged at her then returned with full force. The system had betrayed the Wains, and she had failed to protect them.

Her own disillusionment was still sour in her mouth. She had been driven to social work by a profound guilt because of her own privileged upbringing, and by a hope that she could fill a void in herself by giving something to others. But over the years the hopelessness of the work had eaten away her youthful optimism. She saw so much pain and misery and cruelty that she felt the weight of it would crush her, all her actions a remedy as futile as trying to stem a flood with a finger in the dike.

When a child she'd had removed from his own family had died from abuse inflicted by his foster father, she had wondered how long she could go on. Then what had happened to the Wains had been the last straw.

She had walked away, shutting herself off from human contact like a crab crawling into its shell, but the damage had gone on around her. Rowan Wain and her family were still at risk.

Could Annie live with herself if she turned away again? But if she tried to help them, had she anything to offer? Had she the strength to emerge from her self-imposed cocoon?

The revelation came suddenly. It didn't matter whether or not she was up to the task, or whether her infinitesimal actions would make a dent in the world's ills. All that counted was that she should act.

# 8

As **Babcock squelched** across the rutted ice in the hospital car park, he passed Dr. Elsworthy's Morris Minor in the section reserved for doctors' vehicles. From the rear seat, the dog's head rose like a monolithic monster emerging from the deep. The beast gave him a distant and fathomless stare, then looked away, as if it had assessed him and found him wanting, before sinking out of sight once more. No wonder the doctor had no use for anything as modern as a car with an alarm system, Babcock thought as he gave both dog and vehicle a wide berth. She was more likely to be sued by a prospective burglar complaining of heart failure than to have her car violated.

The sight of his sergeant, Kevin Rasansky, leaning against the wall near the morgue entrance was only slightly more heartening.

"Morning, boss. Happy Christmas," Rasansky called out, seemingly unperturbed by the cold or by the holiday call-out.

Babcock merely grimaced in return. "Don't be so bloody cheerful. What are you doing here? I thought you'd not want to miss Christmas morning with your family."

"Thought you might need a hand. Besides, forgot the batteries for the toys, didn't I? The wife and kiddies aren't too happy with me. And my mother-in-law's there for the duration. Who'd have thought the morgue would be preferable?" Rasansky added as he held the door for Babcock.

Ashamed of the relief he'd felt on leaving the care home, Babcock wasn't about to admit he agreed, especially to his sergeant.

Kevin Rasansky was a large young man with a round countryman's face and clothes that never quite seemed to fit. Beneath his unprepossessing exterior, however, resided a sharp intelligence and a streak of ambition that bordered on the ruthless. Babcock found him useful, but never entirely trusted him.

He knew from past experience that if a successful conclusion to a case meant there was any capital to be gained with the powers-that-be, Rasansky would find a subtle way to claim it. There were the self-deprecating stories told round the water cooler or in the canteen, in which Rasansky would just happen to mention how his own humble insight or suggestion had led his superior officers to make the collar. The said superior officer could then hardly refute Rasansky's version without sounding petty, but Babcock retaliated by making every effort to keep his sergeant firmly in his place. There was no task too unpleasant or menial for Rasansky, but this morning he had been willing to give the sergeant a break.

"Have you been to the scene yet?" he asked as they waited for someone to buzz them through the inner doors.

"First thing this morning."

"Any sign of the media?"

"A stringer from the *Chronicle,* Megan Tully. But it will be old news by the time the paper comes out, and I doubt she can interest a national unless it's a very slow news day." By the *Chronicle,* Rasansky meant the local weekly.

Dealing with the media was always a two-edged sword— the dissemination of information could be helpful to an inquiry, but the untimely release of an investigation's details could be disastrous. Babcock was glad, therefore, to have a few days' grace before deciding what should be released to the public. That way, if they hadn't made an identification by the time the paper went to press, he could use the opportunity to make a public appeal.

"Any luck finding the farm's previous owners?"

"No. House-to-house has had a go again this morning. Apparently quite a few of the surrounding properties have changed hands, and the one neighbor we've been told might have an address is away on holiday."

Babcock absorbed this. It meant they'd have to widen their inquiry, and that meant more manpower. "What about the incident room?" he asked. Late the previous evening, Babcock had organized a temporary incident room at the divisional headquarters in Crewe. "Do we have anyone to spare for slogging round the countryside?"

"We've managed to find a few warm bodies, although not particularly happy ones. They seem to think the villains should agree to a Christmas truce."

Babcock glanced at his sergeant, surprised at the reference. During the Great War, in the first battle of Ypres, the soldiers on the British and German sides of the lines had left their trenches to exchange Christmas greetings and make gifts of their few possessions. Rasansky seemed an unlikely student of history.

"Ah, well," he said instead, "we'd still have to deal with the holiday suicides." With that cheerful pronouncement, the inner doors to the morgue swung open.

Dr. Elsworthy's assistant, a large ginger-haired young woman, led them back to the examination room, saying, "She's just starting."

The doctor acknowledged them with a nod. In her scrubs and apron, with her flyaway gray hair tucked under a cap, she looked years younger, and Babcock was struck again by the strong planes and angles of her face.

But if Althea Elsworthy looked more human this morning, the tiny form on the examination table looked less so. With the removal of the blanket and clothing, the child might have been a tattered scrap of a doll made from leather and hair, or the remains of a small animal left to shrivel by the side of a road. He noticed that there was very little smell, merely a faint mustiness. That, at least, was a relief. For once, he wouldn't have to spend the postmortem trying to work out how to talk and breathe through his mouth at the same time.

When Rasansky shook his head and made a clicking sound of disgust with his teeth, Babcock remembered that the sergeant had an infant at home. If he was ever tempted to envy other people their children, a child's body in the morgue was a sure cure.

He transferred his gaze to the X-rays clipped to the light-board, where the white tracery of bones shone like frost on black velvet.

Elsworthy followed his glance. "Skeleton's intact," she said with her usual economy of words. "No evidence of blunt-force trauma, no previous fractures."

"So what does that leave us?" Babcock asked.

"Suffocation. Drowning. Poisoning. Natural causes." There was a gleam of humor in her eye as she added the last.

"Right." Babcock's lip curled with the sarcasm. "What about stabbing or puncture wounds? Gunshot?"

"Possible, but I've not found any damage to what's left of the tissue, nor nicks on the bones. And I've very rarely seen an infant shot or stabbed. It could have been shaken, of course, but any swelling or bruising of the brain tissue has long since disappeared."

"*It,* you said. Can you tell if the child was male or female?"

"Not conclusively, no. There's not much organic matter left in the pelvic area, certainly not enough to tell if this child possessed a penis. And at this age it's hard to differentiate the skeletal structure.

"But from the clothing, I'd guess female. The DNA testing should clarify it, but you'll have to be patient." The glance the doctor flicked at him told Babcock she knew patience was not his strong suit.

"Okay. Female, then. Jane Doe. Age?"

"From the measurements, anywhere from six months to a year, perhaps even eighteen months. Development can vary greatly, depending both on genetics and the child's health and environment. If the child was malnourished, for instance, she might have been well under the predicted size and weight."

As she spoke, she'd turned back to the corpse and begun probing with tweezers. Her touch seemed surprisingly gentle for such a brusque woman.

"There's no sign of insect activity," she went on, "so I think you can assume that the child died during a period of low temperature and was interred quite soon after death."

Rasansky spoke for the first time. "You think she was abused, then?"

"As I've just said, Sergeant, there's no specific evidence," Elsworthy said testily. "It's quite common that babies who have been abused show healed fractures, but the lack of such doesn't rule out mistreatment. And most people who care for their children well don't inter them in old barns."

Her comment made Babcock think of his aunt's parting words, and he asked the question he'd been holding back: "How long do you think she'd been there?"

Elsworthy frowned and continued her examination in silence for a few moments before she answered. "Probably more than a year. That, of course, is just a guess."

"More than a year? As in five, ten, fifteen, twenty? That's all you can tell me?"

This time Babcock was the object of the doctor's glower. "You wanted miracles? The degree of mummification will have been affected by the amount of lime in the mortar and the stone. The lab results may help narrow your time span down a bit, but in the meantime, you may do better with the clothing.

"Both the sleep suit and the blanket appear to contain some synthetic fibers, and the snaps on the sleep suit are only partially corroded. And"—she paused, ostensibly to probe the child's rib cavity, but Babcock was beginning to suspect she enjoyed teasing him—"best of all, there's still a tag on the sleep suit."

"Wh—"

She nodded towards her assistant. "I've written down the brand information. The manufacturer should at least be able to give you a production span."

"Bloody marvelous," Babcock said with bad grace. Knowing the production span on the suit or blanket would give them a starting point, but not an end point. The things could have been stored away in a cupboard for years before they were used in the makeshift burial. "We'll not be able to reach anyone at the manufacturer's until after Boxing Day, at the least." Tracing that information would be a job for Rasansky.

Ignoring his grousing, the doctor said thoughtfully, "You'll notice that although the child was dressed in a sleeper and wrapped in a blanket, there's no sign of a nappie. That's rather odd, don't you think? It suggests that the child was dressed—or re-dressed—after death. That might indicate care on the part of whoever interred her, or on the other hand, it might be part of a ritual that increases some satisfaction to the perpetrator."

"You're not saying we're dealing with a serial baby killer?"

Elsworthy shrugged. "Unlikely, with the absence of gross injuries, but one should always keep an open mind, Chief Inspector. I take it you've had no luck tracking down the property's previous owners?" she asked, with what might have been a trace of sympathy. "It would seem that either the mortar work was done by one of the owners, or with their knowledge."

Babcock shook his head. "The Smiths, who were apparently an eminently respectable older couple, seem to have vanished without a trace."

As Annie motored north from Nantwich Basin, she felt as if she were leaving a calm oasis. Not that there was much movement evident on the canal, but in her brief stay in the basin she'd felt more at peace than she could remember in a very long time. She'd rung Roger, and although she hadn't reached him, she had left a message suggesting they meet for a Christmas meal. Knowing Roger, he was out walking Jazz, the German shepherd he'd bought himself when she'd left—his consolation prize, he'd told her. She suspected the dog had proved better company.

And she had resolved herself to her fool's errand. There was no reason to think that she would find the Wains' boat where it had been yesterday, or that Gabriel and Rowan Wain would talk to her if she did, but having made the decision to try, she felt oddly euphoric. The glitch in her electrical system seemed to have healed itself. An omen, perhaps, that she was taking the right course.

Bundled in her warmest jacket and scarf, she stood at the tiller, guiding the boat back over the route she had traveled just yesterday. The smoke from the cabin drifted back and stung her eyes, but she loved the smell of it, a distillation of comfort on the crisp, cold air. Over the past few years she had learned to steer instinctively, making infinitesimal adjustments to the tiller with the slightest sway of her body.

She smiled, thinking of her first few awkward weeks on the boat, when she had bounced from one side of the canal to the other like a Ping-Pong ball. The tunnels had been the worst, the unfamiliar darkness skewing her perception so that she continually overcorrected, crashing into the dank and dripping walls.

Although she still didn't like the tunnels, she had learned to cope, and in the process she and the *Horizon* had become an entity, the boat an extension of her body. The boat had her own personality, her moods, and Annie had learned to sense them. Today was a good day, she thought, the tiller sensitive as a live thing, the engine thrumming like a big, contented cat.

All her perceptions seemed heightened. Perhaps it was merely the snow-muffled quiet that made her hearing sharper, the searing blue of the sky that made the scenes unfolding before her seem to jump out in crystalline definition. The snow remade the landscape, masking the familiar contours of the land and the ever-present green of the English countryside in winter. And yet what she could see—the corn stubble, the twisted shape of a dead tree, the fine tracery of the bare, shrubby growth that lined the towpath, the black iron bones of a bridge—seemed more brilliant, more intense.

She passed Hurleston Junction and the temptation of the Llangollen Canal snaking down into Wales, but for once she found escape less enticing than the course she had set. As she neared Barbridge, she began to see boats moored along the towpath, and her heart quickened as she picked out the one she sought at the line's end.

Reducing her speed to a crawl, she slipped the *Horizon* into an empty mooring spot and jumped to the towpath to tie up. When she'd fastened the fore and aft lines to the mooring spikes, she dusted the snow from her knees and studied the *Daphne*.

The wooden hull of the Wains' boat was distinctive, but it seemed to Annie that the bright paint seemed slightly faded, the shine on the brass chimney bands less brilliant than she had remembered. Gabriel had told her once that the *Daphne* was one of the last wooden boats built in Nurser's Boatyard in Braunston.

When Annie had worked with the Wains, Rowan had supplemented the family's income by painting the traditional diamond patterns and rose-and-castle designs on boats, and the *Daphne* had been a floating advertisement for her work. Rowan had also painted canalware, covering the Buckby cans used by the boat people to carry water, as well as bowls and dippers, with her cheerful rose designs.

At their last meeting, Rowan had presented Annie with a dipper she had painted especially for her, her way of communicating the thanks her husband had been too proud and angry to offer.

Not that Annie had expected thanks. Dear God, she had only done what she could to redress the wrong they had already suffered, their unconscionable betrayal by the system that was meant to protect them.

At first Annie thought the *Daphne* was uninhabited. The curtains were drawn and there was no sign of movement. Then she saw the faintest wisp of smoke rising from the chimney, and a moment later, Gabriel Wain emerged onto the stern deck.

He started to nod, the easy greeting of one boater to another, then froze. Expression drained from his face like water from a lock, until all that remained was the wariness in his eyes. His thick dark hair was now flecked with gray, like granite, but his body was still strong. When Annie had first met Gabriel Wain, she had thought him too big to fit comfortably on a narrowboat, but he moved so nimbly and gracefully about the cabin and decks that he might never have set foot on land.

Now he stood, feet slightly apart as he balanced against the slight rocking generated by his own movement, and watched her. When he spoke, his voice held a challenge. "Mrs. Constantine. To see you once, after so long, I might think chance. But twice in as many days? What do you want with us?"

Annie flicked the last of the snow from her trousers and straightened to her full height. "It's not Constantine these days, Gabriel. It's Lebow. I've gone back to my maiden name. And I'm not with Social Services anymore. I left not long after I worked with you. I bought the boat," she added, gesturing towards the *Horizon*. When he merely raised an eyebrow, she faltered on. "It was good to see you yesterday. The children look well. I'm glad. But Rowan—I wondered if I might have a word with Rowan. I thought yesterday— She didn't seem—"

"She's resting. She doesn't need your interference."

Annie took a step nearer the boat. "Look, Gabriel, I understand how you feel. But if she's ill, maybe I could help. I—"

"You can have no idea what I feel," he broke in, his voice quiet for all the fury behind it. "And she's not ill. She's just—she's just tired, that's all." There was the fear again, a chasm yawning behind his eyes, but this time Annie thought she wasn't to blame.

"You know I helped you before," she said more firmly. "You know I was on your side. I might be able—"

"Our side? You, with your tarted-up boat"—he cast a scornful glance at the *Horizon* and spat into the canal—"you don't know anything about our lives. Now leave us alone."

"You can't throw me off the towpath, Gabriel." She knew the absurdity of her position as soon as the words left her mouth. What was she going to do? Call Social Services?

"No." For the first time, there was a hint of bitter humor in the curve of his mouth. "But I can give up a good mooring if you insist on making a nuisance of yourself, woman."

And she could cast off the *Horizon* and follow. Annie had a ridiculous vision of herself trailing down the Cut after the *Daphne* at three miles per hour, a slow-motion version of a car chase in an American film. She sighed, feeling the tension drain from her shoulders, and said quietly, "Gabriel, I know what happened to your family was wrong. I only want— I suppose what I want is to make up for it in some way."

"There is nothing you can do." There was a bleak finality in his expression that made her wish for a return of his anger. "Now—"

The cabin door had opened a crack. The little girl slipped out and Gabriel glanced round, surprised, as she tugged at his trousers leg. She was fairer than Annie had noticed yesterday, and in the clear light her eyes were a brilliant blue. "Poppy," she whispered. "Mummy wants to see the lady."

It had, in spite of Gemma's worries, turned out to be a nearly perfect Christmas. She'd been a little ashamed of her relief when she learned that Juliet and Caspar and their children would be having their Christmas dinner with Caspar's parents. Her heart went out to Juliet—she couldn't imagine how Duncan's sister was coping after Caspar's behavior last night— but she hadn't wanted the couple's feuding to poison her own children's day.

Kit and Toby had slept in, only tumbling downstairs with Tess after Hugh had got the bacon frying and Geordie, her cocker spaniel, and Jack, the sheepdog, had started a rough-and-tumble game in the kitchen. Kit had thrown on jeans and a sweatshirt, but Toby still wore pajamas and dressing gown, and clutched his Christmas stocking possessively to his small chest.

When Rosemary said there would be no presents until after breakfast, not even Toby had complained, although Gemma knew that at home he'd have thrown a wobbly and whinged all the way through the meal.

Half an hour later, replete with eggs, bacon, and sausage, the adults carrying refills of coffee, the dogs damp from a romp in the snow, they all trooped into the sitting room.

Hugh had built a roaring fire and switched on the tree lights, and with the sun sparkling on the snow outside the window, the room looked magical.

Perched on the arm of the chesterfield, leaning against Duncan's warm shoulder, Gemma watched the children. Rosemary had asked Kit to help his younger brother hand round the presents, but as soon as Toby found a few gifts bearing his name, he ripped into them, tossing shreds of paper about like a storm of New Year's confetti. Kit, on the other hand, waited until he'd passed round a few gifts for everyone, then, only at his grandmother's urging, carefully removed the paper from one of his own packages. First he pulled loose the tape, then folded the used paper, then wound the ribbon into a neat roll.

Gemma marveled at the difference in the boys—Toby a miniature marauder, Kit hoarding his gifts while he watched everyone else, as if he wanted to postpone the pleasure for as long as possible. Would he ever dive into anything with abandon, she wondered, without fearing that it would be snatched from him?

But in spite of his habitual caution and the slight shadows round his eyes, she thought he looked happier and more relaxed than he had in weeks. And he had stayed close to Duncan all morning, the tension of yesterday's row apparently forgotten.

Now his eyes widened in pleasure as he finished unwrapping his gift from his grandparents—a trivia game he'd been admiring in the shops for months.

"How did you know?" Gemma asked Rosemary, laughing, as Kit went to give his grandmother a hug.

"A good guess," Rosemary said lightly, but she looked pleased.

"Oh," breathed Toby, his flurry of motion stilled as he uncovered his own from Rosemary and Hugh, a large wooden box filled with multicolored pastels, and a pad of drawing paper. "What are they?" he asked, running his fingers over the sticks. "Are they like crayons?"

"A bit," answered Hugh. "And a bit like chalk. We heard you were quite the artist. I'll show you how to use them later on."

Giving Gemma's shoulder a squeeze, Duncan stood up and rooted under the tree until he found his gift for his father. "I know it's a bit like coals to Newcastle," he said, passing it across with studied nonchalance, but she heard the anticipation in his voice.

Hugh hefted the package in his hand and grinned. "Feels like a book." But when he had peeled off the paper, he sat for a moment, gaping at the small volume, before looking up at his son. "Where did you find this?" he whispered.

Kincaid had come back to the sofa and slipped his arm round Gemma. "A bookseller in Portobello. I thought you might like it." It was, as he had explained to Gemma in great detail, a copy of *Conversations About Christmas,* by Dylan Thomas, one of only two thousand printed in 1954 for the friends of publisher J. Laughlin, none of which was then offered for sale. The text was a segment of Thomas's "A Child's Christmas in Wales," altered by the poet into dialogue form.

"I don't know what to say." Hugh pressed his lips together but didn't quite stop a tremble.

Kincaid cleared his throat and said a little too heartily, "Read it to us, then."

"Now?" asked Hugh, looking at his wife.

Rosemary nodded. "Why not? The turkey's in the oven. We're in no rush."

And so Hugh stood with his back to the fire, a pair of reading glasses on his nose, and, in a credible Welsh accent, began to declaim the lines that took Gemma instantly back to her own sitting room the previous Christmas. Duncan had read the poem aloud to her and the children, and she had imagined a string of Christmases to come, with the boys and the child she carried snuggled beside her.

She shivered and Duncan hugged her a little closer. "Cold?" he murmured in her ear.

She shook her head and put her finger to her lips, listening intently as the words rolled over them, painting pictures more vivid than memories. Even Toby sat quietly, his pastels held tightly in his lap.

Duncan had outdone himself, Gemma thought, as if this Christmas, and this homecoming, had been particularly important to him. He had woken her that morning by setting a box beside her pillow.

"What?" she'd said, blinking sleepily and pulling herself up against the headboard as he sat on the edge of the bed.

"Open it." He was dressed, she saw, but tousled and unshaven, and she guessed he had tiptoed down to the sitting room to retrieve the package.

"Now? But what about the child—"

"This isn't for the children, it's for you. Go on, open it."

She was fully awake now, and her heart gave an anxious little jerk. Pushing her hair from her face, she delayed. "It's bigger than a bread box."

"If you don't open the damned thing, you'll be lucky to get a loaf of bread, much less a bread box," he'd said with mock severity, so she had peeled off the wrapping as carefully as Kit had. "And no, it's not a toaster," he'd added as she saw the appliance label on the cardboard box.

She'd pulled back the box flaps and dug into the nest of tissue paper, easing out first a pottery sugar bowl, then a jug, in the same bright Clarice Cliff pattern as the teapot a friend had given her after her miscarriage.

"Oh," she'd breathed, "you shouldn't have— Wherever did you—They're lovely." The pieces were rare, and bloody expensive, and she guessed he—and their friend Alex—had spent months looking for them.

"You like them?" He'd looked suddenly unsure.

"Of course I like them!" Pulling him to her, she brushed her lips across his stubbly cheek. His skin felt warm in the room's chill, and smelled of sleep.

For just a moment, she'd hoped he'd chosen something a little more romantic, something that represented their future together . . .

Then she'd mentally kicked herself for being a fool. If she wanted something as mundane as a ring, all she had to do was ask and he would take her to the nearest jeweler. Instead, he had gone to a great deal of time and expense to find something that had personal meaning for her—not only a personal meaning, but something that symbolized her recovery. What could possibly be more romantic than that?

Dear God, did she think a little thing like a ring was proof against emotional disaster? Her thoughts strayed to Juliet and Caspar and she shuddered, ashamed of her brief lapse into the pettiness of traditional expectations.

No, ta very much, she would much rather keep things the way they were. To prove it, she'd thanked Duncan with great enthusiasm, and now the memory of that warm half hour made her move a little closer into the circle of his arm.

Later, when the presents had all been opened, Hugh had finished his reading, and the sitting room tidied, they'd had turkey and all the trimmings at the long kitchen table. They'd pulled Christmas crackers to the accompaniment of the dogs' barking, and had all put on their silly paper hats, much to Toby's delight. Gemma knew that Rosemary and Hugh must be worried about Juliet, but they had done their best to make the day special for the children.

When they had eaten as much of the turkey as they could manage, they all pushed back their chairs with groans, and by mutual consent agreed to postpone the Christmas pudding until teatime. Gemma insisted on helping Rosemary with the washing up while the men and boys got out the trivia set. She watched them—Hugh, Duncan, and Kit—as they sat over the game board, their lean Kincaid faces stamped with the same intent expression. And then there was Toby, the odd duckling in the brood. How lucky for him, Gemma thought, that he was not the sort to notice that he didn't belong.

She was glad they had come, she mused as she wiped plates with a tea towel. She hadn't realized until they'd got away just how much they'd needed a change, a break from work for her and for Duncan, a break from school for Kit.

When the phone rang, Rosemary was up to her elbows in the washing-up water. "I'll get it, shall I?" said Gemma, and at Rosemary's nod picked up the handset.

"Gemma?" The word was little more than a whisper, but Gemma recognized Lally's voice. "Look, I don't want my dad to hear me," the girl went on hurriedly. "I'm at my grandma's—my other grandma's. I'm in the loo, ringing from my mobile. Have you seen my mum?"

"Here?" Gemma asked, surprised. "No. Why?" Rosemary had turned to listen, her face frozen in instant alarm, her hands still submerged in the soapy water.

"She left here ages ago, before dinner," said Lally, choking back a little hiccup of distress. "She said she'd forgotten something and she'd only be a few minutes, but she never came back."

*On a blustery day in early spring, he was idling through the covered market in the town center after school, bored with lessons that were too easy, bored with teachers taken in by his excuses, bored with stupid classmates too easily influenced.*

*He moved from stall to stall, examining the merchandise under the watchful eye of the stallholders, enjoying the knowledge that he could easily lift something if he chose. It was all worthless tat, though, not worth the bother.*

*Then a basket beside the fruit-and-veg stall caught his eye. Had it moved? Leaning closer, he heard a high-pitched mewling, and what he'd initially thought was a bundle of yarn resolved itself into a mass of tiny, squirming kittens.*

*"Like a kitten, love?" asked the stallholder, in the too-jolly tone people used with children, as if anyone under the age of reproductive ability was an imbecile. "They're five pounds, mind," she added, with a smile that revealed bottom teeth like leaning gravestones. "Just to ensure they go to a good home."*

*"How old are they?" he asked, touching one of the bundles with a fingertip. A tongue emerged, rasping his bare skin. The kitten's eyes, he saw, were blue, and still slightly clouded, as if it hadn't quite learned to focus.*

*"Six weeks today. They can eat kibble, mushed up with a bit of milk. Would your parents let you have a cat, love?"*

*He smiled, imagining his mother's response if he brought home a kitten. Neither of his parents cared for animals at all, and his mother had a phobia about cats.*

*"Oh, yes," he said. Reaching into his pocket, he pulled out a handful of coins. "I think I've got five pounds. I could*

surprise my mum." He counted out three of the heavy coins, made a face, then began sorting through the small change.

The woman stopped him with a touch on his hand. "No, no, love. That's all right. For you, I'll make it three. No need to spend all your pocket money. Is it the gray one you like?" She plunged her hand into the basket and extricated the bit of gray fluff he'd prodded. "He's a grand one. Can you get him home, or will you have your mum bring you back?"

Giving the woman his best smile, he took the kitten, tucking it into the anorak he wore over his school blazer and pulling up the zip. "I'm sure I can manage. I've got my bike, and I don't live far."

He supported the little body with one hand as he slipped away through the crowd. The kitten wriggled, then quieted, as if comforted by the warmth of his body. "Good luck, sonny," the woman called after him, but he pretended he hadn't heard.

Riding his bike one-handed was easy enough, but instead of turning towards home he rode towards the western edge of town and onto the canal towpath. The days were lengthening, so he still had time before dark, and the ground was dry enough that he needn't worry about splashing mud on his school clothes. He rode north, and when the town had dropped away behind him, he stopped the bike and leaned it against the budding branches of a hawthorn hedge. Just ahead, the canal curved, and the edging had crumbled, providing a fertile hold for reeds at the water's edge.

He came here sometimes when he wanted to think. Hunkering down on a dry hummock among the reeds, he was invisible, but he could hear a boat or pedestrian coming from a good distance away. A faint hum of traffic reached him from the Chester Road and the wind stirred the reed tops, but he found a sheltered spot and folded his legs beneath him. Alerted by the movement, three swans came gliding over, pecking at the tufts of grass lining the canal's edge.

The kitten had been lulled by the movement of the bike, but now it stirred and squirmed, digging tiny needles of claws into his skin through blazer and shirt. Annoyed, he *pulled it out and lifted it by the scruff of its neck, examining it. It hung paralyzed in his grip, its wide blue eyes unblinking.*

*What was he going to do with the thing? The anticipation of his mother's horror had lost some of its appeal. His pleasure would be short-lived. She might screech, but then she would retreat to her room, and he would be left finding a home for the cat, a tedious task.*

*The water rippled as the swans moved away. When the surface stilled, he held the kitten over the canal and studied its wavery reflection. It seemed unreal, a figment of his imagination.*

*Without conscious thought, he lowered his hand. The kitten struggled as it met the water, twisting and raking his wrist with its claws, then the cold closed over the small gray body, and his grip held fast.*

# 9

❧

THE TEMPORARY INCIDENT ROOM at divisional headquarters had been filled with a jumble of scarred and dented furniture not needed elsewhere, and computers had been set up haphazardly on desks and tabletops. Wiring trailed across the scuffed flooring like an infestation of snakes, and Babcock, technophobe that he was, suspected it was almost as dangerous.

It was cold, as it was summer or winter in the nether regions of the old building, and to add an even more festive touch to the atmosphere, the room smelled strongly of potatoes, onions, and dough. Someone had obviously indulged in a morning snack of Cornish pasty. The idea made Babcock's stomach churn.

Ignoring the discomfort, he turned back to the whiteboard set up against one wall and wrote "Baby Jane Doe."

"Unless we hear otherwise," he said, "we are going to assume the child is female."

His team had made themselves as comfortable as possible, and he glanced at them to make sure he had their attention before he continued. He listed the pathologist's conclusions on the board with a dried-out red marker that had an annoying tendency to squeak: "Six to eighteen months old. Interred at least one year, probably during winter. Cause of death not obvious."

One of the detective constables groaned. "You're joking, boss. That's all we have to go on?"

"What? You expect miracles?" asked Babcock in a fair imitation of Dr. Elsworthy, and got a laugh from the group. They'd been grousing among themselves, resenting working on their holiday, and he needed their wholehearted cooperation.

"That rules out the newest owners, the ones doing the construction," said Rasansky. He'd slouched in the chair nearest the board, his long legs stretched out almost in Babcock's path.

"Possibly. Probably. But not the Fosters." Babcock tapped the end of the marker against the side of his nose while he thought. "Although if they'd disposed of an infant in the barn, it seems unlikely they'd have been eager to sell to someone who was going to take the place apart. I'd put them on the back burner for the moment, although we'll need to talk to them again. That leaves—"

"Excuse me, boss." It was Sheila Larkin, the detective constable who had groaned over the postmortem results. She was a sharp young woman and Babcock was always glad to have her on his team, except for the fact that her very short skirts distracted his male officers, not to mention himself. This morning she sat on the edge of a table with her feet propped on a chair, and he had to drag his gaze away from her bare thighs. He wondered how she managed to avoid freezing.

"Isn't it possible," she continued, "that if the Fosters didn't use the barn, the job could have been done without their knowledge?"

"Good point. I don't think our Mr. Foster stirs out of his armchair too often. And I suppose it could have been done at night, in what—an hour or two? I'm not much of a DIY man myself," Babcock added.

"Piece of cake," said Rasansky. "A lantern, a pail of mortar, a trowel. Of course, that's assuming there was already a space in the wall suitable for filling in."

Babcock frowned. "Even so, I doubt whoever did this wandered around with his mortar, hoping he'd run across he perfect spot to inter a baby. This required forethought, and foreknowledge. Our perpetrator had to have been familiar with the barn, and would have to have known when he was least likely to be observed."

"Could a builder estimate the age of the mortar?" asked Larkin, crossing one leg over the other and exposing another few inches of plump white thigh. Travis, his scene-of-crime officer, was riveted, and Babcock wondered if he could have a discreet cautionary word with Larkin without being accused of making inappropriate sexual comments.

"I need to interview Juliet Newcombe again," he said. "I'll have a word with her about it." He turned to Travis. "Any luck with the fingertip search?"

Not the least bit flustered, Travis gave a last lingering glance at Larkin's legs before turning his attention to Babcock. "Sod all, boss. Used condoms, fag ends, lunch wrappers, beer cans. Just the combination you'd expect from a construction site that's also been accessible to teenagers looking to have a bit of fun."

Babcock hadn't expected anything more helpful. He singled out Larkin, who had been assigned to search the missing-persons database. "Any luck with mis-per, Sheila?"

"It's difficult without parameters, boss. I started with the last five years, children under two, confining the search to South Cheshire. No matches, male or female."

"We'll stick to South Cheshire for now, as I think it highly unlikely that someone from out of the area would have known about the barn. But let's go back twenty years. Dr. Elsworthy says the fabrics look to be fairly modern synthetic blends, but twenty years is strictly a guess at this point—we could be looking at twenty-plus. When we get the fabric analysis from the lab, we may be able to narrow it down a bit further."

"Yes, boss," said Larkin, with her usual gung-ho attitude.

He nodded his approval before turning back to the others. "I think our biggest priority, after identifying a missing child that fits our parameters, is to trace the former owners, the Smiths. Kevin, I want you to extend the house-to-house. There's *bound* to be someone who knows where they went."

"I've sent someone round to the big house at the top of the lane twice, but no one's at home," Rasansky said a little defensively. "They're the nearest neighbors other than the Fosters, and the most likely prospect."

"Well, keep trying. But, Kevin," he continued, "I want you to see if you can track down Jim Craddock, the estate agent who handled the Smiths' sale of the property, Christmas or no. And while you're at it, stop at Somerfield's and Safeway, and anywhere else you can think of that carries baby products— Oh, hell." He rubbed at his chin in frustration. "I keep forgetting everything's closed. We'll have to put that off until after Boxing Day. Must be your lucky day, Sergeant."

The look Rasansky shot him was gratifyingly sour, and as everyone turned to his assigned task, Babcock suddenly found himself whistling under his breath.

After the brilliance of sun on snow, it took Annie's eyes a moment to adjust to the dim light in the narrowboat's cabin. The curtains had been pulled almost closed, and a single oil lamp burned on the drop-down table. A low fire smoldered in the woodstove, but the cold seemed dense, as if it had settled in the small space like a weight.

Although Gabriel had built a galley, bathroom, and sleeping quarters into what had once been the boat's cargo space, he had kept the main cabin as unaltered as possible. As Annie looked round, she felt she had stepped back in time.

The woodwork was dark, with trim picked out in a cheery red, and every available inch of flat wall space was covered either with polished brasses or with the laceware china plates that the boaters had traditionally collected. Rowan had once told Annie that she had inherited the pieces from her mother. The back of the cross seat had been embellished with a miniature castle—as was the underside of the drop table, Annie remembered—and painted roses cascaded down a side storage box—all Rowan's work.

But today only Joseph sat at the table, his dark, curly head bent over paper and pencils. He hadn't looked up since Annie had stepped down into the cabin. Gabriel and the little girl, Marie, had stopped on the steps behind her, adding to Annie's sense of unease.

"Hello, Joe," she said. He must be getting on for nine, she thought, a handsome, well-made boy who seemed to have outgrown the problems that had plagued him as a baby and toddler.

He had been two when his parents had first taken him to the local hospital. They'd told the attending doctor that the boy was having fits, and had several times stopped breathing.

After examining the boy, the doctor reported that he could find no evidence of seizures, but that the child had bruising on his arms and legs that might have been due to a violent fit.

Over the next few months, the Wains took Joseph to the hospital again and again, although the staff's findings continued to be inconclusive. Up until that time, the Wains had lived a nomadic life, but because of the child's poor health, Gabriel had found temporary work near Nantwich. Also, Rowan had become pregnant again, and was having a difficult time.

Frustrated and unused to dealing with the hospital bureaucracy, Gabriel Wain had become increasingly belligerent with the doctor and the nursing staff. The boat people had always had a healthy disregard for hospitals, and Gabriel himself had been one of the last babies delivered by Sister Mary at Stoke Bruene on the Grand Union Canal, the nursing sister who spent her life ministering to the needs of the canal community.

On calling up the child's National Health records, the doctor learned that this was not the first time the Wains had sought help for their son. When Joseph was an infant, they had taken him to a Manchester hospital, saying that he couldn't keep food down. Again, no diagnosis had been made.

The doctor's suspicions were aroused, and after a particularly difficult altercation with Gabriel, he had turned Joseph's records over to Social Services.

His accompanying report was damning. He believed the parents were manufacturing symptoms, and possibly abusing the boy, for attention. His official accusation—Annie could no longer think of it as a diagnosis—had been MSBP, Munchausen syndrome by proxy.

It had been her job, as the social worker assigned to the case, to investigate the doctor's allegations.

"You probably won't remember me, Joe," she said now, "but I knew you when you were little."

Joseph glanced at her, then nodded, his eyes downcast again, and from the color that rose in his cheeks she realized that he must be painfully shy. She wondered if the family had stayed in one place long enough for either child to be enrolled in school.

"Your mummy wanted to see—" she had begun, when Gabriel spoke from behind her.

"Through there," he said, gesturing towards the passageway that led to the galley and the sleeping cabins beyond. He stepped down into the cabin, Marie clinging to his leg like a limpet, and the small space seemed suddenly claustrophobic. For a moment Annie felt frightened, then she told herself not to be absurd. Gabriel wouldn't harm her—and certainly not in front of his wife and children.

She followed his instructions, moving through the tidy galley and into the cabin beyond. Here, the curtain had been pulled back a few inches, enough to illuminate the figure lying propped up in the box bed.

"Rowan!" Annie breathed, unable to stop herself. If she had thought the woman looked ill when she had seen her yesterday, today her skin seemed gray, and even in the filtered light of the cabin, her lips had a blue tinge.

Rowan Wain smiled and spoke with obvious effort. "I heard you." She nodded towards the window that overlooked the towpath. "I couldn't let you go, thinking we didn't appreciate what you did for us all that time ago. But there's nothing we need now. We're just fine on our own."

Annie was conscious of Gabriel standing in the doorway, with both children now crowded behind him, but she tried to ignore their presence. As there was no other furniture in the small cabin and she didn't want to talk to Rowan while hovering over her, she sat down carefully on the hard edge of the box bed. Gabriel had made it himself, she remembered, a fine example of his carpentry skills.

"You've got yourself a boat now," Rowan continued with a smile. "You and your husband?"

Facing this woman who had given her entire life to her family, Annie found herself suddenly unable to admit she'd abandoned her husband on what she suspected Rowan would see as a whim. "Finding oneself" was a strictly middle-class luxury. Nor, aware of Gabriel's hostile presence behind her, was she sure she wanted to admit to being alone. "Yes," she said at last, nodding.

"But yesterday you were working her on your own. And well, too."

"My husband—he had some business at our house in Tilston." The prevarication came a little more easily, but then she remembered she'd told Gabriel she'd gone back to using her maiden name. Well, she'd just have to bluff it out as best she could. "He'll be back soon," she said with an internal grimace, knowing she had just marked herself out as someone who used a narrowboat for an occasional second home, a practice that earned little respect from the traditional boater. "I'm surprised I—we hadn't run across you before now."

Rowan looked away. "We were up Manchester way for a while, but the jobs dried up."

From the silence of the generator, the mean fire, and the slight shabbiness of the boat itself, things had not improved on the Shropshire Union. The boat was so cold that Rowan was covered in layers of blankets over the old woolen jumper she wore, and when she spoke, her breath made tiny clouds of condensation. Annie said, "Rowan, if things aren't going well, I could—"

"No." Rowan glanced at her husband as she cut Annie off. "We'll do fine. You should g—"

Annie wasn't going to let herself be fobbed off so easily. "Rowan, you're obviously not well. How long has this been going on? Have you seen a doctor?"

"I'm just a bit tired," Rowan protested, but her voice was breathy, a thread of sound. "With Christmas and all. I'll be fine when I've had a rest."

It was a game effort, but Annie now saw things besides the pallor—the hollows under the woman's eyes, the protrusion of the bones from the stick-thin wrists, the lank hair that had once been glossy.

"Rowan," she said gently. "I think you haven't been well for some time. You must get some help."

"You know I can't." Rowan sat up, grasping Annie's arm with unexpected strength. "No doctors. No hospitals. I won't take a chance with my children."

Annie laid her hand over the other woman's fingers, gently, until she felt Rowan's grip relax. "There's no reason why your seeing a doctor should put the children at risk. They're both well. You must—"

"You know what my records will say." Rowan's voice rose with urgency. "It never comes off—you told me that yourself—even though I was cleared. Someone will come, looking, prying, and this time it won't be you."

Annie closed her eyes and took a breath as the memories flooded back. The case had landed on her desk, one of many, and she'd seen enough abuse in her years as a social worker that at first she'd been predisposed to take the report at face value, a fact that now shamed her. She'd held such power, to have taken it so lightly. If her findings had agreed with the doctors', the Wains' case would have gone to the civil courts. There, the family, marginally literate and with no funds for counsel, would have been helpless against the unlimited resources of the state and the testimony of so-called expert witnesses. It was almost certain that both Joseph and little Marie would have been taken into foster care, and possible that one or both parents would have faced criminal charges.

She had first interviewed the Wains aboard the *Daphne*. She'd been unexpectedly charmed by the boat, and by Rowan's shy hospitality. The first niggle of doubt had crept in as she'd observed a mother whose devoted care of her son seemed in no way calculated to call attention to herself, a father who was surly to her but unfailingly gentle with the little boy. By this time, Joseph's seizures seemed to have stopped, and neither parent displayed anything but heartfelt relief.

Although puzzled as she continued to visit the family, as she watched them time after time with their child, Annie became more and more convinced that the charges against them were unfounded. So she had gone with her instincts, but it had taken her months of investigation, of interviews, of sifting through medical records, to come up with the means to prove herself, and them, right.

Their nomadic life had made the process enormously difficult. They spent little time in one place, had no extended family, no intimate contact with others who could substantiate their accounts of little Joseph's illnesses. But during one interview, Rowan told her about Joseph's first seizure.

They'd been on the Grand Union Canal, below Birmingham, moored alongside several other boats. Gabriel had been on deck and Rowan in the cabin with the sleeping toddler when the boy had stiffened, his back arching, his arms and legs flailing. Then the child had gone limp, his skin turning blue. Rowan had lifted him, shaking him frantically while shouting to Gabriel for help.

Gabe had come plunging down the hatchway with Charlie, a quiet, lanky young man who drifted from one mooring to the next on an old Josher. But when Charlie saw the still child in Rowan's arms, his indolence vanished. "Ambulance training," he'd said shortly. Taking Joseph from Rowan, he'd laid him out on the cabin floor, and after checking his airway, had given the baby a quick puff of breath, then pressed on his chest. Once, twice, three times, and then Joseph's body had jerked in a spasm and he'd begun to wail.

They had never run across Charlie again, however, and Rowan didn't even know if he was still on the boats.

But Annie was determined to substantiate Rowan's story, and her search for the elusive Charlie proved her true introduction to the Cut. She'd begun by car, working in a widening circle from Cheshire, crisscrossing middle England as she tried canal-side shops and marinas, pubs and popular mooring spots, talking to anyone who might have had contact with the Wains or might have news of Charlie.

She soon discovered not only that had she set herself a well-nigh impossible task, but that there were places boaters congregated that couldn't be reached by car. She had almost despaired when a boater told her he knew Charlie; had, in fact, recently seen him on the Staff and Worcs Canal, below Stoke.

The next day Annie had hired a boat with her own funds. She knew her department would never deem it a reasonable expense. But she also realized that somewhere over the past few weeks, she'd slipped over the line between reason and obsession.

She'd had little idea how to handle the boat. Even remembering the mess she'd made of her first few locks made her shudder. Terrified and clumsy, she was kept from swamping the boat or falling from a lock gate only by blind luck and help from fellow boaters. But she had persevered, her enchantment with the Cut growing over the next few days as she worked her way south along the Shropshire Union towards Birmingham. She learned to recognize the Joshers, the restored boats that had once belonged to the Fellows, Morton, and Clayton carrying company, and when one evening she saw the distinctive silhouette of a Josher moored near the bottom of the Wolverhampton 21, her heart had raced. As she drew nearer, she made out the faded letters on the boat's side: *Caroline*. That was the name both the Wains and her boater informant had given her. Charlie did exist, and she had found him. Jubilation fizzed through her.

He was just as the Wains had described him, although not now so young, a thin, freckle-faced man with his sandy hair drawn back in a ponytail. When he understood what Annie wanted, he'd invited her into his tiny cabin for a beer, and he'd given her an account of the incident almost identical to Rowan Wain's. Trying to contain her excitement, Annie wrote out his statement and had him sign it.

"Poor little bugger," he'd said when they'd finished. "It was obviously some sort of seizure. Did they ever get him sorted out? The mother said he'd been unwell as an infant. Gastric reflux. I remember thinking it odd that she knew the term."

Back aboard her hire boat, settled in her cabin with a celebratory glass of wine, Annie tried to work out what to do ext. If Joseph's seizures were real, why had the doctor been so ready to discount his parents' accounts? And was there some connection between the problems he'd had as an infant and his later seizures?

With regret, she'd returned to Nantwich and traded her hire boat for piles of paper. Eventually, her diligence paid off. She found the anomaly in the records from the Manchester hospital where Joseph had previously been treated. One report mentioned an earlier admission, to a hospital near Leeds, where Joseph had been prescribed medication for gastric reflux. And yet in the current doctor's report to Social Services, he stated that Joseph had never been treated for any of the ailments described by his parents. How had he missed it?

Or perhaps more to the point, Annie thought, *why* had he missed it? She knew the system could fail, knew both doctors and nurses were overworked and overtired, but surely such a serious accusation had merited a thorough review of the little boy's case?

Her suspicions aroused, she began interviewing hospital staff and checking the doctor's record. The doctor had a reputation, she found, for his lack of patience with parents who questioned his judgment or took up too much of his time. He had, in fact, made a diagnosis of MSBP in three other cases. Even assuming one believed in the validity of the diagnosis, such a high incidence of the disorder was statistically absurd. All the families had been low income; all had lost their children to foster care.

Annie had, of course, recommended that Joseph and Marie Wain not be added to the council's "at risk" register, or placed in foster care. Joseph's health continued to improve, an occurrence that the other doctors Annie consulted told her was not unusual—sometimes children simply healed themselves as their development progressed.

She had also made a formal complaint against the doctor in question, but no action had been taken by the hospital authorities. And in spite of all her efforts, Rowan Wain's records still carried the diagnosis of MSBP, and the stigma of child abuse and mental illness. It could not be expunged.

Now Annie patted Rowan's hand in an effort at reassurance. "There's no reason anyone should look at the children," she said, yet the scenarios played out in her head. What if Rowan were seriously, even terminally, ill? What if some eager doctor or nurse looked at her records and decided that Rowan—or Gabriel, on Rowan's death—could not provide suitable care? It could start all over again, and this time she would be unable to protect them.

Rowan simply shook her head, as if the effort of speech had exhausted her.

With growing panic, Annie turned to Gabriel. "You must see she can't go on like this. You've got to do something." The sight of the children's anxious faces as they pressed against their father kept her from adding Or she might die, but his expression told her he knew. He knew, but he couldn't risk his children, and the choice was tearing him apart.

"No hospitals," he repeated, but the force had gone from his voice and his rugged face was creased with anguish.

*No hospitals.* An idea took root in Annie's mind. It might work—at the very least it would tell them what they were dealing with.

She gave Rowan's hand a squeeze, then looked back at Gabriel. "What if . . . what if I could find someone to come and have a look at Rowan? What if it were strictly off the record?"

"I'm sure there's no reason to worry," Kincaid said. "You know Jules's temper—after last night, I'm not surprised she couldn't get through Christmas dinner with Caspar. And she's always liked to go off on her own when she's in a funk."

After speaking to Lally, his mother had rung Juliet's mobile number and her home phone, with no response. Then, despite Lally's pleas, she had rung Caspar to confirm the girl's story. Rosemary's mouth had tightened as she listened, then she'd hung up with unnecessary force. "He says it's true," she'd told them. "Juliet walked out without a word to anyone before dinner was even served. He says she meant to inconvenience everyone."

Now his mother shook her head. "I don't like it." Worry

hadowed her eyes, and with a pang, Kincaid saw that she had
ged more than he'd realized since he'd seen her last.

Gemma had gone back to the washing up, but he could
ee that she was listening with quiet attention. A strand of
air had come loose from her clip, curling damply against
er cheek, but he wasn't quite close enough to reach out and
mooth it back.

His father had come to stand beside his mother; Toby had
slipped away from the table and settled on the dog bed, al-
ternating tussling with the three dogs and stroking Geordie's
long ears. And Kit, Kit was watching them, fear flickering
in his eyes.

If Kincaid's job inclined him to glimpse the potential
tragedy in the commonplace, for Kit the possibility was ever
real and ever present. In Kit's world, mothers who left their
children might not return. This was a strain the boy didn't
need.

Inwardly cursing his sister, Kincaid said, "Mum, let's not
call out the cavalry just yet. We know she's taken the car.
She's probably just gone home for a good sulk, and you may
not be doing her any favors by interfering. And in the meantime, Gemma and I can take the boys for a walk while the
light lasts. We'll give the queen a miss, eh?" he added with a
wink at Kit. It was a family joke that the queen's traditional
Christmas Day speech was the perfect soporific.

Gemma nodded towards Toby, who had curled up with an
arm round the cocker spaniel, his eyelids at half-mast. "You
and Kit go," she said softly. "Toby and I will stay here and
keep your mum and dad company."

Tess, Kit's little terrier, raised her head and tilted it expectantly. "Leave her," Kincaid said softly, not wanting to disturb Toby, and Kit signaled her to stay. They slipped into the
front hall, grabbed their coats from the pegs, and eased out
the door, quiet as burglars. The snow still lay bright on the
land, but the light had softened, a harbinger of the early
winter dark. The scent of wood smoke, pure and painfully
sweet, caught at Kincaid's throat.

Without speaking, he led the way around to the back of
the house and picked up the footpath that led across his

parents' field. After all these years, his feet still seemed to know every rise and hollow, and after so long in London, it surprised him how little the countryside had changed. Once he glanced back, but the farmhouse had disappeared behind its sheltering screen of trees.

Tromping along beside him, Kit placed his feet with deliberation, as if the imprint of each boot were of colossal importance. He seemed equally determined not to meet Kincaid's gaze, but after a few moments he said, "Aren't you going to lecture me?"

"I hadn't planned on it." Kincaid kept his tone light. He'd realized, after yesterday's shouting match, that his first priority was to reestablish communication with his son. "Do you want me to?"

This provoked a surprised glance. "Um, no, not really."

"Do you want to tell me what's going on at school, then?" Kincaid asked, just as easily.

Kit hesitated for so long that Kincaid thought he might not answer, but at last he said, "Not now. Not today, anyway."

Kincaid nodded, understanding what was unsaid. After a moment, he squeezed Kit's shoulder. "It's been a good Christmas."

"Brilliant," agreed Kit. Swinging his arms, the boy picked up his pace, as if he'd been given permission to delight in the walk. The tension had drained from him, and suddenly he seemed an ordinary boy, one without the weight of the world on his shoulders—or as ordinary as any thirteen-year-old could be, Kincaid reminded himself.

They went on, the silence between them now stretching in an almost tangible bond. Round spots of color bloomed on Kit's cheeks from the cold and exertion. Then they crested a small hill and saw the sinuous curve of the canal before them, like a hidden necklace tossed carelessly across the rolling Cheshire countryside.

Kit stopped, looking puzzled, then scanned the horizon as if trying to get his bearings. "But I thought— Last night, I thought the canal was running alongside the main road."

"It was." Kincaid stooped and drew a line in the snow with

his finger to illustrate. "That was the main branch of the Shropshire Union, which goes more or less north to Chester and Ellesmere port." He then drew another line, intersecting the first at right angles, and nodded at the canal in front of them. "This is the Middlewich Branch, which meanders off to the northeast, towards Manchester. The two intersect at Barbridge, where we turned onto the main road last night. It's a challenge getting a boat round the bend at Barbridge Junction, I can tell you."

"Can we see?" Kit asked, with a simple enthusiasm that Kincaid had not expected.

"I don't see why not." Having intended to go that way all along, Kincaid was pleased at having found something to interest his son. He led the way through the field gate and down onto the towpath. Here the snow had been compacted by the passage of feet, both human and canine. Bare trees stood crisply skeletal against the snow, and in the distance a trio of black birds circled. Crows, Kincaid thought, searching for carrion, and if he guessed right, not far from the site of last night's grisly discovery.

Not that there was anything left for them to find, of course, but the reminder made him wonder what was happening at the crime scene. Had they identified the child? Old cases, cold cases, were the most difficult. He didn't envy his former schoolmate Ronnie, he told himself firmly. And yet, his curiosity nagged him.

He thought of Juliet, wondering if the image of the dead child was haunting her, wondering if that and worry over the fate of her project might have driven her back to the building site. And what in hell's name was going on between Juliet and Caspar?

"Do you really think Aunt Juliet is all right?" asked Kit, as if he'd read his mind.

"Of course she is. Your aunt Jules is tougher than she looks, and very capable of looking after herself. I'm sure she had a good reason for going walkabout for a bit," he answered, but even as he spoke he realized how little he really knew about his sister.

There was little wind, and in the bright sunshine he hadn't

felt the cold at first. But now he realized that his nose and the tips of his ears had gone numb, and even in gloves his hands were beginning to stiffen. Shoving his hands firmly into his pockets, Kincaid said, "Juliet loved this walk when we were kids. She could tramp round the countryside all day, and in all weathers. She used to say she was going to be an explorer when she grew up, like Ranulph Fiennes." She had been full of dreams, his sister. Had any part of her life turned out as she had imagined?

"But she's a builder instead. Isn't that a funny job for a woman?"

Kincaid smiled. "Better not let Gemma hear you say a thing like that. It's no more odd than a woman police officer. And Jules was always good at making things. My father used to build us stage sets, and Jules would help him."

"You put on plays?" Kit asked, with a trace of wistfulness.

Guilt stabbed at Kincaid. Wasn't he always too busy with work to spend time with his son?

"Shakespeare, usually," he forced himself to answer cheerfully, "given my dad's penchant for the bard. I used to be able to declaim whole bits of *Hamlet,* but I've forgotten them now."

Kincaid had a sudden vision of a summer's afternoon, and Juliet, as Ophelia, sprawled on a blue tarp they had appropriated for a river. "Can't you die a little more gracefully?" he'd groused, and she'd sat up and scowled at him.

"Dead people don't look graceful," she'd retorted, and he'd had plenty of opportunities since to discover that she had been right. He pushed the memory away, searching for a distraction.

Kit provided it for him, pointing. "Look, there's a boat."

They were nearing Barbridge, and Kincaid thought it only due to the slowness of the season that they hadn't encountered moored boats before now. "And a nice one it is, too," he said admiringly as they drew closer. Its hull was painted a deep, glossy sapphire, with trim picked out in a paler sky blue. The elum, as the tiller was called on a narrowboat, was striped in the same contrasting colors, and everything on the boat, down to the chimney brasses, sparkled with loving care. The craft's name was painted on its bow in crisp white script: *Lost Horizon*. A steady column of smoke rose from the chimney, and he heard the faint hum of the generator. Someone was definitely aboard.

As they drew alongside, the bow doors opened and a woman stepped up into the well deck. She was tall, with a slender build undisguised by her heavy padded jacket, and her short fair hair gleamed in the sunlight. Catching sight of them, she nodded, and Kincaid felt a start of recognition.

Last night in church she had seemed an outsider, her shield against the world penetrable only when she sang; here, she moved with the grace of familiarity. Here, he had found her in her element.

# 10

JULIET'S HAND had seemed to turn the key in the ignition of its own accord, her foot had eased in the clutch, and she'd found herself driving. Her reflexes had taken over, funneling her into the most familiar route, up the A529 towards Nantwich.

The rolling meadows of the Cheshire Plain had slipped by, dark stubble now peeking through the snow. At each roundabout she hesitated, thinking she must turn back, but her body seemed unwilling to obey her mind's instructions.

Suddenly, she realized she'd reached the southern outskirts of Nantwich. Swerving the car into a side street, she pulled up against the curb and lifted her trembling hands from the wheel.

What the hell had she done, leaving Caspar's parents like that? She had to go back, had to make some sort of excuse, but what could she say? No excuse would soften Caspar's cold fury; she had done the unforgivable: embarrassing him in front of his parents. And what would she tell the children? That it had been the sound of her mother-in-law's voice as she said, "Juliet, darling, if you could just give the gravy boat a little rinse?"

Rita Newcombe had turned from her state-of-the-art oven to give Juliet a brittle smile and a nod in the direction of the gold-rimmed gravy boat on the worktop, as if Juliet were too dense to recognize a gravy boat when she saw one. Rita,

Juliet knew from experience, hated to risk her manicured nails with washing up, and would no doubt find a good excuse to stick her daughter-in-law with a sink full of dirty crockery when the meal was finished as well.

Juliet had complied, her lips pressed together in irritation, but if Rita noticed her bad grace, she gave no sign. They were having stuffed goose, Rita informed her, a recipe she'd seen in a gourmet cooking magazine, and Juliet doubted the children would do more than push it around on their plates. It would never have occurred to Rita that the children would have preferred plain roast turkey, and if it had been pointed out to her, she'd have announced that the children needed a bit more sophistication—implying that Juliet was falling down on the job at home.

Now it made Juliet flush with shame to remember that when she'd first married Caspar, she'd compared her parents to his and wished hers had a bit more polish, a bit more appreciation for the *finer* things in life, and a little less interest in books.

How could she have been so stupid? And how could she have gone all these years without realizing how thoroughly she despised her in-laws? Rita, with her flawlessly colored hair and trendy jogging outfits—although Juliet had never been able to imagine her actually running, or doing anything else that might cause an unladylike sweat. And Ralph—or *Rafe,* as he insisted on being called—with his paunch and thinning hair, who fancied himself irresistible to anything in a skirt, and flirted shamelessly whenever Rita's back was turned.

The Newcombes had embraced their retirement, trading in their suburban home in Crewe for a modern flat overlooking the locks in Audlem, a pretty town near the Shropshire border. The flat was open plan and too small for the children to stay over, a deficit that Juliet suspected was intentional.

The truth was that her mother- and father-in-law didn't like the disruption of grandchildren—didn't really even like to admit that they *had* grandchildren, because it meant they were losing their tenacious grip on middle age.

Juliet had wiped the gravy boat dry and set it beside the stacked dishes waiting to be carried to the perfectly set table.

As she turned from the sink, she'd glanced into the combined dining and sitting areas. Caspar and his father were ensconced with whiskies in the corner Rita referred to as "the nook," and from the drone of her father-in-law's voice, Juliet guessed he'd launched into one of his interminable golf stories. Sam sat on the floor near the ultrarealistic gas fire, silently picking at one of his shoelaces. And Lally . . . Lally had been curled at her father's knee, tilting her head so that he could stroke her hair.

Then Caspar had looked up and met her eyes, and the venom in his glance struck Juliet like a physical blow. Suddenly her head swam and her heart pounded. She couldn't seem to move air into her lungs. Sweat broke out on her face and arms, trickled down between her shoulder blades.

*Heart attack,* she thought. She was having a heart attack. *Don't be daft,* she told herself, it was just the overheated flat coupled with the stress of her rush of anger. But then a wave of nausea clutched her, and she knew if she didn't get outside that instant she would disgrace herself.

"Sorry," she'd mumbled desperately. "Left something. In the car. Back in a tick." She glimpsed their white, startled faces, turning towards her like sea anemones moving in an ocean current, then she was out the door and down the stairs, gulping clean cold air as she ran.

When she'd reached the car, she'd leaned against it, fists pressed to her heaving chest. Something sharp jabbed her palm, and looking down, she realized that she had somehow, miraculously, snatched up her keys as she ran out the door. They had come in her aging Vauxhall Vectra, thank God, as Caspar's little sports model didn't have room for the kids, and when Juliet unlocked the door and slipped into the driver's seat, it felt like a safe haven.

The car's interior was warm from the sun, and at first she only meant to sit there until her heart slowed and her head cleared. Then it occurred to her that someone might come after her, and she knew she couldn't face anyone quite yet, not even her children, not until she pulled herself together.

So she had driven away, but she hadn't pulled herself together, even now, sitting in an unfamiliar street outside a house where some other family would be having their Christmas dinner. She swallowed hard against the nausea rising again in her throat. The image of Lally at her father's knee, looking at her with alien, sullen eyes, seemed frozen in her mind.

Despair clutched at her. She would lose her children if she didn't get out of this marriage; already Lally was slipping away. Caspar was poisoning her children against her, as Piers had poisoned him, and she felt powerless to stop it. Caspar was weak, susceptible to suggestion, but Piers . . . she knew now what Piers was, she had seen what lurked beneath the charm, and that had been her downfall. Hatred surged through her, corrosive and searing as acid. Her body jerked from the force of it, and for a moment her heart seemed to squeeze to a stop.

But then, slowly, she sank back into her seat. Calm washed through her and everything took on an unexpected clarity. She touched the keys dangling from the ignition with fingertips that felt sensitive as a newborn's.

Caspar was stranded in Audlem, until he had to humiliate himself by begging a ride home from his parents. Piers, as Caspar had told her repeatedly, was spending the day in Chester with his father, a retired barrister. She had the keys to the office, and the freedom to do whatever she pleased, unobserved.

It was time she brought Piers Dutton to account.

The town center was deserted, the shops and cafés tightly, protectively, shut. It was an illustrator's dream, gilded by the afternoon sun, the roofs of the buildings still bearing a confectioners'-sugar dusting of snow, unmarred by the messy unpredictability of human subjects.

Juliet passed the empty space just in front of Newcombe and Dutton, cautiously parking a few streets away. She'd left without her coat, and as she made her way back to Monk's Lane, she soon discovered that the afternoon's clear golden light was deceptive. The cold bit through her thin blouse, and by the time she reached the office, her teeth were chattering. She chafed her hands together, trying to warm them enough to fumble the key into the lock.

Once inside, she stood, shivering with more than cold. She could hear her blood pounding in her ears, feel her heart thudding against the wall of her chest as if she'd been running a marathon.

Light filtered in through the partially opened blinds, and a lamp had been left burning on the credenza against the back wall of the reception area. The space felt ominously still, and smelled faintly of men's aftershave and leather furniture. How odd that she'd never noticed the scent before—had Piers's presence become stronger in her absence?

She told herself not to be silly—she'd been in the office alone countless times and nothing was different. Taking a steadying breath, she reached back and locked the door. No sense in inviting someone to wander in unexpectedly.

It suddenly occurred to Juliet that she was breaking the law. What would her brother think of that? The idea made her smile, and she felt suddenly better.

After considering for a moment, she went to what *had* been her desk and rooted in the drawer for a paper clip. Piers and Caspar had been doing without a secretary since she'd left—she doubted Piers meant to tempt discovery twice—and the neglect was obvious in the desk's cluttered interior. She found what she wanted eventually, however, and straightened out the silver wire, smoothing it with her fingertips.

She'd begun to feel an unexpected excitement, an exhilarating pulse in her veins, dimly recalled from childhood when she and Duncan had embarked on some sort of mischief.

Caspar's office was to the right, Piers's to the left. Juliet turned left without the least hesitation.

"She's lovely, your boat," Kincaid called to the blond woman as he nodded at the long, graceful lines of the *Lost Horizon*. "You must have read James Hilton."

For an instant, her face held the wariness he'd glimpsed the night before. But as she studied them, something in her features softened and she said, "Yes. Although it was years ago. But I always liked the idea of Shangri-La."

"Weren't you in church last night?" asked Kit, surprising Kincaid, who hadn't realized anyone else in the family had noticed this rather odd but striking woman. It was unlike Kit to speak up so quickly to a stranger.

"At St. Mary's? Yes, I was." The woman glanced at Kincaid and inclined her head almost imperceptibly, as if acknowledging their brief rapport. "It was a lovely service. But you're accustomed to it, I'm sure." There was something in her tone that Kincaid couldn't quite pin down—envy, perhaps?

"We're just visiting for the holidays," he told her. "But I grew up here. Not much has changed."

She had left the double cabin doors ajar, and Kincaid became aware that Kit was leaning to one side, trying to peer inside the boat. As he put a hand on the boy's shoulder, preparing to move him on before they infringed on the woman's privacy any further, Kit said, "Do you live on your boat, then?" His face was alight with interest.

"Kit, that's really none of our business," Kincaid said hurriedly. He gave his son's shoulder a squeeze, turning him back towards the towpath, and felt the reassuring solidity of muscle and bone beneath the padded anorak. To the woman, he added, "Sorry. We'd better be off—"

"No, it's all right." She smiled, erasing some of the lines in her face, and seemed to reach a decision. "Yes, I do live aboard. Would you like to see the boat? My name's Annie, by the way. Annie Lebow."

Kincaid introduced himself and Kit, adding, "Are you certain? If it's an imposition—"

"No, really, it's all right. It's nice of you to ask. Sometimes it's a bit like living in a fishbowl. People peer in your windows from the towpath without so much as a by-your-leave. Have you ever been on a narrowboat before?" she asked Kit.

"No, but I've seen them. The Grand Union Canal runs right behind the supermarket where we shop at home. In London," he added, flushing a little at her attention. "Notting Hill. The supermarket's across the canal from Kensal Green Cemetery."

"Oh, yes." Annie Lebow nodded in recognition. "The Paddington Branch. A nice mooring spot. I stayed there for a few weeks once."

"On this boat? You took this boat all the way to London?"

"We've covered a good part of England, the *Horizon* and I. I can show you a map of the waterways, if you're interested. Come aboard and I'll make us a cup of tea when you've had a look about."

Kincaid let Kit climb aboard first, noticing the length of the boy's legs as he stepped up from the towpath and jumped easily into the well deck. When had he grown so tall?

". . . the hull is steel, of course," Annie was saying. "Wooden boats haven't been built since shortly after the war. The *Horizon* is fifty-eight feet long, rather than seventy, but like most narrowboats is only seven feet wide. The traditional boats were usually seventy feet in length, but there are locks on the system that won't take a boat longer than fifty-eight feet, so a seventy-footer can limit your cruising."

As she spoke, she led them through the doors and down two steps into the main cabin. Kincaid ducked automatically, his head just avoiding the low ceiling, then gaped. He was as enchanted as Kit.

The boat's interior was paneled entirely in lustrous wood the color of pale honey, and illuminated by recessed lighting set into the ceiling. A stove was tucked into one corner of the cabin on a tiled platform, while the living area held a small cream-colored leather sofa and matching armchair positioned on a colorful handwoven rug. Bookshelves and storage cupboards had been built into every available nook, and the bits of free space on the walls held china plates with laceware rims. Interspersed about the shelves were a few pieces of traditionally painted canalware, the bright rose patterns of a dipper and water can fitting surprisingly well with the contemporary furnishings.

Beyond the sitting area, a dining table extended from one wall, flanked by two banquettes. The far seat backed up to the galley. And what a galley! It was state-of-the-art, down to the curved granite work tops and oval stainless-steel sink. Kincaid whistled in admiration, thinking of the money required for fittings of this caliber, while Kit muttered "Wow" under his breath. "It's bigger inside than it looks from the outside," he added, still sounding awed.

"A bit like *Alice in Wonderland,* isn't it?" Annie nodded towards the bow. "She only has a foot of draw, but that space beneath the waterline does make a difference. "Go on, see the rest while I put the kettle on."

As they slipped past her in the galley, Kincaid noticed a book on the work top. It was an old but well-preserved copy of *Narrow Boat* by Tom Rolt, a volume he remembered seeing in his father's shop.

The bathroom was as elegant as the lounge and galley, even equipped with a small bath, and the bedroom held what looked to be a full-size bed covered with a crushed-velvet counterpane in dusty mauve. It seemed a surprisingly feminine touch for the woman they had met, and roused Kincaid's curiosity. Her nightstand held a few contemporary novels and a much-thumbed copy of another canal book, *The Water Road* by Paul Gogarty, a well-known travel writer. Kincaid had to resist the temptation to lift the book and flip through it himself.

Beyond the stateroom they found a neatly fitted engine and workroom, and the hatch to the stern deck. All in all, it was a very tidily laid out and maintained setup. It made Kincaid think of Gemma's old flat in her friend Hazel Cavendish's garage, and he could imagine the boat's appeal. If, of course, one were resolute in resisting the accumulation of things, and solitary by nature. There was no obvious provision for guests, although he suspected the dining banquettes converted into a bed.

When they returned to the galley, Annie had shed her jacket and was pouring hot water into mugs. "Here, take your things off," she said. "Just toss them over the sofa. I'm afraid there's no such thing as a cloakroom here." The cabin, with both radiator and woodstove, was warm, and Kincaid was glad to slip off his coat and scarf.

"You've even got a bath in your loo," blurted Kit, when

he'd added his own anorak to Kincaid's. "What do you—I mean, you don't just flush it straight into—"

Annie Lebow came to his rescue matter-of-factly, as if discussing the disposal of sewage was an expected part of everyday conversation. "There's a holding tank. Marinas usually have pumping stations where you can clean out. Nasty job, but it goes with the territory." She set their mugs on the dining table, along with an earthenware sugar bowl and milk jug, then retrieved a map from the nearest bookcase.

The map, like the Gogarty book, was well used, the edges tattered and the creases worn thin. Annie motioned them to sit on one side of the table, but rather than joining them, leaned over from the table's end and spread out the map, facing it towards them. A network of broad multicolored lines snaked across central England. Kincaid quickly found the burgundy thread that represented the Shropshire Union Canal.

Following his gaze, Annie touched the central section of the Shroppie, then traced a path north to Manchester and Leeds, then south again, down the Trent and Mersey Canal to Birmingham, and beyond that, London. "I've done the circuit several times in the last few years," she said. "And the Llangollen Canal, of course, down into Wales, but I seem to keep coming back to where I started. Homing instinct, I suppose, like a pigeon."

"You're from this area, then?" Having added milk to his tea, Kincaid sipped it carefully, feeling the welcome warmth begin to thaw him from the inside out. "I thought I recognized a local accent." As he looked at Annie Lebow in the warm light of the cabin, he realized she was younger than he'd first thought, perhaps only in her early fifties. Too young for retirement, certainly, and he wondered how she could afford the life she led, not to mention a boat of such quality.

"Southern Cheshire, near Malpas," she answered readily enough, but went on quickly, as if it were a subject she didn't want to pursue. Tapping the map with a neatly trimmed fingernail, she said, "There are so many miles of navigable waterway now, more than anyone could have imagined thirty or forty years ago, when the canals were in their worst decline. Of course, it's almost all pleasure traffic now. The working boats are a thing of the past."

"Is that such a bad thing?" Kincaid asked, hearing the obvious regret in her words. "Surely it was a hard life, and the boat people uneducated and illiterate, as well as poor."

"A hard life, but a good one," Annie said, suddenly fierce. "They had their independence, and the Cut. Very few would have chosen to give it up." Then she shook her head and gave a rueful laugh. "But you're right, that's rich, coming from me, with all this." She swept a hand round, indicating the boat and its fittings. "Imagine that the living space for an entire family was seven feet by seven feet, a good deal less than the size of my sitting room. The rest of the boat would be taken up with the cargo. Imagine no electricity, no hot water other than what you could boil on the range, no plumbing"— here she smiled at Kit—"no refrigeration, and the women had to help their husbands with the locks and the cargo as well as caring for their children."

"No baths?" Kit quipped. "No school? That doesn't sound half bad."

"You could probably adapt. After all, the Idle Women did, and most of them came from comfortable homes."

"Idle Women?"

"During the war the government recruited women to work the narrowboats. They were anything but idle—the nickname came from the IW badges they were given by Inland Waterways when they finished their training. No one had ever seen all-female crews before. They caused quite a sensation, but it wasn't long before they earned the respect of the traditional boaters. For many of them, nothing else in their lives ever equaled the experience." Once again a hint of wistfulness echoed in her voice, but she went on with another flash of a smile at Kit. "One of the best-known female trainers was called Kit, like you. Kit Gayford. You should read about her sometime."

"Are you here for long?" Kincaid asked, and saw her hesitate briefly before she answered.

"A few days, I think. I don't keep to a fixed schedule. That's one of the perks of the boating life. You?"

"Just until the New Year. No perks in my job, I'm afraid."

"What is it you do?"

"Civil servant," Kincaid said quickly, and saw Kit's startled glance. "Quite boring, actually."

He tried to work out just exactly what had prompted him to fudge the truth. It was not that he suspected Annie Lebow of criminal pursuits—and his instincts in that department were well honed—but that he still sensed a watchfulness, a wariness, about her, and he didn't want to rupture the fragile connection they'd made.

But even his innocuous response seemed to startle her. She stared at him for a moment, the pupils in her green eyes dilating. Then she stepped back and began folding the map without meeting his gaze again. Kincaid had the distinct sensation of walls going up and alarm bells ringing, and all the camaraderie of moments earlier dissipated like smoke.

When Annie had tucked the map back into its spot in the bookcase, she picked up her barely touched tea and set the mug in the galley sink. The message couldn't have been clearer if she'd shouted.

"Um, I suppose we'd better be going," Kincaid said into the awkward silence. As he stood, he glanced at the window and found an acceptable excuse. "The light's fading. If we're not careful we'll be blundering home in the dark. Thanks for the tea and the hospitality."

Kit looked disappointed, but set his mug in the galley without protest.

"I hate winter afternoons, they draw in so early," murmured Annie, almost as if she were speaking to herself. She stayed at the sink, rinsing cups as Kincaid and Kit put on their coats, but when they were suitably bundled up she wiped her hands on a tea towel and followed them up into the foredeck.

The pale blue dome of the sky had flushed a translucent rose and the light breeze had died, leaving the air utterly still. The boat's mirror image gleamed on the surface of the canal, near and yet enticingly distant. Kincaid had turned to thank their hostess once more when Kit spoke.

"Can I see where you steer, before we go?"

"Kit, I don't think—"

"No, it's all right," said Annie, her mood seeming to shift once again. "You can go along the edge—it's called the gunwale. But be careful not to slip. The canal's not deep, but the water's very cold. You can freeze more quickly than you'd think."

"I won't fall in." Kit grinned at them, then turned and walked lightly towards the stern, his trainer-clad feet sure on the narrow ledge of the gunwale, one hand outstretched so that his fingertips traced the edge of the boat's roof.

As Kincaid made an effort not to hold his breath, he heard Annie's quiet chuckle. "He's a natural. And it helps to be young."

When Kit had reached the stern and jumped into the well deck, Kincaid said, "Still, accidents happen. My sister told me a boy drowned along this stretch of the canal recently. He must have been about Kit's age."

"Is this curvy thing the rudder?" Kit called out, his hand on the swan-necked tiller.

"It's called the elum, in boating language," answered Annie. "Probably a corruption of helm," she added to Kincaid as Kit poked happily about in the stern, examining the ropes and fenders.

Then, to Kincaid's surprise, she said softly, "I might have seen him, the boy who drowned. I was moored not far from here, down near the Hurleston Reservoir. Just at dusk, a boy came running along the towpath. His clothes were wet. He almost ran me down, and he looked . . . wild. Distressed. But I never thought . . . It never occurred to me that it was anything more than kids playing pranks. I moved the boat up to Barbridge that night, and the next morning I left early to cruise down the Llangollen, so I didn't hear what had happened until several weeks later. If I had known . . ." She shivered, crossing her arms over her breasts, and Kincaid realized the temperature was dropping rapidly as the sun set. He could smell the damp rising in tendrils from the water's surface.

"There's no way you could have known what would

happen," Kincaid assured her. He shook his head. "A bad business altogether. Apparently, my niece knew the boy. They were at school together."

"Difficult for her," agreed Annie. "Has she—"

"It's brilliant," called Kit, coming back along the opposite gunwale, interrupting whatever question Annie had meant to ask. He was almost running now, as confident as a tightrope walker.

"Your boat, it's brilliant," he repeated when he reached them. "Or I should say 'she's brilliant,' shouldn't I? Is she easy to steer? And how do you manage the locks on your own?"

Annie answered with indulgent patience. "Most people overcompensate when they first practice steering, but you develop a feel for it after a bit. As for the locks, it takes a bit longer on your own, but you get used to it. And often there are other boaters to help, or bystanders."

Then she seemed to hesitate, as she had when she'd first asked them aboard, but as she studied Kit's eager expression, she gave an almost imperceptible shrug and went on quickly. "Look. You could come back, if you like. We could take her down to Hurleston Junction, through the locks. You could even steer a bit." With a glance at Kincaid, she added, "You *and* your dad, of course, and your mum, too, if she'd like."

Giving no sign that he had noticed the reference to his mother, Kit looked up at Kincaid with an eagerness that was almost painful. "Could we?" he asked. "Could we come back? What about tomorrow?"

Kincaid remembered his mother telling him they'd planned their annual Boxing Day lunch for the entire family at the Barbridge Inn, the pub just round the junction from Annie's mooring. "I think we could work that out," he said, willing to juggle activities in order not to disappoint Kit. But even as he agreed, he felt a fleeting twinge of discomfort as he realized that Kit seemed more at ease with adults than with his cousins. "It's kind of you," he added to Annie. "If you're certain—"

"It's not kindness, it's pure selfishness," Annie said, with a grin for Kit. "I don't often have a chance to indoctrinate a future boater. But you'd better be careful—before you know it you'll be booking family narrowboat holidays." .

"Holidays? Really?" said Kit. "Where do you—"

"Enough." Kincaid gave his son a little push towards the towpath. "We really must go. Gemma and your grandmother will be sending the dogs for us."

Not only was the light fading, but the reminder of the next day's plans had made him think of his sister. The worry that had been lurking in his subconscious now rose to the surface, nagging at him. Had he dismissed Juliet's disappearance from her in-laws' too readily?

He'd asked Gemma to ring him if they heard from Jules, but he knew the mobile reception was spotty this far from town, and he might have missed a call. He was suddenly anxious to return to the farmhouse.

Kit glanced up at him, and seeming to sense his impatience, thanked Annie Lebow with commendable good manners.

"See you tomorrow, then," she called out cheerfully as they jumped to the towpath.

But as they turned away, an impulse made Kincaid glance back. She stood at the *Horizon*'s bow, watching them, with a stillness that was unnerving in its intensity. She might have been enveloped in ice.

Then she broke her pose, lifting her hand in farewell. He returned the salute, chiding himself for being fanciful, but as he walked on, her image lingered as if burned on his retina.

Annie Lebow had a rare confidence and a physical assurance as she moved about her boat, as well as an obsessive enthusiasm when she talked about life on the Cut—a portrait of a woman who had found her place in life. But beneath that veneer, he sensed a melancholy, a shadow of longing. What had been denied her—or what had she denied herself?

Picking the locks on Piers's drawers had been easier than Juliet had expected. Sifting through his paperwork had been much more difficult. It wasn't that it was disorganized, but rather the contrary—everything was kept in meticulous order and seemed quite aboveboard.

After a quick recce, she started with the first client file, reading carefully through each share and unit-trust statement and all the associated correspondence before going on to the next heavy folder.

She grew absorbed, unaware of time passing, and it was only when she glanced absently at the window that she saw the light had begun to fade. Fighting a sudden surge of panic, she took a breath and reached for another file. She couldn't quit, not yet. Urgency gripped her. She might never have another chance at this.

A car door slammed in the street and Juliet jerked, spilling pages across the desk. She listened, but no footsteps approached. Closing her eyes for a moment, she calmed her racing pulse. A few more minutes, and then she would go.

Then, as she gazed at the papers spread across the green baize of the blotter, something caught her eye. She recognized the share issuer, a German high-tech company that Caspar recommended to his own clients, but something didn't seem quite right. She checked the corresponding record of payment again, and frowned. Quickly, she switched on Piers's calculator and entered the amount in euros, then figured the exchange into pounds sterling. "Bloody hell," she whispered. The amount paid to the client was off by a good 10 percent.

She pulled another statement from the loose pages and ran the figures again, with the same results. Chewing her lip in concentration, she carefully gathered up the pages and returned that client's folder to the file drawer. Randomly, she selected another, with similar investments, and did the calculations once more.

"You sodding bastard," she said, this time making no effort to keep her voice down. It was so blindingly simple. Most of Piers's clients were well-off, with multiple investments in both shares and unit trusts. Would any of them bother to match each income check against the exchange rate? Piers had been skimming a cool 10 percent of his clients' earnings, and now she had found the proof.

# 11

*At first the darkness at the water's edge seemed absolute. The sky had filled with mottled clouds, their edges livid with the light of an obscured sickle moon, and little illumination filtered through the overhanging trees.*

*As his eyes began to adjust, however, he could make out a few gleaming patches of the previous night's snow, blotched like alien fungi on the soft belly of the towpath.*

*Carefully, he stepped forward until he could see down into the canal itself. There was no wind and no reflection; he might have been staring into an inky, bottomless void. The sensation was oddly exhilarating, like a glimpse into another universe, and he felt a proprietary surge of pleasure. This was his secret place; he had power here, and the knowledge calmed him.*

*Things were happening that he hadn't anticipated, and while he didn't foresee any real danger, the loss of control made him edgy. Reaching into his coat, he pulled the curved silver flask from his inside pocket and took a sip, then another. Alcohol, he'd learned, was a beautiful thing. Just enough would loosen him up, ease him into a transcendent state where time and action could be manipulated to suit him. Flow, he thought of it, where the ideas that blossomed in his head melded perfectly with his emotions.*

*But he never drank too much. Deliberately, he replaced the flask's cap and screwed it tight. He couldn't afford to be*

*muddled, not now, when he might have to make an unex-*
*pected decision. Nor did he want to lose an iota of the inten-*
*sity of experience, or the clarity of memory. His recollec-*
*tions were kept like the pearls in his pocket, savored, caressed,*
*treasured.*

*So he paced himself, with medicinal discipline. Only once*
*had his control faltered, and that was because he hadn't*
*realized just how intoxicating murder could be.*

Gemma watched Rosemary Kincaid fidget for half an hour
after Duncan and Kit left for their walk. They'd quickly
finished the washing up, and when Hugh had muttered
something about splitting wood and slipped out through the
scullery, Rosemary had murmured, "That's his refuge when
he's worried, the woodshed."

They sat at the kitchen table, nursing mugs of unwanted
tea, while Toby still slept on the dog bed near the kitchen
stove. He looked positively cherubic, his cheeks flushed and
his straw-fair hair tousled, one arm thrown over the patient
cocker spaniel's back. The sheepdog and the terrier had
moved aside, looking slightly affronted at the usurpation of
their warm cushion.

"It's a good thing he hasn't an allergy to dog hair," said
Rosemary, watching him. "Aren't they lovely when they sleep?
When Duncan and Juliet were small, no matter how difficult
they'd been or how tired I was, I would always go in and
watch them for a few minutes after they fell asleep. It helped
keep things in perspective. That was until they started locking
their bedroom doors, of course," she added wryly. "And even
then, you tell yourself that once they're grown, your worries
will be over." She looked wan, and it seemed to Gemma that
the lines bracketing her nose and mouth had deepened since
morning.

"It's not like Juliet, is it?" Gemma asked quietly. "Going
off without telling anyone. Leaving the children." She hadn't
felt comfortable with Duncan's dismissal of his sister's un-
explained disappearance, nor with his admonition to his
parents to ignore it. Of course, she didn't know Juliet as well
as he did, but she seemed a responsible mother, and respon-

sible mothers didn't walk out on their children in the middle of Christmas dinner.

"No." Rosemary gripped her mug until her knuckles blanched. "But then I'd never have thought Caspar capable of the things I heard him say last night. And to think I found him charming, once. He was so earnest. I'm not quite sure when that earnestness turned to self-importance."

The behavior Gemma had witnessed in Caspar Newcombe the previous night had been worse than self-important—it had been vicious. Remembering the near hysteria in Lally's voice, she said carefully, "Rosemary, you don't think Caspar would hurt the children? Lally seemed awfully worried about her father's reaction if he even learned she'd rung you."

"Lally's been a bit prone to dramatizing lately—I suppose it's understandable." Rosemary glanced up at Gemma, guilt in the eyes that were so like her son's. "So at first I thought perhaps she was exaggerating things, looking for attention. But now . . . the thing is, when I spoke to Caspar, I could tell he was drinking. I don't like the idea of him on his own with the children—not to mention the fact that if Caspar's been drinking, you can bet his father has as well, and I hate to think of Ralph driving them home . . ." She stood and took her cup to the sink, then wiped at the already spotless work top with a tea towel. With her back to Gemma, she said, "And Juliet—Caspar was so angry, but cold with it, as if he'd been storing it up."

Gemma glanced at Toby, still sleeping despite the rhythmic thunk of the wood splitter from behind the house, and came to a decision. "How far is it to—what did you say the town was called? Audlem?"

"A half hour from Nantwich. A bit farther for us."

"Look, why don't you and Hugh go and get the children. Bring them here. You can leave Juliet a message saying what you've done, and I'll stay here in case she rings. Caspar *will* let you take the children?"

Rosemary frowned. "I think so, yes. He won't want to make a scene in front of his parents, especially after what's already happened. But if Juliet goes home, and Caspar's there without the children . . ."

"Has he ever hurt Juliet?" Gemma asked gently, trying to mask her own fear.

"I don't think so. But then I assumed they'd just grown a little distant, that the children growing up and Juliet leaving the office were causing a temporary strain."

"This partner—do you think there's any truth to Caspar's accusations? Could Juliet be having an affair with him?" Gemma had met the man briefly after midnight mass the night before. He'd stood with Caspar, oozing the sort of charm that made her instantly wary. She found it hard to imagine a woman as straightforward as Juliet Newcombe being tempted by such goods.

"I don't know," replied Rosemary, her tone bitter. "I'm not sure anymore that I know my daughter at all."

It hadn't taken much argument to convince Rosemary that she should fetch Sam and Lally from Caspar's parents, but when she ended the call to Caspar, Gemma saw that her hands were shaking.

"He was vile," she said, "but he didn't disagree. In fact, he seemed eager to be shot of them."

"No word from Juliet?" asked Gemma.

"No. I can't think—"

"Don't." Impulsively, Gemma hugged her. "I'm sure she's fine. I imagine she just needed some time on her own."

Nodding against her shoulder, Rosemary said, "Thank you. I'm glad you've come." Then she stepped back and began to gather her things briskly. Hugh came in, and when Rosemary explained the situation to him, he instantly agreed that they should go.

Jack the sheepdog watched, sensing an expedition afoot, and began to prance from mistress to master, tail wagging furiously. "No, Jack," Hugh said. "Stay. Guard the house."

His tone woke Toby, who sat up, disoriented and cross from his impromptu sleep. He rubbed his eyes and began to cry. Scooping him up, Gemma sat down at the table, holding him in her lap while urging Rosemary and Hugh to go. A moment later the front door slammed and the house was suddenly silent, except for Toby's grizzling.

"Didn't want a nap," he cried. "Now everybody's gone."

"You didn't take a nap," Gemma assured him, stroking his sleep-damp hair. "You just practiced closing your eyes." She hugged him but he squirmed, refusing to be placated. "Go on, close your eyes," she whispered in his ear. "Just try it."

Forgetting to sniffle, Toby blinked slowly.

"See how easily you can do it?" Gemma asked. "That's from practicing."

He giggled. "That's silly, Mummy."

"No, you're silly. And not everyone's gone. I'm here, aren't I? And that means we can do something special, just the two of us."

Toby slid from her lap, tears forgotten. "Can we do my puzzle?" Although too young to read the Harry Potter books, he was old enough to be susceptible to the product marketing, and Kit's gift of a Harry Potter–themed jigsaw had thrilled him.

"Um, okay," agreed Gemma, deciding she'd worry later about having to dismantle a partially completed puzzle the first time someone needed the kitchen table. "Of course we can."

Toby tore from the room, and a moment later she heard him pounding up the stairs. The dogs, having returned to the warmth of the stove-side bed, glanced up at the noise. Jack and Tess put their heads down again, but Geordie stretched and came over to her, laying his head on her knee. As she stroked his head, she realized this was the first moment she'd had on her own since they'd arrived. She felt a little odd, alone in Duncan's parents' house, as if she were trespassing, but she was glad of the solitude.

Her peace was short-lived, however. She'd just got Toby settled at the table with his jigsaw when the doorbell rang. She had done enough notifications during her days on the beat that she never felt comfortable with an unexpected caller, but this time the instinctive jab of fear was sharper.

It might be Juliet, she told herself, without a key. Assuring Toby she'd be right back, she shut the barking dogs in the kitchen and went to the door, her heart thumping with a mixture of hope and trepidation.

But the man who stood on the porch when she swung

open the door was a stranger. Her first thought was that his slightly battered face seemed an odd match for his well-cut blond hair and his expensively tailored black wool overcoat; her second was that he was rakishly attractive.

Eyeing her with equal interest, he said, "I was looking for Duncan Kincaid. Have I got the right house?" His voice held the drawn-out vowels of the northwest, more pronounced than the faint trace Duncan had retained.

"Yes, but he's not here just now." Glancing at the sky, she saw that it had grown later than she'd realized. She forced a smile and added, "He should be back very soon, though, if you'd like to wait."

The caller glanced at the darkening sky, as if gauging the time, then shook his head. "No, I don't want to impose. Just ask him to call Ronnie Babcock, when he comes in."

"Ronnie Babcock? You're Chief Inspector Babcock?"

He gave her a quizzical look. "Last time I checked."

Gemma flushed. "Oh, sorry. I didn't mean— It's just that Duncan's talked about you." She stepped out on the porch, offering him her hand. "I'm Gemma."

The surprised look that followed this pronouncement was worse than his previous bafflement. Then his face cleared and he shook her hand heartily, smiling at her as if she'd just won the lottery. "The old bugger. He didn't say he was—"

Gemma stopped him before he could go any further. "We're not. Married. But we live together." She felt a flash of fury at Duncan, who had obviously not bothered mentioning her, or their relationship, to his old mate. And why should she feel she had to apologize for the fact that they weren't married?

"Well, he's a lucky man, in any case," said Babcock, making a quick recovery with such charm that her resentment evaporated.

"Look, he really shouldn't be much longer. He's just gone out for a walk, and it's almost dark. Why don't you—"

"Mummy." Toby's voice came plaintively from behind her. "Jack's scratching at the door, but I didn't let him out. Can we finish our puzzle now?"

"My son, Toby," she explained to Babcock, then ruffling

Toby's fair hair, she added, "It's cold, lovey. Go back inside and I'll be right there." She pulled the door a little more tightly closed behind her. Jack's high-pitched bark escalated, and she pictured him hurtling through the house towards the intruding stranger like a black-and-white bullet. Did he bite if not properly introduced?

"It wasn't important. I won't keep you," Babcock told her, and she wasn't sure whether his quick response meant he feared loss of limb or that he might be drafted to participate in puzzle solving.

"Is it about the baby? The one Juliet found?" she asked.

"Well, yes. I thought he might be interested in the results of the—" He paused, and Gemma suspected he was searching for a more delicate way to say "postmortem." Her irritation with Duncan flared again. Not that she could reasonably have expected him to tell Babcock she was a fellow police officer if he hadn't mentioned her at all, but she found being treated like the little woman galling.

"Look," she began. "There's no need to tiptoe about with me. I'm—"

A car, which Gemma had vaguely noticed traveling too fast down the lane, its headlamps unlit in the gathering dusk, turned into the farmhouse drive with a squeal of tires.

Turning to watch, Babcock muttered, "What the hell is he playing at, the mad bastard?" But as the Vauxhall came to a stop and the driver's door opened, it was Juliet Newcombe who climbed out. She walked towards them, her gait a little tentative, like a toddler just finding its balance.

Gemma's first thought was that Duncan's sister was drunk. Her second, as Juliet drew near enough for Gemma to see her pale face and wide, dark eyes, was that she was ill, or very shocked.

Babcock seemed to have come to the same conclusion, saying, "Are you all right, Mrs. Newcombe?"

Juliet stopped, staring at Babcock for a moment as if trying to place him. "Oh. It's Chief Inspector . . . Babcock, isn't it?"

"We've been trying to reach you this afternoon, Mrs. Newcombe," Babcock said pleasantly, but he was scrutinizing her closely, and Gemma knew he would be automatically checking for the smell of alcohol, or the dilated pupils indicating drug use. "We need to get a formal statement from you," he continued, apparently satisfied that he didn't need to nick her for driving while impaired. "About yesterday evening."

"The baby." Juliet's voice held a faint note of surprise, as if she'd forgotten her discovery, then her face creased with concern. "Have you found out anything? Do you know who she is?"

"No, I'm afraid not. But we need contact information for your crew. If you could—"

Gemma stepped into the drive and put an arm round the other woman, feeling her shiver. "Juliet, you're freezing. Come inside. Mr. Babcock, surely she can give her statement in the morning? I can bring her into the station myself, if you'd like."

Seeing him hesitate, Gemma knew his curiosity over Juliet's behavior was warring with the tact necessitated by the fact that he was dealing with a friend's—and a fellow officer's—sister. "That's very kind of you," he said at last, and she breathed an inner sigh of relief. "We've set up an incident room at Crewe headquarters. Shall we say about nine?" He nodded at them. "And tell Duncan to give me a ring, if you wouldn't mind."

"Duncan—where is he?" asked Juliet. "I've been— I've got to—" She broke off as Gemma gave her shoulder a sharp squeeze. However innocent Juliet's actions of the past few hours, Gemma felt instinctively that she didn't want her broadcasting them to Babcock just yet. Fleetingly, she realized that this was what it felt like to be on the other side, and she didn't care for it at all.

"Let's go in," Gemma said, steering an unresisting Juliet towards the door. "You'll catch your death." Over her shoulder, she called out to Ronnie Babcock, "It was nice to meet you. I'll tell Duncan you came by." She pushed Juliet into the house and closed the door on Babcock, who was standing in the drive, staring after them.

Grabbing an old woolly cardigan from among the coats on the hall pegs, Gemma draped it over Juliet's shoulders. "Kitchen," she commanded. "It's warmer in there."

"My parents," Juliet said through chattering teeth. "Where—"

"They've gone to pick up Sam and Lally from Caspar's parents'. Lally rang, saying you'd been gone for hours. They—we—were worried about you."

"I didn't mean— I didn't think—"

"I'm sure you didn't." Gemma herded Juliet down the hall. "Let's get you something hot to drink."

The dogs crowded round as they entered the kitchen, Tess and Geordie sniffing excitedly at a new person, Jack wagging his tail and laying his ears back in fawning devotion. Juliet reached down, burying her hand in his ruff as if finding solace in his thick coat.

Toby was back at the table, his small legs swinging several inches short of the floor. Looking up, he said, "Auntie Juliet!" with as much enthusiasm as if he'd known her all his life. "I've got a Harry Potter puzzle. It's got Quidditch in it."

"Hello, sweetie." Juliet managed a smile, but Gemma could see the effort it cost her. "That's lovely."

"Here. Sit." She guided Juliet into a chair. Fortunately, she had helped Rosemary enough to have an idea of where most things were, and could at least make tea without fumbling about.

As she turned to put the kettle on, the clock over the cooker caught her eye. With a start, she saw that it had gone five o'clock, and a peep at the windows told her that it was now completely dark. She drew the blinds and put another log in the stove while she waited for the water to come to the boil, the busyness an antidote to the disquiet clutching at her stomach. Duncan and Kit should have been back ages ago, surely.

Then she chided herself for worrying. This was Duncan's territory. He knew what he was doing, and he was certainly capable of finding his way home after dark—this rural landscape was alien only to her.

They had probably stopped to watch badgers, she thought, recalling a snatch of a television sitcom she'd once seen about country life. But no, badgers hibernated, she was quite sure, and she was waffling from nerves.

Juliet seemed to be listening to Toby's rather confusing

version of the rules of Quidditch, but she glanced up as Gemma took out the box of PG Tips. "No, wait," she said. "Under the sink. Dad always keeps a bottle of apple brandy there."

Opening the lower cupboard door, Gemma discovered that there was indeed a half-full bottle of Calvados tucked away behind the washing-up liquid. "Handy," she commented as she poured a generous slosh into the mug she'd intended for Juliet's tea.

"His emergency stash. Medicinal, he says. He always gave us apple brandy, lemon, and honey for sore throats when we were kids." Juliet grasped the mug like a life raft and tossed back a swallow. Gasping, she screwed up her face like a child forced to take cough medicine, then took a more considered sip. Color crept back into her cheeks. "You said Mum and Dad have gone to get the children? But Caspar will be furious. He won't let—"

"He will. Your mum spoke to him and he agreed." Gemma didn't add anything else. Having seen a bag of rawhide treats beside the brandy, she fished out three of the pressed bones and distributed them to the dogs. Jack bared his teeth when Geordie and Tess ventured too close, but after circling for a moment, the three dogs found separate corners and settled down with their prizes.

"Mum said she'd bring them here?" Juliet looked both relieved and horrified. "It's not that I want them going home with him," she hastened to explain. "Especially when he's in a foul temper. But—How am I going to explain my leaving to Lally and Sam? I can't—No one will—" She stopped, shivering convulsively.

Gemma slipped into a chair beside Juliet and tipped a much smaller portion of Calvados into her own cup. Someone would be back soon, either Duncan and Kit or Rosemary and Hugh with the children, and she suspected that if she was to get anything out of Juliet it had better be now. Gently, she said, "Why don't you start by telling me?"

Babcock climbed reluctantly back into the BMW and sat for a moment, engine idling, letting the heater blow the remains of the engine's warmth into the frigid cocoon of the car's interior. He slipped on his gloves, then drummed his leather-padded fingers on the steering wheel.

Something was up with Juliet Newcombe and he didn't like it one bit. Nor did he like being brushed off, even when it was done as smoothly as it had been by Duncan's very attractive red-headed girlfriend. She hadn't wanted Juliet to tell him where she'd been, or why she seemed so upset.

His thoughts strayed to Duncan. What had he expected? That his old mate would be living the conventional suburban married life with a bored but well-preserved wife and surly teenagers in public school? But here he was, apparently cohabiting with this fresh-faced woman young enough to put him in the "lucky bastard" category, and she was sharp as a tack, with an engaging directness. He noticed, however, that she'd referred to the towheaded kid as "my son," not "our son." Things were never as simple as they first appeared.

Take the whole situation with Juliet Newcombe. She was the wife of a locally respected financial consultant, recommended for the job on the old dairy barn by her husband's partner, who just happened to live up the lane, and who had not been at home when the uniformed constables did their house-to-house interviews.

Babcock had instructed the officers to keep trying to reach Dutton, but perhaps he should give Dutton a try himself. Dutton was, after all, the ideal person to offer some unbiased insight into Juliet Newcombe's behavior.

"Look. You won't tell anyone else, will you? What I did—it's not exactly kosher." Juliet waited for Gemma's nod before going on, hesitantly. "I went to the office. Caspar and Piers's. I hadn't any intention of driving, even, but when I found myself in Nantwich, I realized that I could get into the office while no one else was there. I could look through Piers's things." She glanced at Gemma as if expecting censure, but Gemma merely nodded again.

"Does this have something to do with Caspar shouting at you last night?" Gemma asked.

Juliet glanced at Toby, who had gone back to his puzzle, humming quietly to himself as he moved the pieces about.

"Yes. But it's not what you think." Her voice was bitter. "When Caspar and Piers first went in together, I thought Piers Dutton was the most considerate man I'd ever met. He'd never let me open his mail, or file his paperwork for him. He said he wanted to save me the trouble. Of course, I knew he'd been on his own before, and it was clear from early on that he was particular—even obsessive—about having things done a certain way. I just assumed he was more comfortable doing things himself. And I wasn't that sure of myself at first—I'd been home with the kids for years when Caspar suggested I come and help out.

"I should bloody well have stayed at home. It's hard to believe now, but I thought I had a good life, a good marriage." She gave Gemma a crooked smile. "You've got the right idea—don't get married to begin with, then it can't go pear-shaped on you."

"It's not quite that simple," Gemma protested. "What changed?" she prompted Juliet, eager to change the subject. "Did something happen with Piers?"

Juliet stared intently at the cottage pattern on her Dunoon mug, as if she might find an answer there. "It was an accumulation of little things, like when you notice a tap dripping somewhere in the house. At first you're not sure you're hearing anything at all, then it grows on you until you think you'll go mad if you don't find the source.

"He'd take the mail before I finished sorting it. He'd shut his door on phone calls with clients. He kept his file drawers locked."

"And Caspar didn't?"

"Why should he? Clients' investment information is confidential, of course, but it's not like it's a matter of national security."

"Not unless you're doing something unethical, or illegal," said Gemma, and Juliet nodded.

"So I started to suspect. I just couldn't work out what he was doing. And all the while I thought I was crazy for even entertaining the idea. Then, one day, when Piers had gone out to lunch, I noticed that one of his file drawers wasn't quite shut. I was standing in his office, trying to decide if it was worth the risk to have a peek, when he came back." Juliet glanced up from the brandy she hadn't tasted since she'd begun to talk. "I remember I jumped, and I must have looked guilty, but he smiled. Piers always smiles. But, just for an instant, I saw something in his eyes." She swallowed. "Afterwards, I tried to convince myself I'd imagined it. I suppose I should be grateful I've led such a sheltered life that at first I didn't recognize it for what it was."

Gemma nodded, understanding what Juliet meant, and why she was reluctant to name what she had sensed. She had seen it, too, only a few times, but those glimpses into the abyss would stay with her for the rest of her life.

Juliet glanced at Toby, who was now flying his puzzle pieces rather than trying to put them together, with suitable sound effects, and seemed oblivious to their conversation. "You don't expect . . . ," she went on slowly. "Not in your friends, acquaintances, business partners . . ." She shook her head as if to clear it. "Not long after that, the way Piers treated me began to change. The friendly hand on the shoulder escalated to pats on the bum; the mildly flirtatious comments got more suggestive. But it was all still subtle enough that I didn't want to make a scene, so I tried to pretend I hadn't heard, or that I hadn't understood what he meant. I started to dread going in to work, or being left alone in the office with him.

"There was something so calculated about it, so inevitable, as if he'd worked out a plan and he never doubted I'd go along. But maybe that's hindsight."

"But you didn't go along."

Juliet met Gemma's gaze, memory like a bruise in her eyes. Her chest rose and fell more quickly, but she kept her voice low. "He cornered me in his office, one day when Caspar was out calling on a client in Macclesfield. I had to kick him to get him to let me go. It was only after that, when he knew he couldn't seduce me, that he started to turn Caspar against me."

# 12

❧

**THE HOUSE STOOD** sentinel at the head of the lane that led to the old dairy barn, the outlines of its four turreted chimneys just visible against the faintly luminescent dusk. The Victorians did themselves proper, Babcock thought as he pulled into the drive, although always at the expense of those less fortunate. He could never see a house like this without thinking of the legions of capped and uniformed maids who had scurried from floor to floor, rubbing their work-reddened and swollen hands against their starched white aprons.

Tonight, however, the house held more than insubstantial Victorian ghosts. Lights blazed from the ground-floor windows, so perhaps he would be fortunate enough to find Piers Dutton at home.

If the house was illuminated, the drive was dark as pitch, he discovered as he climbed out of the car. Muttering under his breath, he picked his way to the porch, where only a dim light burned. If Dutton could afford the upkeep on this pile, surely he could spring for a bulb bright enough to light the entrance, he thought sourly.

Stamping the snow from his feet, Babcock rang the bell. A moment later he was rewarded by the sound of footsteps in the hall, and the massive door swung open to reveal a man he assumed to be Dutton himself. "Can I help you?" the man asked peremptorily, but his tone was more curious than hostile. In designer denim and corduroy, he looked every inch the country gent.

"My name's Babcock. Chief Inspector Babcock. If I could have a moment of your time, Mr. Dutton?"

For just an instant, Dutton's face expressed the alarm felt by the most honest of citizens when confronted unexpectedly by the police. Then he smiled and said, "Ah. This is about all the commotion down the lane, I take it." His accent was the sort of public-school drawl that raised hackles on the back of Babcock's neck, his manner welcoming, with an easy condescension that was more offensive than Tom Foster's outright contempt.

Waving Babcock into the hall, Dutton closed the door against the encroaching cold before continuing. "I was out last night and most of today, so I seem to have missed the excitement. I've only just heard about it from a neighbor."

"Would that have been Mr. Foster?"

Babcock must have given something away in his tone, because Dutton gave a conspiratorial grunt of laughter. "I take it you've met? A half dozen messages on my BT Call-Minder, no less. Tom Foster seemed to be certain I could supply the solution to the mystery."

"And I take it he was disappointed?" Babcock asked lightly.

"Infinitely. Not only did I not know the identity of the mysterious infant, I suggested he should mind his own business and let the police do their jobs."

"That must have gone over well."

"Like the proverbial lead balloon. He rang off in a state of high dudgeon, and I can't truthfully say I'm sorry. Perhaps he won't call back for a bit."

While Babcock might privately agree with Piers Dutton's opinion of his neighbor, he thought Dutton's remarks not only rude, but designed to foster a false atmosphere of camaraderie between them. It made him wonder if the man had something to hide or if he simply manipulated as naturally as he breathed. In any event, it would do no harm to let him think he'd succeeded.

"Considering your spirit of cooperation, I assume you won't mind answering my questions," he suggested, smiling amiably. "So that we *can* do our jobs."

Dutton glanced round, as if considering whether he could keep him standing in the entry hall, then said, "I suppose you'd better come through here." He led the way into a sitting room on the left—or what Babcock supposed should more properly be called a "drawing room." You certainly couldn't say "lounge" in this house.

His first impression, after the relative severity of the hall, was of opulence run amok. The colors ran to rich burgundies and deep blues, and everything that wasn't gilded seemed to be velvet. But then his eye picked out a leather armchair, and he saw rugs in manly Ralph Lauren–esque tartans draped here and there over the furniture. A large Christmas tree stood by the front windows, and the room smelled sharply of fir.

A half dozen candles gleamed from the heavy mahogany mantel, adding to the flickering warmth of the fire burning in the grate. Babcock thought it was a surprisingly feminine touch—he knew very few men who would bother with candles of their own accord—but there was no other hint of a woman's presence.

For all Piers Dutton's apparent disdain for his neighbor, he, like Tom Foster, offered Babcock neither a seat nor a drink. An open bottle of wine stood on a side table, and a half-filled glass on the mantel reflected candlelight from its claret depths; but while Dutton positioned himself with his back to the fire, he didn't pick up his drink.

A laptop computer sat open on the ottoman in front of the leather chair, but the screen faced away from Babcock's curious gaze.

When he was a boy, his great-aunt Margaret, annoyed by his ceaseless questions on one of her infrequent visits, had called him "elephant's child." It wasn't until many years later that he'd read Kipling and discovered the source. Time had not cured him of this malady, but at least now he had an excuse for his persistent curiosity. He'd begun to edge casually towards the chair, as if examining the room, but

Dutton stepped to the ottoman and snapped the laptop shut.

"Very dedicated of you, working on Christmas," Babcock said, giving the computer only a passing glance as he displayed great interest in a series of hunting prints on the wall behind Dutton's chair. "I hope I haven't interrupted anything terribly important."

"Just finishing up a client presentation—a little light relief after a day spent with family." Moving back to the hearth, Dutton regarded him quizzically. "And isn't that a case of the pot calling the kettle black?"

"But I've no choice in the matter," protested Babcock.

"Somehow I doubt that, Chief Inspector." Amusement gleamed in Dutton's blue eyes. Unlike Tom Foster, he seemed to have no trouble remembering Babcock's rank. "You must have minions to do this sort of thing."

Choking back a laugh at the idea of telling Detective Constable Larkin she'd been referred to as a "minion," Babcock said, "The minions have tried several times to contact you since last night, Mr. Dutton. I thought I might get lucky." He slipped off his overcoat and, without invitation, sat on the arm of the sofa and extracted his notebook from his jacket pocket.

"Ah, down to business, then," Dutton said, with an air of mock resignation. "How exactly can I help you, Chief Inspector?"

Babcock had his own agenda, and it didn't include letting Piers Dutton take charge of the interview. "Nice place you've got here." He glanced round the room again, looking as callow and guileless as his battered face would allow. "Although I suspect I'd hate to pay for your central heating. Did Mrs. Dutton do the decorating?"

"I'm divorced, Mr. Babcock. I bought this house after my ex-wife and I separated."

Babcock whistled. "And here I'm stuck paying the mortgage on my semi—either that or splitting the proceeds with my ex if I sell. Not a pretty prospect." He shook his head regretfully, then said, "So you live here all on your own, Mr. Dutton?"

"My son lives with me. My ex-wife and I have joint custody, but Leo prefers staying here most of the time. Boys need their fathers, don't you agree?"

Thinking of what little he had known of his own father, Babcock forced a smile. "No doubt you're right. And you've been here how long?"

"Five years." Dutton frowned, calculating. "A bit longer, actually."

"Then you will have known the Smiths, before they moved away?"

"The people who had the Fosters' place? I met them, yes, but they sold up not long after I moved in. You can't honestly think that old couple walled up a child in their dairy?" Dutton asked, sounding more astonished than horrified. "They were salt of the earth, Farmer Brown and Wife."

"We have to investigate all the possibilities, Mr. Dutton, and it's important that we get in touch with them. Do you know where they went, or how to contact them?"

Piers Dutton raised his brows in undisguised amusement. "Really, Chief Inspector, I've no idea. It wasn't the sort of association one would keep up. And I should think it highly unlikely that they could help you if you do find them. Surely some local kids were responsible, taking advantage of an abandoned building to dispose of an unwanted infant."

"The body was mortared in. A bit much forethought for a teenager, no matter how desperate, I'd say." Babcock found it interesting that Dutton also seemed unaware that the child wasn't a newborn. "Have you not spoken to Mrs. Newcombe?"

"Juliet? No. Although Tom Foster did say that it was she who found this body." He shook his head with a kind of sorrowful majesty. "A bad business, all round. I'm sorry I—" He stopped, his gaze moving past Babcock's shoulder.

At the same moment, Babcock sensed a presence behind him, although he'd heard no sound. He rose, turning towards the doorway, as Dutton said, "Leo. My son, Chief Inspector Babcock."

Babcock saw a young man—no, a boy, he amended after a

moment's assessment, but tall for his age—watching them from the hallway. His eyes gleamed with curiosity, although his face was carefully schooled in an expression of bored disinterest. He was handsome, the angles of his face plainly visible, as his father's once must have been before the indulgences of middle age blurred and softened his features. Babcock wondered how long he'd been listening.

"Sir." Leo acknowledged him with a nod, but didn't come into the room. He turned his attention to his father. "Dad. I'm going out."

"Where?" asked Dutton, but the question seemed perfunctory.

"Barbridge. To meet some of my mates."

"All right, then. Don't be late."

"Yeah," answered Leo, and with another nod at Babcock, disappeared as silently as he'd appeared.

Barbridge was a few minutes' walk, but there was nothing in the hamlet other than the pub, and even had the pub been open, Leo Dutton was too young to be admitted to the premises unaccompanied by an adult. What did his father imagine the boy and his friends were doing?

"Probably wants to show his friends his new mobile," Dutton said, apparently unperturbed by the image of roaming underage boys, cadging beers from those old enough to buy alcohol, and smoking illicit cigarettes, or worse, in the bus shelter.

Perhaps he'd been a policeman too long, Babcock thought, and at any rate it was none of his business. Leo Dutton was too young to have been responsible for an abandoned baby, unless he'd been fathering children in primary school. Babcock was more interested in Juliet Newcombe. "Mr. Dutton, about Mrs. Newcombe. You were saying—?"

"Oh, yes. Sorry. It's just that it must have been a dreadful experience for Juliet, finding that child. I feel a bit responsible, having recommended her for the job."

"Tom Foster seemed to have had some doubt as to Mrs. Newcombe's being capable of doing the work. I'd have thought you'd want your new neighbors to be satisfied with their contractor."

Dutton's heavy face creased in annoyance. "Foster obviously misinterpreted something I said. I'd never have given Juliet's name to the Bonners if I hadn't thought her qualified. There's no questioning her skills . . ."

"But?" asked Babcock, quick to pounce on Dutton's hesitation.

Clasping his hands behind his back, Dutton shifted his stance and looked away. "It's nothing, really."

Babcock didn't respond, letting the silence settle over the room until the sizzle and pop from the hearth sounded as loud as the roar of a brushfire.

Dutton broke the tension, as Babcock had guessed he would. Clearing his throat, he said, "It was a difficult time for everyone concerned, Juliet's leaving. Of course, I wish her success with her venture, for her own sake as well as my partner's. I'd never say anything to jeopardize that. It's just—" His pained expression grew more intense and he cleared his throat again, but this time he held Babcock's gaze, his blue eyes crinkled with earnest sincerity. Then he sighed and went on. "It's just that, emotionally, Juliet can go off the deep end a bit. I'm afraid she's not always entirely reliable."

Lally had pulled a stool into a corner of her grandparents' kitchen, where she perched, isolated as an island in a sea of conversational crosscurrents. For a moment, she wondered what it would be like to be deaf, to watch the movement of mouths and register only meaningless visual static. But even the deaf could read expressions, and that, sometimes, was bad enough.

God, she hated the way they looked at each other, her uncle Duncan and his Gemma. He sat at the far end of the kitchen table, with her grandfather and Kit, while Gemma had just turned from the fridge. Across the hubbub of the room, he inclined an eyebrow, and she gave the slightest of nods, one corner of her mouth lifting in an infinitesimal smile. The communication was more intimate than any touch, and made Lally as ashamed to have witnessed it as if she'd seen them naked. Somehow the fact that she liked Gemma, had felt a connection with her, made it worse.

She couldn't imagine that her parents had ever looked at each other that way, and that realization made her gut clench with a sick feeling she couldn't quite name.

Duncan had been helping her granddad and Kit finish Toby's Harry Potter puzzle while Toby played on the floor with Sam, zooming Star Wars figures around with annoying little-boy sound effects. Now, apparently having received confirmation from Gemma, Duncan stood and scooped Toby up under his arm, announcing, "Bath time, mate." When Toby protested, Duncan tickled his ribs and made growling noises until the little boy squealed with laughter and let himself be carried away, still giggling.

Had her father ever played with her or Sam like that? Thinking about it, Lally couldn't actually remember her father playing with them at all. The attention he'd been paying them lately was a new thing, something that had only started since he'd been so angry with her mum. And although she knew that, when he was nice to her she wanted it to go on, and that made her feel sick in quite a different sort of way.

Gemma followed Duncan and Toby from the room, giving Lally a smile and a feather touch on her shoulder as she passed, but Lally found she couldn't meet her eyes. That left her mum and Nana huddled by the cooker, talking in the sort of low voices that meant they didn't want the children to hear. Nana was using her hands, the way she did when she wanted to make a point, and her mum looked frightened and stubborn, as though Nana was telling her something she didn't want to hear. But there was something more, something in her mother's face it took Lally a moment to recognize—a sort of triumphant excitement.

Lally felt the familiar cramping in her stomach intensify, and the turkey sandwich she'd nibbled at tea rose into her throat. She swallowed hard against the nausea and bit her lip. How could her mother be anything but terrified when her dad was so furious? Why had her mum walked out in the middle of Christmas dinner, knowing how he would react?

When Lally and Sam had arrived at the farmhouse and found her waiting, she'd rattled off a story about having gone back for something at home and then having car trouble. Lally, an experienced liar herself, hadn't believed it for a moment.

If that was true, why hadn't she said she was leaving or rung them? And why were they here now instead of at home? Home, where her dad would be waiting—no, that didn't bear thinking about, either. But she'd told Leo she'd be home, and it didn't do to disappoint Leo.

Of course, she was nearer Leo here than she would be back in Nantwich, but that meant sod-all when she was stuck under the watchful gaze of both her mother and her grandmother. Her chances of sneaking out were pretty much nil—at least on her own.

She cast a speculative look at Kit, still at the far end of the table with Granddad. Sam, who had joined them, was hopping from one foot to the other, jabbing his finger at an empty space he thought might fit the puzzle piece Kit held in his hand. Kit, however, ignored him, and with great deliberation slotted the piece into another spot. He looked up, met her eyes, then flushed and glanced away.

Rejection jabbed Lally like a fist. Her tentative smile died half formed and her eyes stung with sudden, humiliating tears. Jumping from her stool, she slipped out into the quiet solace of the hall. Sound was sliced off in midmurmur as the door latch clicked behind her, and the air felt cold and heavy, a tangible weight against her burning cheeks.

She stood, shivering with the shock of the temperature change, pressing the back of her hand against her nose to stop any more telltale blubbing. What had changed since last night? Kit had liked her, she'd been sure of it, and she'd felt giddy with the unaccustomed sense of power. She hadn't been able to resist showing off to Leo, even though she'd known it was unwise. Animosity had crackled like static between the two boys from the instant they'd met.

But Kit had seemed all right in church afterwards . . . maybe it was just her dreadful family, and the things that had happened today, that had made him want nothing to do with her. Or maybe his dad had had a word with him. When her uncle Duncan looked at her, she felt as if he could see

right through her, and unlike Gemma, there was no understanding in his eyes.

Defiance flared in her. Leaving the hall, she let herself
quietly into the empty sitting room. Only embers glowed in
the hearth, and the tree looked naked, stripped of all its
presents. It was pathetic, Christmas, a stupid sham, when no
one really cared anything about anyone else.

She turned away from the gifts, picking her way across
the minefield of toys Toby and Sam had left littered on the
carpet until she reached the drinks cabinet. Good, it looked
undisturbed. It seemed her grandmother hadn't offered
round the after-dinner sherry bottle. She checked the liquid
level, then tossed back a swallow or two while she thought
what to do. A comforting warmth began to burn in her middle. Dutch courage, she thought it was called, although she
didn't know where the Dutch came into it. After another
sip, she corked the bottle and lowered it carefully back into
its spot.

"Presto," she whispered. The bottle had vanished and
returned, just like her mum. If her mother could simply
walk out, without any explanation, why shouldn't she do
the same?

"What are you doing?" Kit's voice was sharper than he'd
intended. Lally had been behaving oddly ever since she'd
arrived at the farmhouse with Nana and Granddad, and when
he'd seen her leave the room, his uneasiness intensified.
Managing to slip out of the kitchen when his granddad was
occupied with Sam, he'd found Lally by the front door, half
into her pink fleece jacket. At the sound of his footsteps
she'd frozen like a startled hare, but when she saw it was
him she relaxed and shrugged into the other sleeve.

"Going out," she answered coolly. "I should think that's
obvious."

"Now?" Kit's voice squeaked alarmingly and he cleared
his throat before trying again. "Where?"

"Why is it any of your business?"

Unprepared for her belligerence, Kit stuttered, "Because

you didn't tell anyone. And it's . . . dark." His face flamed. God, he sounded a complete prat.

"Dark?" Lally echoed, her voice dripping scorn. "You're telling me I can't go out in the dark, like I'm a little kid? Who do you think you are, coming into *my* grandparents' house, bossing me around, turning your nose up at me?"

"What?" Kit stared at her, completely lost. "But I never—I didn't—"

"You did, just now, in the kitchen. You looked at me like I was something you'd wipe off your shoe." Her voice rose shrilly.

"Lally, what are you talking about?" Kit moved closer, afraid someone would hear them, and caught a faint whiff of her perfume. He shoved his hands into his pockets, resisting the urge to touch her. "Look, I know you're upset about your parents, but I never—"

"What about my parents?" She'd gone quiet again, but her chest rose and fell with the quick rhythm of her breathing and he knew he'd said the wrong thing.

"Nothing. It's just that—I heard them talking just now, your mum and Rose—Nana. They said you were going to stay here tonight, and I thought—"

"Here?" Lally stared at him, uncomprehending. "Sam and me?"

"And your mum." He didn't want to add that Rosemary seemed worried that Lally's dad might do something bad to her mother.

Lally didn't seem to take in the import of what he'd told her. "But I don't want to stay here," she said, stubbornly. "I want to go home. And I promised—"

"Promised what?" Kit pressed when she didn't go on.

She shook her head, lifting her hand to the door latch as if coming to a decision. "I'm going out. I'm going to walk to Leo's, if you really want to know. You can come if you want."

"My dad would kill me," Kit said. He might as well have tattooed "wanker" on his forehead.

"So? My dad gets mad at me all the time." She threw this out as if it were a badge of honor.

His mind flashed back to the afternoon, walking with his dad, talking to the woman with the boat—Annie—and he knew he could never explain that he didn't want to lose what he'd felt.

Sounds drifted down from upstairs: the deeper rumble of his father's voice, Gemma's lighter tone, a laugh. Toby's bath must be finished. They would be coming down again, Toby allowed to stay up a bit longer in his pajamas.

Lally had heard them, too. "Come on, hurry," she hissed at him.

"Wait." Kit reached for her then, his hand finding the thick fleece of her coat sleeve. He couldn't go with her, yet if he didn't, he'd lose all credibility in her eyes. "Don't go tonight," he said, struggling to find a delaying tactic. "Wait till tomorrow. Then I'll go with you."

Lally hesitated, then the energy seemed to drain from her. She looked suddenly younger than her fourteen years, and frightened. Her eyes met his in a plea. "Promise?"

"I promise," Kit said, and wondered just what sort of trouble he'd bound himself to.

# 13

❧

"**I'VE LEFT** a ready meal by the microwave," Althea Elsworthy told her sister, Bea. It was just shy of eight o'clock, and she'd said the same thing, at the same time, every morning for as long as she could remember. It was a necessary part of their ritual, however, and any deviation would cause Bea to grow agitated and have to be calmed down before Althea could leave for the hospital.

"My lunch," said Bea. "Is it mac cheese?" she added querulously, her broad brow furrowed.

"Yes, and I've left an apple for you," Althea answered with a smile. It was always mac cheese, but Bea never failed to ask. In the evenings, Althea tried to vary her sister's diet, but it took coaxing, and she'd long ago decided that the repetitive lunch was a small compromise to make for her sister's continued independence during the day.

Beatrice Elsworthy had been brain damaged since the age of eight, when she suffered a head injury in the car crash that had killed their father. He had been drinking and, against their mother's wishes, had insisted on taking the two girls out for a Sunday afternoon ice cream. At the roundabout nearest their house, he had failed to yield right-of-way to an oncoming lorry. It had been Althea's turn to ride in the backseat; she had escaped with a broken arm and a chipped tooth.

Her father's death had not been punishment enough to assuage her mother's anger. She'd spent the rest of Althea's childhood nursing her bitterness as well as her injured younger daughter, until she succumbed to cancer the year Althea graduated from medical school. Althea had cared for Bea ever since.

Now she settled Bea in her favorite armchair, overlooking the cottage's back garden. Already she had filled the bird feeders and put out nuts for the squirrels on the old tree stump that served as a feeding table. Bea would spend the morning watching the birds and listening to the radio. At noon she would heat her ready meal, and at one she would turn on the telly, already set to BBC1.

The intricacies of the human brain never failed to amaze Althea—why was it that her sister, who was incapable of organizing her own lunch, could name every character on *The Archers,* or describe in great detail who had appeared on the afternoon chat shows on the telly?

Around four, their neighbor, Paul Doyle, would come across for a cup of tea with Bea, and sometimes they would play simple card games for pennies. Nothing made Bea happier than accumulating a pile of gleaming copper coins, and Althea suspected Paul got them new from the bank, although he'd never admitted doing so.

More and more often lately, she found herself rushing to get home before Paul left, to enjoy a drink and a half hour's visit in front of the fire. She and Bea had known Paul and his late wife for years, but it was only since he'd retired from his teaching position at a local school the previous year that he'd begun visiting on a regular basis.

Althea told herself it was only natural to enjoy a little companionship. She had never shared her personal circumstances with any of her work colleagues, nor had she any intention of doing so. Pity was the one thing she couldn't bear. Nor was it justified—she needed Bea just as much as Bea needed her—but her reticence made friendship difficult.

Calling the dog, who got up from his rug by the Rayburn and stretched with a popping of joints, she'd just switched on Radio 4 when the doorbell rang. The dog gave one deep woof and trotted towards the door, his claws clicking on the tiled floor.

Althea frowned. The isolated cottage didn't invite casual visitors, and Paul seldom called round in the mornings. Giving her sister a pat on the shoulder, she said, "I'll be right back, love."

"You won't leave without telling me?"

"No. I promise." Althea followed the dog into the front hall, pushing aside his head so that she could crack open the door, then stared in surprise at the woman standing on her doorstep. It took her a moment to place the face, older and thinner than when she had last seen it, but the name clicked just as the woman said, "Dr. Elsworthy? Do you remember me? It's Annie Le—" She paused, then seemed to correct herself. "Annie Constantine. I'm sorry to bother you at home."

*Not sorry enough to refrain from doing it,* Althea thought, but her curiosity was aroused. She'd dealt with Constantine professionally on several occasions when Social Services had been involved in investigating a death, but hadn't seen her in some years.

She felt the dog's warm breath on her hip and noted the woman's anxious glance in his direction. "Don't mind Dan, he's quite harmless," she said, swinging the door wide enough to allow the dog access to the garden.

"Dan?" asked Annie Constantine, drawing her arms close to her body as the dog pushed past her in pursuit of a squirrel.

Althea smiled to herself. The dog was half Irish wolfhound and half mastiff, and everyone assumed he was called something like Boris or Fang. She had named him Danny Boy, and sang his song to him when they were alone in the car, but she had no intention of sharing her little private joke. Nor was she going to ask the woman in. A stranger's visit would agitate Bea for days.

"What can I do for you, Mrs. Constantine?" she asked, stepping out and pulling the door closed behind her.

"It's Lebow now," she said, explaining her earlier hesitation. "I've gone back to my maiden name."

Not sure whether this called for condolences or congratulations, Althea merely nodded. "Do go on." The previous day's crisp blue skies had given way to tattered gray clouds that mirrored the slush remaining underfoot, and the chill was beginning to seep through her heavy sweater.

"I've come to ask a favor," said Lebow, huddling a bit closer into her fleece jacket, as if preparing for a long stay. Then she told Althea what she wanted.

"I don't see why I have to do this." Juliet Newcombe sounded as truculent as a ten-year-old whisked off to visit an ailing and disliked relative.

Kincaid took his eyes off the road long enough to glance at his sister, who sat beside him in the passenger seat of Gemma's Escort. The day was shaping up to be gray and unremittingly frigid, and even halfway to Crewe the car's heater hadn't managed to dent the chill. Juliet held her coat closed at the throat, as if warding off something more solid than the cold air issuing from the heater vents, and even with her face averted, he could see the dark shadows under her eyes.

His excuse in taking her had been that he wanted to talk to his sister—true—but he suspected Gemma knew him well enough to guess that he also wanted to see what progress the local police had made in identifying the mummified child.

With another glance at Juliet's intractable expression, he said reasonably, "It's routine, I've told you. And as you can't start work again until the police release the crime scene, I should think you'd want to be as cooperative as possible." Then, reminding himself that his objective was to communicate with her, he added, "Look. I know things are a bit rough for you at the moment with Caspar. If there's anything I can—"

She shook her head so violently that strands of her dark hair flew loose from her clip. When she spoke, the words seemed to explode without volition. "There's nothing anyone can do. He's a total shit, and I'm a complete idiot for not having seen it years ago." She stopped, clamping her lips together as if to stop the flow, and shrugged. "But thanks."

"I take it you're not going to go home and kiss and make

up, then," Kincaid said, then asked, "Jules, are you afraid of him?"

Her shoulders jerked, an involuntary spasm. "No. Yes. I don't know. He's never, you know, hit me or anything. But . . . he's changed lately. Those things he said on Christmas Eve . . ." He saw the color creep up her cheeks at the memory. "And then yesterday, things just seemed to get blown all out of proportion. I don't see how I can go home and pretend nothing's happened."

"Has he tried to ring you?"

"I don't know. Not at Mum and Dad's, anyway, and I turned my mobile off. I took Lally's away as well—I didn't want him ringing her. She's furious with me. You'd think I'd amputated an arm."

Kincaid wasn't to be distracted. "You don't think Caspar's worried about you?"

This time Juliet looked at him, just long enough to roll her eyes. "He must know where I am, otherwise Mum and Dad would have called out the cavalry. And besides, where else would I go? It's not like I lead the jet-setter's lifestyle and can run off and borrow a friend's villa in Cap-Ferrat for a few days while I have a think."

Sarcasm had always been his sister's weapon; that, at least, hadn't changed. "Well, you'll have to talk to him at some point. If you like, I can go round with you. To the house, or the office."

"No!" Juliet's voice soared in panic. "I can't speak to him. Not yet. Not until I've worked out what to do. The children— The house— How can I possibly—"

"Jules," he interrupted gently, "you can't imagine the current state of affairs is good for the children."

"No, but . . . I just can't see any options." The car had warmed and she had stopped clutching her coat, but now her fingers picked restlessly at a loose button.

"You ask Caspar to move out. Then you get a lawyer and file for divorce."

Juliet sucked in a breath, as if she'd been punched in the solar plexus.

"That *is* what all this means, Jules. Unless you think counseling or some sort of intervention—"

"Oh, God, no." She gave a bitter whoop and wiped at her eyes. "Caspar in counseling? He'd die first."

"Then—"

"You think everything's so bloody simple, don't you?" Turning to him for the first time, she said, "So tell me how I'm going to support my kids."

"Your business—"

"I just barely manage to pay my crew and keep my head above water. Maybe when this job is finished, there'll be a bit left over, but we were already behind schedule, and now—"

"It's called maintenance, Jules." Kincaid's patience was failing. "Caspar will have to contribute to his children's up-keep. That's only to be expect—"

"You don't understand. You don't know him. He'll find some way to get out of it. Just because you do the right thing, you assume other fathers will do the same." Then she suddenly slumped in her seat and touched his arm. "I'm sorry," she said softly. "That's not fair. And I've never said, about Kit, that I was glad for you, or that I was proud of what you've done for him. I was so busy resenting you for being perfect that I never realized how much I took for granted."

Kincaid gave his sister a startled glance. What had he ever done that she should think him perfect? Was that why she always seemed angry with him?

"I was so naive that I thought all men were like you and Daddy," she went on. "Sometimes I think growing up in a so-called normal family wasn't adequate preparation for life. But you—your experiences can't have been that different from mine. How do you do what you do? Take things like mummified babies in your stride?"

"It's not like that," he responded, stung. "It's not a matter of taking things in stride. It's just that you learn to . . . separate . . . what you see. It's a problem to be solved, and I like knowing that there's something I can do." He wouldn't tell her how often the lines bled, how often the horror crept in on everyday life, especially since he had found Gemma and the boys.

"Power, then. Is that what it is? You like thinking you're an instrument of justice?" She was challenging him again, her earlier moment of contrition seemingly forgotten.

"No." In his early days on the job, he might have been forced to admit that there was some truth in her accusation. Now, however, there were too many days when the beastliness and sheer pettiness he encountered threatened to overwhelm him, when he had to force himself to look for the embers of humanity that sparked among the dregs.

Juliet must have heard the weariness in his voice, because after a quick glance she averted her face again. As he negotiated a roundabout, he sifted through the things his sister had told him, wondering how he could begin to respond. And then, with a spike in his pulse, he realized what she'd avoided so adroitly by turning the conversation to their own family.

"Jules," he said sharply, "those things Caspar said the other night—is there any truth to them? Is that why you won't stand up to him?"

It was not that Ronnie Babcock was unaccustomed to frustration. A good part of policing involved frustration—cases were seldom solved in the day or two allowed in the crime dramas on the telly—but at least there were usually some small avenues of progress.

There would be family, acquaintances, neighbors to interview. Scene-of-crime would have turned up one or two things of possible interest, or the forensic pathologist could tell them the assailant had been right-handed, or the victim had been double the legal limit when he'd been knocked down by a car.

But so far this case had produced nothing but a series of roadblocks. Dr. Elsworthy had sent the child's remains off to the Home Office forensic anthropologist, but Babcock knew it would be another day or two before he could expect a report.

Although scene-of-crime had extended their search from the building to the surrounding lane and pasture, they had turned up nothing more of interest—not that the bits they'd found in the barn itself qualified as interesting, although they had found a stash of vodka bottles beneath some stacked boards in a corner.

Nor had the neighbors who might have an address for the elusive Smiths, the barn's previous owners, returned from their holiday. The manufacturer of the baby's blanket was still closed, and Babcock's old mate Jim Craddock, who had handled the Smiths' sale of the property to the Fosters, was on holiday in Tenerife.

Rasansky's canvass of the local shops that might have sold the child's blanket had proved fruitless as well. In what he knew was an unfair fit of pique, Babcock had sent Rasansky back to reinterview the Fosters, although he suspected Rasansky would probably not find it a punishment—he and the Fosters would probably get on like a house afire.

"Penny for them, boss," said Sheila Larkin, perching on the corner of the desk he'd commandeered in the incident room. She'd made a concession to the cold today, he saw, and wore tights and boots under her scrap of a skirt. "You look like you got out of the wrong side of the bed," she added, eyeing him critically.

"Boiler's still out," he admitted. He'd spent another night on the sofa in front of his sitting-room fire, sleeping fitfully while huddled under every duvet in the house, and had again missed his morning coffee.

"We could do with one of those Caribbean holidays," she said sympathetically, and he noticed that her eyes were a sea green deep enough to swim in. Process of association, he told himself as he blinked and looked away, combined with sleep and caffeine deprivation.

There was only one other officer left in the incident room, collating reports. The case wasn't a high enough priority, and there hadn't been enough information coming in, to justify tying up more manpower. The main phone line rang and Larkin slipped off the desk to answer. She listened briefly, said, "Right, thanks," and rang off.

"Your star witness has arrived," she told him. "Shall I bring her down?"

"No, I think we'll use my office rather than the dungeon. Much more likely to inspire confidence, I should think."

"Does she need inspiring, your Mrs. Newcombe?" Larkin asked as they made their way up to reception. "All we need is her formal statement describing the discovery of the body, and the names of the lads in her crew."

Babcock thought of Juliet Newcombe's frightened face yesterday evening, and of the rather obvious effort Piers Dutton had made to cast doubt on her credibility. "I think it might be a bit more complicated than that," he said, forbearing to add his hope that Kincaid's girlfriend had brought Mrs. Newcombe, as she'd promised. He wouldn't mind another chat with the copper-haired Gemma James.

But when they reached the lobby, it was Kincaid himself who stood beside his sister.

Kincaid, in jeans and a scuffed leather bomber jacket, looked more relaxed than when Babcock had seen him on Christmas Eve, while Juliet Newcombe looked unhappy but less frantic.

When Babcock made introductions, Larkin widened her eyes at Kincaid and said, "Ooh, Scotland Yard! Nice to meet you, sir. If you ever need any help in this part of the world—" Babcock's reproving glare only made her grin unrepentantly as she turned back to him. "You want me to take Mrs. Newcombe's statement, boss?" she asked.

"Why don't you take Mrs. Newcombe to the family room," he suggested. That would allow Larkin to take care of the formalities, and he could take Kincaid to his own office for a natter. There was always a chance that Larkin, for all her cheekiness, would elicit something from Juliet Newcombe that he might not.

Turning to her brother with a distressed expression, Juliet said, "But—I thought you'd be with me—"

Kincaid squeezed her arm. "Don't worry. You just tell the constable exactly what happened the other night. It's only for the record."

"The coffee here is rubbish," Babcock said when Larkin

ad led Juliet away, "but I keep a kettle and some tea bags in my office for special visitors. Care for a cuppa?"

"I'm flattered." Kincaid followed him, and when they were settled in the two chairs on the visitors' side of Babcock's desk, dunking their tea bags in mismatched mugs, he looked round the cramped space. "You've not done too badly for yourself, Ronnie," he commented.

"Don't condescend to me, mate," said Babcock lightly. "You've probably got a suite overlooking the bloody Thames."

Kincaid laughed and shook his head. "Not likely, although you can get a glimpse of the river from my guv'nor's office if you stand on a chair." He fished out his tea bag and lobbed it accurately into the bin. "So, any developments with the case?" he asked, settling back in his chair with his hands wrapped round his mug for the warmth.

"Bugger all," Babcock told him with a grimace. He outlined the results of the pathologist's report and the negative progress in other areas. "I don't suppose you've any suggestions? Not that I'm officially asking for Scotland Yard's assistance, of course."

"Patience, my son?" Kincaid ventured, then held up a hand to ward off an imaginary blow. "No, seriously, I'd say you're pretty well stymied until the neighbors come back from their holiday and businesses reopen. Have you put a notice in the local media?"

"There'll be a story in this week's *Chronicle*. Maybe someone will remember a baby of an unspecified age who disappeared an unspecified number of years ago."

"Stranger things have happened," Kincaid said. "But you might have someone contact you with the Smiths' address. I remember them, you know, although I'm not sure I'd have recalled the name. But the barn was still a working dairy when we were kids. Jules and I—"

"Jules?"

"Sorry, Juliet. Juliet and I used to roam the canal like little fiends, not something you could let your kids do these days. We were chased off by more than one farmer and his dog, but not by the Smiths. They seemed a kindly couple, and although I thought of them as being ancient, I suspect they were only middle-aged."

"You were close, then, you and your sister?" Babcock asked.

Kincaid hesitated for a moment, then said, "There's only three years' difference in our ages and, especially when we were small, our life was fairly isolated, so we spent a good deal of time together. But even then, I'm not sure I really knew her." He shrugged. "And I suppose it's only natural that you grow apart as you get older."

Babcock saw an opportunity to satisfy his curiosity about Juliet Newcombe. "Is she all right, your sister? Yesterday, she seemed more upset than I'd have expected."

"Um, she's having some . . . domestic issues," Kincaid answered after a moment's hesitation.

"Anything to do with this baby?"

"No, of course not." Kincaid seemed surprised by the question. "Although I don't think finding the thing did wonders for her emotional equilibrium."

"Understandable." Babcock grimaced at the memory of the desiccated little form, then turned his mug in his fingers while he considered how much to reveal. "I had a chat with your brother-in-law's partner last night. He's a right tosser. And I got the distinct impression he has it in for your sister."

"Has it in—"

"As in active ill will." Babcock clarified. "As in making an opportunity to suggest she's hysterical and not to be relied upon."

"Why the hell—" Kincaid began, then stopped and sipped carefully at tea that was now tepid. Wariness had slipped over his face like a mask, and Babcock knew he wasn't going to hear everything his friend knew. "Why would Piers Dutton want to undermine my sister?" Kincaid asked after a moment, his voice under control once more.

Frowning, Babcock mused aloud. "Dutton said he'd been in his house five years. But even if the child was buried before that, he could have known about the barn before he moved into the area."

"You're suggesting Dutton had something to do with this baby? But then why would he recommend my sister for the renovation?"

"Well, say he knew the new owners were determined to go ahead with the job. If he was sure the baby would be found, maybe he saw an opportunity to make life difficult for your sister."

"Implicating himself in the process? That's pretty far-fetched, don't you think, Ronnie? And if he was responsible for the baby and he knew the renovation was inevitable, why not just remove the body?"

"Too risky?" Babcock suggested.

"There's only one house between Dutton's and the canal. All he'd need to do was pick a night when he knew his neighbors wouldn't be home. It didn't take Jules that long to chip out that mortar—Dutton could have done it in a few hours, then tossed the body in a ditch somewhere."

Babcock sighed. "That's a point. Tom Foster's not exactly the Cerberus of South Cheshire." Rubbing at his lower lip, he found a spot of stubble he'd missed that morning in his rush to shave in his arctic bathroom. He cast an envious glance at his old friend. Kincaid was one of those men who would look rakish with a day's growth of beard, while he, with his battered face, would merely look like he'd spent the night in a skip. "Still, it's worth checking," he continued. "Dutton was going through a divorce at the time. Maybe he had an illegitimate child he didn't want complicating things—"

"And the baby's mother went along with the interment? Or maybe she's buried somewhere, too? Ronnie, you're building sand castles."

Babcock countered with a grin. "Where's your imagination, lad? All those bureaucrats at the Yard drummed it out of you? For all we know, he's walled her up in the cellar of his Victorian monstrosity. Didn't you read your Poe?"

"You'd better have a little firmer foundation than 'The Cask of Amontillado' before you apply for a warrant to start digging up Dutton's house."

"Okay, okay. Touché. But I think I'll have Larkin do a little research into Dutton's background."

"Your detective constable?" Kincaid raised an amused eyebrow. "Sharp girl. And I do believe she fancies you, you know."

Babcock was momentarily rendered speechless. "You're taking the piss. She's cheeky with everyone, including you—and you're happily attached, I take it. I met your . . . girl-friend?"

"So she said, although I think she'd prefer the term 'part-ner.' And you're changing the subject."

"Even if you were right—and I'm not saying you are—I have enough problems with my ex without getting involved with someone on the job. Although I have to admit, my op-tions for meeting eligible women who'll put up with a cop-per's life are just about nil," Babcock conceded. Even as he spoke he remembered that Kincaid had been divorced, and that he'd heard his ex-wife had died tragically. To cover his momentary awkwardness, he said, "So, how did you get to-gether with your Gemma?"

This time Kincaid's smile was wicked. "She was my ser-geant."

When Althea Elsworthy saw Rowan Wain, she knew. Still, she went through the motions, listening to heart and lungs, checking capillary refill, lips and gums. The woman's la-bored breathing echoed in the boat's small cabin.

The social worker—Annie Lebow, as she was calling her-self now—had given the doctor a brief history of the Wains, explaining why Rowan Wain and her husband refused to seek medical help through the system.

"Munchausen's by proxy?" Althea had said. "Christ. Who made the diagnosis?"

When Annie told her, she shook her head and compressed her lips. "The man's a poisonous toad. I'm not saying that such things don't happen now and again, mind you, parents abusing their children in order to get attention, but it should be called just that—abuse—and dealt with as such. But Sprake pulls MSBP out of his hat whenever he can't diagnose a child or the parents refuse to cooperate with his conception of himself as God."

"And there's no way to have the diagnosis removed from Rowan's records?"

"Not likely, even if the couple had unlimited funds and fancy lawyers. The boy seems all right now?"

"Remarkably well, as far as I can tell," Annie had answered, and Althea nodded. She'd seen cases like that, where a young child failed to thrive, then, without any visible explanation, suddenly seemed to turn a corner. Certainly, both children, seen briefly peeking from behind their father in the main cabin of the narrowboat, had looked healthy, if a trifle thin. Better that, in her opinion, than the pudginess she saw so often these days in children who spent hours in front of the telly.

"Doctor." The whisper of Rowan Wain's voice snapped Althea out of her woolgathering. The thin fingers Rowan placed on her arm were cold and blue as ice. "It's bad, isn't it?"

"Well, it's not good, I'm afraid," Althea admitted. "I don't suppose I can change your mind about going to hospital?"

Rowan gave only the slightest shake of her head, but her eyes were adamant, and filled with a calm acceptance that made the doctor look away. Carefully coiling up her stethoscope and placing it in her bag, she said, "I can try to make you more comfortable. Perhaps some oxygen would help."

"It won't go on any records?"

"I'll see it doesn't."

"Then that would be good. Thank you." Rowan smiled. "Will you speak to my husband?"

"If you'd like, yes." Thinking of the anxious faces of those waiting outside the tiny cabin, Althea was reminded of why she had become a pathologist—she found it much easier to deal with the dead than with the pain of the living. "I'll come back soon," she said. "When I've arranged for the oxygen."

Rowan's eyes were drifting closed; even their short interview had tired her.

When the doctor emerged into the main cabin, she found only Annie and the husband, Gabriel Wain. There seemed to be a tension between them, and Althea wondered briefly if it was due to more than concern.

"I've sent the children up top," Wain said, without offering any pleasantries. He, too, was thin, she realized, with the gauntness of worry, and his dark eyes were as feverish in their intensity as his rough demand when he spoke. "Say what you have to say."

"I suspect you know what I'm going to tell you, Mr. Wain," said Althea, speaking softly enough that she hoped her voice wouldn't carry into the next cabin. "Your wife is suffering from congestive heart failure. I understand your feelings about treatment, and in Rowan's case I must say I fear her heart is too damaged for surgical intervention to be effective, even if it were possible. There are drugs that might help temporarily, but again . . . I've said I'd arrange some oxygen, to make her more comfortable. You do understand that this is strictly my opinion?" she added.

He stared at her. "You're saying there's nothing can be done for her? Even if she went into hospital?"

"In the long term, I fear not."

She heard the quick intake of Annie Lebow's breath and glimpsed her stricken face, but it was Gabriel Wain who held her gaze. His eyes drew her in, and for an instant she felt herself falling into the pit of his grief. But then she saw a flicker of something that might have been relief in those depths, and he seemed to diminish. If the will to keep his wife alive had driven him beyond his limits for too long, it had now released its hold.

"Have you told her," he asked, "that she's dying?"

"Not in so many words, no. Do you want me to speak to her again?"

He drew himself up, once more dominating the claustrophobic confines of the cabin, and his dignity made her suddenly feel an intruder. "No," he said quietly. "I thank you for your help, Doctor, but that burden is mine."

# 14

❧

**THE VICTIM CLUTCHED** his head and staggered, then
swayed and slumped to the floor of the inn's lounge bar, like
a rag doll divested of stuffing. He twitched and, with a final
moan, lay still.

Standing over him, the murderer nudged him with a toe,
once, twice, then, still holding the club, raised his hands above
his head and pumped his arms in victory. He pranced around
the room in an impromptu dance, face obscured by his mask,
ragged clothes fluttering.

"A doctor!" someone called out from the crowd. "Get a
doctor!"

A tall, skeletally thin man in a black top hat pushed
through the bystanders and, kneeling beside the corpse,
opened his large black bag. From its depths, he pulled a jug
of medicine that looked suspiciously like cider, and a pill
the size of a Ping-Pong ball. The doctor held the pill up between thumb and forefinger, displaying it to the crowd, then
pushed it between the unresponsive lips of the corpse.

There was a pregnant pause, a momentary holding of the
collective breath, then the corpse stirred, sat up, and gave an
exaggerated shake. He spat out the pill and took a swig from
the jug, which made him roll his eyes and wipe his lips with
the back of his hand. Then he leapt to his feet and began to
attack his assailant with the same club that had previously
been used against him.

After a frenzied chase round the small open space in the pub's center, the murderer at last fell to his knees, vanquished, and the crowd erupted into cheers. Murderer, victim, and doctor all took bows, then the doctor swept off his top hat and began passing it through the crowd to the accompaniment of clinking glasses.

"That's barbaric," murmured Gemma to Kincaid, who stood beside her at the bar. They'd been queuing for drinks when the play had begun and everyone had fallen silent to watch.

Tossing the change he'd received from the barman into the doctor's hat as it passed by, Kincaid said, "Mummers on Boxing Day are a respected rural tradition. I thought they were quite good, actually."

To Gemma, Boxing Day meant watching football on the telly, which she thought more civilized than pantomimed murder, football hooligans notwithstanding. Toby, who had clamped himself to her and tucked his face away as the villain struck his blows, now tugged on her trousers leg. "Mummy, is the bad man gone?"

Contrite at not realizing he'd really been frightened, she knelt beside him and tousled his hair. "Yes, lovey. It was all just pretend, like on the telly, or a film. See, they're friends again." She pointed to the actors, now engaged in a spirited conversation at a far table, and Toby stood on tiptoe to look.

"The play's medieval, or older," Kincaid explained as he and Gemma collected the round of drinks he'd bought for their table. "Perhaps even pagan—no one seems to know for certain. At least they don't stone wrens these days."

"Stone wrens?" Gemma looked at him askance. "As in little birds?"

"The twenty-sixth of December is the feast day of Saint Stephen, an early Christian martyr who was stoned to death," Kincaid explained as they threaded their way through the crowded room, Toby leading the way. "According to legend, it was the wren that betrayed Stephen to the mob, so boys and young men used to go out on Boxing Day and kill a wren with stones as a sort of retribution. Then they'd affix the little body to a pole tied with ribbons and parade it round the village."

"Ugh." Gemma made a face. "You win. I'll take mummers. But you country people are all a bit cracked," she teased, letting him know he was forgiven for leaving her behind that morning.

She had enjoyed her time with the children—or at least with the younger two. Sam was unexpectedly patient with Toby, and Toby had responded with his usual uncomplicated enthusiasm. Even the ponies had not been too bad: shaggy, friendly creatures who had butted her and nibbled bits of carrot, their warm plumes of breath carrying the beery scent of slightly fermented grain.

But some of her pleasure in the outing had been spoiled by a tension she sensed between Kit and Lally, although they had seemed almost pointedly to ignore each other. It made Gemma uneasy, and she would have guessed they'd had a falling-out, except that once or twice she could have sworn she saw a complicit look pass between them. Had something happened that she'd missed?

Kit had come home from his walk with Duncan the previous evening full of excitement over the boat he'd seen and its owner's invitation to come back for another visit. Was he merely out of sorts because the family's plans for their traditional Boxing Day lunch at the local pub had got in the way of his expedition?

If so, perhaps the inn would make up for it, Gemma thought as she and Duncan reached the table their party had snagged near the fire. In London, going to pubs wasn't a normal experience for the kids, but the Barbridge Inn, like many country pubs that served meals, allowed children in the restaurant area and was family oriented.

The pub was a welcoming place, Gemma had to admit, hugging the canal side in the tiny hamlet of Barbridge, just a mile or two from the Kincaids' farmhouse. Open fires burned in both bars, the rambling rooms were filled with comfortably worn furniture, and the walls were covered with canalthemed prints. There was even a bookcase, filled with used volumes that the patrons traded, and in the central room, a jazz band was setting up for a session.

The musicians were older, all local men and friends of Hugh's, Rosemary explained when Gemma and Duncan had taken their places at the table again. Juliet sat with her back to the fire, as quiet as she had been since her return from the police station, but it seemed to Gemma that she had begun to relax in the warmth and bustle of the pub. Her face seemed softer, less pinched with strain.

The children had taken a small table beside the adults, adjusting their chairs so that they could see the band, but Sam often glanced back at his mother, as if assuring himself that she hadn't vanished.

The band started up just as their food arrived, and they ate the good, plain pub cooking with their feet tapping under the table. After a few bites, Toby abandoned his chicken and chips and stood, jiggling to the beat with the unself-conscious abandon of a five-year-old. It was happy music, Gemma thought, New Orleans–style jazz in an irresistible upbeat tempo, played with professional flair and obvious enjoyment by the band. By the end of the first set, even Juliet had begun to smile.

When the band stopped for a break, wiping sweaty faces with handkerchiefs, the crowd erupted into cheers and applause. Gemma had pushed back her chair, intending to take Toby for a closer look at the instruments, when she saw Juliet's face freeze.

Turning, she saw Caspar Newcombe standing a few feet away. How long he'd watched them while their attention was diverted, she didn't know, but now he stepped up to their table and blocked Juliet's chair.

"I thought I might find you here," he said, quite pleasantly, and gave them all a smile that chilled Gemma's blood. She had seen such control before, and it was much more frightening than any drunken shouting. "You're such creatures of habit, which I suppose is good for me, since you didn't trouble to invite me to your little gathering."

Out of the corner of her eye, Gemma saw that Piers Dutton and his son had apparently come in with Caspar, but

hey were watching from the bar, as if disassociating themselves from impending disaster.

"I thought we might have a little civilized conversation,"
Caspar continued, all his attention now focused on Juliet.
"You've behaved very irresponsibly, you know, and you're
obviously unfit to look after the children. I'm going to take
them home now. You"—he stabbed a finger at her, his careful discipline slipping—"can do whatever you bloody well
like, you stupid—"

"Caspar, don't make a scene," Kincaid broke in, his voice
even but firm. Heads were beginning to turn, and the tables
nearest theirs had fallen silent.

"Me? Make a scene?" Caspar's voice dripped sarcasm.
"And what advice did you give to your sister after she
walked out of my parents' house without a word? Did you
tell her it didn't matter that she insulted my parents and
upset the children?" He was certainly playing the righ-
teously incensed husband to the hilt, but Gemma had the
odd feeling that his performance was not entirely for their
benefit.

"It's you who's upsetting the children now." Hugh rose, as
if determined to step into the breach, and Gemma remembered he had berated himself for not defending his daughter
when Caspar had verbally attacked her on Christmas Eve.
"This isn't the time or place—"

"Shut up. Just shut up, all of you." Juliet sprang up, pushing her chair back with a grating screech that drew the attention of everyone in the room not already mesmerized. "I
don't need anyone to answer for me. You're not taking the
children, Caspar." Her hands were raised, her breathing hard,
and Gemma feared the situation was seconds away from
degenerating into a brawl.

"Sam! Lally!" called out Casper. "Come here. Now."

For an instant, no one breathed. Then Sam moved slowly
to his mother's side. "I—I want to stay with Mummy." He
locked eyes with his father, and after a moment, Caspar
looked away.

"Lally." There was threat in Caspar's voice now, rather
than command. He stepped towards her, hand out.

Lally cast a stricken look at him, another at her mother. Then she scrambled from her chair and ran from the pub.

There was a moment of chaos as everyone in the family shoved and jostled in an instinctive attempt to follow the girl. Then Kit's voice rose clearly above the hubbub, with a ring of authority Gemma had never heard before. "I'll go. Let me talk to her."

Kincaid hesitated, then nodded his approval. Stopping just long enough to grab Lally's jacket, Kit slipped out the side door Lally had taken.

"All right," Kincaid said, taking charge in a manner that brooked no more argument. "Jules, you stay with Sam." He laid a seemingly casual hand on his brother-in-law's shoulder, but Gemma saw Caspar wince from the pressure. "Caspar, you can't force the children to go with you," he continued. "When everyone is a bit calmer, I'm sure you and Juliet will be able to work out a visitation arrangement.

"In the meantime, I just saw the barman pick up the phone. My guess is that he's calling to report a public disturbance. I'd highly recommend you not be here when the police arrive—unless, of course, you want to embarrass yourself further. I'll walk out with you, shall I?"

Kit pushed his way out the door that led to the children's play area at the side of the pub and stopped, getting his bearings. The gunmetal sky had lowered until it met the horizon in a gray sheet, and a fine, freezing mist hung in the air. Traces of glaze had begun to form on the playground climbing equipment and on the branches of the nearby trees. Outside the fenced area, a swath of lawn ran down to the canal side. Mooring rings had been set into the concrete edging, and though every space was filled, the boats were all dark, wrapped and shuttered.

Lally stood on the concrete border, back turned and shoulders hunched, staring into the canal. She must have heard the sound of the door, because she swung round and started picking her way along the edging, away from the pub.

"Lally, wait up!" Kit called. "It's me."

She stopped, nudging a mooring ring with the toe of her trainer, but didn't turn round. "Just bugger off, Kit. Leave me alone."

He let himself out of the playground gate and slid down the lawn. "We can talk," he said, coming to a breathless stop beside her. The concrete felt elusively slippery beneath his feet. "Here." He handed her jacket to her. "I thought you might want this."

"I don't want to talk," she said, but she shrugged the coat on.

"Look, I—" He'd started to say he knew how she felt, but realized that he didn't, not really. How could he, when it hadn't been his parents fighting in front of everyone in the pub?

For the first time, he realized how people must feel when they tried to speak to him about his mother. Their awkward declarations of understanding had made him furious—they couldn't know what it was like, how he felt. But now he saw that it didn't matter that they didn't—couldn't—understand. They genuinely wanted to help and were going about it the best they could.

He also suspected, from his own experience, that even though Lally said she didn't want to talk, she didn't really want to be left alone, either. She had moved on a few steps, to the end of the concrete edging, and stood dangerously close to the lip of the canal. Beyond her, an arched stone bridge crossed the water, giving access to the towpath on the opposite side.

Kit glanced back at the pub. If he went in to say he was taking Lally for a walk, she might disappear. They would just have to trust that he was looking after her. "Come on," he said, and started back up the bank towards the play yard and the road. "Let's have a look at the boats on the other side." He didn't look back, didn't give her a chance to refuse, and after a moment he heard the squelch of her footsteps on the mist-soaked grass. When he reached the road, he slowed a bit and let her draw level, but he still didn't look at her or speak.

At the apex of the bridge, they stopped in silent accord and gazed downstream. On the left-hand side of the canal, a dozen boats were moored end to end along the towpath, like brightly painted railway cars shuffled into a watery siding.

On the right, a cluster of houses backed onto private mooring spaces, and beyond them, a grove of evergreens stood, ghostly sentinel, in the mist. Their trunks were bare and evenly spaced, their tops round and full, so that they looked like Toby's drawings of trees.

"I used to like it when we came here." Lally's voice was soft, disembodied. "Sam and I played on the swings, and in the summer you could see inside the boats at night. I'd watch the families and imagine that their lives were perfect."

Kit knew that game. When he was small, he'd peered in neighbors' windows, wondering what it was like to have brothers and sisters. Then, after Ian had left them, he'd watched families with fathers and wondered why some dads stayed and others didn't. Now, if he glanced into an uncurtained window at dusk, he'd fancy he saw his mother, just for an instant.

He shoved his cold hands a little farther into his jacket pockets. "No one's life is perfect."

Lally turned on him with sudden, blazing fury. "Well, mine sucks. How could my parents be so stupid? And my dad—you don't know what he's like. He'll—"

"Sneaking away to bare your soul, Lal?" The voice was smooth and mocking, and Kit recognized it even as his body jerked from the surprise.

"Leo! You bastard!" Lally whirled round, striking at the boy's chest with her fists, but Leo caught both her wrists in one hand and spun her back like a marionette.

"Shhh," he said. "You don't want to call attention to yourself. I should think there's been quite enough of that in your family for one day." That made Lally struggle harder, but when she saw Kit step forward to intervene, she went limp and Leo let her go.

"Where are you going?" Leo asked, as casually as if he'd run across them in the street rather than creeping up behind them and trying to frighten them half to death.

"For a walk. To see the boats," Kit answered, trying to

make it clear they didn't need company. He started down the far side of the bridge, and Lally followed.

"I'll come with you, then." Leo fell in beside Lally. "My dad's taken Lally's dad to get royally pissed at a more 'accommodating' pub, so I'm all yours for the duration."

"Your dad just left you?" Kit asked, curiosity overcoming his dislike.

"I'm not a baby, like some," Leo snapped, then smiled. "I said I'd walk home. It's not far. You can come with me, and we'll have a look at where Juliet found this famous mummy." He took a packet of cigarettes from the pocket of his peacoat and tapped out two, handing one to Lally without asking if she wanted it. She stopped, touching his hand as she held the end of the fag to the flame, and the casual intimacy of the gesture made Kit feel suddenly queasy.

"You can't go in a crime scene," he said as they merged into single file, now following Leo down the towpath. "Everyone knows that."

"And who's going to see?" Leo shot back. "The police have finished picking up things, and there's only a stupid tape. How is a tape supposed to keep anyone out?"

"You could destroy evidence."

"Ooh, listen to you, Mister Policeman. Taking after your daddy, are you? Anyway, what difference does it make? The thing's probably been there for ages. Just think, Lally—"

"Shut up, Leo." Lally stopped so suddenly that Kit bumped into her. "That's horrid. I'm not going any farther if you don't shut up." The mist had beaded on her dark hair, and now a drop formed on the end of her nose. She wiped her face with the back of her sleeve without taking her eyes off Leo.

"Okay, okay." Leo held up his hands, then took a drag off the cigarette. "Forget it. I've found a new place, anyway."

He and Lally looked at each other for a moment in silent communication, then Lally pushed past Leo and trudged on, her head ducked in misery. Kit was about to reach for her, to insist that they go back, when a boat materialized out of the fog a few yards down the path. He knew it instantly.

Even with her sapphire paintwork dulled by moisture, the

sleek lines of the *Lost Horizon* were unmistakable. Light glowed from within, and smoke hung heavily above the chimney, barely distinguishable from the surrounding fog. Annie Lebow was at home.

Kit's first instinct was to call out. He could show Lally the boat; they could get warm; maybe Annie would even offer them something hot to drink. Then he realized two things simultaneously.

The first was that he didn't want to share anything that was special to him with Leo, and he didn't see how he could make Leo leave them alone. The second was that he'd expected to find the *Horizon* above Barbridge, on the Middlewich Branch, where he had seen her yesterday. Had Annie changed her mind about her invitation? Or perhaps she had never meant it at all.

So humiliated was he by the idea that she hadn't intended to keep their appointment that he stopped dead, wishing himself a planet away. The others halted as well, turning startled faces towards him. Perhaps if no one spoke—if they turned back now—

It was too late. The boat's stern door swung open and Annie Lebow stepped out, a cloth firewood carrier in her hand, and reached for the firewood stacked neatly on the roof of the boat. She paused when she saw the three of them just standing there on the path, then smiled a little hesitantly. Her eyes were a clear green against the gray sky and the gray fleece she wore, and her short blond hair stood on end, as if she'd absently run her fingers through it. "Hullo," she said. "It's Kit, isn't it?" she added as she transferred a few pieces of wood into the carrier.

"You've moved your boat," Kit blurted out, then inwardly cursed himself for a complete idiot. Now she'd think he'd been searching for her, like some kind of stalker.

"Oh . . . yes." She sounded bemused, as if it hadn't occurred to her. "It was a twenty-four-hour mooring, and all the spots at Barbridge were taken. I should have thought to say so yesterday. I'm sorry if you looked and couldn't find me."

"No." Kit saw the possibility of redemption. "No, we

had . . . family things." Belatedly, he added, "This is my cousin Lally. And Leo. We were just walking, and saw the boat."

Annie studied them. "You're wet. And it's freezing. Do you want to come inside?" she added, but Kit could hear the reluctance in her voice.

He imagined the three of them in their sodden, steaming clothes, crammed awkwardly into the *Horizon's* cabin as he tried to make conversation, and shook his head. "No, thanks. We have to get back. But—"

"You could come tomorrow. The weather is supposed to clear. I'll be here, or up at Barbridge. I've some things to . . . to take care of." She sounded as if that surprised her.

"Okay, right." Kit raised his hand in an awkward wave. "See you then." Grabbing Lally's sleeve, he pulled her hurriedly back down the path the way they had come, figuring that Leo could bloody well take care of himself.

But after a moment, he heard the unmistakable rustle of movement behind them, and felt an arm draped across his shoulder.

"Did you have a date, then?" Leo whispered, his breath warm in Kit's ear. "A little old for you, isn't she? Or does that make it more fun?" When Kit tried to shrug loose, he gripped harder. "I think you'd better tell us all about it."

The phone rang, sounding tinny and distant in the mobile held to Annie's ear. She imagined the house at the other end of the electronic connection, pictured Roger swearing as he got up from his laptop and searched for the handset he'd misplaced. But perhaps he'd changed, become more organized, less obsessed with his work, without her there as a foil.

After a moment, however, the answering machine kicked in and she hung up. She didn't want to leave a message—Roger would see her number on the caller ID, and saying "Call me" seemed stupidly redundant. He would ring her back, he always did, although she was no longer quite sure why.

The dark day had faded imperceptibly to night, and Annie had found herself unable to settle to anything constructive. She'd had an unexpected urge to talk to her husband, as if that might help her sort through her jumbled emotions, but now she realized she hadn't any idea what she'd meant to say. She'd never been very good at sharing—that was one of the reasons they'd separated. Why did she think this would be any different?

Wandering from the salon into the galley, she pulled an open bottle of Aussie Chardonnay from the fridge. But as she reached for a glass, she felt the slightest movement of the boat and stopped, puzzled. She knew every creak and quirk of the boat, as if it were an extension of her body, and only registered movement when it was something out of the ordinary. This hadn't been backwash—she'd have heard another boat going by—and she'd checked the mooring lines carefully for slack. Perhaps one of the mooring pins had pulled a bit loose in the wet soil. She would check it, she decided, next time she went out for wood.

The brief interruption, however, added to the uneasiness that had been nagging her all afternoon, and she decided against the wine. She didn't want to feel fuzzy, or to sound muddled if Roger rang her back. Instead, she put on the kettle, sliced half a lemon and a bit of fresh ginger into a mug, then filled the cup with boiling water. The smell of this homemade concoction was always better than the taste, and she held the steaming mug under her nose as she went back into the salon.

The fire burned brightly in the stove and the Tom Rolt volume that Roger had given her lay open on the end table, but even as she curled up on the sofa and lifted the book, her mind wandered.

Although she'd never had children of her own, she'd worked with kids for years and had a well-developed radar for trouble. She'd been drawn to Kit the previous day, although even through his friendliness she'd sensed a reserve that seemed more adult than his years. But today she'd sensed something off, an unhealthy dynamic between the three of them. Was it just an overabundance of adolescent testosterone? The girl—Kit's cousin, he'd said—was far too pretty, and she'd had the haunted look of children who lived

with emotional trauma. Perhaps the boys were vying to protect her, and that, she was sure, was a recipe for disaster.

But whatever it was, she told herself, it was not her
problem—she'd got herself embroiled in enough of a mess
as it was. She'd done as much as she could for the Wains—
she had to let it go.

"Are you sure she's dying?" she'd asked Althea Elsworthy
when they'd reached the car park at Barbridge.

"As sure as I can be without running diagnostics," the
doctor had snapped. "You asked my opinion and now you
don't want to take it?"

"No, I—"

Elsworthy shook her head. "No, I'm sorry. I don't like it
any better than you do. There is a remote possibility that she
could survive a heart transplant. That's assuming that she
could get on the transplant list, with the MSBP strike on her
medical records, and that she'd last until a heart became
available. And all that would depend, of course, on her being
willing to subject herself, and her family, to the system. We
can't force someone to seek medical care, Ms. Lebow."

No, but should she at least try once more, Annie wondered now, to convince Rowan and Gabriel Wain to seek
medical help? She'd tried to tell herself that she could disen-
gage, that isolation would insulate her from pain, but she
had not found the peace she sought. Maybe she'd needed to
discover that no such thing existed. And if she stopped striving for perfection, could she ease a toe back into the water,
so to speak?

The thought made her smile. Roger, journalist to the core,
would tell her that metaphors weren't for amateurs. She
sipped her cooling drink, puckering a little at the lemon's
bite, and when her phone rang, she answered it with unexpected anticipation.

"Two calls in two days?" Roger sounded amused. "What
did I do to deserve such largesse?"

"I just . . . wanted to talk."

"Are you all right?" he asked, the amusement shifting instantly to concern.

"Yes, I think so," Annie said, then laughed at the sound of surprise in her own voice. "Yes. Truly."

"How about dinner, then? I could drive over, pick you up."

She glanced at the clock, then peered out through the half-closed blind covering the cabin window. The fog pressed against the glass, swirling like a sinuous white beast. "The mist has come down. I don't think I dare move the boat, and I'm halfway between Barbridge and the Hurleston Junction. There's no way for you to get to me easily, and besides, the roads may ice." Even as she set out the practical objections, she felt a stab of disappointment. She hadn't expected such an instant response, hadn't realized, until that moment, how much she looked forward to the prospect of sharing her concerns.

"Tomorrow, then?" he asked, and she heard the hope beneath the caution.

"Tomorrow," she said, with certainty.

Kit gasped awake, sucking great gulps of air into his lungs, the hammering of his heart still sounding in his ears. Sitting up, he saw that he'd thrown the covers off and pushed poor Tess to the foot of the bed again. The room was quiet, except for the sound of the younger boys' breathing, and the light coming through the curtain gap was the pearly gray of early morning.

Reassured, Kit reached down to pull up the duvet and scooped Tess to him. The little dog licked his chin with enthusiasm, and he hugged her, rubbing his cheek against the rough, springy hair on the top of her head. He settled back into the pillows, the dog now nestled in the crook of his arm, and made himself examine the nightmare. This one had been different.

He had been walking along the river, behind the cottage in Cambridge where he had spent the first eleven years of his life with his mother, and all except for the last year with the man he had known as his father, Ian McClellan. It was dusk, and he could smell the cold, damp air rising from the river . . . except that in the dream he had suddenly realized that it wasn't the river at all, but a canal.

Then light had spilled out from the cottage window and he had moved toward it, gliding across the familiar lawn as if he were a ghost. All the while the window seemed to recede, but when he reached it at last and looked in, it was not his mother he saw, but Lally. She turned towards him, but her face was pale and featureless, and blood ran from her hands and splashed onto the white floor—

No, it wasn't a floor, but snow, the blood blossoming in the white powder like crimson flowers appearing before his eyes, and he was running, running, trying to catch her, but the snow clung to his feet and his legs grew heavier and heavier. Then the dark figure ahead ducked into an opening, and as Kit followed he recognized his surroundings—it was the yew tunnel that ran alongside his friend Nathan's garden.

Hope had surged in him; this was his place, he could stop her here, keep her safe. But the snow still mired his feet, and even as he wondered how there could be snow inside the tunnel, he realized it wasn't the yew hedge at all, but a canal tunnel, and it wasn't snow closing over his head, but water . . .

Then reflex had jolted him awake, but even the memory of the dream made him shudder. Tess whimpered, and he realized he'd gripped her hard enough to pinch. "Sorry, sorry, girl," he whispered, stroking her, trying to will the fear away. It was just a dream, and it didn't take much to see where his subconscious had picked up the material. His worry over Lally had merely crept across the barrier between waking and sleeping.

She'd been quiet all the way back to the pub yesterday, ignoring him, ignoring Leo's taunts about Annie, and when Leo had finally left them at Barbridge, she hadn't even said good-bye.

They had all been waiting, Duncan and Gemma, his grandparents, Juliet and Sam, but no one had questioned or criticized either him or Lally. On the way back to the farmhouse, and later, as Rosemary had prepared ham sandwiches for tea, the adults had made small talk as if nothing had happened. Kit understood that this was meant to reassure the children, but it hadn't helped him, and he didn't think it had helped Lally, either.

After tea, a friend of Hugh's came to the house and took Juliet into the kitchen for a chat, and although no one said, Kit guessed the man was a lawyer.

Rosemary herded the others into the sitting room for a Scrabble tournament before the fire, but after a bit Lally began to drift away from the board between turns, and at last she disappeared altogether. Kit couldn't concentrate on the board, and when Hugh had trounced him and Gemma beyond redemption, he excused himself and slipped out of the room as well.

The murmur of voices still came from the kitchen, the man's low and steady, his aunt Juliet's rising like a breaking wave. Silently, he'd climbed the stairs, and had seen that the door to Hugh's study, where Lally had slept with her mum the night before, was slightly ajar.

He hadn't known what he'd meant to say, had pushed the door open without thinking, really. Lally sat on the floor, her back to the sofa bed, the left sleeve of her sweatshirt pushed up to the elbow. She was peeling back a strip of bandage from the inside of her forearm, and a trickle of bright blood seeped from beneath the white gauze.

Then, above the bandage, he saw a barely scabbed-over cut, a horizontal slash in the pale flesh, and above that, another, and another—purple scars, straight as rulers.

"Lally, what are you doing?" he cried out, his voice high with shock.

She jerked down the sleeve of her sweatshirt. "Nothing. Don't you knock?"

"I didn't know—" He shook his head. "That doesn't matter. Let me see what you've done to your arm."

"It's just a scratch. It's none of your business, Kit." She crossed her arms tightly beneath her small breasts.

"It's not. I saw it," he insisted. "You cut yourself, and more than once."

They stared at each other, deadlocked, until at last she gave a little shrug. "So?"

Kit gaped at her, unprepared for the enormity of the admission. "But—but you can't do that. You can't hurt your-self."

"Why not?" She smiled, then rocked up onto her knees and raised her chin in defiance. "Don't you dare tell."

"You can't keep me from it," he said, his anger and fear making him reckless.

"Oh, yes, I can." Her eyes were dark with promise. "Because if you tell, I'll do something much, much worse, and it will be your fault."

The memory drove Kit out of bed, but he moved quietly, try-ing not to wake Toby and Sam as he pulled on his clothes. Al-though the travel clock on the desk had stopped the day before, its battery dead, the quality of the light and the stillness of the house told him it was early, perhaps just past daybreak.

He knew he couldn't face the others, that he couldn't sit across the breakfast table from Lally and pretend that noth-ing was wrong. When he was ready, he fished a sheet of pa-per and a pen from his backpack and scribbled, "Taken Tess for walk. Back soon." He picked the dog up in his arms and slipped out of the room, leaving the note on the floor of the hallway in front of the door.

He made it out of the house unaccosted. He'd forgotten Tess's lead, but it didn't matter, he'd no intention of going near a road. The sun hadn't yet risen, but the fog had lifted in the night and the sky was a clear, pale gold, tinted with rose in the east. The air was cold and fresh, as if the fog had scoured it, and when the sun arched above the horizon, the glaze of ice on tree and hedge sparkled like crystal. The beauty of the sight made Kit stop, and he gazed a long mo-ment, as if he could capture perfection.

Then his stomach rumbled, a reminder that time was pass-ing. He knew he should go back—he didn't want anyone wor-rying about him—but when Tess ran on ahead, he followed. Not even the glory of the sunrise had quite dispelled the un-easiness that lingered from his nightmare, and he hadn't worked out what he was going to do about Lally.

Reaching the Middlewich Junction, he turned south, pass-ing by the sleeping inn on the opposite side of the canal. It occurred to him that if he went on, he would find the *Horizon,* and if Annie was up, he could apologize for yesterday. He'd been horribly rude, and he didn't want her to think he hadn't wanted to come back. Maybe they could even set a time for later that day.

He was afraid that yesterday's fog had distorted his perception of the distance, but soon he rounded a curve and saw the *Horizon,* just where he thought it would be. The blue paintwork gleamed in the morning sun, but no smoke rose from the chimney. Fighting disappointment, he went on, just in case she was up but hadn't yet lit the stove. Tess had stopped a few yards back to dig in the edge of the hedgerow, but he let her be, trusting that she would catch him up.

No sound or movement came from the boat, and he had made up his mind to turn back when he saw a huddled shape to the side of the towpath, just past the bow. His steps slowed, mired as if in his dream, but he forced himself to go on. Blood roared in his ears; he fought for breath as his brain processed something far worse than any nightmare.

Annie Lebow lay on the towpath, between the foot track and the hedge. One of her shoes rested a yard from her outstretched leg, and he had to resist the urge to pick it up and slip it back onto her foot. She was on her side, one arm thrown over her face, as if to protect her eyes from the rising sun.

Kit stopped, swallowing hard against the bile rising in his throat. The blood that had pooled beneath the blond spikes of her hair was not crimson, as in his dream, but black as tar.

# 15

❧

**BABCOCK HAD JUST HUNG UP** the phone, after a half-hour argument with the elusive boiler man, when it rang again. His hands already stiff from the numbing cold in his kitchen, he fumbled for the handset without checking the caller ID and barked, "If you're not here in thirty minutes, I'll sue for damages when I've lost fingers to frostbite."

"Um, sir. I can be there in five, but I'm not sure what I can do about the frostbite." It was Sheila Larkin, sounding bemused.

Babcock groaned. Holding the phone with his shoulder, he blew on his fingers. "Sorry, Larkin. I'm still trying to get my bloody boiler repaired. Is there a particular reason you'd want to pick me up at this ungodly hour?" His kitchen clock said straight-up eight, a time when he would normally be coming into the office himself, but a third night spent shivering on the sofa had not started his day well.

"Control hasn't rung you?"

His attention sharpened. "No. What's happened?"

"Body on the canal, boss. A woman."

Babcock's thoughts went back to his conversation with Kincaid the previous day, and their speculation over the fate of the baby's mother. "Buried?"

"No, sir. Lying on the canal path. It looks like someone bashed her over the head with a mooring pin. The boy who found the body identified her as a narrowboat owner named

Annie Lebow. But oddly enough, it's not far from the barn where we found the infant. A bit closer to Barbridge, from what I understand."

"Access?" he snapped, his mind turning to logistics even as he absorbed the shock.

"The constable says we'll have to come in from Barbridge. I'm almost to Nantwich, boss. Shall I—"

"No, thanks. I'll drive myself." Babcock had ridden with Larkin before and decided it was an experience to be avoided at all costs. She drove her Volkswagen as if she were trying to break a record at Le Mans. If anyone was going to subvert the speed laws, he'd prefer to do it himself in the BMW. "What about Rasansky?"

"Hasn't come in yet." Larkin couldn't quite conceal her satisfaction.

"Right," he said. "I'll ring him from the car. See you at the scene," he added and rang off. After a moment's reflection, he decided to take the time to change. There was no point in tramping the towpath in a Hugo Boss suit.

Less than a half hour later, clad more suitably in jeans, boots, and a fleece-lined leather coat, he swung the black BMW into the main street at Barbridge and slowed to a crawl as he looked for a place to park. Both sides of the road, as well as the lay-by near the humpbacked bridge, were filled with panda cars and already-flocking onlookers. He spotted Larkin's green Jetta, pulled rakishly half onto a resident's lawn, but drove past and found a spot behind the pub.

It was at least shaping up to be a halfway decent day, he thought as he locked the car and walked back along the road, if the weak sun held out. There weren't many things worse than trying to do a crime-scene recovery in the rain.

The pub was still locked and shuttered, with the abandoned look that such establishments seem to acquire even when closed for only a few hours. The same could not be said, however, for the houses that surrounded the inn. The occupants stood on porches and postage-stamp lawns, many still in dressing gowns and slippers, watching the police activity with avid interest.

No doubt at least one of these concerned neighbors had rung the media—the vultures would be arriving soon. Babcock stopped to speak to the constable barring access to the pub's play area and the bridge that crossed to the towpath, instructing him to have a patrol car block the top of the lane at the turnoff from the main road. The lane's bottom end, fortunately, dead-ended in a hollow fifty yards or so past the pub. From there one could climb a steep bank up to the section of towpath that ran between Barbridge and the Middlewich Junction.

Turning back, Babcock caught sight of Larkin coming across the bridge. She had her arm round the shoulders of a boy, who in turn held a shaggy brown terrier—it could have been a nice family snapshot, thought Babcock, until he drew near enough to get a good look at the boy's face. He was a good-looking kid, maybe twelve or thirteen, slender and almost as tall as Larkin, with rumpled fair hair. But his skin had the almost translucent pallor of shock, and his pupils were so dilated that Babcock couldn't make out the color of his eyes. Something about the boy tugged at the recesses of Babcock's mind.

"Boss, this is Kit McClellan. He found the vic—deceased," said Larkin.

Babcock saw that the boy's teeth were chattering. "Sheila, you have an emergency blanket in your car?"

"I'll get it." As she left them, Babcock noticed that she had for once dressed appropriately for the weather, in trousers and boots, but he found he had rather been looking forward to the sight of Larkin climbing over a stile in one of her short skirts.

"We'll soon get you warm," he said to the boy, resisting the urge to put an arm round the kid's shoulders. He was not one for cuddling children, or witnesses, although he tried to be gentle. And patient, although that was harder. Just now, he itched to get a look at the body on the towpath, but he knew it would wait, and that his first task was to help this boy recall anything of importance. He touched Kit's shoulder lightly, guiding him down the bridge and onto the grass area near the playground.

"Do you need a lead for your dog?" he asked as Larkin returned with a tiny silver square of insulated blanket. She unfolded the material and draped it like a cape round the boy, who was then forced to free one hand from the dog's coat in order to clutch the fabric together.

"No—I— She'll be fine." The boy lowered the dog to the grass, said, "Tess, down," and gave her a hand signal. The terrier dropped, but kept her bright button eyes fixed anxiously on her master.

"So you were out walking your dog this morning?" Babcock asked, thinking it rather odd for a boy that age to be out so early voluntarily on a school holiday.

The boy nodded, pressing his lips together in an effort to control his still-chattering teeth.

"Why don't you tell me what happened," Babcock prompted gently, and caught a surprised glance from Larkin. Did she think him incapable of interrogating a traumatized kid? "I'm Detective Superintendent Babcock, by the way."

"I saw the boat," the boy said. "I recognized her right off—the *Horizon*—and I thought I might see Annie—Miss Lebow. But when I got closer, there was something on the path, and then I saw—" He stopped, swallowing hard. "I knew she was dead, but I—I went up to her—I had to be sure. Then Tess caught up to me, and I didn't want her to contaminate the scene, so I picked her up.

"There was a farmhouse in the distance, but it was on the other side of the canal and I wasn't sure how to get to it, so I ran back here. The pub was shut, so I knocked on that lady's door." He pointed at a large woman watching them from across the street, a coat thrown over her pajamas, and still wearing pink fuzzy slippers. "I asked her to call the police. When the constable came, I went back with him."

It seemed even kids watched all the crime shows on the telly these days, thought Babcock, surprised at the boy's easy use of the phrase "contaminate the scene." But he had done exactly right, and deserved to be told so. "Good lad. Did you see anything else? Anyone walking along the towpath?"

The boy shook his head.

"The deceased lady—you said you recognized her? Did you know her well?"

"No. My dad and I met her the day before yesterday, when we were out walking. She was . . ." He swallowed again and blinked back tears. Babcock looked away, waiting until the boy went on, with only a slight tremble in his voice. "She was nice. She invited us aboard for tea, and she said if we came back, she'd show me how to drive the boat." The little terrier whined, sensing the distress in her master's voice, and inched forward on her belly. The boy knelt to stroke her and looked up at Babcock through a lock of fair hair. "Can I call my dad now? They'll be worried about me—I only left a note saying I'd taken Tess for a walk, and that was ages ago."

"Where do your parents live?" Babcock asked, wondering if the father could provide more information on the victim.

"London. We live in London. We're only visiting my grandparents for the holiday. I tried ringing from that lady's house, but I couldn't remember the phone number, and my dad didn't answer his mobile."

"I'm afraid you'll have to stay here for a bit longer," Babcock told him. He'd want to have another word once he'd seen the victim, and they'd need an official statement from the boy. "But we'll ring your family, and your dad can come along and wait with you. What are your grandparents' names?"

"Hugh and Rosemary Kincaid." The boy said this with a kind of careful formality, as if it were new to him.

The resemblance that had nagged Babcock all through the conversation clicked into sharp focus. "Good God," he said, as realization dawned. "You're Duncan's son."

Gemma saw Kincaid glance at his watch just as she looked up at the kitchen clock. They'd finished an enormous fried breakfast of eggs, sausage, tomatoes, and toast—God forbid she ate that every morning at home; she'd be the size of a whale and her arteries the consistency of blubber—and had

started on second cups of coffee, but there was still no sign of
Kit and Tess. When they'd emerged from their room, they'd
found his note lying on the hall floor, but they'd no way of
knowing whether they'd missed him by minutes or much
longer.

She was beginning to regret the languorous hour they'd
lingered in bed, the warm nightdress Kincaid had teased her
about so mercilessly the night before lying tangled in a heap
on the floor. "What if someone comes in?" she'd protested at
first, although they'd heard the little boys thundering down
the stairs like elephants on speed.

Kincaid had merely laughed, his mouth against her throat.
"So? Do you think we'll get into trouble?" He pulled away,
examining her, and added thoughtfully, "Besides, I like it
when you blush. Your skin turns a lovely pink, and it spreads
from here"—he touched her cheek—"to here"—then her
throat—"to here." He trailed his fingers lightly across her col-
larbone, then circled her breasts. "Just how far down does it
go? Shall we see?" His lips followed the path he'd traced, and
it didn't take long for Gemma to forget her embarrassment.

Afterwards, she'd lain with her cheek in the hollow of his
shoulder, the length of her body pressed against his warm
bare skin as he stroked her hair. The white curtains grew
brighter, until the room's walls began to glow as if lit from
within. She liked this room, which had once been Juliet's,
she thought drowsily. She liked this house, with its worn and
colorful comfort, and this family, who seemed prepared to
accept her, and her unconventional relationship with their
son, without reservation.

But that thought had reminded her of Juliet's troubles,
and of Lally, and of the baby left in the wall, and by the
time the smell of coffee began to percolate up the stairs,
she'd felt a formless prickle of anxiety.

"We should have bought Kit a watch for Christmas," Kincaid said now, echoing her thoughts. "Only he wants a model
that does everything but talk, so I thought we should save it
for his birthday." He glanced at his own again as he spoke,
then kissed his mother on the cheek as she refilled his mug.
"I'll just—" He stopped as his mobile chirped, unholstering

his phone and clicking it open with more than usual alacrity.

"Ronnie," he said. "Can I ring you back—"

Gemma heard the faint, tinny sound of Ronnie Babcock's voice issuing from the phone's speaker, saw Kincaid's face go blank with shock. She stood, hands gripping the edge of the table, her heart plummeting. "Kit—"

Kincaid shook his head at her and held up his hand, still listening intently. "I'll be there in five," he said at last, and rang off. "Kit's all right," he reassured them. "But he found a body. Annie Lebow, the woman we met on her narrowboat. She's been murdered."

"Oh, God." Seeing the distress in his face, Gemma felt bad for him as well as frantic for Kit. "I'm so sorry. Where did it happen? Where's Kit?"

"Ronnie says Kit found her on the towpath beside her boat, just below Barbridge. That's where Kit is now, at Barbridge." He was already moving, heading for his coat and the door. "I'll be back as soon as—"

"Don't you dare." The fear-induced rush of adrenaline had left Gemma trembling; now fury erupted in its place. Ever since they'd arrived he'd been sidelining her, treating her as if she were competent to do no more than look after the children, and she had let him because she wasn't sure of her ground. But that was going to stop this very minute. "Don't you even think about leaving me home like the little woman," she spat out. "I'm going with you, and you'd better not say one bloody word about it." She stared at him, breathing hard.

Kincaid gaped at her. After a moment, he blinked and said, "Of course you should go. I'm an idiot. Sorry, love." He turned to his mother. "Will you look after Toby for us, Mum?"

"Of course," Rosemary answered. "You go. We'll be fine." And although her face was strained with worry, when Gemma gave her a quick hug of thanks before following Kincaid from the room, Rosemary added in a whisper, "Good for you, dear."

Juliet woke slowly, light stabbing into her brain like an ice pick. But before she squeezed her eyes shut again, she saw enough to bring memory jolting back. She knew exactly where she was and what she was doing there.

She was lying on the badly sprung old sofa bed in her father's study. She had drunk far too many whiskies the night before. She had made up her mind to leave her husband. And beside her lay her daughter, sound asleep. The sofa bed sagged in the center and Lally had slipped towards her, a comforting weight against her hip.

Nausea surged through Juliet and she eased down onto her back again. She lay very still, breathing shallowly, swallowing against the pressure in the back of her throat. After a bit, the sensation eased and she drifted once more into the relief of sleep.

When she woke next, her mind was clearer, although her head still hurt and her mouth felt like the Sahara. Beside her, she heard the soft, steady sound of Lally's breathing. This time, she turned oh so carefully onto her side and, opening her eyes, gazed upon her sleeping daughter's face.

Lally lay on her back, the bedclothes held to her chin with both hands, the dark fan of her lashes casting shadows on her pale cheeks. As a child, she had slept in the same position, as if protecting herself even in her dreams, while Sam had flailed his arms and legs like a swimmer.

Dear God, thought Juliet, how long had it been since she had watched her daughter sleep? And when had her little baby become so beautiful? She reached out and traced the curve of the girl's cheek with her finger. Lally's eyes fluttered at the touch, and for just an instant, her lips curved in a smile of contentment. She pressed her face against her mother's hand, like an infant seeking contact. Then her eyes flew open and Juliet saw the awareness flood in, felt her daughter stiffen and draw away from her touch. Carefully, deliberately, Lally turned her back to her mother and shifted to the edge of the bed, and Juliet thought her heart would break.

*He hadn't imagined the way the blood would smell, or the slick feel of it on his fingers. He hadn't known that the memory of it would keep him awake, tossing and turning* with a strange, jittery discontent that felt like an itch deep in his veins. He'd expected exhilaration, not this half-acknowledged fear that things were spiraling out of his grasp, splintering around him. And yet there was fascination, too, and a new power, waiting like an incubating beast.

# 16

❧

"THE PATHOLOGIST and the scene-of-crime lads should be here anytime," Larkin said as Babcock followed her down the towpath. "Is the sergeant on his way?"

"Oh, he's on his way. Just not here." Babcock edged round a dip filled with standing water, glad he had made the decision to change into boots. It was cold as well, as the porcelain-blue sky of early morning had begun to haze over and a sharp west wind stirred the tops of the hedgerows. When Larkin cast a surprised glance over her shoulder, he added, "I've sent him to oversee a deconstruction crew at the dairy barn. I think we had better make sure there are no more bodies in those walls. And I've put in a request for the equipment we need to scan the floor."

"Bugger," Larkin commented succinctly. "Your Mrs. Newcombe will have a coronary. The sarge is probably not too happy, either."

"I suspect it wouldn't have been Sergeant Rasansky's first choice, but it needs to be done." Babcock wanted to see how Larkin handled herself on a major case. She was buzzed—he could tell that by the contained excitement in her voice and her step—but still she'd been kind and thorough with the witness.

And a good thing, too, as the witness had turned out to be a Scotland Yard superintendent's son. He'd left the boy waiting for his father's arrival in the care of the uniformed constable, but for once he had no doubt that his witness would remain available. Babcock was debating how he felt about having Scotland Yard—and his old mate—breathing over his shoulder in a major investigation when they went round a sharp bend in the canal and he saw the lime-yellow jackets of the uniformed officers in the distance.

"There they are, boss," Larkin informed him.

"I can see that," he answered testily, picking up his pace a bit to keep up with her. He'd slipped up on his daily runs since the divorce, and it was telling.

The boat was half obscured by the knot of officers, but he could see that it was drifting, bow out, into the canal. There was no other sign of disturbance, or even of human habitation. In fact, the stretch of canal might have been lifted straight from a scene in *The Wind in the Willows*. The grass lining the towpath was emerald after the snowmelt, the dried rushes at the canal's edge were golden, and the gleaming water reflected the twisted black trunks and feathery branches of the trees on either side of the path.

Just past the boat, the canal curved again, a seductive lure that compelled one to see what was hidden round the next bend. It was a magical place, not suited for violent death, and for the first time he had a visceral sense of how Kincaid's son must have felt on finding the woman's body.

Nor was it a place suited for investigation. Larkin had been right—he'd seen no access other than the way they had come. He remembered that the boy had said he'd seen a farmhouse in the distance—had he gone some way ahead before turning back for Barbridge?

The officers parted as they drew near, allowing Babcock and Larkin an unimpeded view of the towpath, but it was not until he had moved past them that Babcock saw the crumpled form on the green grass.

Her arm was thrown across her face, as if she were sleeping, but blood had darkened the spikes of her blond hair, and her legs were splayed at an unnatural angle. Babcock knelt and very gently shifted her arm so that he could see her face.

"Jesus fucking Christ!" The shock of recognition made

him feel hollow, and for a moment the face before him blurred and receded. Blinking, he sat back on his heels and wiped the back of his hand across his mouth before looking up at Larkin accusingly. "I thought the boy said her name was Lebow."

"The kid seemed positive in his ID, boss," Larkin said defensively. "And no one's been on the boat yet. Are you saying it's not Lebow?"

He took a last look at the pale face before him. Her eyes were wide, her mouth slightly parted in an expression that might have been surprise. "When I knew her," he said slowly, "her name was Annie Constantine."

Although Gemma was driving, it was Kincaid who flashed his warrant card to the constable guarding access to the lane, and it was Kincaid who explained that he'd been summoned by Chief Inspector Babcock, and that he was the witness's father.

Gemma felt another flash of the anger that had provoked her outburst in the Kincaids' kitchen. What was she, the chauffeur? Never had she felt more sharply her lack of official status in Kit's life, or regretted that she couldn't say "I'm his mum," or at least "He's my stepson." Nor did anyone seem to remember that she, too, was a police officer, and might have something to contribute.

Still fuming, she eased her Escort past the panda cars lining the end of the lane, but when she saw Kit, her irritation vanished and she felt ashamed of her petty feelings.

He was sitting in the grass at the bottom of the hump-backed bridge, knees drawn up, his back against the abutment, his thin face pinched with fright and misery. A silver emergency blanket had slipped from one shoulder, revealing the shaggy brown dog clutched in his lap.

His face brightened as he saw them and he pushed himself to his feet, letting the blanket fall to the ground.

Gemma pulled the car up parallel to an SUV parked at the end of the small lay-by near the bridge.

Kincaid was out of the car before she had come to a full stop, and so reached Kit first. By the time Gemma joined them, he'd grasped his son in a one-armed hug. For a moment, Kit turned his face to his father's shoulder, then he straightened and pulled away, biting his lip.

Gemma wanted to throw her arms around the boy, wanted to hold him tight and stroke his hair and tell him it was okay to cry. But she held back, as she always did, afraid he would feel she was overstepping her bounds, trying to take his mother's place. She contented herself with patting his shoulder as Kincaid said, "Kit, are you all right? Tell me what happened."

Of course he wasn't all right, thought Gemma, but Kit answered with obvious effort. "We were walking. I saw the boat. Then I saw her—Annie. I knew—" He shook his head.

"You didn't see anyone else?" Kincaid asked.

"No. I told the chief inspector."

Kincaid took him gently but firmly by the shoulders and looked in his eyes. "Did you touch anything?"

Gemma's first thought was that this was no time to be worrying about the integrity of the crime scene, but her protest died on her lips as she read the expression on Kincaid's face. It was not the integrity of the scene that concerned him, she realized, but the fact that Kit might have left some trace that would connect him with the woman's death.

"Of course not." Kit sounded incensed, and that, at least, was an improvement. "I know better than that. I kept Tess away, too." Hearing her name, the little terrier raised her head and licked his chin, and Gemma saw that even in Kit's arms the dog was shivering.

"We need to get you both somewhere warm," she said, then, turning to Kincaid, added, "Can't DCI Babcock or one of his officers take Kit's statement at the house?"

"No." The protest came from Kit, not Kincaid. "I want to stay. I told the chief inspector I would. And he said he wants to see you, as soon as possible."

Kincaid glanced at Gemma, his conflict clearly evident. She knew he felt he should stay with Kit—he *wanted* to stay with Kit—and yet he also wanted to go after Babcock, to see the crime scene, to be in on the action. And he was afraid that if he asked her to stay, she'd think him guilty of relegating her to child minder again.

She took pity on him. He did need to talk to Babcock. He had known the victim, and liked the woman—he was connected to this crime in a way she was not. "You go ahead," she said, with a small smile. "Kit and I will wait for you here."

Babcock had just slipped on a pair of latex gloves when the shifting of the uniformed officers heralded another arrival. He glanced up, expecting the SOCOs, or Dr. Elsworthy, but it was Duncan Kincaid. Babcock met his eyes and nodded an acknowledgment.

"You agree with your son, then?" he asked. "This is the woman you met as Annie Lebow?"

After a glance at the body, Kincaid came over to him. "Yes. Have you any idea—"

"You didn't tell me you had a son," Babcock interrupted.

Kincaid looked startled. "You didn't ask. I suppose it didn't occur to me that you didn't know. Does it matter?"

"Your son—Kit—said that the two of you met the victim, and that she'd invited you to visit her again."

Kincaid nodded, but his expression had grown slightly wary. "That was on Christmas Day. She was moored up above Barbridge then, on the Middlewich Branch. She asked us to come back yesterday—she said she'd let Kit steer the boat—but we didn't manage it."

"You didn't know her before that?"

"No. What are you getting at, Ronnie?" Kincaid asked, drawing closer so that he wouldn't be overheard. "And what did you mean when you said the woman we *met* as Annie Lebow?"

Babcock glanced down the path. There was still no sign of the techs or the pathologist. "Sheila," he called out, "can you rustle up an extra pair of gloves and some shoe covers?"

"Rustle up?" Kincaid repeated, one eyebrow raised. "I see you didn't outgrow your fondness for the Wild West."

Larkin, however, complied without hesitation. Digging in

the capacious pockets of her coat, she produced both gloves and elasticized paper shoe covers. "I'm a good Boy Scout, boss," she said with a cheeky grin. "Are you going aboard before the scene-of-crime lads get here?"

Although one of the bow doors stood slightly ajar, there was no other obvious sign of disturbance to the boat. "It doesn't look as though there was a struggle aboard, or a forced entry, so the killer may not have been on the boat at all. And we need a positive ID. We'll be careful." Handing Kincaid the gloves and one set of shoe covers, Babcock fit the other set over his shoes.

After a moment's hesitation, Kincaid followed suit. "You're the boss, mate."

The bow of the boat had drifted back to within a foot of the water's edge, and Babcock wanted to take advantage of the proximity. The hard border of the canal had been overgrown by turf, and as he knelt he immediately felt the sodden grass soak through the knees of his trousers. He leaned out, very much aware that if he fell headfirst into the canal, he would not only be likely to freeze to death, but that if he survived, he'd never live it down. He'd be known as "arse-up Babcock" until they pensioned him off.

His fingers caught the slippery gunwale, and held, but his jubilation was brief as he felt the boat's surprising resistance. For a moment, he hung suspended, knowing that if the boat moved the other way he would go with it; then the fates smiled on him and the *Horizon* slid smoothly into the bank.

One of the uniformed officers stepped forward and grabbed the gunwale so that Babcock was able to reach the rope that hung from the center fender, drifting in the water like a pale snake. The mooring pin that had once held the rope had left dark punctures in the grass, but there was no sign of the pin itself.

The uniformed constable slipped gloves from his pocket and took the rope from Babcock. "I'll take it, sir, until you get aboard and see if there's a spare pin."

Babcock climbed over the gunwale and Kincaid followed, his longer legs giving him the advantage. They both stood still, checking for any sign of disturbance, but Babcock saw no footprints, no mud or blood. The purr of the generator, which he had noticed only peripherally before, was more audible, but still barely louder than a human hum.

Easily locating a spare mooring pin in the tidy well deck, he handed it across to the constable, instructing him, "Place it as far from the original mooring as possible." Kincaid played out several feet of line from the bow stanchion and the officer moved back towards the stern, anchoring the pin well outside the trampled area around the original site.

"That should hold her, sir," the constable called, "even if it does rub up the paintwork a bit."

From this vantage point, Babcock could see faint light shining through the gap left by the open half of the cabin's double doors. He slipped on his gloves and, with a glance at Kincaid, pulled the door wide and stepped down into the salon.

"Holy shit." He stopped so suddenly that Kincaid bumped him from behind.

"My sentiments exactly, when I came aboard before," Kincaid said as Babcock moved aside to make room for him. Although the words were light, Babcock could hear the strain in his voice. He felt it, too, the overwhelming sense of a life interrupted.

Although the fire in the woodstove had gone cold, the radiators still pumped out heat; the lights still shone. A book lay open on an end table beside a half-empty mug of tea. A heavy insulated jacket hung on a hook set into the paneling near the bow doors.

"I'd never have expected a social worker—especially a retired social worker—to have this kind of money," Babcock said, still appraising the luxurious fittings. Put together with the pristine condition of the boat's exterior and expensively quiet generator, it shouted "no expense spared."

"Social worker?" Kincaid was obviously surprised. "She was a social worker? And you knew her?"

"I worked some cases with her. But then I heard she'd retired—oh, five, six years ago. Dropped off the map. Can't

say I blamed her, after the last case we dealt with together."

"Rough?" Kincaid asked.

"She'd placed a child in foster care. The parents were
drug users, couldn't stay clean. You know the story. Then
the foster father killed the kid. I think she blamed herself,
but it was the system." Babcock shrugged. "Sometimes you
just can't get it right."

Kincaid repeated his earlier question. "What did you
mean about her name. Was it not Lebow?"

"You're a persistent bastard." Babcock attempted a smile.
"When I knew her, her name was Constantine. I think her
husband was a journalist, but I'm not sure. She never really
talked about her private life." What he didn't say was that he
had been attracted to her. Not that she had given him any
encouragement, or that he would have done anything about
it if she had. Ironic, that he hadn't known then that all those
years of fidelity were a waste.

He felt another rush of queasiness as he tried to connect
the body on the towpath with the woman he had known. Annie had engaged life with an intensity that was seldom comfortable, and sometimes painful, for herself as well as others,
of that much he was certain.

"Was she divorced, then?" Kincaid asked, snapping Babcock back to the present.

"That could explain the name change, I suppose."

Frowning, Kincaid said, "When you knew her, did you
ever talk about James Hilton?"

Babcock gazed at him blankly, then realization dawned.
"The name of the boat. Yes, we did. I'd no idea she'd remembered." He shook his head, then scanned the cabin, forcing
himself to focus. "Has anything changed since you were
aboard?" The spare contemporary design of the decor made
the small space seem larger, and yet it was warmly comfortable. There were, however, no photographs. Perhaps she had
kept mementos and more personal items in the bedroom.

Kincaid shook his head. "There's certainly no obvious sign
of a struggle or an intruder. I'd guess she was interrupted

sometime last night—otherwise she'd have washed up." He gestured at the mug. "She didn't strike me as the type to leave things untidy."

"No." Babcock walked into the streamlined galley. "There's no sign of a meal, so either she cleaned up before she sat down with her tea, or she hadn't yet eaten." He checked the cupboards and the fridge, finding a few basic supplies, and a generous stock of both red and white wine. "She liked her tipple," he said, examining labels. "And she went to some trouble to get it. This is not the plonk you'd find at your local marina."

"A connoisseur? Or a comfort drinker?" Kincaid mused.

There was no television, Babcock realized. He thought of her, cocooned on her boat in the long winter evenings, and he could imagine that a glass of wine could easily have turned into three or four. "Why such an isolated mooring?" he asked as he moved into the passageway that led towards the stern. "You said she was up above Barbridge when you met her? If she'd stayed . . ."

"You're thinking wrong place, wrong time?" Kincaid shook his head. "With no sign of burglary or vandalism, or of sexual assault, a random killing seems unlikely. And even up on the Middlewich, there wasn't another boat moored in sight."

"So if someone had been stalking her, it wouldn't have made a difference?"

"It's early days yet, to make assumptions one way or the other."

Agreeing, Babcock continued on into the stateroom. It was as neat as the salon, and gave away as little about its occupant. The only photos were black-and-white reproductions of old canal boats. The built-in bed was made, the storage units closed, and there was no sign of personal papers or an address diary. The bedside table held only a book, an alarm clock, and an empty phone cradle. He was about to call out when Kincaid's voice came from the salon.

"There's a mobile phone on the floor, under her chair."

Returning to the salon, Babcock found Kincaid rising from his knees. He had left the phone in place, and almost immediately Babcock spied its silver gleam a foot back from the chair's edge. Kneeling himself, he edged the phone out with the tip of a gloved finger.

"It's closed, so it's unlikely she dropped it in mid-call."

"She might have set it in the chair and forgotten about it when she stood up," Kincaid offered.

Babcock flipped open the phone and checked the last number dialed. The display read "Roger," and the number was a Cheshire exchange.

"Ex-husband?" Kincaid asked, reading over his shoulder.

"I think so." He flipped through the phone's directory; there were no other numbers listed. Taking out his own mobile, he rang control and asked for a reverse look-up on the number.

"Roger Constantine," he informed Kincaid with satisfaction when he'd thanked the dispatcher and rung off. "An address in Tilston, near Malpas." That was the southwest corner of the county, equidistant from both the Shropshire and the Welsh borders.

"As good a place as any to start. Why don't—" Kincaid stopped, and Babcock wasn't sure if it was because he'd realized he wasn't the one giving the orders or if he'd heard the raised voices from the canal side.

"Sounds like we've got company," Babcock said, giving himself time to consider. He wouldn't mind having Kincaid's input, since he had met Annie Constantine so much more recently. And that would allow him to leave Larkin in charge of the scene here. "But you're right," he continued, "visiting Roger Constantine would be the obvious place to start, once I've organized the house-to-house—or maybe I should say boat-to-boat. I take it you'd like to tag along?"

"Boss." It was Larkin, calling from the bank. "The doc's here."

Babcock left the phone for the SOCOs to dissect, making a mental note to tell Travis exactly where they'd found it, then headed for the bow deck, followed by Kincaid.

By the time they reached solid ground, Dr. Elsworthy was already examining the body, her back to them. She had perfected the art of balancing in a flat-footed squat. She wore heavy trousers and a shapeless coat, and a few strands of gray hair had escaped from beneath her woolly gray hat. To the uninitiated, she might be mistaken for a bag lady searching for useful castoffs.

Kincaid, however, seemed unsurprised, and a hush fell over the group as they waited for her to finish.

When Dr. Elsworthy rose at last, her movements seemed slower than usual, and she held her knees for a moment as if they pained her. She turned, stripping off her latex gloves with a snap, and fixed Babcock with a glare. "As you may have gathered, the victim was struck on the back right-hand side of the head with a hard object, possibly your missing mooring pin. The external shape of the wound is compatible.

"Lividity is fixed, and rigor is fairly well established although not complete. I think you can assume death probably occurred sometime between six P.M. and midnight yesterday." Anticipating Babcock's groan, she pointed a finger at him. "You know the mitigating factors as well as I do, Chief Inspector. A night exposed to the elements would have retarded rigor, as would an unanticipated attack. There are no obvious defense wounds or signs of a struggle, nor indications of sexual interference."

As much as it galled him, Babcock knew she was right. If a victim fought his attacker, or ran just before death, the expenditure of ATP in the muscles could bring on almost immediate rigor, while the opposite was true as well. In a victim struck from behind, rigor might be delayed for several hours. There was another factor as well, one that Babcock didn't want to consider, but knew he must.

"Doc, was death instantaneous?"

"That I can't tell you, Ronnie, although I may be able to say more once I get her on the table." Elsworthy sighed and seemed to shrink a little inside her oversize coat. For the first time in Babcock's memory, she seemed human, and suddenly vulnerable. "I can tell you that the position of the body isn't natural—she didn't fall that way after the blow."

Babcock imagined Annie Constantine, snug in her salon,

suddenly feeling the boat drift from the bow. She'd have set down her drink and gone up top, leaving behind her heavy coat. Had she seen that the mooring rope was loose, and perhaps thought her knot had not held? She would have used a pole to push the boat back to the bank, then climbed ashore. Bending to retie the line, she would have seen that the mooring pin itself had gone.

But someone had been waiting, perhaps crouched in the shadow of the hedgerow. Had her assailant sprung out, hit her once, twice, running away as she struggled up and fell again before losing consciousness?

Or had he waited long enough to make sure his blow had done its work, then lifted or dragged her a few feet, to leave her lying as if she had simply fallen asleep?

Beside him, Kincaid spoke quietly, echoing his thoughts. "Why would he—or she—have moved the body? And was she still alive when he did?"

When Gemma had tucked Kit and Tess into the passenger seat of the Escort, she went round to the driver's side and started the car. The engine was still warm, and toasty air blasted from the heater vents. Kit let her fold the blanket she'd retrieved around him without protest, and in a few moments, he had stopped shivering.

"That's better," said Gemma, smiling at him as she warmed her fingers in the airflow.

"You'll use up all your petrol," Kit protested, but without much conviction.

"Better than you catching pneumonia. Or Tess."

"Dogs don't catch pneumonia," Kit retorted with returning spirit, but then his voice wavered and he added, "Do they?" He pulled Tess a little more firmly into his lap.

"I'm sure they don't," said Gemma, who wasn't sure at all, having never owned a dog before Tess and Geordie. "She has a fur coat, after all. Remember how much she loves going out in the garden at home when it's cold?"

Some of the anxious lines in Kit's face relaxed. "She'd watch squirrels in an arctic blizzard."

"And she's never been any the worse for it, so I'm sure

she's fine, now." Indeed, the little dog had closed her eyes, and began to snore very gently.

Gemma chose her next words carefully. She didn't want to damage the rapport they'd established, but something had been nagging at her ever since they'd found Kit's note. "You and Tess were out awfully early this morning," she said, without looking at him. "Did the little boys wake you?"

"No. They were still asleep. It was just that I . . . I had a bad dream." She heard the effort it took him to keep his voice as casual as hers.

For a moment, she watched the wind move the tops of the evergreens beyond the bridge. Then she asked, "Do you want to talk about it?"

"No!" The response had burst from him. "I mean . . . I don't really remember," he added after a moment, moderating his reply.

Gemma didn't press him, but she wasn't sure if her reluctance was due to sensitivity, or the fact that she was afraid to imagine what Kit's nightmares might hold.

Movement in her rearview mirror caught her eye. She watched as a moss-green Morris Minor inched past her in the lay-by, and blinked in surprise as baleful eyes peered back at her from a mammoth gray head resting on the rear seat back. Then the head disappeared as the Morris Minor stopped some yards ahead in a spot kept clear by the uniformed constable, and a figure climbed from the driver's seat. At first Gemma thought it was a rather shabbily dressed man, but a few gray curls peeked from beneath a woolen hat, and she saw a flash of a profile that was definitely feminine. The removal of a black medical bag and the hurried conference with the constable narrowed the identification further. This must be the pathologist. Nothing emerged from the rear of the car, however, and Gemma wondered if she had imagined the beast.

She turned to Kit for confirmation, but his eyes were downcast, and he was stroking Tess's head with a studied concentration.

"I'm sorry about your friend," Gemma said gently. If he

needed to talk about what had happened, she would give him the opportunity.

He nodded, but didn't speak, and Gemma waited with the hard-won patience her job had taught her. At last, Kit's hand fell still and he glanced at her, then away.

"She was all right yesterday," he said, his voice thick with emotion. "If I hadn't— If I'd stayed—I might have stopped it somehow—"

Gemma's breath caught in surprise. "You saw her yesterday?"

"I was with Lally and her friend Leo. She—Annie—asked us to come aboard, but I said no. I didn't want to take anyone else on the boat. I thought—" Kit stopped, flushing, and scrubbed at his cheeks with the back of his hand.

Her own throat tightening, Gemma said, "You liked her, and that felt special. You didn't want to share it with anyone else."

Kit shot her a grateful look and nodded.

"I can understand that," Gemma continued, frowning. "But why do you think it would have changed anything if you'd stayed? Did you see something, or someone, while you were there?" The car had warmed, and she reached out and switched off the ignition.

In the sudden silence, Kit said haltingly, "No. But if he—whoever did that to her—if he'd seen me, he'd have known she wasn't alone, and he might not—"

"No, Kit, you can't think that." Gemma was horrified. What if this woman's killer had expected to find her alone, and discovered Kit there as well?

She swallowed, and made an effort to reassure him. "First of all, even if you had gone aboard, you wouldn't have stayed more than a few minutes. And that was in the middle of the afternoon, wasn't it, when you went after Lally?"

Kit nodded, and Gemma continued, "From what you've told us, I'd say it was very unlikely your friend was killed during the day." The violence of the crime made it more probable that it had been committed under cover of darkness, although there was no guarantee. She suddenly wished desperately that she could see the crime scene and hear what the pathologist had to say. Had the murder been random, combined with a sexual assault or a burglary gone wrong? Or had this woman been targeted?

None of these were speculations she could share with Kit, nor did she feel she could interrogate him about the state of his friend's body. She would just have to wait for Kincaid's report. There was one thing, however, that she could pursue.

"Kit, you said that *he* might not have hurt her if you'd been there. Did you see something that made you think Annie's attacker was a man?"

"No, but . . ." His cheeks grew a little paler. "I suppose I just didn't think a woman could have done . . . that."

Gemma wished she still had his innocence, that she hadn't seen firsthand the damage that women could do. And yet, statistically, he was right—an assault was more likely to have been committed by a male.

From her side mirror, Gemma saw that the pub had apparently stirred to life. A woman came out, bearing a large thermos and a stack of polystyrene cups, and headed towards the nearest uniformed officer.

Raising her hand, Gemma placed the backs of her fingers gently against Kit's cheek, and found his skin still cold to the touch. "Look, the publican's bringing out hot drinks," she said. She recognized the woman who had been serving at the bar the previous afternoon. "Shall I fetch you something?"

"No. I had some coffee earlier." Kit grimaced. "One of the neighbors made a cup for me. It wasn't at all like we make at home." Kit liked to cook breakfast on the weekends, and they had bought an espresso machine primarily so that Kit and Toby could have steamed milk as a special treat, Kit's mixed with a bit of coffee. Homesickness shot through Gemma like a physical pain, and she could only imagine how Kit must be feeling.

"I think I'll have some myself, then. Back in a tick," she added as she took the excuse to slide out of the car, not wanting him to see her face.

She introduced herself to the uniformed officer, showing him her police ID, and to the manageress of the pub. She was sipping what turned out to be scalding-hot and quite respectably good coffee when she saw movement on the bridge. It was the pathologist, trudging back towards her car with her bag, her face set in an abstracted scowl.

"The good Dr. E. looks even less happy than usual," the constable muttered.

"Dr. E.?" asked Gemma. "She's the Home Office pathologist?"

"Dr. Elsworthy." He raised his cup and drained it without a wince before handing it back to the pub's manageress. Gemma thought his mouth must be lined with asbestos. "Ta," he said. "I'd better get back to my post. Don't want the doc to set her dog on me."

"So I did see a dog," Gemma murmured to his retreating back.

The manageress gave her an odd look, but asked, "Is it true that someone's been killed?" It was clear her agenda didn't include the discussion of dogs, imaginary or otherwise. "Do you know who it is?"

"The police won't release that information until family have been notified, ma'am," Gemma answered, avoiding the second question, at least. There was no hope of stonewalling on the first—the human grapevine worked too well.

"I don't know what this will do to my lunch business," the woman said with a sigh. "The roadblock will keep the clientele away."

"I'm sure your customers will find a way to get here. Curiosity will overcome a little minor inconvenience, believe me," Gemma reassured her. "This will be gossip central, once the news gets round, and you might be prepared for some journalists, too.

"That's true." The woman brightened, then frowned again. "I wonder if I've *enough* laid in. I'd better start prep, then." With a distracted nod at Gemma, she turned back to the pub, leaving Gemma with her still-scalding cup of coffee.

"Thanks," Gemma called after her, belatedly. Turning back to the car, she saw that Kit had leaned back against the headrest, his eyes closed, his lips parted in the relaxation of unexpected sleep. He looked as young and defenseless as Toby, and her chest tightened with a fierce, possessive love. She would have done anything to protect him from this— Kit, the last person who needed another blow, another loss, in his short life.

She stood irresolute, not wanting to wake him by getting back into the car, sipping her coffee and gazing at the boats along the canal bank. Lined up nose to tail, they reminded her of a drawing of circus animals leading one another in a parade in one of Toby's books.

She had seen narrowboats on the Grand Union Canal near the supermarket where she shopped at home, but had never been aboard one. Those had charmed her with their rooftop flowerpots and haphazardly strung laundry, their slightly shabby air of rakishness.

Most of the boats below, however, were buttoned up against the cold like sensible matrons, and looked rather forlornly abandoned. But a spiral of smoke issued from the chimney of one of the more colorful crafts, and as she watched, a man came out of the cabin and looked round, briefly, before going back inside.

The sound of a car door slamming made Gemma turn, thinking that Kit had awakened, but to her surprise she saw the doctor climbing from her car once more. This time she held not her bag, but some sort of bulky equipment that on closer inspection Gemma thought was an oxygen tank.

The doctor crossed the bridge again, but rather than turning right, she went to the left, back towards the boats clustered across from the pub. She stopped beside the brightly colored narrowboat Gemma had noticed before and seemed about to call out, but before she could speak, the cabin door opened.

This time, Gemma caught a glimpse of a curly-headed child, then the doctor climbed awkwardly aboard and went inside. Since when, Gemma wondered, did pathologists make house calls?

A touch on her shoulder made her jump, but even as she

drew breath to gasp, Kincaid said, "Sorry, love. I didn't mean to give you a fright. You were miles away."

Turning, she examined his face. His voice had been even, uninflected, but she detected a familiar undercurrent of tension. "Was it bad?" she asked, nodding in the direction of the crime scene.

"Mmmm." He made a noise of assent in his throat. "No sign of sexual interference, though, thank God. At least Kit was spared that. And not much blood, other than beneath the head. But . . ." He stopped, jamming his hands in his coat hard enough to tear holes in his pockets, not meeting her eyes. "But I can't imagine, when he saw her lying there, that he didn't think of his mum. How is he?"

Gemma looked back towards the car. Kit's head had tilted to one side as he'd fallen into a deeper sleep, and Tess had moved to the driver's seat. "He's exhausted," she said. "As much from trying to hold himself together as anything else, I think. We need to get him home."

"Home." Kincaid repeated the word under his breath, frowning, as if making sense of a foreign language, and gazed abstractedly at the canal.

"What—" Gemma had begun, when he turned to her and gripped her shoulders with almost painful force.

"Right," he said. "You're absolutely right. As soon as Babcock gets Kit's statement, we'll pack up and head back to London. There's no reason we should stay here, no reason Kit should be involved in this any further. We can go home."

Gemma stared at him, galvanized by the thought. In just a few hours, they could be back in the safe haven of their house in Notting Hill, removed from thoughts of disintegrating marriages and dead babies, away from the horror of a violent death that encroached on their personal lives.

After all, Duncan and Kit had met the woman only briefly—surely they had no obligation to do more than was legally necessary. And Rosemary and Hugh would understand; they would know that Kit was the last child who should be subjected to such stress.

Glancing towards the car, she saw Kit turn restlessly in his sleep, his lips moving, but the intervening glass muffled any sound. She recalled the things he had said to her in the car, and slowly, reluctantly, shook her head.

"No," she said. "I don't think we can, I think we have to see this through. I think we have to let *Kit* see this through."

"But—"

"It's all mixed up in his mind," Gemma continued, certain that she was right. "This woman's death and his mother's. He feels responsible, as if he somehow failed them both. And if we take him away, he'll just carry that burden with him, wherever he goes. We can't let that happen."

# 17

❧

ALTHEA ELSWORTHY stowed her medical bag in the boot, then climbed gratefully into the relative warmth of the car. Danny, who had sat up at her approach, rested his chin on the seat back and looked at her expectantly. Usually, when she returned to the car, she gave him a biscuit from the large plastic tub she kept on the floor in the front. Of course, he was quite capable of chewing through the container and helping himself, but he was an obedient dog and had never taken advantage of her absence.

"You're a good boy," she said, as she always did, and popped open the tub. Danny took the proferred biscuit delicately, but as he crunched the treat he scattered crumbs and spittle on the towel she kept draped over the seat back for just that purpose.

Ritual satisfied, he settled down again on the seat with his head on his paws, watching her with an eternal canine optimism she wished she shared.

While he trusted that she knew what to do next, she was struggling to understand the action she'd just taken—or perhaps it would be more accurate to say "not taken."

Why had she remained silent? An easy enough explanation was that the first sight of Annie Lebow's body had left her simply too stunned to speak. Her lack of intimation seemed odd now. There had been no frisson of foreknowledge when the call came asking her to attend the body of a woman found dead on the towpath below Barbridge. Most likely a jogger struck down by a heart attack, she'd thought, and had merely been thankful that the location of the body would make it easy for her to call in on the Wains. Not even the sight of the boat had cued her.

But her job required a memory for physical detail, and the fleece top had provided the first jolt of recognition. Then the leather boating shoes, one separated from the foot and lying on its side, as if it had been casually kicked free. After that, the sight of the fair hair, now matted, and the strong jaw, half hidden by the raised forearm, had merely served as confirmation.

Beyond that point, her failure to admit she knew the victim became harder to justify. If Ronnie Babcock hadn't been belowdecks, perhaps she would have spoken to him then, when she'd got her breath back from the first shock. But there had only been his green detective constable, hovering, so she'd waited, trying to concentrate on the task at hand, trying to distance herself from the vision of Annie Lebow's animated face seen just the previous day.

And then, when Babcock had climbed up from the depths of the boat, with him had been a tall, sharp-eyed man whom Babcock had introduced as a Scotland Yard superintendent. No explanation had been given as to why, or how so quickly, the Yard had been called to the scene of a rural suspicious death, but Althea had felt her heart give an unexpected lurch.

She'd realized that if she admitted her recent connection with Annie, she'd have to explain about the Wains.

But now that she'd had a few moments to think, doubt assailed her. Was it just coincidence that Annie Lebow had encountered a family she hadn't seen since she'd left Social Services, then been killed? Could Gabriel Wain have had something to do with Annie's death? And if so, why? Gabriel might have accepted Annie's help grudgingly, but Althea couldn't imagine that he would have harmed her.

With sudden impatience, she thrust her uncertainties aside. She had promised to help Rowan Wain, and now it seemed more important than ever that she keep her word. No matter that she'd have to wade through the local constabulary in order to visit the boat—if anyone inquired, she'd simply tell the truth. She was visiting a patient.

Still, she looked round before getting out of the car, and it was only when the officer watching over the bridge had gone to consult with one of his mates farther up the lane that she retrieved the oxygen tank from the boot and started for the boat. There was no point in complicating matters unnecessarily, she told herself briskly, but she couldn't shake the unsettling feeling that she was being watched.

Although Kincaid usually disliked being driven by someone he didn't know well, he made an effort to relax into the padded leather passenger seat of Ronnie Babcock's BMW. He told himself he should appreciate the chance to concentrate on the landscape and clear his mind for the interview to come.

In the end, it had been Gemma who'd insisted he go with Babcock to see Roger Constantine. Listening in on Babcock's interview with Kit had been enough to convince him that Gemma was right—they couldn't just walk away from this and pretend nothing had happened. And if that was the case, she'd argued, it made sense for him to make use of his connection with Babcock, especially as Babcock seemed willing to accommodate him. He'd just have to be careful to maintain his role as spectator, as he suspected Babcock would draw the line at active interference in his investigation.

"You said this fellow Constantine was a journalist?" he asked Babcock. "I wonder at our odds of catching him at home."

Babcock narrowed his eyes in an effort of recall. "I think I remember Annie saying he was a features writer for one of the major northwest papers. Of course, we could have tried contacting him by phone first, but I'd prefer to break bad news in person if at all possible." It sounded compassionate, but Kincaid knew there was calculation attached—it always paid to see the first reactions of those closest to the victim.

"Then we'll hope he works from home, or that journalists

take a long Christmas holiday." Kincaid resisted the urge to pump an imaginary brake as Babcock slowed sharply for a slow-moving farm lorry. When the way was clear, Babcock downshifted and zipped round it with ease. The road had begun to twist and turn, making an ideal showcase for the BMW's power and maneuverability.

The character of the countryside changed rapidly as one traveled west from Nantwich. Within just a few miles, the land rose from the flat of the Cheshire Plain into gently wooded undulations, and the simple brick farmhouses began to sport brightly colored gingerbread trim. Kincaid had never learned what had inspired the architectural embellishments, but when he was a boy, the decoration had made him think of cottages in enchanted Germanic forests. The childhood that had allowed such imaginings now seemed impossibly distant, and the loss of his son's opportunity for such innocence struck him as forcibly as a blow.

Ronnie Babcock took his eyes from the road to glance at Kincaid. "I know what you're thinking."

"Sorry?" Kincaid responded.

Babcock said, "You're remembering the Ford Anglia I had at school."

Relieved, Kincaid said lightly, "Of course. But I never had the dubious pleasure of riding in it." He recalled the car well, though, a 1966 Saloon special with Venetian-gold paintwork, held together with considerable assistance from baling wire. Ronnie had worked several after-school jobs to save the money for it, and the car had been his pride and joy.

"A good thing, too," Babcock agreed. "I had a passenger or two fall out through the floorboards. I was thinking of building a roof ejector when the old girl finally clapped out on me."

"You've done well for yourself, Ronnie." Kincaid's gesture took in the BMW, but he meant more than that.

Babcock gave a sardonic smile. "I suppose I have. Just look at me now—overworked, with an overly mortgaged unheated house, and no one but an elderly aunt for company. Just what any working-class lad should strive for."

"You're not married, then?"

"Divorced. Just this last year." Babcock's grimace was worth a thousand words. "What about you? Why haven't you and the lovely Gemma tied the knot?"

Taken aback, Kincaid glanced at his friend, but Babcock's eyes were on the road.

"It's complicated," he said slowly. "In the beginning, we were working together, so I suppose we got in the habit of being secretive. You know how it is. It would have been all right for me if it had come out, just a bit of nudge, nudge, wink, wink from the worst tossers in the locker room, that sort of thing. But for Gemma, it would have meant a permanent shadow on her career. There would always have been whispers that she'd slept her way into promotions, no matter how capable she proved herself." Even now, the unfairness of it made his blood pressure rise, and he shook his head in disgust before going on. "So when she made inspector and transferred to another posting, we more or less kept on as we were. But then . . ." Kincaid hesitated.

"Then we found out that Gemma was pregnant. We moved in together, but I—I think neither of us wanted to feel that—"

"Marriage was a necessity of circumstance?" Babcock finished for him when he halted again. "That would have been a blow to your pride."

Kincaid nodded, feeling his face flush at the accuracy of the hit. "Just so. It seems unutterably selfish now."

Frowning, Babcock said, "But it's been some time, hasn't it? I met your younger boy, when I came to the house."

"Oh, no," Kincaid hastened to explain. "Toby is Gemma's son, from her first marriage. We—Gemma lost our baby, halfway to term. That was a year ago."

"Oh, Jesus." Babcock looked at him, his battered face creased in sympathy. "That's a bloody shame."

Not trusting himself to accept the commiseration, Kincaid went on, "Since then, we've just sort of muddled along, the four of us living as a family. Not unhappily," he amended, afraid his words had implied that. "It's just that—I don't know if she'd have chosen differently, you see, if it hadn't been for the child." Kincaid realized it was the first time he'd admitted his fear, even to himself, and he felt suddenly as exposed as if he'd laid bare his chest to the knife.

"You could ask her," Babcock suggested, as if it were the most reasonable response imaginable.

"Christ, no." Kincaid shook his head. "I'd be forcing her into a corner then, and if she told me what I wanted to hear, I'd never be sure if she was being honest or just kind." He thought of her refusal to discuss trying for another child, and felt cold.

He searched for a change of subject, glad that Babcock was momentarily distracted as he downshifted and left the A49 for a B road signposted NO MAN'S HEATH. "That sounds a desolate place," Kincaid offered, a little too quickly.

"A bit Shakespearean," Babcock agreed. "But there's a nice pub there, as it happens. That's why I came this way, I suppose. Old habits." With that ambiguous and uninviting comment, he fell silent, leaving Kincaid to gaze at the scenery and wonder about his friend's reticence.

They were nearing the Welsh border, and he could see that it had snowed more heavily here. Snow still lingered on the eaves of the isolated farmhouses, and as they passed through the pretty redbrick hill town of Malpas, the anti-icing grit crunched under the BMW's tires.

A few miles farther north, the tree-lined lane dipped and curved into the hamlet of Tilston. Although they slowed to a crawl, reading the address plaques on the cottages and suburban bungalows lining the road, they still missed Roger Constantine's house the first time past. The steep entrance to its drive faced away from them, so that they only saw the address when they had turned around at the postage stamp of a village green and come back from the opposite direction.

In a village of cottages and suburban bungalows, the Victorian lodge stood on a high bank above the road, screened from below by the large trees and shrubs of a mature garden.

"Blimey," Babcock said eloquently as they bumped up the narrow gravel drive and pulled to a stop on the forecourt. "Nice digs for a journalist, wouldn't you say?"

Kincaid had to agree. The house's brick facade was a mellow rose rather than the harsh burnt red used often in Cheshire and North Wales, and the gleaming white trim looked freshly painted. "Maybe he's sold a few exclusives to the *Sun*," Kincaid quipped.

"My ex-wife would have killed for this," Babcock muttered as they climbed from the car and crossed the raked gravel of the drive.

Kincaid merely nodded. He felt the weight of the coming interview descend on him—he had never learned to bear bad tidings easily. He took a preparatory breath, but before they reached the porch, the front door opened and a large German shepherd charged out at them. Kincaid's life flashed before his eyes in the instant it took him to see that the dog was firmly attached to a lead held by a slight man with trimmed white hair and beard.

"Can I help you?" the man asked, reining the dog in with an admonishing "Jazz, easy."

The dog subsided into a sit at the man's left knee, but whined in protest.

"Are you Roger Constantine?" Babcock asked warily, having backed off a pace.

"Yes. What can I do for you?" Constantine was frowning now, and it occurred to Kincaid for the first time that in their casual clothes neither he nor Babcock radiated official import. The man probably thought they were selling double glazing.

Babcock took out his warrant card and displayed it as carefully as if Constantine were holding a loaded gun instead of the now-panting dog. "I'm Chief Inspector Babcock, Cheshire constabulary, and this is Superintendent Kincaid. Sorry to barge in on you unannounced—"

"Look, if this is about the gang story, I've already told your colleagues I can't divulge—"

"No, this is a personal matter, Mr. Constantine. If we could speak to you inside." Babcock made a statement of the question, and the first flash of uneasiness crossed Constantine's face. Kincaid saw now that the white hair and beard had given a misleading impression of the man's age;

Constantine's face was unlined, and the eyes behind the gold-rimmed spectacles were sharp and a very pale blue.

"All right," Constantine agreed reluctantly, and in an aside to the dog added, "You'll have to wait for your walk, Jazzy." He turned to the door, motioning to them as he opened it. When he noticed Babcock still hesitating, he said, "Oh. Don't mind the dog. He's quite friendly, really."

Kincaid went first, holding out a hand, palm down, for the dog to sniff. While the dog investigated the scents on his clothes, his tail now wagging, Kincaid took in the interior of the house with equal interest. An archway opened the central hall onto a sitting room to the left. Deep gold walls and white trim set off the gilded frames of pictures and mirrors and a beautiful black-and-white tile floor. Small touches—a potted fern on a stand, a few items of well-made caned furniture scattered among heavier items—hinted at the Victorian history of the house.

Through an open door on the right, he glimpsed a plum-colored dining room filled with rich mahogany furniture, then Constantine was ushering them into a combined kitchen–sitting room at the back of the house.

Immediately, he saw that they had stepped offstage. This room, while expensively done with the requisite Aga and custom cabinetry, was cluttered with books and papers and used mugs. A laptop computer stood open on the large oak table, and a dog bed festooned with chew toys lay near the stove. The room still held the comforting breakfast scents of toast and coffee, with a faint underlying note of dog.

"I suppose you'd better sit," said Constantine, scooping papers from two chairs and dumping them onto the already overflowing surface of a Welsh dresser. "Jazz, lie down on your bed," he commanded the dog.

He took the chair by the laptop himself, and waited with an air of contained impatience for them to get on with whatever it was they wanted.

After a relieved glance at the dog's retreating hindquarters, Babcock began, "Mr. Constantine, am I right in thinking that at one time you were married to Annie Constantine?"

Constantine frowned. "What do you mean, 'were married'? We're still married."

Babcock flicked a startled glance in Kincaid's direction before continuing. "Then you and your wife maintain separate domiciles?"

"Yes. She lives aboard her boat, although I don't see why our marital arrangements are any business of yours. What's going on here?" There was tension in his voice now, a thread of fear beneath the annoyance. Constantine was a journalist; although Babcock hadn't identified Kincaid as Scotland Yard, he would realize that two senior police officers even of local jurisdiction didn't make routine inquiries.

"But your wife uses the name Lebow?" Babcock used the present tense carefully.

"Sometimes. It's her maiden name. Look, what's this about?"

The dog, which had been watching with its head on its paws, sat up and whined.

Babcock sat forward, his eyes fixed on Roger Constantine's face. "Mr. Constantine, I'm sorry to tell you that your wife was found dead this morning."

"What?" Constantine stared at them. Light caught the reflective surface of his glasses, momentarily masking his eyes. "Is this some sort of joke? I just spoke to her last night. There must be a mistake."

"No, sir. Mr. Cons—"

"It can't have been Annie." Constantine gripped the edge of the table, as if assailed by sudden vertigo, and it occurred to Kincaid that in his experience, women often accepted the news of a tragedy more quickly than men. It was as if women carried with them a constant intimation of mortality, while men assumed that both they and their loved ones were invincible.

"I knew your wife, Mr. Constantine," Babcock said quietly. "I worked with her several times before she retired from Social Services. I identified her body myself."

In the silence that followed, Kincaid imagined he heard the painful beat of his own heart. Then the dog rose, and the click of its nails on the tile brought a faint relief. It crossed to its master and laid its head on Constantine's knee.

The man loosed one visibly trembling hand from the table and buried it in the ruff of the dog's neck. "Oh, no. Christ. What—" He swallowed and tried again. "What happened? Was she ill? Was there an accident with the boat?"

A slight nod from Babcock surprised Kincaid, but he took up the cue. It was a useful technique, handing off the questioning from the person who had broken the news. "It looks as though your wife was attacked, Mr. Constantine. Sometime yesterday evening. What time did you speak with her?"

"Attacked? But why would—"

"I know this is difficult, Mr. Constantine," Kincaid said. "But if you could just bear with us. It's important that we get the details." He held Constantine's gaze, and after a moment Constantine nodded and seemed to make an effort to pull himself together.

"It was—it must have been about eight. We'd just come back from our after-dinner walk. I was surprised when I saw it was Annie ringing, because she had just called the day before, to wish me happy Christmas. But she said she wanted to make a date for dinner—tonight—I was supposed to see her tonight." Shaking his head, Constantine pulled off his glasses and rubbed at his reddening eyes.

"Did she give a particular reason?"

"No. She just said she wanted to talk."

Kincaid thought about the reserved woman he had met, and he couldn't help comparing the almost Spartan neatness of the *Lost Horizon* with the jumble of this room. It seemed an unlikely juxtaposition. "Mr. Constantine, I know you said you and your wife lived separately. Would you say you were estranged?"

"No. At least not in the ordinary sense of having had a quarrel or disagreement, if that's what you mean." Constantine seemed almost eager to talk now. "I know our living arrangements seem odd to other people, but our lives just diverged. She likes being on her own—she had some things she needed to sort out, after she left her job. And I was happy enough to stay on here, to look after the house. We were—we never saw a need to consider divorce."

"But you talked often?"

"Fairly often. Sometimes I wouldn't hear from her for a few weeks. That usually meant she was having a bad time." Constantine looked from Kincaid to Babcock. "You're certain she didn't—"

"There's no question that your wife harmed herself, Mr. Constantine," Kincaid said, and saw an easing of the other man's features. Why this should be a reassurance, why suicide should seem worse than murder, he didn't know— perhaps it was that the suicide of a loved one carried with it such responsibility for those left behind.

"Then if she— Was she robbed? I kept telling her— She didn't have anything of value really, but the boat itself—" Constantine stood suddenly, running both hands through his already bristling white hair as if he could no longer contain his agitation.

Babcock stepped in. "There's no sign that anything was taken from the boat, or from your wife's person. We will, of course, need you to look things over for us at some point to confirm this."

"But then—" Constantine's eyes were wide, the pupils dilated. The dog nudged his knee, whining, but he ignored it. "Then what the hell happened to my wife?" he said, his voice rising. "What aren't you telling me?"

Babcock hesitated, and Kincaid guessed he was weighing the disadvantages of revealing the manner of death against his obligation to provide information to a grieving spouse. Constantine had said nothing to indicate any knowledge of the circumstances, and they wouldn't be able to keep it to themselves for long in any case. "Your wife's body was found on the towpath, not on the boat, Mr. Constantine," Babcock said at last. "Someone hit her over the head."

"Oh, Jesus." Grasping the chair back, Constantine eased himself into it again without looking, like a blind man. "Why would anyone want to hurt my wife?"

"We were hoping you might be able to tell us that."

"Annie never harmed anyone— For God's sake, she hardly spoke to anyone." Constantine's tone was accusatory. "She wasn't—tell me she wasn't—" His face lost its little remaining color.

With surprising gentleness, Babcock said, "Your wife does not appear to have been sexually molested."

Constantine dropped his face into his hands and sat, unmoving.

After a moment, Kincaid rose and went to the sink, finding a glass in the second cupboard he opened. As he filled it from the tap, he noticed a dusting of fine white hairs on the dark blue tile of the work top. It appeared that Roger Constantine and his German shepherd shared their household with a cat. He wondered if the cat had been Annie's, and if so, why she had left it behind. He could imagine her with a cat, a tidy beast that echoed her reserve.

The water from the tap was icy and he held the glass for a moment, feeling the coolness against his fingertips as he gazed out the window above the sink. It overlooked the side garden, a swath of green winter grass studded with the bare silhouettes of fruit trees. In spring, when the trees were in bloom, it must be magnificent. What could have moved Annie Lebow to give all this up for life on a seven-by-sixty-foot boat, no matter how well outfitted?

He returned to the table and touched Roger Constantine on the shoulder. Looking up, Constantine took the glass and drained it as thirstily as a parched wanderer in the desert.

"Thanks," Constantine said hoarsely as he set the empty tumbler on the table, then rubbed the back of his hand across his tear-streaked cheek. "I'm sorry, I didn't think—there's tea if you want."

"No, we're fine." Kincaid sat again, this time in the chair nearest Constantine, and took the liberty of stroking the dog's thick coat. "Mr. Constantine—Roger—do you mind if I call you Roger?" Without waiting for Constantine's assent, he went on, "Roger, do you and your wife own this house jointly?"

Constantine looked a little surprised at the question, but

not alarmed. "No. Actually, it's Annie's family home. She inherited the place when her parents died. Merchant pirates, she liked to call the Lebows. Her great-great-great-grandfather started with one ship out of Liverpool, and had built this place as a weekend getaway in the country by the time he retired."

"Quite an accomplishment."

"Yes, but Annie was always a little ashamed of the family history. She felt their fortune was built on exploiting the poor. I think it's one of the reasons she went into social work—as a sort of penance."

That would explain a good bit, Kincaid thought, including the means for the early retirement and the fact that even her self-imposed exile had reflected the best money could buy. He wondered if she had seen the irony of it.

It also opened up a Pandora's box of questions, and he saw Babcock sit up a bit straighter, suddenly alert with interest.

"Your wife owned this place in its entirety, and she was content to let you stay here like a lodger?" Babcock raised a skeptical eyebrow.

"Yes. We were married, for God's sake," Constantine answered defensively. "I told you—"

"It's a nice deal, you have to admit." Babcock shook his head. "My ex should have been half so generous. And who stands to inherit, if your wife was the last of her family?"

"I do, as far as I know." Constantine stared at him, the color rising in his fair skin. "You're not suggesting I killed my wife for this house! That's obscene."

The dog tensed at his master's tone, its hackles rising, and began a low, steady growl, just above the threshold of hearing. Withdrawing his hand, Kincaid wished he hadn't sat quite so close to the beast.

"It is a substantial property," said Babcock, undaunted. "Worth a pretty penny on the market, if one were a bit short of the ready. Did you carry life insurance on your wife, by the way?" he added conversationally.

After a moment, Constantine answered reluctantly. "Yes. We insured one another, years ago, when we were first married.

It's a small premium—I've never thought to change it." He looked from Babcock to Kincaid, outrage turning to appeal. "Jesus Christ. You can't think—"

"Mr. Constantine," asked Babcock, "what did you do last night, after your wife rang you?"

For the first time Kincaid thought he glimpsed a flicker of terror in the man's eyes. "Nothing," Constantine said. "I mean, I was here, working on a piece." He gestured at the books and papers covering the table. "I'm up against a deadline."

Babcock's smile held all the warmth of a shark bite. "Is there anyone who can verify that, Mr. Constantine, other than your dog?"

# 18

❧

**THE TAG END** of the crime-scene tape rose and fluttered, briefly animated by a gust of wind, then it dropped, hanging limply beside its anchoring stake as though exhausted by its effort. Gemma and Juliet Newcombe stood outside the tape's boundary, surveying the ruin of Juliet's building site.

A sea of muck stretched before them, the sodden ground pockmarked by the treads of heavy equipment and human boots. The prospect was as desolate as the moon, and a good bit messier. Figures in overalls came and went from the shell of the dairy barn, and the sporadic sounds of hammering and banging echoed like shotgun retorts in the cold air.

Juliet stared, her face stamped with dismay, then fury seemed to propel her into motion. She ducked under the tape and set off across the muck like a Valkyrie going to battle. Gemma, with a wince of regret for her London shoes, followed more carefully, wondering what she had got herself into.

Even though she'd urged Kincaid to go with Chief Inspector Babcock, she hadn't been prepared for the frustration that had gripped her as she watched them drive away.

On returning to the farmhouse, it had been a relief when Rosemary and Hugh insisted on taking the children into the shop with them. Juliet had said quietly that she meant to get some things from her house, as she knew Caspar had an appointment out of Nantwich that morning. Juliet hadn't asked for help, but her nervousness had been obvious, and when

Gemma offered to accompany her, she accepted without argument.

First, however, Juliet had been determined to check on her building site, in hopes that the police would be finished and she could get her crew back to work. That that wasn't going to happen anytime soon was all too obvious.

"Hey, you!" A beefy man wearing a police safety jacket thrown over his suit had spied Juliet. Breaking off his conference with one of the overalled men, he charged towards them. "What the hell do you think you're doing? Can't you see this is restricted?"

"What the hell do you think *you're* doing?" Juliet shouted back. "This is my job site. What are you doing to my building?"

The man didn't need the police jacket for identification—he had "copper" written all over him, subtitled "copper in a bad temper over his assignment." His face took on a deeper hue of puce. "Look, lady—"

"It's not 'lady,' " Gemma said icily, stepping forward. "It's Mrs. Newcombe. And I'm Detective Inspector James, Metropolitan Police."

"Yeah, right, and I'm the Queen Mum," he answered. "I'm not going to tell you two a—" He stopped, his mouth hanging open unflatteringly midword, and the florid color drained from his face. Gemma had pulled her identification from her bag and raised it to his eye level.

"Shit," he said succinctly, then looked even more horrified. "Sorry, ma'am. I didn't realize—"

"Whatever happened to community policing?" Gemma asked with cutting sarcasm. "Where I come from, we generally try to establish a good relationship with the tax-paying public, as difficult as that may be."

"I didn't know—"

"I don't care if you thought we were the local bag ladies." A glance at Juliet's anxious face reminded Gemma that, while she might be enjoying this little skirmish, it wasn't doing anything to ease her companion's mind. She summoned a smile. "Look. Sergeant, is it?" It was an educated guess, considering that Babcock had left him overseeing a less than glamorous job while the DCI hared off after a fresh murder, and his instant deferral to her rank made it unlikely he was an inspector himself.

"Rasansky, ma'am," he answered, tight-lipped.

"Sergeant Rasansky, what *is* going on here? Have you found something new?"

"No, ma'am. The DCI ordered a deconstruction crew. Waste of time, if you ask me."

"Deconstruction?" Juliet grasped Gemma's arm. "What does that mean?"

"Just what it sounds, I'm afraid," Gemma answered with a sigh. "It means that Chief Inspector Babcock thinks there's a possibility that where there was one body, there might be more. It wouldn't be the first time."

"But—" Juliet took an involuntary step forward, but stopped when she saw Rasansky's glare. "But that mortar work over the old manger was the only sign of disturbance—"

"Nevertheless, he's got to be thorough." Gemma thought of the horrors discovered in the garden and cellar of Fred and Rosemary West's Gloucestershire home, a lesson no British police officer was likely to forget. Babcock didn't know enough at this point to rule out multiple murders.

"But this will delay construction for months. The Bonners might even pull out altogether." Juliet looked close to tears. "Can't I at least oversee what they're doing so that they damage things as little as possible?"

Her distress seemed to soften Rasansky's attitude. "I'm sorry, miss. It's strictly authorized personnel. But this crew's good, and I'm sure you'll be compensated for any damages." He seemed to have recovered some of his assurance, however, and fixed Gemma with a hard stare. "If you don't mind me asking, ma'am, what's the Met got to do with this?"

"We're consulting with DCI Babcock," she said briskly. "I'd like to have a look round the perimeter while I'm here, but you needn't trouble yourself. I'll let you know if I have any further questions." She nodded at him while taking a firm grip on Juliet's arm and turning her in the direction of the canal.

Juliet began to protest as Gemma led her towards the humpbacked bridge. "What are we—"

"I've no authority to pull rank on him, or to poke about, and I'd just as soon he not realize it," Gemma whispered. "But I do want to have a look at the canal from here."

They picked their way through ruts and pools of slush until they reached the old stone bridge. "It doesn't go anywhere," Gemma said in surprise when they stopped on the slight rise at the bridge's center. A green-and-brown checkerboard of fields stretched away on the other side, bordered by a distant line of trees.

"It does." Juliet smiled a little for the first time that morning. "It gives access to the towpath. There are any number of bridges like this on the waterways."

Gemma turned, slowly, as the wind tugged at her coat with probing fingers. The haze that had dulled the morning at Barbridge had condensed into solid cloud, and the gray bowl of the sky seemed to press down on the landscape. The canal beneath them, unruffled by the wind, held the sky in mirrored perfection.

To the north, a half dozen narrowboats were lined up opposite the towpath, their primary colors glowing in contrast to the dullness of the day.

"Permanent moorings," Juliet explained. "Leased from the landowner."

From this perspective, Gemma could see that the dairy barn would have a view of these boats, and of the pretty stone bridge, and of the curve of the canal in either direction. Perhaps the place was more desirable than she'd imagined, but that wasn't what piqued her curiosity.

She pointed to the north. "How far to Barbridge from here?" The distance had seemed to flash past coming by road, and she thought the canal ran more or less parallel.

"I don't know," Juliet answered. "A mile. Maybe a little more."

Gemma frowned. "Is there any way to get to the canal by road between here and there?"

"No. You'd have to cut across the fields. Why?"

"It just seems odd to me," Gemma said, shrugging. "Two bodies within such a short distance of each other, and the second following so soon on the discovery of the first." She urned to Juliet. "Did the woman who was found this morning have any connection with your building site?"

"Not that I know of. But—are you suggesting her death had something to do with the discovery of that baby's body?" Juliet's voice rose on a note of horror.

"No, no, I'm not suggesting anything, really, just thinking aloud. There's no need for you to be concerned."

But Juliet was shaking her head. "That's too much. If something else holds up this job, I don't know what I'll do. I know that sounds horribly selfish, and it's not that I don't care about that poor woman who was killed last night. But I can't make payroll for my crew, and if I lose them, I'm as good as finished."

Recognizing the signs of imminent panic, Gemma realized she'd have to put her speculations aside. She threw an arm round Juliet's shoulders and turned her back towards the car, saying, "Never mind that now. The first thing we have to do is get your things. Then we'll think about what's next."

The cabin door swung open before Althea could knock, and Gabriel Wain pulled her inside, roughly. The salon curtains were tightly closed, and a single lamp cast a circle of yellow light on the drop-down table. The room was as cold as it had been the previous day, and the fire in the stove burned low.

Althea's eyes were still adjusting to the dimness as she heard Gabriel's hoarse voice in her ear. "Is it true? Is it true what they're saying? That she's dead?" His fingers dug into the flesh of her upper arm.

"If you mean Annie Constantine, yes, she's dead."

For an instant, she thought she would cry out from the pain in her arm. Then he released her, turning away, and it seemed to Althea that he shrank before her eyes.

Cradling the oxygen tank against her chest, she rubbed at her arm with her free hand. Now she could see that the children were huddled on the bench by the table, their eyes enormous in frightened faces. There was no sign of Rowan.

Gabriel spoke to his son without turning back. "Joseph, go up top and tidy up. We'll need to pump out and fill the water tank. And take your sister with you."

The children stood obediently, and as they edged past Althea, she had to resist an unexpected urge to touch the boy's curling hair. When they had gone, Gabriel Wain faced her once more, his expression unreadable.

"I'm sorry for the trouble you've taken," he said. "But we won't be needing what you've brought." He nodded at the oxygen tank.

Althea's heart thumped. "Your wife. Is she—"

"Much the same. She'll be all right."

She stared at him. "But she won't. I thought I explained—" Then she realized what he had meant when he spoke to the children, and to her. "You can't think of leaving," she said, shocked.

"It's best," he answered shortly. "Now if you'll—"

"Mr. Wain, I don't think you realize how . . . difficult . . . things are going to be for your wife. I can help her. Why would you refuse her that?"

"We can't be doing with interference. The police—"

"Why would the police need to speak to you? What happened to Mrs. Constantine was dreadful, but surely no one would think it had any connection with you."

He rubbed a hand across his unshaven chin. "You can't know that. I— When she came to the boat, on Christmas Day. We had words."

"Words?"

"A row. It was Rowan who insisted she come aboard. I'd told her we wanted nothing to do with her, to leave us be. Why should she come poking into our lives, after all this time?"

"She only wanted to help you."

"And where does that leave us now?" he hissed at her, and she heard the despair.

"With me." Althea said this with more assurance than she felt. But even as she wondered if this man could have done such a terrible thing to Annie Constantine, she rejected it. She would swear the news had been a blow.

Then doubt niggled at her. Could he have argued with Annie again, struck her in a fit of temper, then left her, not realizing how badly she was injured?

"Gabriel. Did you see Annie Constantine last night?"

"No. I never laid eyes on the woman after the two of you left the boat yesterday." He met her eyes, and she thought she heard a note of pleading under the roughness of his tone.

"Then you have nothing to worry about," she said.

He turned away, suppressing a bitter laugh. "Would that were true." The boat rocked gently as the children moved about above decks. "I tell you we have to go. The children— we can't risk staying."

Althea considered, running over the possibilities in her mind. He could move the boat, and she could meet them at some prearranged mooring to change out the oxygen—but no. She shook her head at her own stupidity.

"Did anyone hear you arguing with Annie that day?" she asked.

"Likely the whole of Barbridge."

"Then you can't leave. Don't you see? The police will be interviewing everyone in the area. Someone is bound to tell them they heard the two of you in a slanging match, and they'll take your flight as an indication of guilt. It wouldn't take them long to track you down—the waterways are finite. You'll have to bluff it out."

"But—what would I say?"

If Althea had needed reassurance, it was the ingrained honesty of a man who couldn't manufacture a lie. "Tell them it was a boater's row. Say she moored badly, and scraped your boat. It wouldn't be the first time tempers were lost over a bit of bad steering."

Gabriel was nodding, agreeing with her.

"Was anyone close enough to hear differently?"

"No, I don't think so."

"Then maybe they won't take it further. And you mustn't volunteer that you knew her." Even as she spoke, Althea wondered what had possessed her. She, who had spent most of her working life helping the police.

"I'll get Sam's things if you'll gather up Lally's," Juliet told Gemma as they climbed the stairs to the first floor.

The house seemed unsettlingly quiet, unwelcoming, and Gemma thought she must have absorbed some of Juliet's

nervousness. They had checked to make sure there was n
sign of Caspar's car at either house or office before goin
in, and even then they had stood in the entrance hall, listen
ing, before doing a quick recce of the downstairs rooms.

Chiding herself for being overimaginative, Gemma aske
as briskly as she could, "What sort of things should I get?"

What did it matter if Caspar Newcombe did come home
she told herself. Juliet certainly had every right to be there
and to take whatever personal things she needed.

Unfortunately, Gemma had seen the results of too many
domestic disputes to be entirely comforted by her own
commonsense advice.

"Oh, just undies, a change of jeans and jumpers." Juliet
pointed to the first door on the left of the upstairs hall. "God
knows, whatever I chose would be wrong; I thought you
might do better." The strain between mother and daughter
had been evident that morning, and Gemma had sensed Juliet's relief when her parents had taken the children.

Although she felt much better qualified to pick out boys'
things than girls', Gemma followed Juliet's direction without protest. Lally's door was closed, and on it she had
tacked a sheet of paper with a carefully hand-drawn skull
and crossbones. Beneath the graphic, she had printed KEEP
OUT, then below that, in parentheses, (THAT MEANS YOU,
SAM!).

"Sorry, love," Gemma whispered, and turned the knob.
The door swung open and she stood on the threshold, expel-
ling a breath of surprise. She had been expecting openly expressed rebellion—what she found was a room that seemed to
bear little imprint of its teenage occupant.

The walls were rose, the duvet a floral mint-and-rose print,
the upholstered armchair by the window a coordinating
mint-and-rose stripe. A few stuffed animals sat grouped at
the head of the hastily made bed; the framed prints on the
walls were variations on horses grazing in dreamily impres-
sionistic meadows. These were a child's things—had Lally
held on to them by choice? And if so, why?

The room was too tidy as well, except for a few items of
clothing tossed haphazardly on a bench at the foot of the bed

and the snaggletoothed appearance of dressing-table drawers not quite shut.

Sniffing, Gemma caught the faint drift of cheap perfume, the sort that teenage girls bought at Woolworth's or the Body Shop with their pocket money, and the normality of it eased her disquiet. She was letting her imagination run away with her again. She certainly didn't know Lally well enough to make judgments based on something as superficial as her lack of boy-band posters and black drapes.

The sound of Juliet moving around in the next room, opening and shutting doors and drawers, spurred her into action. Juliet hadn't given her a bag, so the first thing was to find a holdall or suitcase.

Rummaging through the wardrobe, the best she came up with was an empty, slightly worn backpack. Setting the pack on the bed, she quickly riffled through the chest of drawers, pulling out folded panties and bras that were little more than bits of lace and padding. She smiled a bit, remembering when she had worn such things so proudly and she and her sister had fought over who needed them most.

When her hands were full, she turned back to the bed and saw that the pack had tipped over, spilling a brightly colored bit of paper or foil onto the floor. She reached for it absently, then froze as her fingers closed round the small packet and she realized what she held.

It was a condom, wrapped in colored foil.

Gemma dumped the neatly folded clothes on the bed and reached for the backpack. She felt inside, exploring the depths until she found the pocket that had come open.

A sharp edge jabbed her finger, and she pulled out more condoms, a half dozen, their foil wrappers as cheerful as confetti. Sinking down onto the edge of the bed, Gemma thought furiously. Surely the novelty condoms were every schoolgirl's idea of sophistication, passed giggling from friend to friend at lunch break. Possession didn't necessarily mean that Lally had a use for them.

She slipped the condoms back into the bag and picked up the clothes, then stopped, her nose wrinkling. There was something else, a hint of a familiar smell.

This time she protected her fingers with a handkerchief, searching more thoroughly and feeling along the seams of the innermost pockets. Her diligence rewarded her with a bumpy, thumbnail-size packet of cling film. Carefully, she peeled back the clear layers of plastic, but her stomach was plummeting even before she saw what the film held. Tablets. White, unstamped, some oval, some round.

They could be anything, of course, but Gemma suspected the ovals were Xanax, or a similar tranquilizer, and the round tablets Ecstasy. The round tablets were unscored, and had that slightly homemade look. In any case, she was quite sure neither of the pills was something Lally should have.

But there was still something more; the smell was stronger now. She felt again, and her fingers closed on a softer packet. She knew what it was before she saw the contents. Pot, and a sizable amount.

She sat, staring down at what she held, until Juliet's voice came anxiously from the hall. "Gemma, are you almost ready? We need to go, soon."

With a jerk, Gemma shoved the drugs into her pocket and stuffed the clothes into the pack, all the while swearing under her breath. She called out, "Coming," as she hurried to pull jeans and tops from the drawers, adding them to the pack until she thought she had enough for a few days' wear.

Then she stopped, her hand on the doorknob, and took a breath. What the hell was she going to do about this?

How could she tell Juliet what she had found, today of all days? And how could she not?

"Juliet . . ." Gemma paused, concentrating on stirring the too-hot-to-taste bowl of leek soup before her on the small café table. Suspecting that Juliet had subsisted through the morning on nothing but nerves and multiple cups of coffee, she'd insisted that they get some lunch once they were safely away from the Newcombes' house.

Juliet had agreed, if reluctantly, and within a quarter of an hour they were seated in the tiny tea shop called the Inglenook, just up Pillory Street from the bookshop. It was a bit late for a cooked lunch, but the proprietor had suggested his wife's prizewinning soup, and the steam rising from Gemma's bowl smelled heavenly. And it was just as well, she thought, that they'd missed the height of the lunch crowd, as only one other table was occupied, providing the opportunity for a fairly private conversation, if only she could figure out what to say.

It had taken her only a moment's contemplation to realize that she couldn't, in good conscience, ignore what she'd found in Lally's room. She put herself in Juliet's place—what if someone discovered evidence that Kit had been using drugs, and didn't tell her or Duncan? She would want to know, and would be slow to forgive anyone who kept it from her.

That decision made, her first instinct had been to tell Duncan and let him deal with it. She'd realized quickly, however, that that was merely cowardice on her part.

Gemma took a tiny sip of the soup, which was as good as it smelled, then made another stab at finding an opening. "It's difficult, isn't it, knowing what to do with teenagers, even under the best of circumstances?"

Juliet looked up from her soup, one dark eyebrow arched in surprise, and Gemma was struck by her sudden but fleeting resemblance to Duncan. More often, she'd seen Rosemary in Juliet, and occasionally a smile or a tilt of the head that made her think of Hugh. "I suppose so," Juliet said slowly, rotating her spoon. "Lally was such a sweet child, always eager to please. And now—sometimes I wonder what happened to that little girl, if she's even still there."

Hearing the pain in Juliet's voice, Gemma knew she'd struck a nerve. "I doubt Lally knows herself." She ate a little more of her soup, then broke off a piece of crusty brown bread and peeled the foil cover from a packet of butter. "When I was Lally's age, I remember my mum telling me I must have been abducted by aliens." Juliet smiled, and encouraged, Gemma went on. "Was Lally having a difficult time even before things got so rough with Caspar?"

Frowning, Juliet said, "I don't know, really. It seems as if this entire year's been hard for her, but now I wonder if there were signs earlier and I simply missed them."

Gemma thought of how blind they had been to the problems Kit was having at school, and swallowed a little too hastily. She coughed until her eyes watered, but waved of Juliet's concern.

Then she thought about Kit's association with Lally, and felt a clutch of dread. Surely they could trust him not to get involved with drugs, whatever he might feel about Lally—he'd always seemed such a sensible boy. But a sliver of doubt wedged in her heart like an ice fragment, and she found she'd lost her appetite.

"Of course, it's been worse since Peter died," said Juliet, and Gemma looked up in surprise.

"Peter?"

"A friend of Lally's at school. Peter Llewellyn. He drowned in the canal. There was . . ." Juliet pushed her plate away, as if she, too, suddenly found it difficult to force food down, no matter how good. "There was alcohol involved. It was such a shock—Peter was the last boy anyone would have expected . . . And Lally, Lally seemed to take it very hard, but she wouldn't talk to me about it."

Gemma saw her opening. "Was there anything else indicated in the boy's death?"

"Anything else? What do you mean?" The baffled tone told Gemma that Juliet wasn't going to make this easy for her.

"Drugs. Did they find drugs in Peter's system?"

"No." Juliet shook her head. "No. Not that I heard. And I can't imagine that they did. These kids, they're just babies, really. I mean, experimenting with alcohol is one thing, but—"

"Jules." Gemma found herself using Duncan's nickname for his sister, an intimacy she wouldn't have contemplated an hour ago. "There's something I have to tell you."

Juliet looked at her, her dark gray eyes dilating with apprehension, but she didn't speak.

Glancing round the room, Gemma saw that the only other customer, a woman in the back corner, had taken out her mobile phone and was murmuring into it. The proprietor had disappeared into the kitchen. Still, she leaned forward and lowered her voice. "I'm sorry. There's no easy way to say this. But when I was getting Lally's clothes, I found some things in her backpack. Drugs."

"What?" Juliet said, blankly. Then, "No, that's not possible." But in spite of her protest, her oval face paled. "Did you say her backpack? Lally has her backpack with her."

"This was an old one, in the wardrobe. The one I put her clothes in."

Blowing out her lips in a little puff of relief, Juliet tried a smile. "Lally hasn't used that since last year. She must have loaned it to someone who left the things in it, by accident."

Gemma reached out and laid her fingers lightly on Juliet's wrist. "Juliet, I really am sorry. But no one forgets they've left things like this lying about. The pills, maybe, but not the other. There was marijuana, too. And even if Lally was keeping the stuff for someone else, she's involved in something dangerous. You had to know."

"Pot?" whispered Juliet, her argument abandoned. "And what sort of pills?"

Gemma sighed. "I suspect some of the pills might be a 'pam drug, Valium or Xanax. Tranquilizers. Do you or Caspar have a prescription?" When Juliet shook her head, she went on. "The other tablets look homemade—I suspect they're Ecstasy."

"But that's not all that bad, is it?" Juliet asked, her voice rising on a shred of hope. "I mean—I read about raves—" She brought her hands together, twisting them in her lap as if one were seeking comfort from the other. They had begun to tremble. "Oh, Christ," she whispered. "I can't believe it, there must be some mistake."

Gemma couldn't bring herself to mention the condoms, not now.

Silence descended on their little table. Their unfinished bowls of soup had cooled; the scattered crumbs of bread lay drying on the cheerful tablecloth. Closing her eyes, Juliet sat so still she might have fallen asleep. The woman sitting alone finished her conversation and snapped her mobile phone closed, glancing curiously at Gemma and Juliet as she made her way to the register.

The owner emerged from the kitchen, engaging the woman in friendly banter as he rang up her bill—she was obviously a regular customer.

Opening her eyes, Juliet fixed Gemma with a burning stare, and under cover of the voices of the owner and customer, said quietly, "I'll kill her." Spots of color flared high on her pale cheeks.

"No." Gemma had been thinking furiously, ever since she'd found Lally's stash. "Juliet, wait. I'm not suggesting you ignore this—God forbid—but I think you should hold off for a few days before you talk to her about it." It seemed to Gemma that both mother and daughter were stretched to the breaking point, and that a confrontation might have disastrous consequences.

"Things are so unsettled just now—I'm afraid you may both say things you'll regret. Wait at least until you've worked out a plan for you and the children, and until you've told her what you mean to do. Looking round, Gemma saw that the café's owner had disappeared into the kitchen. She reached into her pocket and passed the bags surreptitiously across the small table. "Deal with this when you're calmer."

Juliet gazed wide-eyed at what she held. Then she stuffed the bags into her handbag. Her shoulders slumping, she said, "Promise me this time. Promise me you won't tell Duncan."

"So what did she look like?" Lally sat back on her heels and looked at Kit across the opened case of the latest Harry Potter. They'd spent most of the morning, and the last hour since lunch, unpacking and shelving the boxes of books in the small back room of the bookshop. "Was there blood?"

"Just bugger off, okay?" said Kit. "I don't want to talk about it."

Dropping her gaze, Lally ran a fingertip over the slightly dusty spines of the books left in the box. He thought he'd discouraged her, but after a moment she said more quietly, "Did she—did she look like she was asleep?"

The change in her tone made Kit look up. "No. Why?"

"I just wondered, that's all." She gave an elaborate shrug and stretched, showing a sliver of midriff. "God, I'm dying for a ciggie."

"Don't be daft," Kit said crossly, although he was glad enough of the change of subject. "You shouldn't smoke, and I don't think we're supposed to go out." Lally had been complaining since Rosemary had ignored Lally's plea for hamburgers and brought in sandwiches instead, and the constant harping was giving Kit a pounding headache.

"Why shouldn't we?" Lally protested. "They're treating us like prisoners." She pulled out another half dozen books and stacked them carelessly on the edge of the table. "Shouldn't we get a trial first?"

Both Rosemary and Hugh had been tactful enough—none of the children had actually been forbidden to go out of the shop, but tasks had been found to keep them busy from the minute they arrived. And although nothing had been said, Kit suspected it was because the adults didn't want Lally or Sam to see their dad. He also knew that Lally's mum had taken away her mobile phone—that had been the other subject of Lally's ongoing complaint—and he guessed that Rosemary and Hugh were worried that Casper might come into the shop and demand to take the children, as he had yesterday in the pub.

Rosemary had given a little start every time the bell on the shop door rang, and Hugh had come down often from his small office on the first floor, making some excuse to check on them, once stopping to give Kit an awkward pat on the shoulder. Kit had caught Rosemary watching him as well, with a mixture of kindness and concern in her eyes that made him feel slightly uncomfortable and funnily warm at the same time.

Unlike his cousin, Kit was happy enough to stay in the shop. He liked the slightly musty smell emanating from the used-book section; he liked the higgledy-piggledy unevenness of the floors and the walls; he liked the weight of the books in his hands and the lure of the bright covers, the promise of adventures that would take him out of

himself. He didn't mind being kept busy, either—tha
held the recurring visions of what he had seen that morn
ing at bay.

"Watch the books," he said sharply as the stack behind
Lally's head teetered.

"I don't care about the bloody books," she retorted, bu
pushed the volumes back from the edge of the table and
straightened them a little. She gave Kit a sly glance from
under the wing of dark hair that had fallen across her face.
"We could just slip out the back door."

"No." Kit collapsed the box he'd emptied with a little
more force than necessary. "And even if we did, where are
you going to get cigarettes? You can't buy them."

Lally grinned. "Oh, there are always places where you can
get things. You know the pub round the back of the shop?
This bloke that works behind the bar, he'll buy them for me if
I give him the money."

"But that's—" The bell on the shop door jangled, startling them both, then Kit saw Lally relax as a distinctly female voice answered Rosemary's greeting. So she was
nervous about her dad after all.

"It's Mrs. Armbruster," Lally whispered. "She'll talk
Nana's ear off for an hour. Come on. If we go now, we can
be back before anyone notices we're gone."

"What about Sam and Toby?"

"Granddad took them upstairs to play draughts. They
won't be looking for us. Come on." She stood and moved
lightly towards the door, her trainer-shod feet soundless on
the wooden floorboards.

"Lally, no, wait." Kit pushed himself up, but his feet
seemed to have tangled themselves together and he stumbled
awkwardly. "We shouldn't—they'd worry—"

She stopped, her hand on the knob of the back door. "I'll
go on my own, then. You can cover for me." Her eyes held
disdain, and a challenge.

Kit flushed, shamed at being treated like a child. But
worse was the thought of Lally alone on the street. What if
her dad saw her and snatched her up? Then he, Kit, would be

responsible for losing her. If Lally was determined to go out, he would have to go with her.

"Make it quick," Kit hissed at her as they stood on the pavement outside the pub. It was a quiet time of day, and he could see through the leaded window that the bar was almost empty. "How are you going to manage this, anyway? You can't go in."

They had gone out without coats, and he was already shivering. The sky had darkened to the purple-gray of tarnished silver, and he thought he could smell snow in the air.

"You'll see." Lally tugged down the hem of her cotton sweatshirt, raised her chin, and pulled open the door. Stepping over the threshold, she called out, "Can I use your loo?"

Through the window, Kit saw the barman look up. He had spots on his pudgy face, and was probably not much more than eighteen.

"Sorry, love." The barman shook his head as he wiped a cloth across the bar top. "You're underage. Find the public toilets, or go to the Crown. They'll let you in."

Making a show of jiggling impatiently, Lally said, "Please. I'm desperate. I don't think I can make it that far. I'll be really quick."

"Oh, all right. But shut the bloody door, and hurry up."

Lally flashed Kit a smile and slipped inside. He saw her disappear into a passage that led towards the rear of the pub. After one more flourish with his cloth, the barman reached for something under the bar, then stepped casually into the same passage.

A moment later, he reappeared, then Lally emerged and quickly crossed the room, hands in the pockets of her sweatshirt. "Ta, love," she tossed cheekily over her shoulder as she pushed her way out the door.

"That's Sean," she explained as they started back towards the bookshop, Kit hurrying her along with a hand on her elbow. "Lives down the road from us. He'd do anything for me." Lally fished a packet of Benson & Hedges from her sweatshirt pocket and began peeling the cellophane from the top. The wind caught the ephemeral scrap as she tossed it away, spinning it like a bit of tinsel come to life before it disappeared.

Pulling a cigarette from the pack and a plastic lighter from her pocket, she slowed and ducked under a shop-window awning. "Wait," she said, holding the cigarette to her lips and shielding the tip with her hand as she flicked the lighter.

"Lally, stop pissing about. You can't stand here in the street and smoke. Someone will see you." Nervous impatience edged Kit's voice.

"So? What am I going to do? Wait until we get back to the shop and have a smoke in the back room? That was the point of this whole exercise, remember, for me to have a smoke." She inhaled and leaned a little farther back into the awning's cover, watching him with narrowed eyes before looking away.

Kit stared at her profile. For just an instant, he had the oddest sensation that he was seeing her as she might look in ten years, or twenty, the delicate contours of her face drawn and hardened by time and experience.

But he said only, "They'll miss us. What on earth are we going to say if they've been looking for us?"

"I'll think of something," she snapped back at him. "For God's sake, Kit, don't be so wet. You sound just like my friend Peter. 'Don't smoke, Lally,'" she mimicked. "'Don't drink, Lally. Don't do this, don't do that. You might get into trouble, Lally.'" Dropping her half-smoked cigarette, she ground it viciously into the pavement with her heel. "It was all bollocks. In the end, he was no different— No, he was worse." She glared at Kit, as if daring him to argue. Her eyes brimmed with unshed tears as she turned away, starting back towards the shop.

An icy dart of rain stung Kit's cheek, then another. It had started to sleet. Running after her, he struggled to find his voice. "Why? Why was he worse?"

The rising wind snatched her words, throwing them back at him in a gust of disembodied fury. "Because. Because he was a fucking hypocrite, that's why."

# 19

❧

"**He's lying,** I'd say." Babcock gave a last glance at the house before turning the BMW into the main road.

"About last night?" Kincaid snapped the lock on his seat belt and turned the heater vent—now spewing frigid air—away from his face. "Yes, I think so," he agreed. "And maybe more besides, but something about the last question really put the wind up him."

He was still sorting his own impressions of Roger Constantine, and found himself missing Gemma. They used each other as sounding boards, and no idea was too far-fetched to be tossed into the pot. Ronnie Babcock, however, had proved himself a good listener. "Constantine seems a clever man, though," he allowed himself to muse aloud. "You'd think if he meant to kill his wife, he'd have a ready-made alibi."

As they left the leafy village of Tilston behind and the heater began to generate some welcome warmth, Babcock said, "But what if it wasn't planned? What if Annie didn't just ring him to set a date for dinner? After all, we only have his word for that. What if she dropped a bombshell? Told him she wanted to meet and discuss a divorce? No more living the good life in the Victorian villa for poor Roger." He gestured behind them. "Not only would he lose the house, but I'd wager he could never afford to keep up a comparable lifestyle on a journalist's pay. Now he gets it all, plus the life insurance, with no strings attached. I'd say he had a good deal to lose."

Kincaid considered this, frowning. "Or what if it was just the opposite—she rang up and said she was coming home, for good? In the five years she's been gone, he may have come to like the status quo very well. Maybe he didn't want her to come back. Either way—"

"Either way, he's got a motive, but the logistics are difficult. Say he was surprised by her phone call, whatever the content, and wanted to talk to her in person. I'm not sure he could have driven from Tilston to Barbridge in last night's fog, much less have found his way to the boat, especially if he didn't know exactly where she was moored."

They had just swept round a ninety-degree blind turn on a lane not much wider than the car. Kincaid shuddered at the thought of driving this road at night, in bad conditions. It was possible, but was it likely? "Was the fog as heavy to the west?" he asked.

"I don't know, but we'll find out." Babcock slipped his phone from his pocket and hit speed dial. "Sheila? Are you still on the boat? Okay, listen. I've some things I want you to check. I need to know if last night's fog extended as far west as Tilston. What?" He glanced at Kincaid and grinned. "I know you're not the weather bureau," he continued. "But we're going to need someone from that area to knock on doors, chat up the neighbors about Roger Constantine. We need to know any tidbits of gossip, as well as whether anyone noticed his movements last night. And if you get on to Tilston, I'm sure the locals can tell us if they had a pea-souper last night.

"Oh, and when you've got that sorted, pull any financial records you find on the boat—in fact, pull any sort of papers you can find. And what about the house-to-house in Barbridge?"

A tinny squawk of protest issued from the phone's speaker and Babcock rolled his eyes. "Of course you can do all that," he said soothingly. "I've great confidence in you. I'll ring you when we get to the station. 'Bye now."

"Complaints, complaints," he said to Kincaid as he flipped the phone closed. "I'm sure we never whinged like that. What's happened to the copper's work ethic?" He slowed, and Kincaid saw that they'd once again reached the junction for No Man's Heath, the village with the reputed pub. "Now," Babcock continued, a gleam in his eye, "what do you say to a ploughman's lunch?"

Sheila Larkin swore under her breath. Who did the DCI think she was, bloody Wonder Woman? Not that she wasn't used to him expecting her to be in two places at once, but he'd been enjoying bossing her about in front of his mate, and that she resented.

She'd been looking round the narrowboat's galley when her phone rang, and now, as her stomach growled in protest, she eyed with longing an unopened packet of ginger biscuits in the cupboard. The temptation passed quickly, however, and she shut the cupboard door. It wouldn't seem right, taking food from a dead woman, no matter if everything in the kitchen eventually got chucked in the bin.

Taking her notebook and a pen from her coat pocket, she jotted down Babcock's list of tasks. The first thing was to ring Western Division and set the inquiries in Tilston in motion.

When Control had put her through, she asked the duty sergeant to send an officer who knew the village—that would increase their odds of getting useful information. She asked about the fog as well, and the sergeant told her that the previous night it had been heavy in western Cheshire and on over the border into Wales. That was one question answered right off the bat, she thought, ringing off with satisfaction.

Then she went back to the task of searching the boat for anything that might shed light on the victim, or the circumstances of her death. She had begun in the salon, the careful survey of which had taken only a few minutes—Annie Lebow had obviously been an enthusiastic proponent of the simplified life.

Thinking of the suburban semidetached house she shared with her mother in North Crewe, Sheila sighed. If anything happened to her or her mum, it would take the police a week just to go through the sitting room. It wasn't that either of them was particularly fond of clutter, it was just that accumulation seemed to overtake them, and neither had the time to deal with it.

They rubbed along together pretty well, she and her mum. Her mum, Diane, had been only seventeen when Sheila was born, and her dad had buggered off without ever doing the right thing, so it had been just the two of them for as long as Sheila could remember.

She was perfectly happy to go on sharing a house with her mum. She paid her share of the mortgage and the rates and the groceries—not that either of them was home to eat all that often, or even to see each other, for that matter. Her mum was a nurse who worked night shifts in accident and emergency at Leighton Hospital, so the two of them could go for days communicating only by notes left on the door of the fridge.

Still, even when the house was empty, there was the feel of another person's presence, and Sheila found that comforting, especially after a difficult case.

Now, as she moved into the bedroom—or master stateroom, she supposed it was called—it seemed to her that she could feel loneliness settle over her like a pall. Any envy she'd felt over the dead woman's posh living situation vanished. Annie Lebow had created a cocoon for herself: beautiful, expensive, and emotionally isolated.

She soon found, however, that Lebow's spare lifestyle had advantages. A section of panel in the stateroom dropped down to form a desk, and the space behind the panel held organizing nooks and niches. In these she easily found such paperwork as Annie Lebow had seen fit to keep.

A leather-bound accordion file held carefully sorted bills for a credit card and a mobile phone, as well as the last several quarterly statements for a number of investments. In another nook, she found a personal address book, also leather bound.

Tucked inside the book's front cover were a half dozen loose photographs. All featured the boat, and from the background foliage, looked to have been taken in spring or summer. Only one, however, showed the victim.

Annie Lebow stood at the helm, her right hand resting

lightly on the end of the S-shaped tiller. Her bare arms and face looked tanned, her expression relaxed, with a hint of a smile touching the corners of her mouth. It seemed to Sheila that she had been gazing at whoever held the camera with a slightly tolerant affection.

Although the photo was undated, Sheila guessed it was several years old, perhaps taken when Lebow had first ac-quired the boat. Her hair had been longer and darker, the planes of her face softer, less pronounced, and the more Sheila gazed at the image, the more she thought there was a sort of tentative pride in the way the woman held the tiller.

Sheila took a last look at the photo, then grimaced and snapped the book closed. She had looked at Annie Lebow's body and felt the shock and anger she always experienced at a murder scene. She had riffled through the woman's clothes and most intimate possessions, and had still managed to keep a distance between herself and the victim. That separa-tion was a learned skill, a necessity of the job that she struggled to maintain.

But as Annie Lebow met her eyes in the photograph, Sheila felt a connection. The crumpled body on the path had become a woman who had lived and worked and slept and dreamed, who had inhabited this small space, however lightly. In that instant of association across time and space, Annie Lebow had become real to Sheila, and her death had become personal.

She wore boots, trousers, and a heavy woolen coat, but even from a distance and out of uniform, he could tell she was a cop. There was something in the way she moved, confident but alert, that marked her like a brand.

As he moved around the boat, from one small task to an-other, he watched her. She'd come up the towpath from the direction of the crime scene, and after handing a parcel to one of the uniformed officers standing guard in the parking area, she'd made her way along the houses that lined the Cut just below Barbridge.

When the woman with the frizzy hair and the pink dress-ing gown had come out to speak to her, panic rose in his throat. It was all he could do to keep himself still, to concentrate on what the doctor had told him. It would do no good to run. He couldn't disguise his family or his boat, and the Cut was a small world. Once before, fear had driven him to take the *Daphne* into Manchester's industrial slums, but things were different now. Even the inner-city parts of the Cut were changing as the old warehouses became desirable "waterside properties." And no one had been looking for him then.

The woman in the pink dressing gown gestured, and even from a distance he could hear her raised voice. He didn't need to make out the words. Bending over the strap he was repairing, he kept his eyes down and whistled tunelessly between his teeth. The soft turf of the towpath muffled footsteps, but he didn't need sound to track the policewoman's progress. When, a few moments later, a voice called out, "Mr. Wain?" he looked up with feigned surprise.

She stood on the towpath, across from the bow. Up close, he could see that she was pretty in a snub-nosed sort of way, and that she was a bit older than her bouncy stride had led him to expect. Intelligence gleamed from her eyes, and his heart sank.

He nodded, his hand still on the strap, as if he were impatient at the interruption. "Aye. What's it to you, miss?"

"Detective Constable Larkin, Cheshire police." She held up an identification card, though she must have known he couldn't read it at that distance. "Could I have a word?"

"Nothing's stopping you," he said, and began to coil the straps.

Shifting her weight ever so slightly to the balls of her feet, she squared her shoulders. "I suppose you've heard that a woman died last night, just down from Barbridge." She nodded in the direction of the bridge. "Her name was Annie Lebow."

"Aye?" he said again, standing and brushing the palms of his hands against his trousers. Now he'd put her at a disadvantage. She had to tilt her head back to look up at him.

"Did you know her?"

He shrugged. "You meet a lot of folks on the Cut."

Larkin pulled a photograph from her coat pocket and held

out to him. Gabriel had no choice but to lean over the gunwale and take it. He squinted at the print for a moment, then handed it back. "The *Horizon*. You should have told me the name of the boat. It's boats I remember, more than names or faces."

"You're saying you did know Ms. Lebow?" asked the detective.

"In passing." He felt the sweat forming under his heavy fisherman's jersey, as if the sun had suddenly come out, and hoped she couldn't see the dampness on his brow. For a moment he was tempted to tell her the whole truth, just to have it over with, to stop the pressure squeezing his heart, but he knew he couldn't. Not with Rowan and the children at stake.

Larkin nodded back towards the houses in Barbridge. The woman in the pink dressing gown was still standing in her garden, he saw, watching them. The old biddy must be freezing herself by now, just to satisfy her curiosity. "Mrs. Millsap says you had a row with the deceased, on Christmas Day."

Gabriel made a swift calculation. Mrs. Millsap might have heard raised voices, but she couldn't have made out what was said, not from that distance. "The bloody woman scraped my boat," he admitted, sounding aggrieved. "Reversed right into it, the silly cow." He leaned over the gunwale, pointing at a long abrasion, just above the *Daphne*'s waterline. He'd done the damage himself, banging into the side of Hurleston Locks a week ago, and he hadn't had the heart or the energy to repair it.

"Not to speak ill of the dead," he added, "but I was that pissed off."

"Did you threaten her?"

"Threaten? I told her to watch where she was bloody going, if you call that a threat."

The detective studied the scrape, then shook her head, as if commiserating. "Then what happened?"

"She said she was sorry, she'd been distracted. And she offered to pay for any repairs, I'll give her that. But I told her no, there was no need, I could fix it myself." He looked up at the leaden bowl of the sky. "Have to wait until it's a bit drier though."

"So you parted amicably? On good terms?" she added.

He should have been used to it—people assuming boaters were stupid, or at least illiterate. Illiterate they may have been, for the most part, but they had never been stupid, and Gabriel's parents had made sure that he learned to read well. They had known that times were changing, that hard work and a knowledge of the Cut would no longer be enough.

Controlling a flare of anger, he said, "Not on ill terms. Look, it was just an ordinary row, the sort that happens if someone cuts you off at a lock, or leaves the lock against you. What has any of it to do with this woman dying?"

"Annie Lebow died violently, Mr. Wain. We have to investigate anyone who might have wished her harm."

"You're saying you think I'd kill a woman I hardly knew over a bit of scraped paint?" His anger was righteous now, and he didn't trouble to keep it in check. "That's downright daft."

"We have to ask. You can understand that. We also have to ask where you were last night."

"I was here, with my family. But I'll not have my family brought into this. It's nothing to do with—"

"For the moment, we just need to know we can speak with you again. You weren't planning on leaving Bar-bridge?"

Seeing the detective give a covert glance at her watch, Gabriel realized she'd finished with him, and was more than likely trying to work out how to juggle more tasks than she could manage in a given amount of time.

Relief flooded through him, so intense it left his hands shaking. She would, no doubt, be checking his story with anyone else she could find to speak to along this part of the canal, but none of the nearby boats was occupied, and he doubted if anyone other than the Millsap woman had witnessed Annie's visit on Christmas Eve.

He shoved his telltale hands in his trouser pockets and nodded brusquely. "We've no plans to move on, for now," he said, and it struck him, as he watched her walk away, that he had no plans at all. For him, time had stopped here in Barbridge, and his future had ceased to exist.

Kit followed Lally back towards the shop, struggling to keep up with her pace. He was still trying to work out why she was angry with him, and what any of it had to do with her friend Peter, but the taut line of her back offered no helpful clues.

"Lally!" he called out as they neared the back door of the bookshop. "Wait. Can't we talk?"

She slowed, but kept her face averted. "There's nothing to—"

Kit caught a shadow of movement out of the corner of his eye, then Leo stepped in front of them, as if he'd appeared from out of nowhere. "What's the matter, Lal?" he said. "You and coz have a falling-out?"

Lally gave a little yelp of surprise, then turned to face him, hands on her hips. "Bloody hell, Leo. Are you trying to make me wet my knickers? And no, we haven't had a falling-out, but even if we had, it's none of your business."

Leo didn't take up the challenge. Instead, he said, "Where have you been?" and to Kit's surprise he sounded more worried than belligerent. "I've been ringing you since yesterday and your mobile goes straight to voice mail."

"You didn't leave anything . . . personal . . . in a message?" Lally's voice had suddenly gone breathy with panic. She pulled them into the doorway of the next-door shop's back entrance, and Kit realized that was where Leo must have been waiting. "My mum took my phone yesterday. She doesn't want me talking to my dad. That's why I didn't call."

"Couldn't you have used someone else's phone? What about coz here?"

Kit wondered if Leo had guessed that he didn't have a phone and was deliberately trying to humiliate him. "I left it at home," he said, as nonchalantly as he could.

"Liar." Leo rolled his eyes. "No one leaves their phone, not even the übergeeks." He turned his attention back to Lally. "I hitchhiked into town last night and waited by the Bowling Green. Surely you could have got out for a bit."

"She won't let us go home, my mum. We're staying at my grandparents'."

"All the better, then." Leo sounded as if she'd just won the lottery. "That makes us practically neighbors. Come out tonight, when everyone's gone to bed. We could meet at the old dairy, see where your mum found the mummy. It's a good place to have a nip, and I've got some really brilliant st—"

"You don't understand," Lally said vehemently. "After what happened this morning, my mum and my grandparents aren't letting any of us out of their sight."

Leo stared at her. "What? What are you talking about? What happened this morning?"

"You don't know?" Her satisfaction was evident. "Kit found a body. On the canal, just below Barbridge." Lally gave Kit a proprietary glance that he didn't find the least bit flattering. "It was the woman we met on her boat yesterday. Someone killed her."

"No way." Leo glanced from Lally to Kit, his eyes wide with disbelief.

"Way," Lally retorted, with taunting smugness. "She was—"

"Lally, we've got to go," broke in Kit. He wasn't sure how much Lally had actually overheard from the grown-ups that morning, but he couldn't bear the thought of her reciting Annie's injuries to Leo. "We should have been back ages ago," he urged, reaching for her arm to pull her towards the door. But then he saw Leo's expression, and his fingers fell away, suddenly nerveless.

Lally shrugged away from them both. "All right, all right. Don't get your knickers in a twist."

As she turned towards the bookshop door, Leo called out, "At least say you'll try tonight. Just ring me to say when. You can use your grandparents' phone without being overheard— get lover boy here to create a diversion," he wheedled. "You could come, too," he added to Kit, the animosity of a moment ago seemingly forgotten. "We'll show you a good time, won't we, Lal?"

"Shut up, Leo." She was angry again, and Kit was as lost as before. He was glad, however, when she pulled open the

bookshop door and shoved him inside, closing it firmly behind her.

The storeroom was empty. Kit leaned against the door,
listening, his heart pounding. But a steady hum of voices
came from the front room, one of them the unmistakable
drone of Mrs. Armbruster. They had made it back without
their absence being noticed.

The sudden relief gave him courage. He turned to Lally,
who had sat casually on a box and was picking at her finger-
nails. When she looked up at him with a challenging half
smile and said, "See?" he snapped back without thinking.

"Is Leo your boyfriend?"

"No!" Caught off guard, she'd spoken with unaccustomed
vehemence.

"Then how come you do whatever he says?"

"I don't." She must have seen the disbelief in Kit's eyes
because she went on. "It's not like that. You don't understand. It's just that Leo . . . knows . . . things . . ."

"What sort of things?"

Lally met Kit's eyes, and for just an instant, a frightened
child looked back at him. Then the barriers sprang up again,
as tangible as shutters, and as she turned away she said,
"Nothing. Nothing at all."

# 20

❧

"**You'll be all right?**" asked Gemma, turning to Juliet as they stopped outside the small shop and office Juliet rented in Castle Street, tucked away behind the town square.

They had walked down Pillory Street from the café, and when Juliet had hesitated as they passed the bookshop, Gemma had urged her on, saying, "I'm sure the children are fine. It might be best to wait a bit before you see Lally, don't you think?"

"I suppose so," Juliet agreed with a sigh. "Although I'm not sure waiting a few hours will make it any easier to talk to her and pretend I know nothing. God, she must think me a fool," she added, her anger returning.

"I've no more experience than you, but I suspect that most fourteen-year-olds think their parents are fools, on a good day." Gemma had given Juliet's arm a squeeze, and got a small smile in return.

Then Juliet had insisted that if she couldn't do anything for the children, she must update her crew and try to contact the Bonners, the clients who had commissioned the reconstruction of the barn.

Gemma, afraid that Juliet's shop was the first place Caspar would look for her if he was in a temper, felt uneasy about leaving her there on her own. "Don't worry," Juliet assured her, pointing to a battered van parked half on the curb in front of the shop. "My foreman's here, and I'd like to see

Caspar try anything in front of him—Jim does kickboxing in his spare time. When I've finished, I'll have Jim walk me up to the bookshop. I can get a ride back to the house with Mum or Dad."

Gemma hesitated, afraid of overstepping bounds, but after considering what she'd already had to tell Juliet that day, decided in for a penny, in for a pound. "Juliet, you know that whenever you decide to talk to Caspar, Duncan and I can be there to back you up. You don't have to do it on your own."

With her hand on the knob of the shop door, Juliet turned back. "I—I'm not sure I'm quite ready. But thanks."

Gemma stood watching until Juliet had gone inside the shop, her uneasiness not dispelled. But she couldn't stand guard over an unwilling subject, and besides, Caspar had never actually harmed Juliet, or even made outright threats. Perhaps it was just the shadow cast by Annie Lebow's murder that was making her feel so unsettled.

That, and the fact that she'd once again found herself a spare cog. Juliet had her business to see to, the children were with Rosemary and Hugh, and Kincaid was still off somewhere with Ronnie Babcock, no doubt indulging in a bit of male bonding.

As she walked slowly towards the car park at the end of Castle Street, she saw that the shops and businesses that had characterized the street nearer the town center were soon replaced by well-kept Georgian residences. Some of the houses were occupied by solicitors and insurance agents, but the commercial use didn't mar the serene feel of the tree-lined street.

It made her think of Islington, where she had lived in her friend Hazel Cavendish's garage flat, and she felt a pang of nostalgia for a life that had seemed simpler, at least in retrospect. But that simplicity had been deceptive, she reminded herself, and if her life had been less complicated, it had also been less rich.

She wouldn't willingly trade the life she led now—in fact, she found it hard to envision anything other than the hustle and bustle of the Notting Hill house shared with Duncan and the boys. And if she sometimes wished that Duncan hadn't felt obligated to take her and Toby in, she tried to put the thought aside. She couldn't change what had happened, or bring back the child she had lost.

She felt a cold kiss of moisture on her cheek, like a frozen tear. Looking up, she saw a single snowflake spiraling down, but the sky looked less threatening than it had earlier, when she and Juliet had felt a spatter of sleet as they walked from the car park to the café.

Although Juliet had given her an illustrated map of the town and suggested she take a walking tour on her own, when Gemma reached the car park, she stood and gazed across the road at the River Weaver. She imagined the canal, running parallel a half mile to the west as it passed the outskirts of the town, then leaving the course of the river and angling northwest towards Barbridge and distant Chester—the same canal that passed Juliet's dairy barn, and the scene of Annie Lebow's murder.

It was a coincidence, surely, that the remains of the child, perhaps long buried, should lie so near the place where a woman had died violently sometime last night. She could see no logical connection, but still it nagged at her. Suddenly, she felt she had better things to do than sightsee.

The same uniformed constable she had spoken with that morning was still restricting access into Barbridge, but he recognized Gemma and waved her through. The crime-scene van was still parked near the bridge end, and she knew the local force would try to limit traffic through the area until the SOCOs had finished.

She found a place to leave her own car, then spoke to the officer who was monitoring pedestrian movement over the bridge and onto the towpath. "What about boats?" she asked him, when he'd checked her identification.

"Not much traffic this time of year," he answered. "And we've had someone stationed at the Middlewich Junction, to warn the boaters off, as well as down at the Hurleston Locks, below the crime scene. I've mostly had to turn back gawkers who have walked in to visit the pub," he added, gesturing at the Barbridge Inn.

Thanking him, Gemma crossed the humpbacked bridge and climbed down the incline to the towpath. There was only one boat moored below the bridge, a matte black vessel with small brass-rimmed round portals, like multiple eyes. Gemma peered curiously at the portholes as she passed, but the interior curtains were drawn tight, and both fore and aft decks were closed in with heavy black canvas. The boat looked deserted, and unpleasantly funereal.

The two boats moored on the other side of the canal were more cheerful, painted in traditional reds and greens, but they appeared just as devoid of human presence.

Gemma walked on, following the sharp curve of the canal to the left, and as the boats and houses of Barbridge vanished behind her she felt she'd entered a different, secret world. There was nothing but the wide curve of the water, always turning sinuously just out of sight, and the black tracery of bare trees against the gray sky.

The place seemed to her unutterably lonely—and yet she could feel the pull of it, the desire to see always what lay round the next bend. And she could imagine that in summer, when the trees were thick with leaf and the air soft and drowsy, it would be enchanted.

Looking down, she saw that that rutted path worn into the surrounding turf held a collage of footprints—a nightmare for the scene-of-crime team. She went on, conscious of the sound of her own breathing, and of the occasional faint rustle of the wind or a small creature in the surrounding woods. When a trio of swans appeared round the next bend and glided towards her, she felt an unexpected easing of tension. They were company, even if not human.

She spoke to them, feeling slightly foolish, and they changed course and came towards her, swimming in formation, trailing geometrically perfect wakes behind them. When they saw she had no food to offer, however, they quickly abandoned her, picking desultorily at the rushes lining the banks.

"Silly cow," Gemma admonished herself aloud. What had she expected, a conversation? A look at the heavy cloud layer drawing nearer the horizon told her that her window of opportunity might not last. If she was going to see anything she had better get a move on, and not fritter away her time idling with swans.

She set off again, her stride more purposeful, and after a few more bends the canal straightened a bit, and hedgerows began to replace the trees. Ahead, Gemma saw a black iron bridge that possessed none of the grace of the old stone hump-backed bridges, and to one side, a gnarled and twisted black silhouette of a tree that rose in unnatural parody.

And beyond that, she glimpsed the first fluorescent lime-green flash of a police officer's safety jacket. She had reached the crime scene. After identifying herself, she stood for a few moments at the perimeter, watching. The technicians were still searching for trace evidence, combing through every blade of grass and every twig of hedgerow. The deep blue boat floated serenely against the bank, as if removed from the fuss, but as Gemma looked more closely she could see the dusting of print powder on the sides and decks. There was no sign, of course, of the victim's body, only a dark patch in the turf, unidentifiable as blood from where Gemma stood.

"The lads have finished inside the boat, if you want to have a look," the officer told her, but Gemma resisted the temptation. She knew Babcock's crew would have been over the boat thoroughly, and that was not why she'd come.

"Is there some way I can get past, without contaminating the scene?" she asked. The hedgerow looked as impenetrable as Sleeping Beauty's briar thicket.

"There's a stile a few yards back—you'll have passed it. It's a bit overgrown, but I think you could get over it into the field." He didn't ask why, and although she suspected he could tell her what she wanted to know, there was no substitute for seeing the lay of the land herself.

"Thanks," she said, adding, "I'll give you a shout if I get stuck," and got a friendly and appreciative grin in return.

A few moments later, she found the stile, and was glad enough that the curve of the hedge hid her from the constable's sight. "Overgrown" had been an understatement, she thought as she pushed aside branches and placed a foot on the raised step. She swung the other leg awkwardly over the top and found herself hung, straddling the fence, the back of her coat caught on a bramble. "Bloody country," she swore, wishing she were double-jointed as she reached round to free the snag from her back. When she finally clambered down, as graceful as a ballerina in lead boots, she could feel her face flushed pink with aggravation and embarrassment. Now she'd just have to hope she didn't meet an irate cow.

She discovered soon enough that her nemesis was mineral rather than animal. The field had been plowed, and although sprouts of bright green winter grass grew on the raised ridges, the furrows held a porridge of slush and mud. Gemma trudged on, her boots growing heavier with every step, until the hedgerow diminished to a few strands of wire fencing and she was able to climb back to the towpath. Ahead, she saw the now-familiar shape of a stone bridge, half hidden by the curve of the canal.

As she came round the bend, she saw the redbrick building hugging the rise on the opposite side of the canal—Juliet's dairy barn. She had reached the far side of the bridge that went nowhere.

Getting onto the bridge itself required climbing over another stile, but this time Gemma managed a bit more gracefully. From her vantage point at the top of the bridge, she could see the activity still under way at the dairy, but there was no sign of the irascible sergeant she and Juliet had met that morning. She thought that without him to play watchdog, she'd have no trouble getting inside the building, but first she meant to finish what she had come to do.

She stood at the parapet and looked back the way she had come, at the still reach of the canal, empty now of any movement save a faint ripple in the rushes lining the bank. Then she turned, and crossing the bridge, looked south. In the distance, she could see the rising bank of the Hurleston Reservoir, stark after the tree-lined curves she had seen to the north, and she knew that beyond that lay the Hurleston Locks and the entrance to the Llangollen Canal, and farther still, the village of Acton, and Nantwich.

Close by, in the lee of the dairy barn, a half dozen

narrowboats were moored opposite the towpath, like a gay trail of ducklings, and she could see where a path led from the dairy's lane along the edge of the field, allowing access to the boats. But the deck doors were sealed tight or covered with canvas, and no smoke rose from the brass-ringed chimneys. Gemma doubted that Babcock's men had found any witnesses there.

Why had Annie Lebow chosen such a deserted stretch of the canal in which to moor her boat? Did it have some connection with the proximity of the dairy barn?

Or look at it another way, Gemma thought. If Annie had been accustomed to mooring her boat there when she came to the Barbridge area, had she seen something at the barn? And if that was the case, could the discovery of the child's body have brought her to the killer's attention?

But for all they knew, Gemma reminded herself, the baby might have been interred in the barn wall long before Annie Lebow had even bought her boat. She shook her head in frustration. She was hypothesizing without hard data, a dangerous thing.

But her walk had netted her one thing more than muddy boots and fingers that were starting to go numb. She knew concretely what she had guessed from looking at the map—that whoever had attacked Annie Lebow had come either from Barbridge or from the lane that led down to the dairy barn. Of course, it was possible that someone could have walked the towpath from as far away as Nantwich to the south, or from above Barbridge to the north, but in last night's heavy fog, she thought it very unlikely—as unlikely as the idea that the killer had blundered his or her way across the fields and through wood, fence, and hedgerow to the path.

That, however, was as far as supposition could take her, but she realized she was not willing to stop there. Once back at her car, she'd run down Kincaid and Ronnie Babcock, and see what they had turned up. It was time she did what she did best, putting the pieces together.

But even as she started towards the towpath, she hesitated. Turning, she gazed once more at the redbrick barn.

There was still no sign of Sergeant Rasansky, and it looked as though the deconstruction crew was winding down. There was no one who knew her history to call her curiosity morbid—why shouldn't she see the last resting place of the mystery child for herself?

*That was one of the things he hated about women. The way they said one thing and meant another. Or the look, the one they gave you that was worse than words, but kept you from striking back, because there was nothing concrete you could name.*

*It made him think of his mother, when he had continued to wet the bed long past the age when it might be excused.*

*She'd waited until he left his room, then slipped in, bundling up the fouled sheets and putting on new ones. He watched her sometimes, from round the corner in the hall.*

*Later, when she would pass by him, she'd give him a look that said she knew what he'd done, and without a word spoken, she had entrapped him in a conspiracy of shame.*

*Furious, he eventually began to deliberately soil the bed, his way of taking back his power, over her, over his own body. But somehow his mother had seemed to know. She simply stopped changing the linen, and a night spent on sodden, stinking sheets made that game not worth playing.*

*And still she had smiled and said nothing.*

*Time had worn her down. She'd tired of the game, and he of her, and he had let her go.*

*But not this time, not this one. This one, with her sideways glances and treacherous tongue—oh, he knew the signs, the signals, all too well. But she would not slip away from him like quicksilver through his fingers. He would make sure of that.*

By the time Kincaid and Babcock returned to Crewe Station, the incident room was humming with a gratifying level of activity. Both Larkin and Rasansky were back and occupied at separate desks, but one look at Rasansky's sour face told Kincaid he didn't have anything positive to report.

"No joy with the deconstruction, I take it?" Babcock asked, as if he, too, was guessing what the answer would be.

"Bloody waste of time," grumbled Rasansky. "Not to mention the fact that I think I've developed double pneumonia." His nose had taken on a Rudolf-like hue, but Constable Larkin, for one, displayed no sympathy.

"I can't think why you're sorry you didn't turn up another body," Larkin said tartly, eyeing them over the stack of papers she'd loaded onto her desk. "Or were you hoping for mass infant graves?"

"Any luck tracing the infant we did find?" Babcock asked, warding off argument.

"We've started tracing birth records for the county, going back fifteen years," said Larkin, "as I doubt the blanket and clothing are older than that. No hits so far, but it will take some time just to process the county records. And that's not taking into account the fact that the birth might have been unregistered."

"What about midwives?"

Larkin nodded at a uniformed constable ensconced at a desk in the corner, phone glued to his ear. "We're checking with locally registered midwives, although they're usually pretty good about getting the birth records filed. Still, slip-ups can happen." She shrugged, adding, "We'll canvass the local doctors, too, just in case someone made a home delivery off the books."

"And we still haven't found the Smiths?" Babcock asked, scowling, but Larkin didn't look intimidated.

"Sorry, boss. I've got someone checking every few hours to see if the couple who supposedly kept up with the Smiths have come back from holiday. We've left word with their neighbors, a note on their door, and a message on their answer phone."

Kincaid, who had propped himself on a desk and faded unobtrusively into the background, spoke up. "Have you contacted the Yard to see if they have a record of any similar cases?"

"Yesterday." Rasansky's irritated look said he didn't appreciate being told how to do his job, however politely.

"When I sent out a description of the infant and its clothing to all agencies."

Pacing, Babcock said, "We're bloody handicapped without more information from the Home Office. Surely the forensic anthropologist can at least give us an idea how long that baby was buried. Ring them again, will you, Sheila? And while you have them on the line, ask if they can do a facial reconstruction."

"Don't all babies that age look pretty much alike, boss?" Larkin asked, raising a carefully shaped eyebrow.

"Just do it. What about the DNA sample Dr. Elsworthy entered into the system?"

Larkin shook her head. "Too soon to have checked it against the database." She gave him a measuring glance. "Looks like that leaves us with the media, boss. Who gets to chat up Lois Lane from the *Chronicle*?"

Watching the glance that passed between them, and Larkin's slight nod in Rasansky's direction, Kincaid guessed there was unspoken context to her query. From what he'd seen of the sergeant, he suspected that Rasansky would make the most of the importance of the case—and of his part in it—and that that served Larkin and Babcock very well.

"Right then, Kevin," Babcock said to Rasansky. "Give little miss reporter the child's approximate age and clothing description, and have her ask if anyone knows of a child who mysteriously disappeared in the last few years. We'll have someone man a designated contact number when the story runs. But for God's sake, tell her to keep the buried-in-the-wall part out of it for now."

Larkin straightened her files with a thump. "Can we get on to the good stuff now, boss? I know we have to trace the child, but that little girl's been dead a long time, and we had a murder on our doorstep this morning. What did you find out from the husband?"

"A dodgy setup, if you ask me. He lives in her house—a Victorian lodge that would make a fitting residence for the chief constable—and apparently lives at least partly off her money. He's certainly not going to lose financially by her death, as he's her heir, and he hasn't an alibi for last night. He says she rang him, wanting to talk, and they made a date to meet for dinner tonight."

"Prime suspect, then?" asked Larkin. "I pulled every bit of paper that looked even remotely relevant off the boat."

"Motive, possibly," answered Kincaid, "and it will be interesting to see what you turn up. But I don't know about the feasibility. I'm not sure he could have got to the boat in last night's fog, or even to the Cut—much less found the boat even if he knew exactly where to look."

"What about the door-to-door in Barbridge?" asked Babcock. "Any luck there?"

"More like boat-to-boat." Larkin grinned. "I did find one old biddy, a Mrs. Millsap, who said she overheard the victim having a row with a man on a boat moored by the pub, on Christmas Day. He was still there, and I spoke to him. His name's Gabriel Wain, and he says Ms. Lebow scraped his boat and they had a bit of argy-bargy over it. He showed me the damage. But then he said she'd offered to pay for any repairs, and apologized, and that was that. I've made a note of it, but it didn't seem the sort of thing that would lead to sneaking up on someone days later and bashing them over the head."

Kincaid frowned. "He said Annie scraped his boat?"

"Yeah. When she was mooring next to him," Larkin clarified. "A nice long patch on the bow."

"That's odd." Kincaid rubbed his chin as he thought, feeling the stubble that was just beginning to break through the skin. "I watched her maneuver the *Horizon* myself, and I'd have said she was a very competent boater."

By the time Gemma neared Barbridge again, this time relatively unscathed by her encounters with stile and hedge, she felt chilled to the bone. She wasn't sure, however, how much of her discomfort came from the physical cold and how much from the memory of the gaping hole she'd seen in the wall of the old dairy.

With the departure of the sergeant, the lads working deconstruction had been happy enough to let her have a look round the interior as long as she didn't interfere with their grid. She'd only ventured in far enough to see the place where Juliet had found the infant, and that glimpse had made her realize that although she'd sympathized with Juliet's experience, she hadn't, until that moment, understood the visceral horror of it.

Gemma wondered if Juliet's clients, who had envisioned turning the old structure into a warm family retreat, would ever regain their enthusiasm—or if Juliet would find any pleasure in completing the job, assuming she had the opportunity.

The day seemed to have softened, a slight rise in temperature transmuting the sleety pellets of early afternoon into fine beads of moisture that soaked into her clothing and coated her hair. It seemed likely that dusk would presage a recurrence of the previous night's heavy fog.

The thought gave Gemma a prickle between her shoulder blades, a rise of the hair on her neck. She jerked round, as she had more than once on her walk back from the barn, but there was no one on the path. Shaking herself, she picked up her pace. The curve of the stone bridge was now in sight; in just a few moments she would be snug in her car and laughing at her paranoid fantasies of being followed.

But she stopped just short of the steps leading up to the road, arrested by the sight framed in the weathered stone arch of the bridge. A small girl, perhaps not much older than Toby, sat at the canal's edge a few yards beyond the bridge, huddled under an enormous black umbrella. She held a fishing rod in one hand, but both girl and line were so still they might have been sculpted.

A boat was moored nearby, its colors softened by the mist, but Gemma realized it was the one she had seen the forensic pathologist visit that morning. Her curiosity aroused, she watched for a moment, then walked slowly forward until she emerged from beneath the bridge.

The girl looked up at her approach. Her curling hair was darkened by the damp, but nothing could dim the brilliant cornflower blue of her eyes.

"A bit wet for fishing, isn't it?" Gemma asked, stopping a few steps away.

The child regarded her seriously. "Poppy says the fish bite better in the rain. I think it's because they can't tell where the water ends and the air begins." She was older than Gemma had first thought; the gap left by the loss of her two front teeth had begun to fill in.

Moving a bit closer, Gemma dropped into as graceful a squat as she could manage, her face now level with the girl's. "What do you catch?"

"Roach. Perch. Bream. Sometimes gudgeon."

Gemma's face must have reflected her distaste, because the girl gave a sudden peal of laughter. "They're tiny things, the gudgeon," she explained. "But you have to use maggots to catch them and I don't much like that. I don't like cleaning the fish, either, but Poppy says it's no different from peeling potatoes or cutting up a hen."

"Can you do that, then?" asked Gemma, impressed. Although Kit was quite skilled in the kitchen, Toby was just mastering making toast and sandwiches, and was certainly never given a sharp knife.

"Not as well as my brother," the girl answered. "I can make smashing mac cheese, though. Much better than fish, but Poppy says we shouldn't pay for food that we can provide ourselves." There was no resentment in her tone.

Gemma realized that it wasn't this child she'd glimpsed opening the door to the doctor, but a boy perhaps a few years older. "Are there just the two of you, you and your brother?"

The girl nodded. "That's Joseph. I'm Marie," she added, favoring Gemma with a grave smile.

"I'm Gemma." Gemma rocked back on her heels, trying to find a more comfortable position without actually letting the seat of her trousers come in contact with the damp turf.

Marie detached a hand from the fishing rod and held it out. The small, calloused fingers felt icily cold in Gemma's, but the child seemed unaware of any discomfort.

Nodding towards the boat, Gemma said, "You and your brother live on the boat with your dad?"

"And our mum. But she's dying," Marie added, in the

same matter-of-fact tone. "Mummy and Poppy don't know that we know, but we do."

Gemma gazed at the girl, at a loss for a response. At last she said, "Has your mum been ill long?"

"I'm not sure." A small crease marred Marie's smooth brow. "But I think she's tired. It's just that she doesn't want to leave us."

"I can understand that," offered Gemma, her heart contracting. "She must love you very much."

Afterwards, Gemma could never guess what signal alerted the child, but Marie suddenly ducked her head round the edge of her umbrella and looked up the towpath. In the distance, Gemma saw a man and a boy, their arms filled with firewood, walking slowly down from the Middlewich Junction.

"That's my poppy coming," said Marie, tucking herself back under the black umbrella like a retreating tortoise. "You'd better go." The cornflower-blue eyes that met Gemma's were as calm and ancient as the sea. "He doesn't like us talking to strangers."

# 21

❧

GEMMA FOUND CREWE Police Station without trouble, and the temporary incident room more easily still. Although the duty sergeant had given her directions, she could have followed the scent trail of stale coffee, half-eaten takeaways, and slightly damp wool, carried on the murmur of multitudinous voices muttering into telephones. Her spirits rose at the familiarity of it, and as she entered the basement room, the sight of the battered desks and snaking telephone and computer wires brought a smile to her lips. She might have felt a fish out of water these last few days, but here she belonged.

She saw Kincaid before he saw her. He was perched on the corner of a desk occupied by Ronnie Babcock, who was leaning back in a battered chair, phone glued to his ear. Kincaid was listening, brow creased, as if trying to make out the unheard end of the conversation. Glancing up, he saw Gemma, grinned and started to rise, but she motioned him to stay where he was and crossed the room to him.

A few of the officers occupying the other desks looked up as she passed. Most were too occupied with their own tasks to display much curiosity, but the young constable who had been so kind to Kit that morning looked up from a stack of papers and gave Gemma a smile of recognition. Sheila Larkin was her name, Gemma remembered.

The sergeant she'd met at the building site was there as

well. He looked no more pleased to see her than he had earlier, but if he'd meant to protest her presence, he was stopped by his ringing phone. Gemma couldn't resist giving him a cheeky little wave, and was rewarded by a full-wattage scowl.

Gemma's shoulder brushed Kincaid's as she reached him. In such surroundings the contact seemed unexpectedly intimate, but she resisted the urge to touch him even as she felt a flush of pleasure in her cheeks.

"Where have you been?" he asked softly, his breath tickling her ear.

"Tell you later," she whispered back, ignoring the rise of gooseflesh on her arms as she tried to catch the drift of Babcock's conversation.

"Right. Okay. Thanks, Doc," Babcock was saying. "Let me know if anything else comes in. Yeah. Sorry about the balls-up."

Kincaid raised an interrogatory eyebrow as Babcock rang off. "Balls-up?"

"It seems the good doctor didn't appreciate us ringing up the forensic anthropologist directly. Not that he was willing to tell us anything. There are channels," he added with mock severity as he nodded a greeting to Gemma.

"So did your pathologist come up with the goods?" Kincaid asked.

"With as many variable parameters as you'd expect from two experts hedging each other." Babcock ran his hands through his thick fair hair, making it stand on end, then leaned back in his creaking chair, hands behind his head. "The bone doctor estimates, from the amount of decomposition and given the circumstances, et cetera, et cetera, that the remains had been in place at least five years. He confirms that the child was female, age less than one year. No obvious cause of death. But before you conclude that we're not much further ahead"—he waggled an admonitory finger at Kincaid, as if he had protested—"the Home Office lab boffins have had some luck with the clothing. The blanket was manufactured for several years in the midnineties, and sold through a number of local outlets."

"My sister said the blanket looked like one she'd used with her own kids, but she couldn't remember if it was Sam or Lally's," Kincaid said. "But if it was available in the mid-nineties, it was most likely Sam's. Of course," he continued, "there's nothing to say that the blanket was acquired for this mystery infant during the period it was initially sold, but that at least gives us an outside limit on the time of death."

"More than five years, less than ten, if you put the blanket and bones together," Babcock agreed, but he didn't sound greatly encouraged. The creases at the corners of his blue eyes deepened as he frowned. "Dr. Elsworthy also informed me that she's already conducted the postmortem on Annie Lebow. I can't think why she didn't let me know she'd scheduled it so quickly. I should have been there."

"Any unexpected results?" Kincaid asked.

"Apparently not. Death due to blunt-force trauma." Babcock couldn't quite control a grimace.

Eyeing his friend with concern, Kincaid said, "Perhaps the doctor was sparing your feelings, Ronnie, by not asking you to attend the p.m. As you knew the victim."

Babcock tilted his chair back into its upright position. "I never thought I'd see the day when Dr. E. worried about treading on anyone's sensibilities. In fact, she seemed definitely off-kilter at the crime scene this morning. Maybe she's ill."

"It's not her that's ill. At least I don't think so," Gemma amended, as both men stared at her in surprise. "I saw her this morning, while I was waiting with Kit. When she came back from the scene, she sat in car for a bit, with this big dog, as if she were deliberating something. Then she got out again and walked down to one of the boats moored across from the pub. She was carrying an oxygen tank." Gemma could see now, from the puzzled expressions on their faces, that she was going to have to admit to her afternoon's snooping. "I walked the towpath this afternoon, from Barbridge to the dairy barn, just to get a picture in my mind of how the places fit together. When I got back to Barbridge, I met this little girl who was fishing beside the same boat the doctor visited this morning. The girl said her mother was dying, so it must have been the mother the doctor was going to see—though I must say I never knew of a pathologist making house calls."

"You're quite certain it was Dr. Elsworthy?"

Gemma bristled under Babcock's skeptical regard. "Yes. I asked the constable on duty who she was, when I saw her go to the boat. She's not someone you'd easily mistake."

"And the boat? You're sure it was the same boat?"

Before Gemma could reply, Kincaid said with some asperity, "Of course she's certain, Ronnie," then he turned to Gemma, frowning. "You said you wanted to see how the two places fit together. But we don't know of any connection between Annie Lebow's murder and the remains found in the barn."

Unwilling to air any far-flung theories in front of Ronnie Babcock, Gemma merely shrugged. "It just seemed odd, that's all. I only wanted—"

"Boss." Sheila Larkin got up from her desk, picked her way through the obstacle course of cables until she reached them, and waved a handful of loose papers at Babcock. "Boss," she repeated, making sure she had his full attention, "I've been looking through some of the things I found on Annie Lebow's boat. It seems she had considerable investments with Newcombe and Dutton, here in Nantwich." She glanced at Kincaid. "Is that any connection with your sister, Mrs. Newcombe?"

"My sister's husband's firm," Kincaid confirmed easily, but Gemma detected a faint note of surprise in his voice. "But you said Annie worked here in Nantwich, before she left Social Services, didn't you, Ronnie? So I suppose it's not unlikely she'd have dealt with Newcombe and Dutton."

"Newcombe and Dutton have any number of well-heeled clients in this area, and it seems that Annie Lebow certainly fit into that category," said Babcock, steepling his fingers together. "The question is whether the disposition of those investments on her death gives her husband a motive for killing her."

Gemma heard the last words only vaguely, drowned out by the rush of blood in her ears. As Babcock took the papers from Larkin and began to flip through them, she grasped Kincaid's arm. "We'd better leave the chief inspector to it," she said, forcing a smile that made her face ache. "Your mother's expecting us to pick up the children."

"But I thought she and Dad were taking them home from the shop," Kincaid said, sounding baffled.

"Change of plans," Gemma answered, still smiling. When Babcock turned away for a moment to speak to another officer, she dug her fingers into the flesh above Kincaid's elbow until he winced. When he glanced at her in surprise, she mouthed, "We need to talk. Now."

After hasty and slightly awkward good-byes, Gemma hurried Kincaid to the Escort, which was parked on the double yellows near the police station and was remarkably ticket free.

The car's interior still retained a little welcome heat, but Gemma shivered as they buckled themselves in. Kincaid turned to her, looking concerned. "What's going on, Gem? Are the kids—"

"They're fine—"

"Then what is it? What have you been up to? Why were you checking out the crime scenes this afternoon?"

Gemma shook her head. "It's nothing to do with that. Look, is there someplace we can stop and talk?" she asked, knowing she couldn't explain and drive at the same time. The early winter dusk was coming on fast, the mist was thickening, and she'd felt a slight glaze beneath her feet as they walked across the pavement.

"But you said we needed to pick up the boys—"

"It was just an excuse."

He stared at her, his mouth open to form another question, then suddenly nodded and settled back in his seat. "Okay. We can stop at the Crown in Nantwich. It's halfway to the house, and we ought to be able to have a quiet word in the bar."

As they walked across the darkening square towards the old inn, Gemma thought of Christmas Eve, when she'd imagined she'd seen Lally and a boy who might have been Kit slip furtively into the shadows of the Crown's coach entrance. But she'd been mistaken, she reminded herself, as the children had been waiting for them in church. She dismissed the memory with a shrug as Kincaid led her into the hotel's lounge bar.

The warmth generated by the crush of bodies and the blazing fire struck them like a wave, and Gemma was already shedding her coat as they squeezed round a small table in a corner. The firelight sparkled like gems from the leaded glass of the front windows, a cheerful counterpoint to the hum of conversation, but Gemma watched anxiously as Duncan fetched their drinks from the bar. Now that she'd had time to think, she wondered just exactly what she was going to say.

Perhaps she should have spoken to Juliet first, tried to convince her to share what she'd learned about Newcombe and Dutton with Duncan.

As Kincaid returned to the table, carrying a pint for himself and lemonade for her, she took a breath and began. "There are some things you need to know about your sister."

"You bastard! You can't mean it." Juliet rose from the sofa and backed away from Kincaid as if he'd struck her.

"Jules, see reason, will you? And keep your voice down." As soon as he and Gemma had reached the house, he'd maneuvered his sister as unobtrusively as he could manage into the unoccupied sitting room, but if she was going to shout at him, the whole family would be trooping in to see what was wrong. Not that he'd mind an audience, except for the children's sake, but he had no doubt that she would.

"Reason?" Juliet had come up against the other chesterfield, but showed no inclination to sink into its cracked leather depths. "The only reason I can see is that I should never have told Gemma, and she should never have told you. How could you possibly think I'd agree to implicate my husband in a murder inquiry?"

"You'd not be implicating Caspar in anything. It's his partner who's done the fiddling, according to what you told Gemma," he countered, trying to keep his patience. Although Gemma had warned him Juliet would react this way, he hadn't been prepared for her fragility, or for the edge of hysteria in her voice. He went on quietly, trying to stay reasonable himself. "Look, Jules. You've said you've seen proof that Piers Dutton was skimming money from his investors' accounts. If Annie Lebow was Piers's client, and if she somehow found out he was cheating her, he'd have had a bang-up motive for killing her. You can't—"

"I don't care. I won't help you ruin Caspar's business for some pie-in-the-sky idea of yours—"

"You don't care?" Standing, he crossed to the hearth and stabbed at the cold grate with the poker. "How can you say you don't care that this woman was murdered? You didn't meet her. You didn't see her body lying on the towpath this morning, or see Kit's face after he found her."

For the first time, Juliet looked ashamed, but she didn't relax her stance. "That's not fair. That's not what I meant and you know it. You always twist things. But I won't have the children jeopardized. Have you thought what it would mean for Sam and Lally if their father's business and reputation were ruined? They're your niece and nephew, for God's sake, or had you forgotten?"

The fairy lights on the Christmas tree in the corner twinkled, but the room was as cold as the fire, and Kincaid remembered, suddenly, the bitter arguments he and his sister had had in this room over long-ago differences. "Of course I hadn't forgotten," he said, tasting the ashes of one more unresolved quarrel. "But those things might not happen, and even if they did, they're not insurmountable. You can recover from a financial crisis, from a damaged reputation—even from a failed marriage—and the children can deal with more than you think. But nothing can give Annie Lebow's life back to her, and I won't let go any opportunity to find her killer."

They stared at each other, deadlocked, and after a moment Juliet's eyes filled with tears. "You're a self-righteous shit, Duncan. You always were. You can say what you want, but I'll deny I found anything."

"It doesn't matter. Ronnie Babcock can get a warrant to search Newcombe and Dutton's files on the basis of the connection between the firm and the victim. All he needs is a nod in the right direction. And he'll be interviewing Piers and Caspar, regardless."

Juliet shook her head, once, and wrapped her arms tightly around her thin body, as if the cold had seeped into her bones. "Don't think I'll forgive you for this."

He sighed, his anger evaporating. "I'm sorry, Jules, but I haven't a choice. Now will you make the call, or shall I?"

There was something in the quality of silence that told Caspar the moment he opened the door that the house was empty. He stood for a moment in the foyer, listening, trying to define the difference. Had the mere physical presence of the children in their rooms, of Juliet working on her accounts at the kitchen table, created a resonance he had never noticed?

It wasn't that he'd really expected his family to have come home, he told himself as he hung his coat carefully in the cupboard, it was just that the habit of having them there was so ingrained in his mind that it took a conscious effort to refute it.

Even though he'd already had a few drinks at the Bowling Green with Piers, he went into his study and poured himself a good finger of Cardhu single malt. It was a whisky he hadn't tried before, recommended by Piers, and he'd treated himself to a bottle partly because he knew the expense would annoy Juliet—just as his retreating to his study to have a drink as soon as he got home had annoyed Juliet.

Now he stood, irresolute, unable to decide whether to sit at his desk, although he really had no pressing work to do, or to wander into the kitchen or sitting room. He could turn on the telly, after all, without being sniped at by the children for interrupting one of their programs, or nagged to help them with their schoolwork. He could make himself cheese on toast for supper, if he chose, and leave the washing up for tomorrow, or even the next day, without Juliet giving him the evil eye and an exasperated sigh.

But there didn't seem much point in doing any of those things if there was no one to object, and he felt suddenly, frighteningly hollow, as if his insides had been scooped out like the pulp of a ripe melon. Afraid his legs wouldn't support him, he groped for the arm of his chair, and after lowering himself carefully into it, topped up his glass with another inch of Cardhu.

The neat whisky seared his throat and warmed his gut, and after a few sips he began to feel more substantial. The house wouldn't be empty for long. Piers had warned him over their drinks that if Juliet was determined to split up, then he must get custody of the children, and that her financial status should be enough to convince a court that he was the more responsible parent. Caspar had agreed, adding that he'd see her stripped of every penny, but only now did he begin to wonder what he would do with the children if he had them. Juliet had managed and organized and seen to all their needs, and for just an instant his own ignorance terrified him.

Then he shrugged and knocked back the remainder of his drink. Lally and Sam were old enough; they could manage without such coddling. What was important was that Juliet be made to see the error of her ways, and to pay.

A small bloom of satisfaction began to replace the emptiness in his gut. He had been right to listen to Piers. Piers had seen Juliet for the manipulative bitch she was when Caspar had still been duped, and it was Piers who had kept him from following blindly while she made a mockery of him.

And it was Piers who had had the good grace not to say "I told you so," but had smiled with the sort of sympathy only another man could offer, and had promised him that together they would work everything out.

# 22

✤

**BABCOCK REACHED NANTWICH TOWN** center at half past eight the next morning to find the premises of Newcombe and Dutton still locked, blinds closed. He strolled across to the churchyard, taking up a position on a bench that would allow him to keep an unobtrusive eye on the firm's door. The morning was gray, the remnants of the previous night's fog still hovering round the rooftops and the massive square of the church tower, and it wasn't long before the chill of the bench slats worked its way through his overcoat. He'd begun to contemplate the advisability of adding a pound or two of padding to his backside when a shiny new Land Rover (both adjectives oxymorons when combined with Land Rover, in Babcock's opinion) pulled into the firm's parking area and Piers Dutton climbed unhurriedly out.

Babcock found it interesting that it was Dutton who'd arrived first to open the office, when Caspar Newcombe lived just a short walk away. But perhaps investment advisors, unlike police officers, relaxed their schedules during Christmas week. The development suited him well enough, however, as he wanted to interview Dutton on his own.

He gave Dutton a few minutes to get settled so as not to give the impression he'd been waiting to pounce. He wanted the man relaxed, at least in the beginning.

While he waited, he popped knuckles stiffening from the cold and ran over the conversation he'd had with Duncan

Kincaid the night before. It was a tricky situation. Not only had Kincaid told him about his sister's suspicions against her wishes, but Babcock didn't know Juliet Newcombe well enough to judge her credibility. For all he knew, she might have made the entire business up to satisfy a personal grudge.

When the office blinds snapped open, Babcock took it as his cue and, prizing himself off the bench, crossed Churchyardside to the office, at the end of Monk's Lane. A bell chimed gently as Babcock pushed open the door and stepped into the reception area. Piers Dutton came out of an inner office, looking surprised to see him, but not alarmed.

"You're the early bird, Chief Inspector," he said genially. "What can I do for you?"

"Just a quick word, Mr. Dutton, if you don't mind."

"No further along, are you, in finding the elusive Smiths?" Dutton asked as he waved Babcock towards the room from which he'd appeared. "Can I get you a coffee?"

"Yes, thanks." Babcock, never a morning person himself, had not expected such cordiality from Dutton. He wasn't about to refuse what he suspected would be good coffee, however, especially as he was half frozen.

Following Dutton, he looked round the man's private office with interest. He'd been right about the coffeemaker. A sleek German contraption that looked as if it might run on rocket fuel took center stage on the credenza against the back wall, and the smell emanating from it was enough to make Babcock light-headed.

The rest of the furnishings matched the credenza, never a look that appealed to Babcock personally, but the patina of the wood and the thickness of the carpet beneath his feet shouted money, as he supposed it was meant to do. The maize-colored wall behind Dutton's desk held a single painting, an ornately framed study of a bay horse and spaniel in the style of George Stubbs. But the more Babcock studied the jewel-like depth of the colors and the exquisite execution of the brushwork, the more he began to wonder if it actually *was* a Stubbs, and he whistled soundlessly through his teeth.

"There you are, Chief Inspector." Dutton handed him a coffee, in a bone-china cup and saucer, no less, and looked at him quizzically.

"Just admiring your painting, sir," said Babcock, going for the country-bumpkin air. "Reminds me of a picture I saw once in London, at the Tate. By George Stubbs, I think it was."

Dutton turned to gaze at the painting, but didn't quite manage to hide the flicker of pleasure that crossed his face. "Very astute of you, Chief Inspector. It *is* a Stubbs. A family heirloom, actually, but I keep it here where I can enjoy it most."

Babcock rather doubted that, as Dutton's back would be to the painting as he sat at his desk, just as he doubted the painting was a family heirloom, but he looked suitably impressed. "Not worried about theft, then, sir?" he asked, eyeing the office window, which looked directly out onto the parking area and, beyond that, the town square.

"Our security's quite good," said Dutton. "And I don't bandy the painting's provenance about. Very few people are aware of its value." He eyed Babcock curiously, and while Babcock felt he might have erred in displaying interest in the painting, he found it telling that Dutton hadn't been able to resist bragging about his possession.

Dutton poured his own coffee, then seated himself in one of the two visitors' chairs, motioning Babcock to take the other one. It was a gesture designed to make Babcock feel comfortable, one Babcock imagined Dutton used when he was working a client up to an agreement, and he wondered why the man had changed his tactic after the subtle condescension he'd displayed during their first interview. It could be that the mention of the painting had made Dutton feel he deserved to be treated as a social equal—a thought that made Babcock want to grind his teeth—or it could be that Dutton was nervous about something. Babcock's curiosity rose another notch.

"Actually, Mr. Dutton, it's not the Smiths I've come about," he said. Having sipped the coffee, and found it as good as it smelled, he balanced the delicate cup on his knee. "Do I take it you haven't heard about yesterday's murder?"

"Murder?" Dutton gazed at him blankly.

"A woman named Annie Lebow was found murdered beside her narrowboat, quite near your house, in fact." When Dutton still registered nothing but puzzlement, Babcock added, "I believe you might have known her as Annie Constantine. She was one of your clients."

"What?" Dutton's eyes widened, and Babcock could have sworn he saw real shock, quickly camouflaged, in the slackening muscles of the man's face. "Of course I know Annie Constantine," Dutton said slowly. "Don't know why she started calling herself Lebow, when she and her husband aren't even divorced." He shook his head, as if he couldn't quite comprehend what he'd heard. "Dead, you say?"

"Can you account for your movements night before last, Mr. Dutton?" asked Babcock, tiring of the man's baffled-squire act when he felt quite sure there was lightning calculation going on behind the blue eyes.

"My movements? Why on earth would you need to know that?" Although he sounded incensed, Dutton's china rattled in his hand. He leaned forward to set the cup and saucer on the edge of his desk, sloshing coffee as he did so.

"Routine inquiries," Babcock said, knowing it would irritate Dutton. "But I'm sure you want to cooperate in any way you can."

"Of course," Dutton agreed heartily. "But I hadn't met with Annie Constantine for at least a year, so I don't quite see—"

"Were you at home the night before last, Mr. Dutton?"

"I— No, actually, I met friends for dinner, at the Swan in Tarporley. We finished about half past ten, and I drove home. The fog was drawing in, so I thought it best to get off the road before the visibility worsened." Now Dutton was volunteering information, an indication that he was definitely off balance. "Especially as I'd had one or two glasses of wine over the limit," he added, imparting the confidence with a slight twinkle, one sophisticated man to another.

Babcock didn't return the smile. "And when you arrived home, can anyone vouch for your movements? Your son, perhaps?"

Dutton's careful bonhomie vanished instantly. Blanching, he said furiously, "I won't have you grilling my son, Chief Inspector. I can't think why you believe any of this is necessary—"

"The victim has considerable money invested with your firm, I believe?"

Reaching for his coffee again, Dutton seemed to make an effort to recover some of his assurance, but Babcock caught the sudden scent of his expensive aftershave, mixed with sweat. "Since when is that a crime," Dutton said with forced lightness, "or anyone else's business?"

"When we've received information indicating that you might have been defrauding some of your clients, Mr. Dutton. If you were stealing from Ms. Constantine and she found out, that would certainly give you a motive. It appears you had opportunity, and the means were easy enough to hand."

Dutton gave an unexpected bark of laughter. "So that's your theory, Chief Inspector? And your source would be Juliet Newcombe, I take it?" He shook his head, a fond uncle expressing disappointment. "I expected better of you. Look, I've tried to be discreet about this whole business, for Caspar's sake, but you must know that the woman is seriously unbalanced. She developed a sort of unhealthy . . . obsession . . . with me." He looked away, as if embarrassed by the admission. "When I didn't respond, she began to retaliate. She . . . imagined things. That's why I encouraged her to leave the office, to set up on her own. I put clients her way. I tried to protect my partner as best I could, but in the end, I had to tell him what was going on."

It was slick, it was plausible, and it was recounted with just the right degree of reluctance, and Babcock found that he didn't believe a word. For the first time, he felt certain that Juliet Newcombe had been telling the truth and that Dutton had manufactured her infatuation with him as a shield. Had her husband actually believed him?

But if Juliet Newcombe had held such dangerous knowledge, why wasn't she dead, rather than Annie Constantine? Was it because Dutton hadn't been sure what Juliet knew? Or because he guessed her loyalty to her husband would keep her quiet?

If that was the case, could Annie Constantine have found out something from Juliet that aroused her own suspicions? Was there a link between the two women that Juliet hadn't revealed? And did any of this connect in some way with the infant buried in the barn, so near Piers Dutton's property?

Dutton was watching him, as if assessing his reaction, so Babcock said sympathetically, "How very difficult for you. But I'm sure you can understand that we will have to audit the records of your transactions on Ms. Constantine's behalf."

"I understand nothing of the kind." Dutton's smile, which had never reached his eyes, disappeared entirely, and his tone could have frozen a hot geyser. "You have no right to my clients' confidential files, Chief Inspector, and if you persist, I'll have to bring in my attorney."

Babcock finished his coffee with deliberation, enjoying the last drop, then reached into his jacket pocket and removed a folded paper. "Then you can show him this. It's a warrant authorizing our fraud team to search your records. They should be here"—he glanced at his watch—"any moment now. If you don't mind, I'll just make myself at home until they arrive. And while we're waiting," he added, pulling a notebook from his pocket as well, "you could start by giving me the names of the friends you dined with in Tarporley."

Althea found Gabriel Wain waiting for her in the lay-by across the canal from his boat. He stood like a brooding hawk, hands in the pockets of his coat, shoulders hunched, glancing from the boat to the lane and back again. Although he waited while she found a spot for her car at the bottom of the lay-by, he shifted his stance uneasily, his impatience seeming barely contained. Her heart constricted as she reached him. Had Rowan taken a turn for the worse?

But before she could ask, he spoke, the words spilling out as if he could no longer contain them. "The police have been. I said what you told me, that the Constantine woman had reversed into the *Daphne* and scraped her bow. It seemed all right."

"Well, then, that's—"

"No, no," he broke in impatiently. "Later, a woman came while I was away gathering firewood. Police or bloody social worker, one or the other. I only saw her from a distance, but I can smell it, the nosiness, the do-gooding. She was talking to Marie, this woman, asking her questions. Then when she saw me coming, she left."

"What did she ask, did Marie say?"

"Only that she was a 'nice lady.' I've told the girl time and again not to speak to strangers—"

"Leave her be, Gabriel," said Althea, thinking furiously. "She's just a child, and she's not the issue here." If the police were suspicious of Gabriel, wouldn't Babcock have mentioned something when she'd spoken to him the previous afternoon?

Was it possible that Babcock had got wind of her involvement and had kept things from her deliberately? He had, after all, gone over her head to speak to the forensic anthropologist about the mummified infant.

What if Babcock had discovered Annie Lebow's connection with Gabriel and his family? And if the police learned of the past accusations against Rowan and Gabriel, would Social Services be far behind?

She met Gabriel's eyes, saw the raw fear there, and knew her decision had made itself. For just an instant, a detached part of her mind wondered how she had got from a woman who'd spent her life refusing any commitments other than the care of her sister, to this reckless person who was willing to risk career and reputation to help people she hardly knew. But then she heard herself say, "Gabriel?" and the voice of reason vanished like a will-o'-the-wisp.

"Gabriel," she repeated, more forcefully. "Listen. About the children. I think you should let them come with me for a bit." She forestalled the protest she saw forming on his lips, all the while wondering how she would juggle her work a the hospital, how she would handle things at home. Shoul she call in and say she was ill? Would the children be al right if she left them with Beatrice? Could she ask Paul fo help?

"If the police come back, they might bring someone from Social Services," she continued. "If the children weren' here, at least we'd have a chance to forestall things. I've some connections—"

"But Rowan—she couldn't bear to let them go. Every minute she has—" He stopped, eyes reddening, and looked back towards the boat. "How could I even . . ."

"I know," Althea said, gently. "But what if they took the children away? I can't imagine anything worse for Rowan than that. And if they come . . . if they should take you in for questioning, the children would see . . ."

"They've never spent a night away from this boat," Gabriel protested fiercely. "They don't know anything else."

A wave of sadness swept over Althea. She reached out and touched his arm, a contact neither of them would have accepted even a few moments before. "Gabriel, things are going to change. Whatever happens, things are going to change."

"You couldn't have gone with him, you know," Gemma told Kincaid quietly. They had arrived at Crewe Police station after breakfast to find Babcock already gone. "You're too close; you know that. With Juliet involved, we'll be lucky if the DCI doesn't boot us out altogether."

They moved to an unoccupied desk in the corner of the incident room, and she knew that the sense of the investigations flowing around them must be as frustrating for Kincaid as it was for her. He took the swivel chair, the cracks in its faux-leather seat mended with packing tape. Scowling, he drummed his fingers on the sticky surface of the desk. She knew that he knew she was right, but she also knew that admitting it would make him even more irritable, so she let it drop.

The choleric Sergeant Rasansky had been out as well,

and it had been DC Larkin who'd told them that Babcock had already gone to interview Piers Dutton, warrant in hand, with the fraud team scheduled to meet him there at a prearranged time. Impressed with his efficiency, Gemma had said, "He's got skates on, your guv'nor."

Larkin had shaken her head. "You'd not have wanted to cross him this morning. He was up half the night getting that warrant, and he'll be paying back favors until doomsday. Piers Dutton has a lot of influence in this town." She gave Kincaid a searching look. "I hope you're right about this. The fraud lads won't be happy if he's given them a false lead, either."

With that disapproving comment, she'd gone back to her desk and her reports, and although she gave them the occasional curious glance, she didn't protest their presence. But a few moments later, a phone call took all her attention.

Gemma watched her, liking the young DC's brisk manner, and when Larkin rang off, she navigated her way across the floor obstacles and perched on the edge of the constable's desk. "Anything interesting?" she asked.

Larkin hesitated, then gave a slight shrug, apparently deciding that if they were in Babcock's confidence she might as well share. "That was Western Division. The constable who most often patrols Tilston knows Roger Constantine. Says he keeps to himself, but according to neighbors, he's been seen occasionally having dinner in the pub with a younger woman."

Kincaid had joined them in time to hear her summary. "That gives him motive in spades," he said, looking distinctly more cheerful. "But we know Annie rang him at home that night—could he have driven from Tilston to Barbridge in the fog after that? And if so, could he have found the boat?"

"She might have given him specific directions," suggested Gemma, but Kincaid was already frowning.

"I'd think that unless he was very familiar with that stretch of the Shroppie, he'd quite likely have ended up in the Cut rather than alongside it. You've seen how it twists and turns along that stretch. Unless—"

He stopped as Larkin's attention shifted towards the door. Turning, Gemma saw not Babcock, but Sergeant Rasansky looking happier than she'd imagined possible.

"What's up, Sarge?" asked Larkin, sounding equally surprised. "You look like the proverbial cat in the cream."

"I found the bloody Smiths." Rasansky nodded at Kincaid and Gemma, and seated himself on the edge of Larkin's desk, regardless of carefully arranged paperwork. "Settled in a retirement flat in Shrewsbury—not a bad place if you like that sort—"

"Sarge," Larkin interrupted, and Gemma guessed Rasansky had a tendency to be long-winded when he had an audience. "What did they say about the baby?"

He clicked his tongue. "Shocked, absolutely shocked. I thought the missus might have a coronary on me, poor old dear. Husband had to sit her down and fetch a glass of water. They said they'd no idea how something like that could have happened in their barn, and they certainly hadn't lost any infants. Their grandkids were ten and twelve when they moved away, so I suppose that lets them out as potential parents." He scanned the room, ignoring Larkin's look of disappointment. "Where's the boss?"

"Still interviewing Piers Dutton. So what's all the fuss about, then?"

Rasansky hesitated, as if debating whether he was willing to lose the cachet of telling Babcock first, but the temptation of listeners on tenterhooks proved too much. "Well, I thought it was a bust, but they insisted on giving me tea and cakes, for all the trouble I'd taken to drive there."

Larkin, sitting just out of her sergeant's line of sight, rolled her eyes, and Gemma suppressed a smile. From the comfortable curve of Rasansky's belly and the crumbs dotting his tie, this wasn't an unusual occurrence.

"Good thing, too," Rasansky went on, "because it was only when the old man had calmed down and had a few minutes to think that he remembered he'd had some masonry work done in the old dairy, not too long before they decided to sell the place. Hired a fellow off the boats, name of Wain."

He pulled a notebook from his jacket pocket and made a show of consulting his notes. "Gabriel Wain. Now all we have to do is find this bloke—"

"Oh, Christ." Sheila Larkin's normally rosy cheeks had gone pale. "Gabriel Wain. He was right under our noses the whole time, and I didn't bloody see it."

"What are you talking about?" broke in Kincaid.

"His wife's name is Rowan—it must be." She shook her head, impatient with their lack of understanding. "I interviewed him. His boat's moored at Barbridge, and a woman who lives along the canal said he had a row with Annie Lebow on Christmas Day. He said she'd scraped his boat— he even showed me the damage—and it seemed plausible enough. I didn't—"

"Sheila, I've told you you're too gullible—" Rasansky began, but Kincaid cut him off.

"You're saying that the same man who might be connected with the baby had an argument with Annie Lebow?"

Larkin nodded miserably. "There's more. I was reading through the victim's case files—Annie Constantine, as she was then. I had them sent over from Social Services. I was just skimming, really, so I didn't—" The color had crept back into her cheeks, but this time it was a blush of embarrassment. "I didn't make a connection.

"There was a case, not long before Constantine retired. The mother was accused of MSBP—Munchausen syndrome by proxy. She kept telling the doctors that her little boy had fits and stopped breathing, but they couldn't find anything, so the doctor in charge of the case referred it to Social Services. Annie Constantine had the case dismissed, so I didn't pay all that much attention. But the thing is, the woman had a second baby while the case was under investigation, a little girl called Marie. And the mother . . . the mother's name was Rowan Wain."

The gears in his brain visibly clicking, Rasansky said, "The Smiths sold up five years ago, so it must have been a bit longer than that when they had the work done in the dairy. Mr. Smith said it was dead of winter—he worried about the mortar setting in the cold."

"That would fit with what the pathologist found," Kincaid put in. "No sign of insect activity on the corpse."

Sheila Larkin scrabbled through the papers on her desk until she found the file she wanted, then scanned the pages, running down the text with her forefinger. Her nail, Gemma noticed, was bitten to the quick.

Larkin stopped, her lips moving with concentration as she read to herself, then looked up at them. "The timing might fit. Constantine worked the case the year before she left the job."

"So this Wain bloke, or his wife, was abusing the older kid." Rasansky sounded positively gleeful at the prospect. "Then they start on the baby, but this one dies. Wain just happens to be working in the dairy, repairing a bit of masonry, so he thinks, 'Bob's your uncle,' the perfect opportunity to dispose of the body, no one the wiser. And they're gypsies, these boat people. No one keeps track of their kiddies, so afterwards they move on and no one notices they're one tyke short."

"Except Annie Constantine," Larkin said softly. "When she met up with the Wains on Christmas Day. If that was why she argued with Gabriel Wain, if she threatened to go to the authorities—"

"Motive." Rasansky ticked one meaty forefinger against the other. "And he certainly would have had opportunity—if anyone could have found her boat in the dark, it was this Wain fellow. He must know the Cut like the back of his hand."

Larkin glanced at the clock on the basement wall. "Where the hell is the guv'nor? I don't know if he's going to kill us or kiss us, but we've got to get Wain in—"

"There's only one problem with all this," broke in Gemma. They all turned to stare at her.

She had been listening, first with a rush of relief that perhaps none of this would touch Juliet after all, then with growing dismay as she put the pieces together.

"More than one, actually. First, Annie Constantine had the case dismissed, and from what you've just said, the doctors never found evidence that the child was physically abused.

Basically, they were accusing the mother of making up his illness, to get attention for herself."

As Larkin nodded slowly, Kincaid raised an eyebrow. "And?"

"And," Gemma said, "Marie Wain is alive and well, and as bright and healthy a seven-year-old as you could imagine. I've met her."

# 23

❧

BABCOCK HAD COME into the station whistling under his breath, having left Piers Dutton shouting at some solicitor's poor secretary and the fraud team beginning a systematic removal of his files. All in a good morning's work, he'd told himself. He was liking Dutton more and more for Annie Lebow's murder, and the fact that he'd developed a healthy distaste for the man only added to his satisfaction. Police officers, of course, were supposed to be unbiased, but he'd yet to meet one who didn't enjoy making a collar on a bastard like Dutton.

Now, if he could just sort out this business with the baby—

The whistle died on his lips as he caught sight of the posse gathered round Sheila Larkin's desk. Larkin, Rasansky, Kincaid, and the lovely Gemma, all watching him with expressions that boded no good.

"You lot look like a convention of funeral directors," he said as he reached them, his heart sinking. "What's happened, then?"

It was Kincaid who told him, concisely, ignoring increasingly evil looks from Rasansky, who would rather be the bearer of bad news than shoved out of the picture altogether. Larkin was chewing on a fingernail again, a habit he thought she'd broken.

"Guv—" Rasansky began when Kincaid had finished his summary, but Babcock held up a hand for silence.

"Just let me think a minute, Kevin." He patted his coat pockets, as he always did when faced with a problem, then remembered, as he always did, that he no longer smoked. He settled for nicking a pencil off Larkin's desk and rotating it in his fingers as he said, "Okay, so this Wain fellow can't have murdered his baby daughter. But it can't simply be coincidence that he did mortar work in the dairy near the time the infant must have been interred, or that he knew Annie Lebow, or that he had a public row with her a day before she died."

"Maybe he didn't kill his own daughter," said Rasansky. "Maybe it was someone else's daughter that he conveniently walled up in that barn—"

"Then why were no baby girls that age reported missing?" broke in Larkin. "And how would Annie Lebow have known that when she met up with him again?"

"She kept her own counsel, Annie," Babcock replied. "She might have known all sorts of things she didn't put down on paper." He tapped the report on Larkin's desk with the pencil end. "And if he had nothing to do with her death, why did he lie about knowing her when he was first questioned?"

"That's easy enough," said Gemma. "If he'd been in trouble with the law before, especially if he and his wife were unjustly accused, he'd not want to call attention to himself. That's understandable."

Babcock looked at the two women, wondering why they seemed to be defending a man Gemma had not even met. "Well, he's going to regret it," Babcock said crossly. He dropped the pencil on the desk and watched it bounce, his visions of an easily solved case evaporating. "We're going to talk to him again." Turning to Rasansky, he added, "Kevin, I'll need you to stay here to liaise with the fraud team. I'm not giving up on Dutton yet." Then, to Larkin, "Sheila, you've met Wain; you'd better come with me." He eyed his friend. "And I suppose the two of you want to tag along?"

Kincaid met his eyes with no trace of humor. "Ronnie, I want to see this case solved as much as you do. Maybe more."

"All right," Babcock agreed, against his better judgment. It would be a wonder if Wain didn't make a run for it when he saw four coppers descending on him like storm troopers. "We'll make a bloody party of it."

Kincaid realized he'd seen the boat, both on Boxing Day and on the following morning, after Annie Lebow's murder, but he'd paid no attention other than to notice the trickle of smoke from the chimney.

Now he noticed that it was an old boat, perhaps even pre-war, and painted in the traditional style, although it looked as though it had been neglected recently. But a wisp of wood smoke spiraled from a chimney whose brass rings still gleamed, and the scent was sharp on the still, damp air.

They crossed the bridge and stepped down to the towpath single file, with Babcock leading, but when they reached the boat, it was obvious that the four of them couldn't crowd into the well deck.

Babcock stood back and nodded at DC Larkin. "You've met him, Sheila. You make the contact."

Larkin glanced at him, and whatever passed between them seemed to give her confidence. Although it must have been awkward, with everyone watching, she climbed from the towpath into the well deck nimbly enough, then squared her shoulders and rapped at the cabin door.

"Mr. Wain," she called out, "it's DC Larkin. I—" The cabin door swung open before she could say more.

The man who stepped out, blinking in the gray light, was tall and well built, with the sort of musculature that comes from hard physical labor rather than time spent in a gym. His dark hair was still thick, but flecked with silver, and his cheeks were sunken, his dark eyes hollow, as if he'd suffered a recent illness, or grief.

Yet his stance, as he surveyed them, was defiant, and he answered Larkin brusquely. "I know who you are, Constable. I thought we'd finished our business."

"So did I, Mr. Wain, until I found out you lied to me." There was a note of personal injury in Larkin's voice that made Kincaid think of the way Gemma sometimes made an intense connection with a suspect. "You said you only met Annie Lebow when she scraped your boat," continued Larkin, "but in fact you knew her very well."

Kincaid saw the shock ripple through the man's body, saw him tense with the automatic instinct to flee, then saw him force himself to relax.

"This is my boss, by the way." Larkin gestured at Babcock, reinforcing her position. "Chief Inspector Babcock. And this is Superintendent Kincaid, from Scotland Yard, and Inspector James."

At the mention of Scotland Yard, Wain rested his fingertips on the top of the boat's curved tiller, as if for support, but when he spoke his voice was steady. "I knew her, all right, I'll admit that. But this is why I didn't say." His gaze took in all the gathered officers, and Kincaid thought he saw a flash of recognition as his eyes passed over Gemma, but the man didn't acknowledge it. "I knew, when I heard she was dead, that you'd pick me out. I've had dealings with the police before. I know you lot go for the easiest target, and you don't care about the truth."

"Why don't you try me and see," said Larkin, resolute as a bull terrier. "What did you argue with Ms. Lebow about on Christmas Day?"

"I don't know any Lebow. She was Annie Constantine to me. I hadn't seen her in years, since she got the case against us dismissed. That day, I think she was as surprised to see me as I was to see her. She seemed pleased, asked after the children, wanting to see how they were doing.

"But I couldn't have that, do you see? It brought it all back, that terrible time. When she came back the next morning, I'm ashamed to say I shouted at her, and she was hurt. She said she'd never done anything but help us, and it was true. I'd take the words back, if I could."

Wain's words rang with sincerity. Still, Kincaid had the sense that he was somehow skirting the truth.

"And she didn't ask you what you knew about the infant found in the wall of the dairy barn where you worked?" asked Larkin.

Kincaid knew instantly Larkin had made a mistake, that

the timing was wrong. Juliet had only found the child's body on Christmas Eve. It was highly unlikely that Annie could have learned about the baby by Christmas morning. In fact, they had no proof that she had ever known.

"What?" Wain looked stunned. "What are you talking about?"

Taking a step nearer the boat, Babcock intervened. "The body of a female infant was found mortared into the wall of the old dairy just down the way."

"The Smiths' place?" Wain asked, and seeing Babcock's nod of confirmation, went on, "I did some work for them, yes, but I didn't—you can't think—" He stopped, shaking his head, as if speech had deserted him.

"I don't know what to think," Babcock said conversationally. "It seems a bit much to believe that someone else did mortar work in that barn without Mr. Smith noticing. Or that someone else took advantage of your work to add a little of their own and you didn't twig to it."

Gabriel Wain's face hardened. "You can't possibly know that this"—he stopped, swallowing—"this child was put there during the time I did the work for the Smiths. I was only there a few days."

He was right, and Kincaid could see that Babcock knew it. They had no physical evidence that could link Wain directly to the body, nor any explanation as to why or how Wain could have acquired the child. Not only that, but Kincaid had dealt with a good number of perverts over the course of his career, and while they sometimes presented a very plausible persona, there was always something just slightly off about them. He'd developed radar of a sort for the unbalanced personality, and he didn't read the signs in Gabriel Wain.

Babcock, apparently realizing that he couldn't push further without more to back up any accusations, changed tack. "Where were you night before last, Mr. Wain?"

"Here. With my wife and children."

"The entire night? Can your wife vouch for you?"

"You leave my wife out of this," Wain said, angry again. "I won't have you hounding her. She's been through enough."

"Mr. Wain." Gemma's voice was quiet, gentle almost, but it held everyone's attention. "Where are your children?"

Kincaid realized that he'd not heard a sound from the boat, or seen a twitch of the curtains pulled tightly across the cabin windows.

"Gone to the shops."

"And your wife?"

He hesitated, looking round as if enlightenment might appear out of thin air. "Resting," he said at last.

"And the doctor who visited you yesterday, she's treating your wife? That would be Dr. Elsworthy, I think?" Gemma glanced at Babcock for confirmation.

Babcock stared back. "Elsworthy? Here? *This* was the boat she visited?"

This was a train wreck, Kincaid thought, looking on in horror, a massive miscommunication. Neither Babcock nor Gemma could have known the doctor's patient and Gabriel Wain were connected.

Babcock, however, made a recovery that any good copper would have envied. After a muttered, "Jesus Christ," under his breath, he turned to Wain and said in a tone that brooked no argument, "I think you'd better start by telling me exactly how you know our forensic pathologist."

Babcock waited until he was in the privacy of his office before he rang Althea Elsworthy. He tried the hospital first, but was not surprised to be told she'd called in, pleading illness, an occurrence apparently so noteworthy that her colleagues in the morgue had taken wagers on whether she'd been struck down with plague or dengue fever.

This seemed to be his day for calling in favors. It took a bit of wheedling and downright arm-twisting, but in the end he ran down her home telephone number, and the vague direction that she lived "somewhere near Whitchurch."

Hoping the phone number would be sufficient, he dialed and listened to the repeated double burr. No answer phone kicked in, and he was about to give up when the ringing stopped and her familiar voice came brusquely down the line. "Elsworthy."

"Babcock," he replied, just as succinctly, and when there was no response, he sighed and said, "Don't you dare hang up on me, Doc."

There was another silence, then she said with resignation, "I take it you've seen Gabriel Wain."

"Oh, yes. And aside from the fact that you've made a first-class idiot of me, do you realize you could be struck off for this? Colluding with a suspect in a murder investigation? Keeping vital information from the police?"

"Chief Inspector, you have every right to be angry with me. But I'm a doctor first and a pathologist second, although I suppose it has been a good many years since I've been reminded of it."

"I think you had better start from the beginning," he said, his patience forced.

"Gabriel didn't tell you?"

"I want to hear it from you." And he did, not just to verify Wain's story, but because he still couldn't quite believe that the Dr. Elsworthy he had known had strayed so far off course.

"I knew Annie Constantine when she worked for Social Services. Not well, but I found her competent, and professional, and we got on together. The last case we worked together was a bad one, though—the one where the child was killed by his foster father, do you remember?

"I could tell Constantine was having a difficult time, possibly even suffering some posttraumatic stress, so I wasn't all that surprised when a few months later I heard she'd taken early retirement. After that, I didn't hear from her, or of her, until two days ago, when she showed up at my door as I was leaving for the morgue.

"How she got the address of my cottage, I don't know— perhaps she had some of the same connections as you, Chief Inspector." For the first time, he heard a trace of her wry humor.

"She seemed quite distraught," the doctor continued, "and wouldn't be brushed off, so in the end I agreed to listen to her. She said she needed help, that one of her former clients was gravely ill but refused to seek any medical treatment. Then she told me what had happened to Rowan Wain and her family.

"Well, I know the doctor who filed the MSBP complaint against Rowan. He's a self-serving little shit who, when a case is beyond his competence, looks for someone else to blame."

Babcock, who had never heard the doctor swear before, found himself slightly shocked.

"It wasn't the first time he'd used a diagnosis of Munchausen by proxy," she said, an undercurrent of anger in her voice, "and the other parents might have been blameless as well, but they didn't have Annie Constantine to go to bat for them. They lost their children.

"As Constantine spent time with the Wains, she became convinced that the boy, Joseph, really had suffered from life-threatening seizures, and that the parents had only turned to the medical establishment in desperation.

"It seems she made a crusade of proving their innocence." Elsworthy paused, and Babcock imagined her frowning, as she did during a postmortem when she didn't like what she was seeing. "I suspect she needed a crusade," she went on, slowly. "The murdered foster child had been in her care, and when the natural parents reported after their visitations that they suspected abuse, she dismissed their claims as no more than a manipulative effort to get their child back. They were drug users, you see, and not terribly dependable."

Babcock had worked that case, and remembered it all too well. The natural parents had lashed out at everyone involved in a fury made all the more vicious by the fact that they, too, had failed their child. No wonder Annie Constantine had felt a need for atonement.

"Her determination paid off," Elsworthy continued. "Eventually, she found corroboration, both from witnesses who had seen the seizures and in hospital records that the doctor reporting the suspected abuse had somehow missed. She got the case dismissed."

"So how does all this tie in with what happened these last few days?" asked Babcock.

"Chance," said Elsworthy. "It was pure chance that she motored past the Wains at the Middlewich Junction on Christmas Eve. It's surprising, I suppose, that she hadn't run into them before. The waterways are a fairly self-contained world.

"She spoke to them, and although the children seemed well, she thought Rowan looked really ill. The more she thought about it, the more concerned she became. It was when she went back that she and Gabriel had the row, but in the end he agreed to let her see Rowan, who had worsened even in that short time. Annie became convinced that Rowan would let herself die from an untreated illness rather than expose her family to the system again. That's when she came to me, asking me to examine Rowan, off the record."

"And was she right? About Rowan's illness?"

Elsworthy sighed and lowered her voice, as if she didn't want to be overheard. "Unfortunately, she was more than right. Rowan Wain is suffering from advanced congestive heart failure. She might have been helped, if it had been caught early, but even then she would have had to agree to a transplant. Now it's much too late for that, even were she willing."

Babcock digested this. "So Rowan Wain really is dying?"

"Yes. All I can do is make her a bit more comfortable. I promised Annie Constantine I would do that, and that I would treat Rowan without calling in the authorities. Then, when Annie was killed, I felt I had to honor my obligation, both to her and to Rowan . . ."

It was, Babcock suspected, as close to an apology for her behavior as he was going to get. "And when you heard Annie Constantine had been murdered, you never thought Gabriel Wain might be involved?"

"No! Why would Gabriel Wain want to harm Annie? He owed her his family, and more."

"What if Annie discovered he was connected with the infant we found in the barn?"

"Gabriel?" The doctor's voice rose in astonishment.

"He did mortar work in the dairy not long before the Smiths sold the place. We've narrowed the time frame for

the interment to between five and ten years, so it would
fit."

"I don't believe it," Ellsworthy said with utter commit-
ment. "I don't believe Gabriel Wain could have murdered a
child. It's bound to be coincidence, Chief Inspector, just as it
was coincidence that Annie met the family again on Christmas Eve."

*And coincidence that two days later she was dead,* he
thought, but he didn't say it aloud. There was no use preach-
ing to the converted. Instead, he asked, "Doc, did Annie
Constantine say anything to you about the child in the barn?
Or you to her?"

"No, she didn't mention it. And neither did I," she added,
sounding incensed that he should question her discretion, as
if she hadn't violated a half dozen ethical rules in the last
few days.

"One more thing, Doc," he said lightly, as if it were of no
great import. "Do you have the children?"

The silence on the other end of the line was so profound
that for a moment he thought she had severed the connection. Then he heard her draw in a breath. "Yes. Yes, I have
the children. I thought it best, under the circumstances." She
hesitated again, then said quietly, "Ronnie, leave them be.
And promise me that if you feel you must take Gabriel Wain
in for questioning, you'll let me know. Someone needs to
stay with Rowan."

"If you'll make me a promise, Doc," he returned, unable
to imagine calling her by her first name. "Tell me the truth
from now on."

He'd just rung off when he heard a tap on his door and
Sheila Larkin peered in. "Got a minute, Guv?" When he
nodded, she came in and sat demurely in his extra chair. She
was dressed rather sensibly again today, in trousers and a
warm jumper. A good thing, he supposed, especially as
they'd stood around on the freezing towpath for half an eter-
nity, but he found he missed watching her struggle to sit in
a short skirt without revealing her knickers. "So has our doc
gone completely off the rails, then?" she asked with relish.

"She had her reasons," he said, surprising himself. "And they're mine to know," he added, putting Larkin firmly in her place, then grinned. "But you can run down a couple of things for me."

"Yes, sir, Guv'nor, sir." Larkin saluted.

"I want you to find out anything you can about the doctor who filed the MSBP allegations against Rowan Wain. And then I want you to find out what happened to the parents of the little boy who was beaten to death by his foster father."

Babcock was treating Kincaid and Gemma to the dubious pleasure of a late lunch at the Subway shop near the Crewe railway station when his phone rang. It was Rasansky, sounding jubilant.

"Preliminary from the fraud lads says you were right, Guv," he said. "They've just reviewed the Constantines' files and a few others, but it looks as though Dutton has been skimming. It's certainly enough to have another word."

Surveying the remains of his chicken breast on Parmesan bread, Babcock bundled it into its wrapper and tossed it into the nearest bin. "I'm on my way. Meet me there, and bring a couple of uniforms along for backup, just in case."

"What's happened?" Kincaid asked even before Babcock had disconnected. "Is it Wain?"

"No." Babcock couldn't resist a smile. "It's Piers Dutton. It seems your sister was right." He watched the emotions chase each other across his friend's face—first satisfaction, then dismay as he realized the implications. "And no," he continued, forestalling what he knew would come next, "you can't come with me to interview him, either of you. You'll just have to trust Cheshire CID to manage."

Kincaid's struggle not to argue was visible, but he was too experienced an officer not to know the difficulties his direct involvement could cause.

Gemma, Babcock saw, had shown no pleasure at Juliet Newcombe's vindication. She listened without expression, all the while carefully folding the paper wrapper round her barely touched food.

"Why don't the two of you wait for me at the station?" he suggested. "You can help Larkin with the files. Just don't let her boss you around too much," he added. "She'll be insufferable if she thinks she can lord it over two detectives from the Big Smoke."

Piers Dutton had stopped protesting the ransacking of his office. He stood in the reception area, watching tight-lipped as uniformed officers carried out the remainder of his files in boxes, and didn't acknowledge Babcock's entrance with so much as a blink.

"Sorry about the inconvenience," Babcock said cheerfully. "Moving is always so disruptive, wouldn't you agree, Mr. Dutton?"

Dutton compressed his lips further, but the silent riposte wasn't in his nature, and after a moment he gave in to the temptation to retort. "You'll be hearing from my solicitor, Chief Inspector. And don't think you won't regret this."

"I'm surprised your solicitor isn't here already. Have a bit of trouble running him down?"

"He was on holiday," Dutton admitted reluctantly. "Not that it will matter, as there's no question that what you're doing here is illegal."

"I can see why he wouldn't be anxious to give up his post-Christmas amusements to deal with your spot of trouble."

"Now see here, Babcock. I've rung your chief constable—"

"Yes, I've rung him myself, *Mr.* Dutton. He wasn't too keen on the idea that he'd been playing golf with a swindler, especially as it seems you convinced him to make one or two small investments." Babcock shook his head in mock dismay. "You wouldn't have been so foolish as to skim a percentage off the chief constable's account?"

Dutton quite wisely clamped his mouth closed on that one, but Babcock thought he looked a little pale. "And by the way, Mr. Dutton," he added, "I don't appreciate being threatened. I think you'll find that sort of thing doesn't win you any friends—especially if I should mention it to the custody sergeant at Crewe headquarters."

"What are you talking about?" Dutton's voice rose to a squeak of panic.

"You're going to be our guest, Mr. Dutton, while we talk about Annie Lebow."

"But you can't—"

"I can. Twenty-four hours without charge, and then we'll see where we are." Babcock stepped closer, into the other man's comfort zone. "You're going to tell me about every contact you ever had with Annie Lebow, or with anyone connected with Annie Lebow. And then you're going to take me through every second of your time the day before yes—"

"Boss?" Rasansky pushed open the door. "Mr. Newcombe's here. He wants to—"

But Caspar Newcombe didn't wait to have his mission announced. Shoving Rasansky, who outweighed him by a good two stone, aside, he barged into the room.

"Hey, you can't—" Rasansky began, but Newcombe had already turned to Babcock.

"You're in charge here? What is this? What do you think you're doing?" He was wild-eyed with outrage, and his breath told Babcock he'd had a fortified lunch. "This is our business. You can't just take things away. Piers, you'll tell them—"

"Mr. Newcombe." Babcock stepped back, out of range of Newcombe's uncoordinatedly swinging arms. He knew Caspar Newcombe by sight, had even been briefly introduced to him once over drinks at a Nantwich pub, but he doubted the man remembered his name or title. "I'm Detective Chief Inspector Babcock. Did your partner not tell you we had some questions about his accounts? Or that one of his clients was murdered night before last? And that unfortunately, it appears that Mr. Dutton had been helping himself to a percentage of her profits without permission?"

"What?" Newcombe's thin face went slack with shock. "You can't be ser—"

"Annie Lebow. Or Annie Constantine, according to your records. Mr. Dutton will be helping us with our inquiries."

Newcombe turned to Dutton like a child asking for reassurance. "Piers, this can't be true—"

"I'm afraid it is true that Annie Constantine was murdered, Caspar, but I had nothing to do with it," Dutton said, his voice even, soothing.

"And you haven't—"

"Of course not. I'm sure the police will find it's all a misunderstanding, perhaps a bookkeeping error. Juliet sometimes—" Dutton stopped and shrugged, and Newcombe nodded, accepting the implication without protest.

He turned back to Babcock and regarded him owlishly. "Night before last, you say?"

"Yes."

Newcombe drew himself up to his full height. "Then you have no reason to harass my partner, Inspector. Piers was with me the entire evening."

From the corner of his eye, Babcock saw the flash of dismay on Dutton's face.

Juliet wanted nothing more than a hot bath. Her entire body felt as if it had been stomped on by a rugby team, due, she suspected, to her daylong efforts to put a good face on her rising internal panic.

She'd begun by taking her foreman, Jim, to the building site, and while she viewed the aftermath left by the deconstruction crew with horror, he'd stood shaking his head in a wordless dismay that made her feel even worse.

Leaving him to it, she'd retreated to her van and, forcing a smile on her face, had rung the Bonners in London and told them cheerfully that it would take only a few days to get back on schedule.

Her clients were already jittery over the idea that their future home had been used as a burial ground for a child, and Juliet was afraid that with the snowballing delays, they might cut their losses and pull out altogether. When her thoughts strayed down that path, her heart began to pound.

*Keep things in proportion,* she'd told herself, turning up the van's heater in hopes that air from the still-warm engine would stop her teeth chattering.

There would be other jobs. She and the kids wouldn't starve—they could stay with her folks as long as necessary,

and it was only her pride that would suffer. And if worse
came to worst and her business failed, she could find another
job. She had skills; she'd managed Caspar's office efficiently
enough—in spite of Piers—and she'd made a good bit on the
side doing small fix-up projects for friends.

Somehow, she had to get herself through the day. Confine
her thoughts to minutiae, concentrate on the sequence of
steps required to get her project back on course.

For a moment, her hatred of Piers Dutton squeezed her
chest like a python, and she swallowed against the bile rising in her throat. It occurred to her that she'd never known
true hatred before. If she'd thought about it at all, she'd
imagined it as cleansing, a pure emotion unadulterated by
the burden of fairness or compassion.

But it was corrosive, spilling over into every facet of her
life, poisoning all her relationships. It kept her from forgiv-
ing Caspar his weakness; it kept her from telling her brother
and Gemma that she understood they'd only done what they
felt they must. And it was keeping her from reassuring her
children that she loved them, especially Lally.

The thought pierced her heart. She'd sniffed, wiped her
eyes, and gone back to the job site determined to do better,
to keep focused on the things that really mattered.

But by midafternoon, when she'd picked Lally and the
two younger boys up at the bookshop, her daughter's sullen
withdrawal only made her angry again.

She knew Lally had been hurt by her grandfather's sin-
gling out Kit for this morning's trip to Audlem—she'd felt
a stab of jealousy herself that shamed her—but all her at-
tempts at engaging the girl in some sort of ordinary conversation had failed so miserably that even the boys had become
quiet, embarrassed.

When they reached the house, they'd found Kit and Hugh
just back from their expedition, red cheeked and irritatingly
cheerful. Hugh had lit the fire in the sitting room, and had
dared the boys and Lally to take him on at Monopoly, but
Lally had disappeared upstairs, refusing to join in. When Juliet called after her, she'd pretended not to hear.

Juliet sank down on the bottom step, desolation settling

over her. She tried to force her cold fingers to unlace her work boots, but stopped halfway through. Suddenly even the longed-for bath seemed more than she could manage. Perhaps she'd have a nip from the bottle of brandy her dad kept under the kitchen sink, just to get herself going, she thought, and she'd just pushed herself upright when the doorbell rang.

She knew, with the absolute certainty born of dread, who it was. The dogs barked in chorus, and when her dad looked out of the sitting room, she waved him back and said, "It's for me."

Opening the door, Juliet stepped out onto the porch and faced her husband.

Her first thought was that he looked diminished, much less frightening than her imagination had painted him after his attack on her in the pub. His chest seemed to have sunk, his cheeks were unshaven, but his eyes glittered so feverishly that any hopes she had had that he'd come to apologize were quickly dashed.

The muscles in his jaw worked as he said, "They've taken him in. Piers. To the police station. They say he cheated this woman who died, and others, too. Piers!" Outrage warred with disbelief in his voice.

"Caspar—" She reached out, moved by unexpected pity, but he jerked his arm away from her fingers as if stung.

"It's your doing," he spat at her. "You'd stoop to anything to get back at him for rejecting you, even ruining the business, ruining me. And now the police suspect him of *murder*."

Juliet let her hand fall to her side. So she had been right all along. The police wouldn't have taken Piers in for questioning unless they'd found evidence to support her suspicions. Jubilation flared through her, but it faded in an instant and she felt merely tired and infinitely sad. There was no joy in vindication, not at this cost, but the oddest thing was that her fear had vanished.

Piers couldn't hurt her now, and in defending him even in the face of reason, Caspar had lost his power over her.

"I didn't mean to hurt you, Caspar," she said. "I'm sorry."

"Sorry? You bitch. You—"

She stopped his venom with a wave of her hand, and felt like Moses parting the Red Sea. Her head was suddenly clear. "I've started divorce proceedings. My solicitor will contact you. In the meantime, I want you out of the house. The children and I will be moving back in until things are settled. I'll give you twenty-four hours to get your things. After that, if you come near us, except for arranged visitations with the children, I'll take out restraining orders against you."

He stared at her, uncomprehending. "You can't—"

"I can." She looked at her husband one last time, then stepped back into the house and closed the door.

It was only as she turned round that she saw Lally standing at the foot of the stairs.

"I got two of the big houses," shrieked Toby, almost upsetting the game board in his excitement. "I win."

"You can't win yet, silly," Sam told him. "Not until everyone runs out of money, and that can take *days*."

Hugh, who had been coaching Toby on his moves, stepped in. "It's all right, Toby. You can buy lots more houses, and railroads, and you may beat us all yet." He winked at Kit over the little boy's head, and Kit grinned back.

Kit still felt a glow of pleasure from their morning, spent exploring the stair-step locks in the pretty town of Audlem, south of Nantwich. Hugh—he still didn't quite feel comfortable calling him "grandfather"—had talked to him as if he were an adult, drawing him out about his opinions and interests, and had then taken him for lunch at a pub in the village of Wrenbury. Only thoughts of Annie Lebow and the *Horizon* had marred Kit's enjoyment, and he'd tried hard to keep them at bay.

Now, as Hugh urged Toby to roll the dice again, Kit made an effort to join in, but he kept thinking about the raised voices he'd heard a few minutes earlier, and the slamming of the front door. Hugh, too, kept glancing at the sitting-room door, and Kit sensed his enthusiasm for the game was at least partly an attempt at distracting them from whatever scene had taken place on the front porch.

And where, he wondered, was Lally?

"Sam," he whispered, "take my turns for me, will you? I've got to go to the loo." Then he was up and slipping from the room before anyone could protest, or Toby could follow.

The air in the front hall felt frigid compared to the warmth of the sitting room. No sound came from the kitchen, where the dogs were having a kip by the stove. Not wanting to disturb them, he climbed the stairs quietly, although he couldn't have explained quite why he felt the need for stealth.

When he reached the upstairs hall, he saw that the bathroom door was closed, and as he moved closer he heard faint splashing, and smelled the scent of bubble bath wafting from under the door. He doubted it was Lally in the tub, although the fleeting image conjured up by that thought made his skin prickle with embarrassment.

Hugh's study, then, where Lally and Juliet had been sleeping? The door stood slightly ajar, but when he looked in, the sofa bed was tucked away, and only the clutter of Hugh's books and papers hinted at its occupancy.

Perplexed, Kit wondered if Lally had been in the kitchen all along, but decided that while he was upstairs he'd grab a book he'd been reading that he'd promised to show Hugh.

He flung open the door to the room he shared with the other boys, with none of the care he'd taken in the study, and froze.

Lally, crouched on his bed with her hand plunged into the depths of a backpack, jumped as if she'd been shot.

"What are you doing in here?" she hissed at him.

"It's my room," he said, incensed. "What are *you* doing in here?"

"Trying to get away from my fucking mother, that's what." Lally eased her hand from the backpack, but stayed in her crouch, clutching the pack to her chest like body armor.

"Why?" asked Kit, still not following the plot.

"Because I hate her," said Lally, vicious.

"You don't mean—"

"Yes, I do mean it." Her eyes filled. "I hate her. I wish she were dead."

Kit crossed the room in two strides. When the edge of the bed stopped his forward momentum, he reached out and slapped Lally across the face, hard. Only then did he realize he was shaking with anger. "Don't say that. Don't ever say that. You don't know what it means."

He waited for her to hit back, to tell him to sod off, to yell for help, but she only stared at him and whispered, "And you don't know what she's done." The tears that had threatened spilled over, making glistening trails across the white handprint on her cheek, and Kit felt ashamed.

"Lally, I'm sorry. I didn't mean to—it's just that—"

"She's ruined everything. Why couldn't she just leave things alone? We were all right the way we were."

Feeling helpless now, Kit sat down beside her. He pulled her hand from the pack and held it between his own. "Look, I know your parents aren't getting on, but whatever happens with them, you'll be okay." Her hand felt like a live thing between his, a small creature caught unawares, still with terror.

"I won't." Her eyes met his, and in them he saw a certainty that chilled him.

Before he could speak, she pulled her hand away and zipped the pack. "I'm going out tonight," she said dully. "As soon as it's dark."

"You can't," he protested. "Your mother's practically had you under lock and key, even in the daytime."

"She can't watch me every minute. And she can't stop me walking out the door."

"Why do you have to go out? Tell me what's going on—"

"Why should I?" she said, defiant now. "Why should it matter?" It was a challenge, and Kit knew suddenly that if he failed her now he would never make it up.

"God almighty, he's one slick bastard." Kevin Rasansky shook his head, half in obvious disgust, half in admiration. He'd just come from the interview room where Babcock had been questioning Piers Dutton for the last few hours, and had apparently picked out Gemma and Kincaid as the most appreciative audience.

They had settled into the temporary incident room, lending a hand where they could, both chafing at the inactivity and their lack of command, but unwilling to leave. Gemma had taken Sheila Larkin's desk, as the DC had gone to meet Roger Constantine at the morgue. She was thumbing through files she knew Larkin had already scanned while keeping an uneasy eye on Kincaid, who had gone broodingly silent as the hours passed. It worried her, and she had to keep herself from overcompensating with cheery conversation.

"And now he's got his high-priced lawyer, I doubt we'll keep him twenty-four hours," Rasansky continued, seeing that he had their attention.

"But surely with the evidence in his files—" Gemma began, but Rasansky interrupted her.

"Oh, no doubt we'll get a fraud charge somewhere down the line, but it may take months to build a solid case. And in the meantime, his alibi for the night of Lebow's death is at least convincing enough that I don't think the boss will charge him without corroborating evidence. His friends confirmed that he had dinner with them in Tarporley, and that he didn't leave the pub until well after ten. They also admitted, a bit reluctantly, that he'd had a good bit to drink, and probably shouldn't have driven. And if he was that cut, how likely is it that he stumbled his way down the towpath in the fog, pulled Lebow's mooring pin loose, and waited patiently for her to come out and see what was amiss?"

"Then what about Caspar Newcombe?" asked Kincaid. Babcock had told them about Caspar's hastily proffered alibi for his partner.

"Dutton says he admires his loyalty, but that Newcombe's gesture was 'misguided.' The man's an idiot, if you ask me," Rasansky added, and Gemma wondered if he'd forgotten that Caspar Newcombe was Kincaid's brother-in-law. Anyone with the barest minimum of tact would have stopped at the expression on Kincaid's face, but Rasansky barreled on. "We've applied for a warrant for Newcombe's files as well, and we've padlocked the premises in the meantime. If we're lucky, we'll get both the bastards for fraud." He smiled at them, pleased at his prediction.

Gemma had managed a strangled "Yes" when, with great relief, she saw Sheila Larkin come in through the door. Larkin stopped, belatedly, to stomp caked snow off her boots onto the industrial carpet. "Bloody snowing again," she said as she reached them, and when Gemma started to get up, she waved her back into her chair. She tossed her padded coat over a vacant desk and continued to Gemma, "You're welcome to it. I've got to use the computer. Any luck with Dutton?"

"The DCI is still in with him."

Larkin made a face. "Bugger all on this end, too, except in the process of elimination. I met Roger Constantine at the morgue for the formal identification." She propped a hip on the desk, pushing a paper stack out of the way. "He was pretty cut up, poor bloke, so I thought I'd take advantage of his *fragile emotional state*." This last was said in obvious quotes, and Gemma suspected it could be attributed to Babcock.

"He was shocked to find his neighbors had been gossiping about his occasional dinners in the pub with the young woman—turns out she's his goddaughter. But he did admit, with a bit of encouragement, that after his call from Lebow on the night she was killed, he spent the rest of the evening visiting a neighbor. It seems her husband was out of town, but she's willing to back him up if need be." Shrugging, Larkin added, "Can't say I blame him for having a bit on the side, if they'd been separated for five years. It's only human, isn't it? But he says he'd have taken her back in an instant if that's what she'd wanted."

"That's all very well after the fact," Kincaid said sharply. "But we can't be sure that Annie Lebow didn't threaten to pull the plug on his finances that night—maybe she found out about the neighbor and didn't take quite such a philosophical view. And we can't discount the possibility that said neighbor was in on it with him. Maybe she plans to leave her husband when Constantine inherits."

"You're as cynical as my guv'nor," Larkin said, dimpling at him. "But that doesn't tell us how he drove from Tilston to Barbridge in blinding fog, then found his way along the towpath to the boat. And he seems more a cerebral type, if you know what I mean. If he were going to kill her, I can't see him bashing her over the head. I'd bet he'd plan ahead, and make it look like an accident, or suicide. After all, she had a history of depression."

"You've an evil mind." Kincaid looked inordinately cheered, and if Gemma hadn't been so relieved at the lifting of his mood, she'd have felt a stab of jealousy.

"What about the other leads the guv'nor asked you to follow up?" put in Rasansky, breaking up the party to which he hadn't been invited.

"No joy. The doctor who made the MSBP diagnosis was on duty that night, with multiple witnesses. And as for the parents of the child who died in foster care, the mother committed suicide a couple of years ago, and after that the father went completely off the rails. He's serving time for aggravated assault and dealing." Even Larkin's cheeky demeanor seemed dampened by the recital of this sad little story. Standing, she said, "I'd better get these reports entered and printed before the boss takes a break from his interview."

While Larkin made her way to a vacant computer terminal, Rasansky pulled Kincaid aside and began questioning him about procedures at the Yard. Gemma suspected he was trying to impress Kincaid, with an eye to a transfer, and judging from Kincaid's air of polite forbearance, he'd come to the same conclusion.

Trying to put from her mind the thought of the parents whose child's death had deprived them of any reason to pull their own lives together, Gemma restraightened the papers Sheila Larkin had shoved aside. Lifting the top page of the stack, she saw that it was part of Annie Constantine's report on the Wain case. Gemma had read the narrative earlier, remarking on the clarity of the writing, and Constantine's obvious compassion. She wished she had met her. Even after her years on the job, the finality of death never failed to jar her; the human mind was so geared to think in the future tense, about opportunities yet to come. But there would be no to-morrows for Annie Constantine, and Gemma felt a personal pang of loss.

Now she glanced through the narrative idly, half listening to Kincaid and Rasansky's conversation, half worrying about the latest development with Caspar Newcombe and Kincaid's reaction to it.

Then a sentence caught her eye. She stopped, rereading, feeling a frisson of shock travel up her spine. Closing her eyes, she brought back the image of the little girl, fishing under her large black umbrella.

It couldn't be. And yet— Once more she read the descriptions of the Wains' children, so carefully noted by Annie Constantine, and she knew that she was not mistaken.

The little girl she had met was not Marie Wain.

# 24

As soon as Gemma said they had to pick up the children, he knew that it was an excuse. He stared at her, questioning, but she just gave a slight shake of her head.

Frustration gripped him. He didn't want to leave until he'd talked to Babcock himself, found out what he'd managed to get out of Piers Dutton. At least so far it didn't sound as if Dutton had implicated Caspar in the fraud scheme, but if Caspar *was* involved . . . It would mean disaster for Juliet, and it would be his fault.

And if Dutton was cleared of Annie Lebow's murder, had he brought it about needlessly? Not that Dutton didn't deserve a good prison term for the scams he'd pulled on his clients, but was it worth the damage to Juliet? Perhaps his sister had been right all along—he was a self-righteous bastard, concerned only with being seen to do the right thing. The fact that Caspar Newcombe was a fool didn't make it any better.

Gemma had slipped into her coat and was glancing at him anxiously while making chitchat with Sheila Larkin. What had she found that she couldn't say in front of—

The thought that struck him sent the blood from his head. Why had Caspar volunteered an alibi for Dutton? What if it wasn't Dutton who needed an alibi, but Caspar himself?

What if Caspar had discovered that Annie Lebow meant to shop Dutton for cheating her, and had decided to make sure she didn't have that chance? There was not only the business at stake, but Kincaid had begun to think that Caspar would do anything for Piers Dutton. Dutton, obviously, had not been so willing to do the same for him.

Suddenly as eager to be away as Gemma, he got his own coat and interrupted Gemma's conversation with Larkin. "Tell your boss to ring us if there's any news," he told the DC, and although she looked surprised at his abruptness, she nodded.

"Will do."

Taking Gemma's arm, he hurried her up the stairs and out into an early dusk. The swollen clouds seemed to hang just above the rooftops, pressing down with a momentous weight, and fine snowflakes stung their cheeks like microscopic shards of glass.

"Is it Caspar?" he asked. "What have you found?"

"Caspar?" Gemma looked up at him, shielding her eyes against the snow. "What are you talking about?"

Relief flooded through him. He'd been paranoid, that's all, and he was suddenly reluctant to share his suspicions. "What is it, then?" he asked, but she'd broken away, dashing for the car and plunging into the driver's seat.

She had the car started before he'd closed his own door, in gear before he'd buckled his seat belt. "Gemma, where's the damned fire?"

Gemma eased into the congestion of Crewe's late-afternoon traffic without looking at him and said, "Marie Wain." When he stared blankly at her, she added, "It was there all along. Annie Lebow spent time with the children, when she was arranging care for Rowan. She should have seen it."

"Gemma." He reached out, covered her hand on the steering wheel with his own. "Will you please tell me what the hell you're talking about?"

This time she glanced at him as she downshifted for a traffic light. "Marie Wain—the little girl I met—isn't Marie Wain. It's right there in Annie's notes on the original case. Gabriel and Rowan Wain's baby girl had brown eyes, like her brother, like her parents. The girl they call Marie has eyes as blue as delphiniums."

He took this in. "But . . . the girl was just a baby the last time Annie saw her, when she closed the case. She might have been mistaken—"

"No. Babies' eyes are sometimes a cloudy, indeterminate color for the first few weeks. But after that you can tell— And with blue-eyed children it's easier— You could see that Toby's eyes were unmistakably blue within a day or two."

"Are you suggesting the Wains switched their child with someone else's? And no one noticed?" The full import hit him. "If that was the case, then the baby in the barn could be—"

"I don't know." She accelerated a bit too fast, and the Escort's back tires slid a little on the glazed pavement. "But we're going to find out."

"Gemma, if you're right, we should have told Babcock."

"Not until we talk to Gabriel Wain."

Squeaky clean and dressed in jeans and a nubby jumper, Juliet came downstairs to find her mother home from the bookshop and rushing round the kitchen like a whirlwind.

"I've put some things out for the children's tea," said Rosemary. "There's a cauliflower bake I had in the freezer, and some things for salad. If you can just—"

"Mummy, please. I can manage," Juliet interrupted, but without heat. Her parents had a long-planned dinner engagement with friends in Barbridge, and she knew Rosemary was overcompensating. "Go. Have a good time. We won't starve." Giving her mother an impulsive hug, she caught the familiar scent of Crabtree & Evelyn's Lily of the Valley, and was oddly comforted.

What scents would her own children associate with her, she wondered, when they were grown? Sweat, brick, and sawdust?

"Are you certain?" asked Rosemary, touching her cheek. "Duncan and Gemma should be back soon."

"Yes. And if you don't get Daddy out of the house, he'll get sucked back into the perpetual Monopoly game. I'm glad you're not going far, though. It's shaping up to be a foul night."

She had bundled her mother into her coat and waved both parents off at the door, like a mother sending kids off to school, when the phone rang. Her first instinct was to reach for her mobile, then she realized she'd left it with her work clothes upstairs, and it was the house phone ringing.

The children were all in the sitting room, and when neither Lally nor Sam—who usually responded to a ringing phone with Pavlovian promptness—appeared, she padded into the kitchen herself. Lifting the handset, she gave her parents' number.

"Juliet? Is that you?"

Surprised, she recognized her friend Gill, who had a fine-arts shop near the square in Nantwich.

"Gill?"

"I've been ringing and ringing your house, and your mobile," Gill went on. "And then I thought to try your parents."

Juliet felt a little lurch of unease. Gill would never go to such trouble for social reasons, and it was past time for her to have closed up shop and set off for her cottage near Whitchurch. "What is it? Has something happened?"

"It's Newcombe and Dutton. The building's on fire. The fire brigade's there but they haven't got things under control yet. I don't think anyone is inside, but when I couldn't reach you or Caspar—"

"Caspar? You rang his mobile, too?"

"Yes. You mean he's not with you?"

"No. Gill, look, I'm sorry. I've got to go. I'll ring you later." Juliet hung up before her friend could respond. She couldn't answer questions, not now. Her knees felt weak with panic. Having heard the alarm in her voice, Jack got up from his bed by the stove and came over to her, wagging his bushy tail and watching her with his alert sheepdog eyes.

"It's all right, boy," she said, trying to reassure herself as well as the dog, but she had to grasp the kitchen table for a moment. What if Caspar had done something stupid? What if Caspar was in that building?

She had to go. She had to see what was happening.

Purpose galvanized her, channeling the rush of adrena-

ine into flight. It was only as she was into her coat and
halfway out the door that she remembered the children.

"I have to go out. There's a fire." Kit's aunt Juliet had run
into the sitting room, banging the door so loudly that all the
children jumped. "Lally," she said breathlessly, "Kit. You
look after the boys. Sammy, you do what your sister tells
you. I'll be back as soon as I can."

With that, she was gone, and the children sat staring at one
another in frozen surprise until Sam said, "A fire? What's she
talking about? Why would she have to go? Do you think it's
our house?"

"Of course not, silly," answered Lally. "She'd have said."
She caught Kit's eye, then added as she uncurled herself
from the corner of the chesterfield and stood, "I have to go
out, too. Kit, can you look after Sam and Toby?"

"But I don't want—"

"Mum said for you to do what I told you. Don't argue.
And don't snitch, or you'll be sorry."

Without another glance at the younger boys, she slipped
into the hall and started tugging on boots and coat.

"Lally, this is daft," protested Kit, following her. "It's
dark and it's snowing. Where do you have to go that's so
important?"

Pulling a fleece hat from the rack by the door, she said,
"I have to meet Leo. I promised. I—it doesn't matter. I don't
have to tell you why."

There was something in her face that frightened him, a
recklessness—no, more than that, a desperation. It made
him think that if he let her go alone, she might not come
back.

And that meant he had no choice. "All right," he said.
"I'm coming with you."

Gemma had taken the pocket torch from the door of the car,
but once they left the bridge for the towpath, they discovered it only made the visibility worse, trapping them in an
illuminated cone of swirling snowflakes. They moved into
the shelter of the bridge, then switched the torch off and

stood until their eyes adjusted. Beside her, Kincaid was a comforting presence.

The snow made a curtain on either side of the stone archway, but the flakes were bigger and softer than when they had left Crewe, and when Gemma stepped out into the open she found she could make out the outline of the canal's edge, and the shapes of the boats huddled against it. Then she saw a sliver of light, the glow of a lamp seeping through a gap in curtains pulled tight over a porthole, and she knew the *Daphne* was still moored where she had last seen it.

She moved forward, Kincaid near enough behind her that she could hear him muttering as the snow soaked through his shoes. When she reached the boat, she stopped, feeling the warmth of his body as he halted behind her and gave her shoulder a brief squeeze.

This time, she didn't call out, but felt for the gunwale and climbed carefully into the well deck, then made room for Kincaid to do the same. Knowing the slight movement of the boat under their combined weight had announced their presence, she rapped sharply on the cabin door. "Mr. Wain, it's Gemma James. We need to talk to you."

The door opened quickly, to Gemma's surprise, and Gabriel Wain looked out at them without speaking. After a moment, he stepped back and down, and she saw that three steps led into the tiny cabin. Gemma caught her breath as she peered in, thinking for an instant that she had happened upon a child's playhouse. The space was so tiny, so cleverly arranged, and so welcoming with its dark-paneled walls decorated with gleaming brasses and delicate lace-edged plates. There were homely touches of red in the curtains and the cushions on the two benches, a fire burned in the cast-iron stove tucked neatly into the corner nearest the steps, and a lantern hung from a hook in the sloping paneled ceiling.

But everything drew the eye towards the painting on the underside of a folding table now stowed in its upright position. A pale winding road, flower lined, led to a castle dreaming on a hilltop. The colors were brilliant, the grass magically green, the sky a perfect blue, the clouds a luminous white, and the detail and perspective were the work of a master artist.

"My wife's," said Gabriel Wain, his voice filled with un-expected pride. "There's no one on the Cut paints in the old way like my Rowan."

Gemma now saw that there were other pieces on display bearing Rowan's signature touch—a metal canalware cup in blue embellished with red and yellow roses, a water can, a bowl.

"You'll let the cold in," Wain added, nodding towards the door behind Gemma.

She started, realizing she'd stood frozen, with Kincaid trapped behind her, and stepped down into the cabin proper.

"You've kept the cabin in its original state," Kincaid said as he came down after her, his admiration evident. He nodded at the passageway leading towards the bow. "But you'll have built more living quarters into the old cargo space?"

"This boat was the butty of a pair, originally, so the cabin was larger," Wain agreed. "But you didn't come out in this weather to admire my boat, Mr.—Kincaid, is it?" He didn't invite them to sit.

Gemma moved a bit farther into the center of the cabin and knew, from the way Kincaid positioned himself behind her, that he meant for her to take the lead. Gathering herself, she said, "Mr. Wain, we need to know what happened to Marie."

Wain stared at them, his eyes widening. He'd been wary, she thought, but he had not expected this. "Marie? She and Joseph are with the doctor. She'll have told you—"

"No," said Gemma, and although she hadn't raised her voice, Wain stopped as if he'd been struck. "I want you to tell us what happened to *Marie*."

The silence stretched in the small space, then Wain re-covered enough for an attempt at bluster. "I don't know what you're on about. Marie's staying with Dr. Elsworthy, just for a few—"

There was movement in the passageway, and a woman came into the cabin. Standing beside Gabriel, she laid thin fingers on his arm, the touch enough to silence him.

She had once been pretty, thought Gemma, but now she

wore death like a pall. Her clothes hung loosely on her gaunt frame, her lank hair was pulled back carelessly, her skin tinged with gray. With her free arm she cradled an oxygen tank like an unnatural infant, tethered to her by a plastic umbilicus that ended in the twin prongs of a nasal canula.

"You must be Rowan," Gemma said gently. "I'm Gemma James, and this is Duncan Kincaid."

"You're with the police?" asked Rowan Wain.

"We're police officers in London, yes," Gemma temporized, wishing she and Kincaid had discussed beforehand how they meant to handle this, "but we're not here officially."

"Then you've no right to be asking—"

"Gabriel, please." Rowan used his arm for support as she lowered herself onto a bench. "It's no use. Can't you see that?" She looked up at him imploringly. "And I need to tell it. Now, while I can."

Gabriel Wain seemed to shrink before Gemma's eyes, as if the purpose that had sustained him had gone. He lowered himself to the bench, beside his wife, and took her hand but didn't speak. The only sound in the small space was the rhythmic puff of the oxygen as it left the tank.

"She was so perfect." Rowan's lips curved in a smile at the memory. "After Joseph, we were terrified it would start again, the vomiting, the seizures. And it had been a hard pregnancy, with everything that had happened." She stopped, letting the oxygen do its work, closing her eyes in an effort to gather strength before going on. "But she ate, and she slept, and she grew rosy and beautiful, with no hint of trouble.

"Then, on the day she turned eight months old, I put her down for her afternoon sleep, just there." She gestured at the passageway, and Gemma saw that a small bed was fitted into one side, just the size for a baby or a toddler. "I was making mince for tea," continued Rowan. "It was cold that day, and I knew Gabriel had been working hard." Her expression grew distant; her voice faded to a thread of sound. "Gabe had taken Joseph with him. Joseph was almost three by then, and he was so much better, we didn't worry as much. He liked help-

ing his papa with his work, and I was enjoying the bit of time
to myself.

"I was singing. With the radio. A man Gabriel had worked
for had given him a radio that ran on batteries, so it was a
special treat to listen. It was a silly song. I don't know what
it was called, but it made me happy." She hummed a few
breathy bars, and Gemma recognized the tune—ABBA's
"Dancing Queen."

"I know the one you mean," she said, and Rowan nodded,
as if they had made a connection.

"I was thinking of what I might paint that night, when the
children were in bed." Rowan stopped. Her face grew even
paler, her breathing more labored.

Moving towards her, Gemma said, "Are you all right? Let
me—" But Rowan lifted her hand from her husband's and
waved her back.

"No. Please. Let me finish. I had the mince almost ready.
The light was going, and I realized it was past time for Marie
to wake. I wiped my hands on the tea towel and went in to her.
I was still singing."

Gabriel shook his head, a plea of denial, but he seemed to
realize he was powerless to stop her. Bowing his head, he
took her hand again and they all waited. Gemma could feel
Kincaid's breath, warm on the back of her neck as he stood
behind her.

"I knew straightaway. In the verses I learned as a child,
the poets always compared death to sleep, but you can't possibly mistake it. Even under her little pink blanket, she was
too still. When I touched her, she was cold, and her skin was
blue."

No one spoke. The hypnotic hiss of the oxygen regulator
filled the room, until it seemed to Gemma that it synchro-
nized with her heartbeat. She realized her cheeks were
damp, and scrubbed at them with the back of her hand.

She had held her own child in her arms, so tiny, so perfect, and knew one couldn't mistake the absence of life. "I'm
so sorry. That must have been terrible for you," she said, and
her words seemed to give Rowan a last burst of energy.

"I tried. Oh, I tried. I did everything we'd been taught

with Joseph. I puffed my own breath into her lungs until I could feel the rise and fall of her chest under my hand, but it was no use. We were down near Hurleston, and there was no one moored nearby to call for help. By the time Gabriel came . . ."

"I found them," said Gabriel hoarsely. "Rowan holding little Marie to her breast. It was too late. Too late," he repeated, his face etched with pain. "And then I realized what would happen if anyone knew. We would lose Joseph, too, and Rowan might go to prison. I couldn't let that happen.

"I knew I hadn't much time. Rowan washed her, and dressed her in her best little suit."

"No nappy. That's why there was no nappy," Kincaid said softly, as if he'd just remembered something that had bothered him, and Gabriel nodded.

"It was full dark by that time. I wrapped her in her blanket and carried her to the old dairy. We couldn't risk Rowan coming, and besides, there was Joseph to look after." Now that he'd begun, Gabriel seemed to feel the same relief as his wife, the long-dammed words flowing from him.

"I'd been working that week for old Mr. Smith. The dairy hadn't been used as such for years, but he'd got in mind to sell the place, and much of the mortar work was crumbling. I'd not quite finished the repairs, so I'd left my tools. Everything was to hand. There was a manger, half hidden behind some old milking equipment and bits of cast-off furniture—I'd seen it when I'd checked for damage. I made—I did the best I could for Marie—" He stopped, swallowing, his face nearly as ashen as his wife's. "And then I closed her up, safe, where nothing could get at her, and I put everything back the way it was before.

"The next day I took my pay from Mr. Smith. I didn't want any talk—nothing out of the ordinary. Then we left the Shroppie, went up north, mostly, where no one knew us. But somehow it got harder and harder to stay away. Maybe it was meant we should be here when she was found."

"But I don't understand," said Gemma. "Your daughter, the girl you call Marie, who is she?"

"I can't tell you who she is," answered Gabriel. Then he

must have seen something in Kincaid's expression because he added, quickly, "I don't mean I *won't* tell you. I mean I *can't,* because I don't know. But I can tell you where she came from. That first year or so, we lived in fear, thinking someone would find our baby, would somehow connect her with us. But we couldn't leave the boat—we had nothing else—so it seemed easiest to disappear in the cities. The canals run through the worst parts, the old warehouses and slums, and they'd only begun to be called 'waterfront properties.' " There was a hint of derision in his voice.

"We were in Manchester—I'd found some day work in a factory there—but the warehouses near the mooring were squats, taken over by drug users, prostitutes, runaways sleeping rough. Rowan got to know some of the women; she helped them when she could. One day they told her they'd found this girl dead, apparently from an overdose, her toddler crouched beside her body."

"The mother wasn't much more than a child herself," put in Rowan, a spark of pity in her eyes. "And the baby, she looked as if her mother had tried to care for her, in spite of everything. She was well fed, and as clean as could be expected. But she was that frightened, poor little mite, and no one would call for help—the squatters didn't invite the police or the socials onto their patch for any reason—and no one would take her. So we did." Rowan said it as if it had been the simplest thing in the world, and the memory made her smile. After a moment she went on. "She was about the age our Marie would have been, and now . . . She *is* Marie. She doesn't remember anything else. This life is all she knows. And we—she is our daughter, just as if I'd borne her myself."

All the protests ran through Gemma's head. If the mother had been identified, there might have been a father to take the child, or grandparents, all with more right than Gabriel and Rowan Wain. And yet . . . would anyone have loved her more?

Breaking into Gemma's musing, Rowan asked quietly, "How did you know? About Marie?"

"It was her eyes. In Annie Constantine's notes, she said Marie's eyes were brown."

Rowan sighed. "Dear God. I never thought. I never knew she wrote things like that about the children."

Moving Gemma aside, Kincaid spoke to Gabriel, his voice hard. "Did she see it, too? Annie Constantine, when you met her again on Christmas Day? She saw the children that day, and again when she came back with Dr. Elsworthy. Was that why you argued, because she realized Marie wasn't your daughter? And then, if she learned about the infant found in the barn, she would have put two and two together. You would have had to stop her, whatever it took."

Gabriel loosed his hand from his wife's and stood. The two men faced each other across the small confines of the cabin, and Gemma felt a sudden surge of claustrophobia, as if all the air had been sucked from the space.

But there was no defiance in Gabriel Wain's stance, and when he spoke his voice rang with desperation. "No. I'd swear she didn't know. And if she heard little Marie had been found, she never said." Resting his hand on his wife's shoulder, he went on, his words a plea. "I'd not have hurt her, even so."

The possibilities ran through Gemma's mind. Annie might not have seen the girl for a changeling at first, but what if something had triggered a memory on Boxing Day morning, when she'd brought Dr. Elsworthy to see to Rowan? Had she come back, later in the day, to confront the couple?

No, not Rowan. Rowan would have told her the truth—she owed Annie Constantine that, and she had been ready to tell the truth. But if Annie had spoken to Gabriel alone . . . How far had Gabriel Wain been willing to go to protect his family?

Yet they had no proof. And if they made an accusation against Gabriel, there could be no reprieve for this family, or for Rowan, who had so little time.

Gabriel regarded them in silence. He had put himself at their mercy; now he could only wait. But Rowan said, "What will you do?" and there was hope in her voice for her children, if not for herself.

"I—" Gemma hesitated, painfully aware of the risk in

either action. But then she knew, with sudden clarity, that she wouldn't sacrifice this family without proof of Gabriel's guilt. And that meant they had to find out who had killed Annie Constantine.

The fire was guttering by the time Juliet reached Nantwich and found a place for her van outside the ring of fire engines and snaking hoses. Two firefighters still stood, directing streams of water into the sodden remains of Newcombe and Dutton. She pushed through the crowd of onlookers until she saw a familiar face.

"Chief Inspector! What happened? Did you— Was anyone—"

"There was no one inside, Mrs. Newcombe," Babcock hastened to reassure her. "As to what happened, we released your husband's partner about an hour before the blaze began. The door was padlocked, as we hadn't got all the files out, but someone remedied that with a pair of bolt cutters." He surveyed the damage with disgust. "It was lucky all of Monk's Walk didn't go up."

"You think Piers did this?" Juliet's first relief was replaced with uneasiness.

"It would seem the logical assumption, yes. There's only so much even a high-priced lawyer can do if there's sufficient evidence of wrongdoing. It would have been worth the risk to get rid of it. A can of petrol tucked under an overcoat—" He shrugged.

"You're sure the fire was set, then?"

"You could still smell the petrol. I've sent a car to Mr. Dutton's house. If he's not at home, do you know where we might find him?"

"I— His parents live in Chester. I don't know where else he might go," Juliet answered, but she was thinking furiously. This seemed much too blatant for Piers. He was a string puller, a manipulator—direct action was not his style. And looking at the smoldering, blackened shell of what had been Newcombe and Dutton, she sensed there had been more at stake than covering up evidence.

"—looks worse than it is," Babcock was saying. "Even though some of the papers were strewn around the office, you'd be surprised at what we can re—"

But Juliet didn't hear the rest. Muttering "Excuse me," she eased through the crush and slipped into the tree-covered tunnel of Monk's Lane. Only light powder had drifted through the foliage, and it crunched under her feet as she ran.

By the time she veered into North Crofts and reached her front porch, a stitch in her side made her bend over, gasping until it had passed. Then she saw that the door stood slightly ajar. Her heart thumping with fear, she pushed it open and walked into her house.

It took her a moment to identify the unfamiliar smell. Petrol. Dear God. Her feet felt weighted now as she followed the scent, and the wet footprints, down the hall and into the kitchen.

Still wearing his coat, Caspar stood at the kitchen sink, scrubbing at his hands. He looked up when she came into the room, but didn't seem surprised to see her. "It won't come out," he said. "I can't get it out."

"Caspar, what have you done?"

He turned back to his scrubbing, his words made indistinct by the sound of the running water. "They let me watch while they carried out the files. But they didn't get them all, so they put a padlock on the door and said they'd come back for the rest in the morning.

"Some of Piers's things were left. I wanted to see for myself. To prove you wrong. So I went back as it was getting dark. When no one was watching, I cut the lock."

"*You* cut the padlock?" Juliet said. This was a man who was known for his inability to change a lightbulb.

Caspar, seemingly unaware of the incredulity in her voice, went on. "I found your bolt cutters in the garage. I put them under my coat. A flimsy thing, the lock. It was easy, like slicing butter. Once I was inside, I made sure the blinds were closed tight, then I used a torch to look through Piers's files." He turned to her, heedless of the soapy water dripping from his hands, down the front of his coat and onto the floor.

"He was cheating them. Almost all of them." His eyes were dark with shock. "I couldn't believe—I couldn't—I came back from the house and got a can of petrol. I scattered the papers from the files. I thought if I set them alight—"

"Good God, Caspar, you could have been killed!" Juliet shouted at him. "Pouring petrol and setting it alight! Are you completely mad?" She shook her head in disgust. "And for nothing. You couldn't have saved Piers. The police already have enough evidence to build a case against him; the rest was just icing on the cake. You might have got by, but now they'll have you for arson and destroying evidence, and anything you could have salvaged from the business is ruined. What in bloody hell were you thinking?"

Caspar collapsed into the nearest chair, like a scarecrow in a cashmere overcoat. Water still trickled from the tap, an echo of the tears flowing unchecked down his cheeks.

"I thought we were— I thought Piers would have done anything for me. I thought that if I burned the office he'd be—" He sounded baffled by his own emotions. "I just wanted to hurt him, Jules, that's all."

Kit followed Lally down the lane, trying to keep up with her when he felt blind and disoriented and she seemed able to see in the dark. Gradually, the snow grew lighter, diminishing to a few dancing flakes, and Lally's outline solidified.

"Where the hell are we?" he asked, panting, when he managed a few paces by her side. They'd turned right out of the farmhouse drive, rather than left, the way he'd become accustomed to going in the car.

"Shortcut to Barbridge. You'll see. We'll come out at the bridge over the canal."

"Lally, you said you had to meet Leo, but I thought you hadn't talked to him. I mean yesterday you seemed—I don't know—pissed off. And you haven't been allowed to use the phone—"

"Doesn't matter," she said shortly. "Remember yesterday he said for us to meet him? He will have waited last night. He'll be there tonight."

"But I don't un—"

"I have some things of his. Or at least, I'm supposed to have some things of his. The problem is, I don't." She giggled, the sound brittle as glass. "And Leo never stops until he gets what he wants."

"What do you mean, things of his. What sort of things?"

Lally slowed enough to look at him. "Oh, Kit, don't be so dense. Pills. And other stuff. You sound just like Peter."

"Peter?" Kit struggled to place the name. "Your friend who died?"

"Drowned. He drowned," said Lally, with a vehemence Kit didn't understand. "You even look a bit like him—that schoolboy-innocence thing."

Kit felt the blood rise to his face, but before he could protest, she went on, "Leo called him a ponce, but he wasn't. He was just . . . gentle. He was smart, and he was funny, and he could tell how I was feeling, you know? Without me saying." Lally's steps lagged until Kit had to slow his own. "And he knew how to touch me. It wasn't that he'd been with other girls, it was just that he seemed to know what I was thinking, every minute, and he—"

"There's the bridge," Kit said, knowing it was idiotic but desperate to stop her saying more. He hadn't realized Peter had been *that* kind of friend, and he didn't want to think about what Lally had been doing with him—but then she'd said that *he* reminded her of Peter—

After that thought he no longer felt the cold, and was glad the darkness hid his blush. "About Leo," he said, trying to focus on the other thing Lally had said. Somehow he found he wasn't surprised that Lally had been holding drugs, or that Leo had given them to her. "You said you had Leo's stuff, but you don't anymore. Why not?"

"Because someone went through my fucking backpack and took it." The swearing didn't quite hide the fear in her voice. They'd reached the stone arch of the bridge, and instead of crossing it, Lally leapt down onto the canal towpath like a mountain goat. "It must have been my mother, but then why hasn't she said anything?" she went on. "She should have killed me, grounded me for life, and then some."

Kit was forced to follow her again, single file, and her words came back to him in bursts, carried by the wind.

"Won't Leo be worried about you getting in trouble?"

"No—can't be traced to him, can it? He'll want me to get it back, or make it up—"

"What do you mean, make it up?" asked Kit, not liking the sound of that at all.

But Lally only muttered, "You wouldn't understand," and kept walking, head down, as if suddenly afraid she'd said too much.

It was dark, so dark that Kit could only make out the water to his left as a deeper blackness. When something white flapped at them from the void, he jumped, grabbing Lally's shoulder and pulling her to a halt. "What the—" Then, as his eyes adjusted, he realized where he was and what he was seeing. Beneath the wind he heard a creak of mooring ropes, saw the faint gleam of letters materializing against a dark hull. It was the *Lost Horizon,* and the streamer cracking in the wind was a loose end of the blue-and-white crime-scene tape wrapped round the boat. He was standing within inches of where Annie Lebow's body had lain.

"Christ, Lally." Kit thought he might be sick. "What do you mean, bringing me here?" he shouted at her. "Don't you know—"

"Sorry, sorry." Lally pulled at his jacket. "We're not stopping here, but we have to go past. I didn't think. Come on. We have to hurry." She tugged at him until he stumbled after her, trying to shut out the images crowding into his mind: Annie, lying in the emerald grass of the towpath . . . his mother, lying against the white tile in their kitchen . . .

Then he was caught in the rushing corridor of his dream, running, running, trying to get help, while the room where his mother lay receded endlessly in front of him.

Lally's shaking him brought him out of it.

"Kit, what's the matter with you, for God's sake? We have to climb the stile here. Come on." Lally turned and vaulted halfway up, one leg over, and it looked to Kit as if she were disappearing into the hedge. He followed her, clumsily, the brambles scratching his hands. Jumping down on the far side, his feet sank into snow that had settled in the lee of the hedge.

Lally was moving up the hill, opening a gate and motioning him through. The surface under his feet grew firmer, and he realized they were on a bridge, crossing back over the canal. "Where are we?"

"My mum's dairy. Don't you want to see where they found the dead baby?"

"No!" Kit said, then amended, "It's a crime scene."

"So what's a little tape?" Her teeth flashed as she glanced back at him. "Besides, it's only a couple of minutes from Leo's house, and this is where he said to come."

Squinting at the outline of a peaked roof against the lighter sky, Kit caught a flicker of artificial light lower down, a match or lighter, or a quickly covered torch.

"He's here," said Lally, her voice gone suddenly flat. She stepped over the crime-scene tape that had drooped between its stakes.

"Took your time, didn't you?" said a voice from the darkness. Leo stepped out of the barn's entrance. He drew on a cigarette and the tip's brief flare lit his face at odd angles, so that the planes stood out like shapes in a Cubist painting.

"Aren't we going in?" asked Lally, with what Kit now recognized as manufactured disinterest.

"Nothing to see but some crumbling mortar. Disappointing." Leo shrugged. "I should know. I waited last night."

"My mum didn't let me out of her sight last night. It's only because she went out that we could come tonight."

"Did you bring it?" Leo asked, as if her excuses were meaningless static, and Kit felt Lally go suddenly still.

"No. It's at our house. My mum won't let Sam and me go back there. She doesn't want us to see our dad."

"So they haven't kissed and made up, your parents?" There was something in Leo's voice that made the hair on Kit's neck stand up.

Lally took a little hiccupping breath. Dead giveaway, thought Kit. Instinctively, he reached for her, a protective hand on her shoulder.

She stepped away, but not before Leo had seen. There was

a new tension in his posture, but he said lightly, "Is this your hostage, then?"

"What do you mean?" Lally asked.

"Coz, here. It's a good night for a boys' night out. What do you say, coz? I've a bottle of Absolut tucked away—no need to chill it in this weather. We can go to the clubhouse."

"Leo—"

"Not you, Lally." His voice was suddenly hard. "I said 'boys' night out.' Go home. Go home and start thinking how you're going to get your mother to let you back into your house."

"Leo, I—"

"That's the bad thing about letting people in on your secrets, Lal." Leo spoke the words with a smile, but Kit knew it was a threat. "You can never be sure they'll keep quiet."

"Go on, Lally," said Kit, knowing only that he wanted her to get away, and that he meant to find out what Leo was holding over her. If it was drugs, Leo would implicate himself if he told. But had he seen the scars on her arms?

"But—"

"You heard the man," echoed Leo. "Run along now. There's a good girl."

"You're a bastard, Leo," said Lally, her voice shaking, but she turned away, without another look at Kit, and in an instant was lost in the darkness.

Kit's mouth went dry as he realized he wasn't sure he could find his way back on his own. Follow the towpath, that was all. If he'd done it once, he could do it again.

"Not having second thoughts, are you, Kit?" Leo put the emphasis on his name, now that Lally was gone. "Come on, have some fun. I thought you city boys were sophisticated."

"I don't—"

But Leo threw an arm over his shoulders, propelling him away from the barn, and Kit realized that not only was the other boy a good six inches taller, but he was stronger than he looked. "It's not far. Just across this field and into those trees up ahead. I've got a special place. I found it not long after we moved here. I could never see what my dad wanted with this old pile of a house, but the property had its unexpected bonuses," he continued conversationally, but he didn't let up his grip on Kit's shoulder.

"Why's Lally afraid of you?" said Kit, determined to take control of the situation, in spite of the hand at his back.

"Afraid of me?" Leo sounded hurt. "Lally's not afraid of me. We look out for each other, that's all. She has some habits that need to be kept in check. And I make sure she doesn't get involved with people who might not be good for her. She's a bit fragile. I wouldn't want someone to take advantage of her."

"I'm not going to take advantage of her," Kit said angrily. He tried to shrug away, but Leo's fingers gripped like steel.

"But you like her. Admit it."

They entered the woods. The darkness closed in until there was nothing in Kit's universe but Leo's hand, and Leo's voice.

When he didn't answer, Leo said, "That's a shame. Peter liked her, too."

# 25

❧

**"I DON'T LIKE IT,"** Kincaid said as soon as they had stepped back onto the towpath. "What if we're wrong and we haven't told Babcock? We're obligated, and even if the Wains are telling the truth, Ronnie will spend valuable time and resources trying to solve the case—"

"You'd sacrifice this family to save police resources?" Gemma stopped, turning to face him, and even though he couldn't see her face clearly, he could hear the censure in her voice. "Gabriel Wain would lose his wife *and* his children—because wherever little Marie came from, she *is* his child," Gemma went on.

"Babcock may get there by himself. He has access to the same records you saw. And if he does, and realizes we withheld information—"

"What? Your reputation would suffer a little damage?"

"And yours," he retorted, stung. "We could both face disciplinary action."

"If you think that matters more than people's lives, then you're not the man I thought."

Kincaid heard echoes of his sister's condemnation, and thought of the consequences of his insistence on doing what he thought right.

"Twenty-four hours," he said. "We'll sit on it for twenty-four hours, see what progress Ronnie Babcock makes on the Lebow case. We've got to make sure that Gabriel Wain is not connected to Annie Lebow's death. You have to give me that."

"Yes." Gemma sighed and turned away, and as Kincaid followed, she added reluctantly, "I suppose I do, although I don't believe he's guilty."

They crossed under the bridge, each occupied with his own thoughts, but as they emerged from the shelter of the arch, a figure came hurtling out of the darkness and cannoned into Gemma.

Gemma and her assailant went down in a tangle of arms and legs, both swearing, and Kincaid recognized the other voice.

"Lally? What in hell's name are you doing here?" he said as he lifted his niece, allowing Gemma to get to her feet, if a little ungracefully. "You could both have gone in the canal."

"Uncle Duncan?" the girl said tremulously. He could feel her shoulders shaking beneath his hands, and her teeth were chattering. "What are you doing here? How did you know? I didn't know if I could find you in time—"

"What do you mean, in time?" Kincaid said, fear shooting through him. "What's happened? Where are Kit and the little boys?"

"Toby and Sam are at the house, but Kit—" Lally mumbled something he couldn't understand, then began to sob convulsively.

"Lally, where's Kit?" He increased the pressure on her shoulders, shaking her, but she only sobbed harder.

"Lally, Lally." Gemma gently disengaged the girl from Kincaid's grasp. "It's all right." She wiped the tears from Lally's cheeks with the palms of her hands. "You just have to tell us what's happened, so we can take care of it." There was an undertone of panic in her voice, but still it seemed to calm Lally.

"We met Leo. I— He wanted Kit— He sent me home, but I'm afraid of what will happen to Kit. That night with Peter, he made me leave, and then—"

"And then what?" Gemma prompted when Lally stopped. "It's okay. You can tell us. You won't be in trouble."

"Leo had some stuff. Vodka, that's all. But he wanted me to help him get Peter drunk. And Peter went along with it. But then Leo told me to go. And Peter—" She held her hands to her face and her sob drew out to a little keening wail.

"Peter?" said Gemma, but the pieces were cascading in Kincaid's mind.

"Peter? The boy who drowned?" He remembered Annie telling him, that day on the boat, about the boy she'd seen running along the towpath, his clothes wet, and how she'd assumed, when she'd heard later about the boy who drowned that night, that it was he she had seen.

"How did you know about Peter?" asked Lally, shocked enough to stop crying.

Kincaid made an effort to match Gemma's patience. "Lally, on Boxing Day, do you remember when you and Kit met Annie Lebow? Was Leo with you?" When she nodded, he took a breath and said, "Did she speak to him?"

"No, not really." Lally wiped her nose with the back of her hand. "But he seemed anxious to get away. I thought he was just bored—he doesn't like grown-ups much."

Kincaid's thoughts raced. What if it had not been Peter Llewellyn Annie saw running that night, but Leo Dutton? Leo, dripping wet from holding the other boy under the water? And what if Annie had recognized him and realized her mistake? Gemma was staring at him, baffled, but he couldn't take the time to explain.

"Lally, start from the beginning. If you thought Leo had something to do with Peter's death, why didn't you say?"

"Because I wasn't sure at first. And then, when I started to suspect, Leo said— I didn't want—"

Leo had made her think she'd be held responsible for Peter's drowning if she tried to implicate him, Kincaid guessed. He couldn't let himself wonder why Leo would have hurt Peter Llewellyn, or why he might want to hurt Kit. There wasn't time. "You said you left Kit with Leo? Where did you meet him?"

"We met at the dairy barn. But that's not where—Leo will have taken him to the clubhouse."

"Tell me exactly where it is, this clubhouse."

"It's on Leo's dad's property, almost right on the canal, but you'd never see it if you didn't know it was there. Leo says it's an old tollhouse, but I don't think they'd have put a tollhouse so far from the junction."

For just an instant, Kincaid heard his father in the girl's slightly pedantic explanation, and his heart softened towards her. "It's all right, Lally," he said, trying to reassure himself as much as her. "We'll find them."

Pulling out his mobile, he dialed Babcock.

The building was a windowless brick cubicle, about eight feet square, with a small door sagging half off its hinges. When Leo steered him firmly through the doorway, Kit's head just missed the lintel. Once inside, he saw that half the roof was gone. The snow-heavy clouds showing in the gap cast a diffuse light that just allowed him to make out shapes.

Leo flicked on the torch, and the shapes resolved into up-turned packing crates and some old blankets made into a nest. "Have a seat," he said, in a tone that made it clear it was not a request. "It's not elegant, but it's mine," he went on, as Kit sank reluctantly onto a packing crate. "I don't think my father even knows this is here; he's never explored the property. The country-squire thing is just for show.

"No glasses, I'm afraid," he added as he produced a bottle of vodka from behind one of the crates. "Bottoms up."

He sat beside Kit and took a healthy swig, then passed the bottle on. Kit tipped the bottle up, compressing his lips so that only a little liquid trickled into his mouth. It was foul, like drinking petrol, and it was all he could do to not spit it out.

"No cheating," Leo said. "That's expensive vodka, not mouthwash. Drink it down." When Kit forced down another sip, he took the bottle back and drank again. "I might have had something more to your liking if Lally hadn't gone and lost my stash."

"Lally couldn't help it." The liquor burned all the way to Kit's stomach, and made him feel reckless. "Her mother hasn't let her near their house."

"Defending her again?" Leo's voice was cold. Kit knew he'd made a mistake, but he stared back at the other boy, refusing to back down. "She does the damsel in distress well," Leo went on, as if musing aloud. "Good old Peter certainly fell for it. But she wasn't so innocent, was she?"

"I don't know what you're talking about," Kit answered, although he was afraid he did.

"She's a slut," said Leo, suddenly harsh. "And worse than that, a careless slut. She should never have left condoms in her backpack where I would find them."

"But weren't they for—I thought you and Lally—"

"It wasn't like that!" Leo shouted, the anger that had been simmering beneath the surface of his offhand manner suddenly boiling over. He stood, pacing in the cramped space, and Kit began to feel really frightened.

"Oh, I could have done it, whenever I wanted," Leo went on, his voice calmer, but Kit could hear him breathing hard. "But we were different, special. And then she ruined it because she felt sorry for pretty-boy Peter, just like she does you."

Kit knew that Lally hadn't gone with Peter because she felt sorry for him, and he didn't think she liked him because she was sorry for him, either.

Understanding came to him with a sickening jolt. Lally had refused Leo, telling him their relationship was too special for sex. Leo had believed her, accepted it, until he discovered she'd been sleeping with Peter Llewellyn.

And then Peter had died.

"I'm going." Kit pushed himself to his feet, his heart thumping.

"Suit yourself," said Leo, with a return of his mocking manner. "Think you can find the towpath in the dark?"

"How hard can it be?" asked Kit, trying to match him for nonchalance. In the faint light from Leo's covered torch, he found the door. But as he stepped out, Leo switched the torch off, and the dark descended like a cloak.

Kit stood still, fighting panic. He thought back to the way they'd come, parallel to the canal as they'd crossed the field and entered the wood, then turning gradually to the right. They had come straight to the door side of the shed, which must mean that the way to the canal lay round the back of the cubicle.

He felt his way round the building, then carried straight on, brushing the tree trunks with his fingertips. After a few yards, the trees thinned, and he thought he smelled the mossy scent of water, even beneath the sharp tang of snow in the air. Yes, he could see it now, the water reflecting very faintly the overcast sky.

Relief quickened his steps, and it was only when he reached the water's edge that he realized the towpath was on the far side, and there was no bridge.

He couldn't be that far from the dairy barn, though, if he just followed the water. The ground was tussocky, but he could man—

The shove caught him in the middle of the back like a cannonball. He had only an instant's sensation of falling, and then the water closed over him, cold enough to freeze his heart.

Ronnie answered on the first ring. "I was just on my way to you. There's been—"

"Ronnie, we're going to need backup." Kincaid paused, taking the phone from his ear while he spoke to his niece. "Lally, can you get to this tollhouse from the Dutton place?"

"There's a track, from the gate at the back of the garden through the woods."

"It's Kit," he said to Ronnie again. "It's looks like Leo Dutton may have been involved in Annie Lebow's murder, and now he has Kit—"

"*Leo* Dutton? But he's just a kid. Why would—"

"Ronnie, there's no time." He gave Babcock the best directions he could, adding, "You'll need a torch."

"I'm just leaving Nantwich," said Ronnie. "Can I pick you up?"

"No. We're at Barbridge. We'll take the car round and be there before you. And, Ronnie, call for uniforms."

At the shock of the water, Kit had instinctively opened his mouth and inhaled. He thrashed wildly, struggling towards the surface, and when his head broke water he gagged and spewed up canal water mixed with the little vodka he'd drunk. Still coughing, he tried to catch his breath, then discovered he could stand. But the cold was quickly numbing his arms and legs—if he didn't move he'd be paralyzed.

Through the water streaming from his hair, he could make out the near bank. His arms felt leaden, but he forced himself to reach out in a long swimmer's stroke. When his fingers touched firm bank, he grasped with all his strength. Then a crushing weight came down on his hand.

Yelling, Kit wrenched his hand free and, with a lunge, wrapped both his arms round Leo's ankles, pulling with all his might.

The force of it toppled the other boy, but he fell back, rather than into the canal, and by the time Kit had managed to clamber onto the bank on his hands and knees, Leo was already back on his feet.

With a grunt more vicious than any swear word, Leo pulled back a booted foot and kicked Kit hard in the chin.

Kit's head snapped back. Then he was lying in the grass, coughing on the metallic taste of the blood flowing from his lower lip. His head buzzed from the impact, and he shook it like a punch-drunk boxer as he hauled himself back up to his knees and then stood, staggering unsteadily.

He tensed, balling his fists as he waited for the next blow, then realized that Leo was moving away from him, back towards the shed.

"You bastard!" he shouted, and started after him. The fact that he had a chance to run, to get a head start, was banished by his fury as quickly as it had crossed his mind. No one was going to try to drown him, then kick him in the face, and get away with it. He stumbled forward, hampered by the sodden, icy weight of his clothes and shoes, and by the ringing in his head. "Is that what you did to Peter?" he gasped. "Did you push him in and hold him under?"

Then Leo disappeared round the corner of the shed and Kit stopped, suddenly uncertain. But before he could decide whether to follow, Leo reappeared and walked towards him.

Even in the dim light, Kit could see what Leo held in his hands.

He stared down the barrel of the shotgun, then into Leo's eyes, and he knew he was dead.

"Lally, stay in the car. Wait for the police." Kincaid had driven down Piers Dutton's drive until the Escort's wheels spun and stuck. The house was dark, so he knew there'd be no help from that quarter, and that they'd have to make it the rest of the way on foot.

His niece had gone quiet in the backseat, her silence more disturbing than her earlier tears. But now she said, "No," in a voice as implacable as his own. "You won't find it without me. I'm coming." Then she was out of the car and running across the back garden that lay to the left of the drive, and all they could do was follow her.

Kincaid knew she was right, and that she had relieved him of making the choice of risking her safety at the expense of Kit's.

"Don't use a torch," Lally called back to them. "It'll confuse you. Just stay close to me."

She slipped through a gate at the back of the garden and into what seemed at first glance to be impenetrable scrub. But as they followed her through the gate, he saw that a barely discernible path, no wider than a deer trail, led through the woods.

Once he heard Gemma stumble and curse, but when he reached back to steady her, she whispered, "No, I'm fine. Hurry." The path twisted and turned, but Kincaid's sense of direction told him they were heading towards the canal at a slightly oblique angle.

The path curved once more, and Lally came to a dead stop. When they cannoned into her, she steadied herself, then raised a hand to motion them to silence. Ahead, Kincaid could see a small brick building, but it was dark and there was no sign of movement.

Lally let out an audible breath and moved forward, skirting the shed on the left as she headed towards the canal. "They're not here. What if we're too—"

Kincaid and Gemma had stepped up to flank her, so that when she froze, they saw the tableau before them in the same instant.

Kit stood to one side of a slight clearing ahead of them. Ten feet away, on the clearing's far side, Leo Dutton held a raised shotgun.

"You'd better stop where you are," Leo said, so casually that Kincaid knew he had heard them before they saw him. "That's what I call in the nick of time. And, Lally, you brought the cavalry, clever girl."

"Leo, I— Don't hurt Kit. He hasn't done any—"

"Shut up." With the barrel of the gun, Leo motioned to Kit to move closer to the others. Then he rotated slightly, so that he could cover them all evenly. "So now you're a snitch, Lally, as well as a thief and a liar. But this time you can't take it back. You can't make it up to me."

"I can. I'll do whatever you want—"

"What? You think it's that easy? That I'll just let you lot walk away?" Leo's voice rose, and the barrel of the shotgun came up with it.

"You won't gain anything by hurting us, Leo," said Kincaid, as levelly as he could manage. If he could keep the boy talking, he might be able to contain him until backup arrived. "The police already know you drowned Peter Llewellyn and you killed Annie Lebow. She recognized you on Boxing Day, didn't she, when you and Lally and Kit stopped at the boat? She'd seen you the night Peter died.

"You were wet because you'd had to hold Peter under, weren't you? It was harder than you'd thought to drown someone. Annie said you were 'wild-eyed'; maybe you hadn't known what it would feel like to kill another human being. She thought, when she heard about the drowning later, that it was Peter she had seen, and that she might have helped him."

"She stepped right into my path, the stupid cow. She saw my face. That day on the towpath, while Kit here was making chitchat, I could see her looking at me, trying to make the connection."

"You killed her?" Kit's voice was high with shock, and

Kincaid realized his mistake. Kit had guessed about Peter, but he hadn't known enough to put the pieces together about Annie. "You killed Annie!" Kit was shouting now, blazing with rage. "She was a good person. She never did anything to hurt anyone. She didn't deserve to die. And you— I saw her. I saw what you did to her." Kit charged towards the other boy, in his fury oblivious to the danger.

"No!" shouted Lally, and launched herself at Kit.

In that instant, a twig cracked. Kincaid just glimpsed Ronnie Babcock stepping into the clearing as Leo whirled towards the noise and the gun discharged.

The boom reverberated, deafening in the still night air, but beneath it Kincaid heard Ronnie's grunt of surprise. Gemma ran towards him even as he fell.

"Don't move. Nobody move," commanded Kincaid. Lally had pushed Kit down and they both froze in a crouch. Leo still held the gun, but he was visibly shaking. "Easy, Leo, easy," Kincaid said, then to Gemma, "How bad is it?"

She'd knelt, slipping off her coat and pressing it to Ronnie's midriff. Her face looked white in the gloom as she glanced up at him. "We need help. Quickly."

Kincaid prayed that the gun had been filled with birdshot, that it had not been tightly choked, that the boy's aim had been off. Ronnie groaned and Gemma murmured something he couldn't hear.

Slowly, carefully, Kincaid turned back to Leo Dutton. The gun was double-barreled. Had the boy loaded both chambers? "Leo. Put the gun down. If you do it now, that was an accident. We all saw that. But if you let a policeman die, it's murder."

"You said the police already knew about Peter and that woman," Leo countered. "So what do I have to lose?" But some of the bravado was gone; he sounded, for the first time, like a frightened teenager.

"Oh, they know, but that's not the same as proof, is it? Not even Lally can prove you killed Peter Llewellyn. It's only conjecture on her part. And there's no forensic evidence linking you to the murder of Annie Lebow, and no witnesses. Anything you've said tonight will be inadmissible in court.

"But even if the police could connect you to these crimes, you're a juvenile. You might get a few months in a psychiatric ward, then probation. Your father can pull strings." Kincaid could only hope that Leo didn't know his father was facing indictment for fraud, and that the influence Piers Dutton had wielded among the rich and powerful in the county might soon be a memory.

He glanced over at Babcock, who lay alarmingly still. Gemma shook her head at him, a signal of distress.

Kincaid dropped his voice, mustering every ounce of persuasion he possessed. "But if you let the chief inspector here die, not even your father can protect you. It won't matter what you do to the rest of us. And there isn't anywhere you can run that they won't find you."

A flash of light came from the woods, then another, followed by the faint echo of voices. Leo glanced towards the sound, the whites of his eyes showing, then back at Kincaid. He shifted the gun until it pointed not at Kincaid, but at Kit. "I could shoot him. You know I could. And you couldn't stop me."

Despair washed over Kincaid, followed immediately by an incandescent anger. He would not let this monster take his son. He tensed his body, ready to throw himself at the boy, but said, "You won't."

The moment stretched until Kincaid thought his heart would stop. Then Leo let the gun barrel drop until the end touched the ground. He laughed. "No, I don't suppose I will. But I had you." Turning to Kit, he said, "And you. I had you. A few seconds, a little pressure on the trigger. That's all it would have taken, and you knew it. I won. Don't forget it."

# 26

❧

It was after midnight by the time Kincaid managed to get to Leighton Hospital.

Although Kevin Rasansky had secured the crime scene competently enough after the ambulance crew had taken Babcock away, it had been Babcock's superintendent who had met them at Crewe Police Station to take statements from Kincaid, Gemma, Lally, and Kit, and to oversee the booking in of Leo Dutton. Special arrangements would have to be made for the boy's custody, as he was a juvenile, but for now he was safely ensconced in an interview room with a constable on the door.

Piers Dutton had been contacted and had arrived, at first too shocked to bluster, but the last Kincaid had seen of him, he'd been on his mobile, calling solicitors and his father, the judge.

Having obtained dry clothes for Kit from one of the officers, Kincaid had rung his sister and was surprised to find that she, too, was at the police station, assisting her husband in making a statement concerning a fire at Newcombe and Dutton. Once Lally had given her statement, he had taken her to meet her mother in the lobby, and Juliet had hugged her daughter as if she would never let her go. When Lally had at last pulled away and asked, "What about Daddy?" Juliet had simply told her he would be staying for a bit, helping the police.

"I can take Lally and Kit home," Juliet had offered. "And Gemma, too, if you're not ready, Duncan." She paused. 'Your friend the chief inspector—"

"I'll stay," Gemma had said. "I can drive you to hospital."

"No, go on, the boys need you," he'd told her, but the truth was that if the news was bad, he wanted to be on his own when he heard it. He'd tried ringing the hospital several times, but they'd refused to tell him anything about Babcock's condition. "I'll call you as soon as I know anything." He'd brushed his lips against her cheek and given Kit a quick hug.

Now, as he entered the waiting room outside intensive care, his stomach clamped with dread. By the time the medics had arrived, Ronnie had lost consciousness, and Gemma's hands and arms had been covered with his blood.

The small room was filled with men and women with tense white faces, sitting and standing, clutching polystyrene coffee cups like talismans. He recognized many of them, officers both plainclothed and uniformed, whom he had seen in the incident room and at Crewe station.

"Is there any news?" he asked, and one of the women shook her head.

"No. He's out of surgery, but they won't tell us anything. Sheila's gone to bully the doctor." She managed a faint smile.

It was only then that Kincaid realized he hadn't seen Larkin at the crime scene or the station—she must have gone directly to hospital.

He found a vacant spot of wall and leaned against it, settling in to wait with the others. The woman who had spoken offered him coffee from an urn on the table and he accepted, knowing it would be swill, but, like the others, needing something to hold in his hands.

It was another half hour before the doors swung open and Sheila Larkin came through. Her skin was pasty with exhaustion, her eyes ringed with smudged mascara. His heart plummeted, and he heard little gasps of dismay travel round the room like a wave.

But then she was shaking her head and wiping her eyes, half laughing and saying hurriedly, "No, no. He's all right. The doctor says he looks like a sieve, but that he was too bloody-minded to die on the operating table. He's going to be okay. He's going to be okay."

# 27

❧

NEW YEAR'S DAY dawned clear and unseasonably mild. After breakfast, Kincaid started to Leighton for one last visit with Ronnie Babcock. He'd been every day, but had found his friend sedated and sprouting enough tubes to qualify as the Bionic Man. The nurses had insisted he was improving, however, and promised that today would see some of the tubes out and the pain medication reduced. "He may be a bit bad-tempered, though," the head sister had added with a grin.

Bad-tempered would be welcome, in Kincaid's view, as long as his friend was conversant. He and Gemma and the boys would be heading back to London that afternoon, and Gemma having agreed that they should tell Babcock the Wains' story, he would much prefer to do it in person.

He found a space in the hospital's still-slushy car park. Passing through the area reserved for hospital personnel, he glanced at a Morris Minor and started as deep brown eyes in a large shaggy head stared back at him. Remembering Gemma's description of Dr. Elsworthy's dog, he laughed, and as the windows were half down, said, "Hello, boy. Are you waiting for your mistress?"

The beast's ears went back, and the car rocked as the giant tail thumped. Kincaid took that as a good sign, but wasn't quite brave enough to put his hand through the window to pet the dog. The pathologist needn't worry about car burglars—not that it looked as though there was anything in it worth stealing.

Once inside, he found his friend indeed looking more chipper, sitting up in bed and, although still hooked to a drip, missing the gastric tube that had been snaked from his nose.

"Jelly," said Babcock disgustedly when Kincaid commented on his improved status. "That's what they call real food. Lemon-flavored jelly and a can of some revolting boost drink."

Kincaid grinned. "I'm sure you'll be up to steak and whisky tomorrow."

Babcock rolled his eyes but said, "Well, eventually, or so they say, thank God. It seems they were able to repair all the major bits." Sighing, he added, "I just want to go home. This place smells like a funeral parlor." He gestured at the bouquets covering every available surface. "All my officers, sucking up. My ex-wife even sent a meager offering, although she didn't come to wish me well in person. Probably a good thing—the sight of her might have set me back days."

He paused, resting for a moment as Kincaid pulled up a chair, then said, "Your sister sent a card, by the way. Very kind of her, considering the fact that we've charged her husband with arson. How is she doing, after all this?" Although shadowed, his blue eyes showed the concern that had made Kincaid like Ronnie Babcock from the day he'd met him.

"She seems to be coping. The dairy renovation's going again, and with a streak of mild weather she might even get it back on schedule. And she's started divorce proceedings. I don't know how things will work out."

"Your brother-in-law is an idiot," Babcock said testily. "She deserves better."

"Yes." Kincaid's agreement was heartfelt. She'd deserved better from him, too, and he meant to remedy that.

"I heard you, that night." Babcock's words snapped his attention back to his friend.

"What?"

"Telling Leo Dutton he'd get away with murder if he

urned himself in. Mind you, I'm not criticizing. I'd have
done the same, and it probably saved my life. But that's not
going to happen, not if I have breath left in my body. I don't
care if he is only fourteen. He's vicious."

"A bad seed?"

"Born or made, I don't care. But I will find evidence to
link him to those crimes, no matter how long it takes. The
high-flying solicitor Piers Dutton wanted for his son
turned down the case," he added with a smile of satisfaction. "Seems he wasn't confident of papa's ability to pay,
considering his present difficulties."

"Not surprising, but good news."

"It would make me even happier if I could link Dutton
Senior to the baby."

"Ronnie." Kincaid adjusted his chair. "You won't."

"What are you, clairvoyant?" Babcock asked, but the
acerbity was a bit forced, his voice going thready. He was
tiring.

"No," Kincaid told him. "Just listen."

While he talked, Babcock's eyes drifted closed, and when
he'd finished, his friend lay still for so long that Kincaid
thought he had fallen asleep.

Then Babcock opened his eyes and fixed Kincaid with a
blue glare. "Let sleeping dogs lie, then? Is that what you're
suggesting?" Before Kincaid could protest, Babcock silenced
him with a wave. "I daresay you're right. Annie Constantine
believed in the Wains, and although she may have been com-
pensating for past mistakes, she was a good judge of character. It sounds as if that family has suffered enough.

"But before you go thinking I've gone soft, I've more reasons than the kindness of my heart for not pursuing it." He
ticked them off on his fingers, making the drip dance. "Even
if I could get CPS to take on the case, I doubt any jury would
convict. It would serve only to get Social Services involved
and lose the man what family he has left.

"And most important, I've enough on my plate trying to
get Piers and Leo Dutton banged up for a good long time. I
don't need to waste time and resources on something with
no return."

Kincaid grinned. "Said like a good bureaucrat. But you are a softie."

"There's a caveat," Babcock countered. "I need to tell my aunt Margaret. She said when I told her about the case that someone had grieved for that child, and it seems she was right." He thought for a moment, the creases in his face deepening. "And there's one other person should know the truth."

Before Kincaid could question him, there was a light tap at the door and Sheila Larkin came in. She wore a short skirt, a fuzzy pink jumper, and patterned tights, and the sight of her round, snub-nosed face seemed to bring the color back to Babcock's cheeks. "Oh, am I interrupting?" she asked, looking prepared to back out again.

"Not a bit." Kincaid stood, offering his chair. "I've got to dash. We're off home to London this afternoon, after my mother's traditional New Year's lunch."

Larkin took the chair, producing a bunch of carnations she'd held behind her back.

"Don't tell me you've brought flowers," Babcock groaned. "You know I hate flowers."

"Couldn't get the single malt past the matron." Larkin winked at Kincaid, suppressing a smile. "Besides, I thought the more miserable I made you, the sooner you'd get yourself back to work. There are going to be dire consequences if you don't, boss."

"What?" said Babcock, taking the bait.

This time Larkin's grin threatened to split her face. "Rasansky's going to get himself promoted to chief superintendent, that's what. He's already taken over your desk."

Juliet was loading the children's things into the van when she saw Duncan turn into the drive. She stopped, shielding her eyes from the sun, and watched him get out of the car.

"Here," he said as he reached her. "Let me help." He lifted the last bag with a surprised "Oof," and hefted it into the van. "What have you got in here, rocks?"

"Probably a few. It's Sammy's. He tends to accumulate things."

"You're going home, then?"

She had given Caspar the last few days to get his things out of the house and to make arrangements for somewhere else to stay, but this afternoon she and the children were going back to North Crofts. "Yes. At least for the time being."

"Chief Inspector Babcock sends his regards."

"How is he?"

"Recovering." Duncan said it lightly, but she heard his relief. She studied her brother, realizing that for the first time, free of the lens of resentment, she was seeing him as he really was. He was no superman to be lived up to, but just an ordinary man—although sometimes an annoying one—with troubles of his own. And she loved him.

"I'm glad about your friend Ronnie," she said. Then, "Duncan, what will happen to Caspar? Will he go to prison?"

"I don't know. His sentencing might be lenient if he makes a good plea for disturbance of the balance of his mind, especially as, so far, the police have found no evidence linking him to Piers's fraud scheme." He looked away, then went on a little awkwardly. "Jules, I'm sorry—"

"No. Don't say it. You were right. Even though Piers wasn't guilty of murder, he deserved to be caught out."

He nodded. "What will you do—about Caspar, I mean? Mum says he's been ringing every day, wanting to reconcile. Will you take him back?"

She watched a car travel down the farm lane and disappear round a curve as she thought about it. "No. I might forgive what he did to me, eventually. But the children—he twisted them. He played them against me for his own emotional gratification. I should have stopped it long ago, but I didn't. It's going to take a lot of work on my part to remedy the damage."

She had begun that very morning, taking Lally into the upstairs bathroom and locking the door. She pulled the bags Gemma had given her from her pocket, and when Lally's startled eyes met hers, she'd emptied both bags carefully into the toilet and pulled the chain.

"No more," she said. "From now on, I'm going to be watching you like a hawk, and if I even suspect you're doing anything like this, I'll lock you up until you're toothless. Is that understood?"

Lally nodded, wordlessly, but the relief in her eyes had been clear.

Now the front door opened and Lally came out with Geordie scampering at her heels. She'd been grooming him, with instructions from Kit, and the little dog's silky coat glistened in the sun.

"He's lovely, isn't he, Mum?" called out Lally, and when Juliet saw the uncomplicated smile of pleasure on her daughter's face, she thought that perhaps all things were possible, even new beginnings.

Gemma sat at the kitchen table drinking tea with Rosemary. The past few days had been good, and it surprised her now that she had ever wondered if she would fit in here. Even Juliet seemed to have forgiven her breach of confidence, and had hugged her tightly when she and Sam and Lally had left just after their New Year's lunch.

Duncan had gone with Kit to take Tess and Geordie for a last walk, and Hugh, who had taken Toby under his wing as if he were his own grandchild, was leading the little boy round and round the field on one of the Shetland ponies. Even from the kitchen she could hear Jack's barks and Toby's shrieks of excitement, and was grateful for the pony's placid temperament.

"They're getting on well, aren't they?" said Rosemary, echoing her thoughts. "Hugh's missed having little ones, with Lally and Sam getting older."

"He's good with the children."

"Too good, I sometimes think," answered Rosemary, laughing. "He's a child at heart. I don't suppose that's altogether a bad thing, although there have been times when it has tried my patience sorely. But we've rubbed off on each other, over the years." She set down her cup and studied Gemma as if debating something, then said, "It's been good to see you and Duncan together. You're truly partners, in a way that he and Victoria never were. Nor could they have been, I think, even if things had turned out differently."

Gemma flushed. She had always supposed Duncan's parents would compare her to Vic, and find her lacking. "I—"

But Rosemary cut her off, shaking her head. "Forgive my being blunt, but it's a gift, what you and Duncan have. It shouldn't be taken lightly. It's a balancing act, I know, juggling the different pieces of your life, but don't let this pass you by, or let loss harden you against it."

Gemma went still inside, and when she met the older woman's gaze she felt as if she had been stripped naked, and was suddenly ashamed.

Then Rosemary smiled. "He's not perfect, I admit, even though he is my son. But then I should think perfection would be very hard to live with."

They took the footpath across the field, towards the Middlewich Junction, letting the dogs run free. The ground had begun to dry and the going was easier than it had been in the snow.

Tess stayed close to Kit, her eyes on her master, but Geordie zigzagged in front of them, sniffing the ground excitedly. Then a low-flying bird caught the cocker spaniel's eye and he froze, his docked tail straight out, one paw raised.

"Look, he's pointing," said Kit. "He does that at home when he sees squirrels."

"Cocker spaniels are flushing dogs, not pointers," Kincaid commented, "but he doesn't seem to know the difference."

He surveyed the rolling Cheshire landscape with a pang, wondering when he would see it again, and why he had waited so long to come back. Glancing at his son, he asked, "Do you like it here?"

"Yes. It reminds me of Grantchester, a bit." Then Kit added thoughtfully, "But I'm not sure I'd want to be reminded, not all the time. And I miss our house, and Wesley, and the park, and the market on Saturday—"

"Okay, okay," Kincaid said, smiling. "I get it. I'm glad. I miss it, too. I'll be glad to get home."

They walked on in easy silence, then, as they climbed down to the Middlewich towpath, Kit said, "Will Lally be all right?"

Kincaid considered what to say. "I think so. But it wouldn't hurt to keep in touch, let her know you're there. She is your cousin, after all."

When they reached Barbridge he stopped, looking down the Shropshire Union and thinking of the associations that stretch of the canal must have for Kit, and would have now for him, as well. "We should go back."

But Kit surprised him, saying, "No. I want to go on, just for a bit."

"All right." Kincaid shrugged assent, wondering if this was Kit's way of laying his demons to rest. The dogs ran ahead and Kincaid followed his son's determined stride as they left pub and moorings behind. The curving reaches of the cut looked enchanted in the early-afternoon sunlight, a place of dreaming stillness, impervious to violence.

Kit's steps slowed as they rounded a now-familiar curve and saw the *Horizon* still at her mooring. The crime-scene tape was gone, but the blinds were tightly closed, and it seemed to Kincaid that the boat had already taken on a neglected air.

"What will happen to her?" asked Kit.

"I should imagine Roger Constantine will sell the boat, after a time. I can't imagine that he would want to use it. It's too much Annie's."

"Ghosts," Kit said softly, and with a last look, called the dogs and turned away.

Glancing at the boy's quiet face, Kincaid asked the question that had been haunting him. "Kit, when you said those things to Leo, about Annie not deserving to die, you were thinking of your mum, too, weren't you?"

"I suppose I was," Kit admitted, and after a moment added, "It's funny. The dreams have stopped."

"What dreams?"

"I'd been having dreams, about Mum, for a long time. Bad ones. Every night." His expression told Kincaid he wasn't going to say more.

"But not since the night with Leo?"

Kit shook his head. "Is it true what you said that night, that nothing will happen to him?"

"No. Now that the police know he was responsible for those deaths, they'll do all they can to find evidence that will tie Leo to the crimes. And I don't think a court will let him off lightly."

"It's not enough."

"No."

"He'll hurt someone else, eventually. He likes it."

Startled by his son's insight, Kincaid said, "Yes, I suspect he does. But we'll do our best to stop him doing more damage."

Kit nodded and walked on without speaking, but his silence was companionable, so Kincaid ventured, "I know it must seem a minor thing now, but about school . . . Do you want to tell me why you were having trouble? Besides the dreams?"

Shrugging, Kit said, "There were these boys. They were bullying me. But it doesn't seem important now." He looked up at Kincaid. "You know what Leo said, there at the last? Well, it's not true. He didn't win. I did."

# Epilogue

❧

"**GOOD GOD,**" said Althea Elsworthy. "How on earth did the boatmen ever get their horses across this thing? The beasts must have been terrified."

"I expect they used blinders," answered Gabriel. "Might be useful for people as well," he added, with a hint of teasing.

They stood in the stern well deck of the *Daphne,* Gabriel holding the tiller, Althea on one side and the children on the other. They were crossing the Pontcysyllte Aqueduct over the Dee Gorge on a crisp, clear day in early February. The great stone pillars of Thomas Telford's engineering marvel spanned over a thousand feet, one hundred and twenty-six dizzying feet above the ground.

"Rowan loved this place," Gabriel went on. "She was born not far from Wrexham, and she always said she felt freer here than anyplace else in the world."

The great iron trough was just a bit wider than the seven-foot boat, flanked on one side by the towpath the nineteenth-century boatmen had needed for the sturdy horses that pulled the boats. Now people walked the towpath for the thrill, but Althea thought she was doing very well to let herself be carried across in what seemed the relative safety of the boat's well deck. She had a mission, however, and was not about to be deterred by a small discomfort with heights.

On a bench at her side rested two urns, one large, one small. They had come to disperse mother's and daughter's ashes over the expanse of the Dee Gorge.

Rowan had died in her own bed on the *Daphne* in mid-January, with Gabriel and the children at her side, and Althea standing by to make her passing as comfortable as possible. She had been at peace, Althea thought, knowing her children were safe, and no longer burdened by a secret grief. When she still had the strength to talk, she'd made Althea promise to take in hand the children's education.

"The world's changing," she said. "We were the last of our generation, and past our time. The children will need to make a life outside the boats, and for that they need proper schooling."

"I could help Gabriel find steady work here, so that the children can enroll in school," Althea had agreed, liking the thought of continuing her connection with the children, and with Gabriel, whom she had come to like and respect.

"Unless you want to teach them yourself. That boyfriend the children have told me about could help you—"

"If you mean Paul, he's no such thing," Althea had protested, but she had flushed, and Rowan had smiled, pleased. Soon after that she had drifted into the twilight of coma, and then she had slipped away.

Althea had paid for Rowan's cremation. She had also, after a visit with Ronnie Babcock before Rowan's death, paid for the cremation of the remains of Baby Jane Doe. None of her colleagues knew what she had done for Rowan, and if anyone thought it odd that she had claimed responsibility for the body of the unidentified child, they hadn't remarked on it.

Rowan had not questioned Althea's knowledge of the child's identity, and had seemed to find solace in knowing her baby would at last have the acknowledgment she deserved.

Gabriel, however, had required an explanation.

"It's in his hands, then," he'd said with a stoic resignation, when Althea had explained about Babcock.

"Yes. But he's a good man, Ronnie Babcock, and he was a friend of Annie Constantine. He'll not bring any harm to you and the children." After that, there had been an easing in Gabriel, even through his grief over Rowan.

"Are we at the middle yet?" asked Joseph, who had been watching their progress across the aqueduct carefully. Gabriel checked aft, to make certain there were no boats coming behind them, then killed the *Daphne*'s engine. The boat drifted to a stop, suspended in the air. At first the silence seemed absolute, then gradually Althea's ears became attuned to the sigh of the wind, the twitter of birds below, and what she imagined was the very faint groaning of the structure that supported them, almost as if the bridge were breathing.

"Are you ready?" asked Gabriel, and the children nodded, their faces solemn. Gabriel handed them their mother's urn, and took little Marie's for himself. Together they removed the seals and, at a nod from Gabriel, let the ashes drift into space.

They all watched in silence until the last particle vanished, then Althea took a small box from her coat pocket. She had made a request of Roger Constantine, and although puzzled, he'd willingly complied. Now Althea lifted the lid from the box, and with a swing of her arm, scattered the contents as Gabriel and the children had done.

"Top of the world, Annie," she said.

Turn the page for a sneak peek
at the next thrilling
Gemma James/Duncan Kincaid mystery
**WHERE MEMORIES LIE**
coming out in hardcover
from William Morrow.

# Prologue

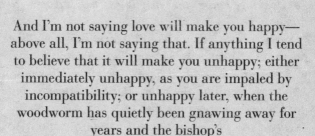

And I'm not saying love will make you happy—
above all, I'm not saying that. If anything I tend
to believe that it will make you unhappy; either
immediately unhappy, as you are impaled by
incompatibility; or unhappy later, when the
woodworm has quietly been gnawing away for
years and the bishop's
throne collapses. But you can believe this and
still insist that love is our only hope.

Julian Barnes
*A History of the World in 10½ Chapters*

*October, 1945*

**ERIKA WOKE,** *her body jerking to the whump of the
bomb, the flash of light from the incendiary flickering
against her closed eyelids. She threw back the covers
and had reached for David to shake him awake when*

*she realized the night was silent. No sirens, no rumble and thump of guns. Rubbing at her sleep-fogged eyes, she saw that light from the street lamp at the corner of Kensington Park Road was shining through the gap in the bedroom curtains, etching a pattern lucid as moonlight across the counterpane. It must have been that gleam that had insinuated itself into her subconscious—or perhaps a reflection from the moving lights of a passing car. She had yet to become accustomed to the unshuttered headlamps. Even in her waking hours the brightness caused her to flinch.*

*She lay back against the pillows, heart pounding painfully in her chest, cursing herself for a fool. It was over, the war—had been over for months now, London preternaturally quiet. Her mind knew it, but not her body, nor her dreams.*

*David lay on his back, still as marble, the rise and fall of his chest invisible even in the light that spilled through the curtains. Again she felt the irrational spike of fear. Reaching out, she laid her fingers ever so lightly against the thin skin on the inside of his wrist, feeling for the reassuring steady beat of his pulse. This was a habit she'd developed during the Blitz, a compelling and irresistible need to assure herself that life was not so easily snuffed out.*

*The rhythm of David's breathing became suddenly audible, and beneath her fingertips she felt the tension of awareness flood through her husband's body.*

*"I'm sorry, darling," she said. "I didn't mean to wake you."* She heard the tremble of longing in her voice, barely controlled, but David's only response was to slip his hand from hers, and turn away.

# 1

The vast stucco palaces of Kensington Park Road
and the adjoining streets had long ago been
converted into self-contained flats where an ever-
increasing stream of refugees from every part of
the once civilized world had found improvised
homes, like the dark-age troglodytes who
sheltered in the galleries and boxes of the
Colosseum.

Sir Osbert Lancaster
*All Done From Memory, 1963*

**THE DAY WAS** utterly miserable for early May, even
considering the expected vagaries of English weather.
At a few minutes to four in the afternoon it was dark
as twilight, and the rain came down in relentless,
pounding sheets. The gusts of wind had repeatedly
turned Henri Durrell's umbrella wrong side out, so he
had given up, and trudged down the Old Brompton

Road with his head down and his shoulders hunched against the torrent, trying to avoid losing an eye to carelessly wielded umbrellas that had proved stronger than his own, and dodging the waves thrown up by passing automobiles.

Pain shot through his hip and he slowed, wincing. He was seventy-five, as much as it galled him to admit it, and the damp did quite unpleasant things to his joints, even without the stress of an unaccustomed jog.

What had he been thinking? He should have stayed at the V&A until closing, then perhaps the worst of the storm would have blown through. He'd met a friend at the museum's café for Saturday afternoon tea, always a pleasant treat, but his haste in leaving had been inspired by his desire to get home to his flat in Roland Gardens and its seductive comforts—his book, a stiff whisky, the gas fire, and his cat, Matilde.

Jostled by a hurrying passerby, Henri stopped to recover his balance and found himself gazing into the windows of Harrowby's, the auction house. A poster advertised an upcoming sale of Art Deco jewelry. An avid collector, Henri usually kept up with such things, but he had been away for a spring holiday in his native Burgundy—where the sun had shone, thank God—and missed notice of this one.

The auction was to take place a week hence, he saw with relief. He could still buy a catalogue and peruse it thoroughly—if he hadn't missed the four o'clock closing time, that is. A quick glance at his watch showed one minute to the hour. Henri shook his wet umbrella, showering himself in the process, and dashed through Harrowby's still-open doors.

A few minutes later, he emerged, cheered by his acquisition and a friendly chat with the woman at reception. The rest of his walk home seemed less laborious, even though the rain had not abated.

He toweled himself off and changed into dry socks and slippers, with Matilde impeding the process by purring and butting against his ankles. He decided on tea rather than whisky, the better to ward off a chill, and when the pot had steeped he lit the gas fire and settled himself in his favorite chair, the catalogue resting carefully on his knees. It was beautifully produced, as Harrowby's catalogues always were—the house had never been known to lack style—and Henri opened it with a sigh of pleasure. Making room for the insistent cat, he thumbed through the pages, his breath catching at the beauty of the pieces. He had taught art history before his recent retirement, and something about the clean innovative shapes of this period appealed to him above all other.

Here, the master artists were well represented; a diamond and sapphire pendant by George Fouquet, a diamond cocktail ring by Rene Boivin—

Then his hand froze as an entry caught his eye, and his heart gave an uncomfortable flutter. Surely that couldn't be possible?

He studied the photo more closely. Henri appreciated color, so diamonds alone had never thrilled him as much as pieces that set platinum against the red, blue, or green of rubies, sapphires, or emeralds, but this—

The brooch was made of diamonds set in platinum, a double drop that reminded him of a waterfall or the swoop of a peacock's tail. The curving style was unusual for Art Deco, where the emphasis had been highly geometric. But the date of the piece was late—1938—and the name—the name he recognized with a jolt that sent the blood pounding through his veins.

Shaking his head, he stood, dumping Matilde unceremoniously from his lap. Then he hesitated. Should he ask to view the piece before taking any action? But no, the auction house would be closed now until Monday, and he doubted a mistake in the provenance, or in his memory.

He slipped the catalogue carefully back into its bag and carried it into the hall, where he donned his wet boots and coat once again, and reluctantly left the shelter of his flat.

"Why the bloody hell did it have to rain?" Gemma James dropped supermarket carrier bags on her kitchen table and pushed a sodden strand of hair from her face. Rivulets from the bags pooled on the scrubbed pine surface. Grabbing a tea towel, Gemma blotted up the water as Duncan Kincaid set down his own load of dripping plastic.

"Because it's May in London?" he asked, grinning. "Or because the patron saint of dinner parties has it in for you?"

She swatted at him with the damp towel, but smiled

in spite of herself. "Okay, point taken. But seriously, I meant to do the flowers from our garden, and now that's out. Not to mention that between boys and dogs, the house will be a sea of mud."

"The boys are with Wesley, probably making themselves sick on Wesley's mother's sweets and watching God knows what on the telly. As for the dogs, I will personally wipe every trace of muck from errant paws, and I can run down and get flowers from one of the stalls on Portobello." He slipped his arm round her shoulders. "Don't worry, love. You'll be brilliant."

For a moment, she allowed herself to rest her head against his shoulder. His shirt was damp from the rain, and through the fabric she could feel the comforting warmth of his skin. She leaned a little closer, then forced herself to squelch the thought that there were better ways to spend a rainy Saturday afternoon with the children out of the house.

They had begun as partners at Scotland Yard, then against her better judgment they had become clandestine lovers until her promotion to inspector and transfer to Notting Hill Police Station had separated them professionally. With no barrier to their relationship, they had moved in together, each bringing a son from a previous marriage and complications that at times had seemed insurmountable. But they had got through these challenges, including the mid-term loss of the child they had conceived together, and since their visit to Duncan's family in Cheshire this last Christmas, the dynamics of their cobbled-together family seemed to have meshed more smoothly.

It was a stroke of luck that had landed them in a house in an upmarket area of Notting Hill they would not normally have been able to afford, even with Kincaid's higher superintendent's salary. The house belonged to Duncan's chief superintendent's sister, whose family had gone abroad on a five-year contract, and Duncan and Gemma had been recommended to her as the ideal tenants.

Gemma had never thought she would adjust to life in Notting Hill, so different was it from the working-class area of London where she had grown up, but now she found that she loved the house and neighborhood so passionately that she couldn't imagine leaving, and the end of their lease hovered in her mind like a distant specter.

What she hadn't learned to love was the art of formal entertaining, and tonight she'd agreed to host a dinner party, the anticipation of which had sent her into a paroxysm of nerves. The guest list included Chief Superintendent Denis Childs—Duncan's guv'nor and their landlady's brother—along with his wife, whom Gemma had never met; Superintendent Mark Lamb, Gemma's boss, and his wife; Doug Cullen, who was now Kincaid's sergeant; and PC Melody Talbot, who worked with Gemma at Notting Hill.

Doug Cullen and Melody Talbot didn't know each other well, and Gemma was indulging an impulse to play at matchmaker, although Kincaid had teasingly warned her that she'd better be prepared to deal with the consequences of meddling.

She sighed and straightened up, gazing at the abundance spilling from the carrier bags onto the kitchen table. There were fillets of fresh salmon, lemons, frilly bunches of fennel, and tiny jewel-like grape tomatoes, as well as bread from her favorite bakery on Portobello Road, several bottles of crisp white wine, and the makings for enough salad to feed an army. The desert she had bought ready-made—to her shame, baker's daughter that she was—a beautiful fruit tart from Mr. Christian's Deli on Elgin Crescent. Attempting to bake would definitely have sent her over the edge into blithering idiocy.

"It all looked so easy in the cookery book," she said. "What if the Chief Super doesn't like it? Or what if he tells his sister we've made a wreck of her house?"

"You can't call him *guv'nor* at dinner, you know. You'll have to practice saying *Denis*." Kincaid gave her shoulder a squeeze and began pulling groceries from the bags. "And as for the house, it looks better than it did when we moved in. The food will be fabulous, the table stunning, and if all else fails," he added, grinning, "you can play the piano. What could possibly go wrong?"

Gemma stuck out her tongue. "Something," she said darkly, "always does."